CROSSFIRE

- - -

Book I of The Rhidge

A.G. KARINE

CROSSFIRE
Copyright (c) 2021 by Crossfire Publishing LLC

First Paperback Edition: November 2021

Cover Design by: Bookscovered.co.uk

ISBN 978-1-7377591-0-2

Visit the author's website at www.agkarine.com

*For my husband
you are my crossfire*

Table of Contents

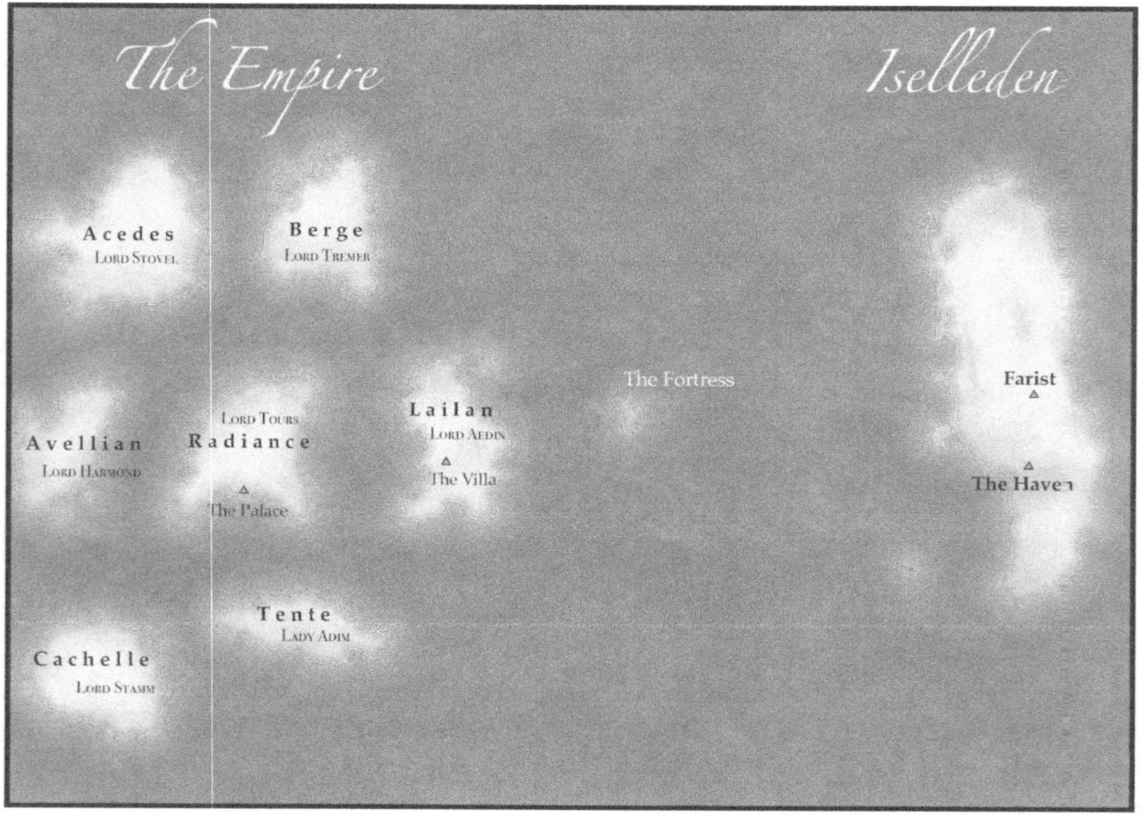

The Empire
Iselleden
Acedes
Lord Stovel
Berge
Lord Tremer
Avellian
Lord Harmond
Radiance
Lord Tours
The Palace
Lailan
Lord Aedin
The Villa
The Fortress
Farist
The Haven
Tente
Lady Adim
Cachelle
Lord Stamm

Prologue

IN HER DREAM she was running.

Her feet pressed into wet, long grass unbroken by rocks; her breath came easy. A light, airy fabric clothed her body and flowed with a life of its own. She was alone in an unfamiliar valley, but unafraid.

Vibrant snow-tipped mountains rose in time with each step, climbing higher and higher, blinding the sun. The crests grew, blocking the light. Snow from their peaks fell gently as the world turned and a cage of earth, dew, sweat, and bitter cold surrounded her—wrapping and embracing her in a warm void.

Gwyneth woke to the darkness of reality.

She was alone. A foreign bed of finely threaded cotton sheets held her, grabbing at her arms like an anchor as the ship swayed drunkenly. Her mind mimicked the motion.

The extinguished candles hung like ghosts in the moonlight. There was a window—it was small but she knew others didn't have the luxury. And yet, with each rocking of the waves, its hinges squeaked and clicked, calling to her in mockery.

It is said that wealth comes with a price. Such a price indeed— Gwen had hardly thought straight in the past seventy-two hours.

The band of precious metal gripped her finger possessively, its diamond and sapphires biting into her skin as she pressed her hands together. Sadistically, she wished the skin to break. To feel the pain of the stones cut her and evoke some form of emotion—anger, madness, despair.

But she was hollow. The bitter draught she had swallowed had yet to come to full force.

He had stolen her.

They had told her the trip was a three-day journey to the island of Lailan. It was the first night, a late hour, close to morning.

He had not come. She didn't know if she expected him to, because of the haste of it all, but she nonetheless feared it. Just as she had feared every glance and touch—despite how sparing those were.

This was a deal, her father had reminded her, a sanctified act, yes, but a deal. He had promised to bless them with worldly goods. He had promised them positions in the palace and the benefits of noble connection.

But Gwen had seen the rawness in her father and brother's faces as she had boarded the ship; had seen Daniel—a shadow in the back of a crowd of unfamiliar faces. There had been a pain in their expressions that neither gold nor status could salvage.

She would not be coming back.

And she was alone.

Something like thick oil eased painfully into the recesses of her stomach.

He had stolen her.

Chapter One

THE NUMBNESS OF shock, which had helped me survive the journey to Lailan, was wearing thin. There was a spark of hatred smoldering in my stomach, threatening to break.

We sat in the carriage as it rocked up the hill—silent and sweating in the humid air. Through the window, the expanse of sea stretched out like an azure blanket. It seemed to engulf everything—even the light of the sun was unable to penetrate the deep blue of the harbor.

It was magnificent and heartbreaking. I hated it for its beauty.

The island of Lailan was a gem within the seven islands of the Empire. And I was its new mistress—the Lady of Lailan.

My new husband sat mute, staring out the opposite window. The carriage swerved on a sharp switchback—I gripped the seat as the world swayed—and my view turned to an endless wall of thick, waxy leaves, tangled trees, and bright flowers.

It was a far cry from the icy, dark mountains of my home on the island of Berge.

I stole looks at him as we continued to climb. The infamous Lord Aedin, who had been little more than a distant figure about a week ago… and who was now my husband.

He seemed to wear a perpetual expression of stern boredom, as if nothing would ever please him. The sharp angles of his face were handsome and cold and I wondered if he was even happy at the prospect of being married. I hadn't recalled him once admitting a smile throughout the small ceremony.

Aedin's dark eyes flashed to mine. I flushed and looked away, opting again for the harbor view.

Regret was etched on my heart. I remembered Daniel's warm, loving gaze—I would never see him again.

A line of sweat trickled down between my breasts. Shifting uncomfortably in the layers of cotton and my finest furs from home, I eyed my husband's black, linen shirt with envy. The sleeves were rolled up, exposing the firm, bronzed skin of his forearms. His long fingers tapped impatiently on his knee, a faint crease on his brow—as if he was also eager to end this journey.

We reached the crest of the hill and my stomach recoiled at the sight of the rocks just below. As the carriage slowed, I straightened in anticipation, wiping the back of my hand across my forehead. Gods above, it was so hot!

Thick, iron gates were pushed open as our vehicle entered a large courtyard filled with foreign plants and grand fountains. Tall trees with great bare trunks shot into the sky, massive leaves dotting the tops. A wide stone fountain sat in the middle of the yard—large enough to be considered a pond.

A line of men and women stood before a pair of heavy wooden doors. I brushed back another bead of sweat, marveling at the warm painted walls of stucco that extended in the distance.

This was my new home.

The carriage jolted to a stop and all eyes shifted to us.

Aedin descended, straightened his tall frame and held out his hand. With one hand on the carriage door, the other in his grasp, I prayed my legs wouldn't give in. The prayer was answered as my feet crunched against the gravel and I dropped his hand.

I could already feel a sun rash forming on my skin as the line of servants and staff bowed before us.

The tall, blonde man that had shadowed our entire journey to Lailan emerged from the carriage behind ours, squinting in the bright sun. "Good to be home again," he muttered, shooting me a wry grin.

I had forgotten his name and I wasn't sure that I agreed, so I grimaced in response.

"My lord." An older woman came forward to curtsy before Aedin. Her wrinkled skin was the color of the rich, dark earth.

Aedin nodded at her respectfully. "Gwyneth, may I present my personal secretary and steward of the villa—Mary Turnleaf."

"I am honored to meet you and look forward to serving you, my lady. Welcome to the villa." Mary bent her knee in my direction, her quick brown eyes appraising and steady.

"Thank you," I said, inwardly cringing at the sound of my new title.

Aedin waved his hand towards the line of people. "This is our staff, who manage the day-to-day running of the villa, and our guards, led by Mr. Marks, whom you have already met."

The blonde man offered a brisk bow, clad in the same dark uniform as the men lining the door. "We are here to serve you, my lady."

"It is good to be back. A month was too long to be away," Aedin said quietly, his eyes warmly appraising the staff and guards. "Marks"—he raised his voice—"I will leave for Tahuna around noon. Until then, please train the guards."

"Yes, my lord." Marks fingered the long sword buckled at his hip and walked over to the guards standing at attention.

We slowly made our way down the line of staff, Mary introducing each one as they curtsied and bowed in greeting. I nodded civilly, trying to maintain some composure at the realization that I now lived in a home with servants.

Only a week ago, we had struggled to buy bread for our small family. Now, the coins we had saved were irrelevant. My family had all the bread they needed—and I had a luxurious villa with a distant husband.

Mary led us wordlessly through the wide doors and into a long hall open to the island air. Lamps hung from the wooden beams that supported the roof, swaying in the gentle breeze of the passageway. Arching columns revealed an atrium garden teeming with life and birdsong.

We turned left and walked along whitewashed walls, mostly bare save for some tapestries. Our footsteps echoed intrusively against the shaded stones. There was a peaceful stillness that hung in the moist, damp air. Although we had left the sun's merciless heat, I was still melting under my furs.

Mary opened the door to a small sitting room filled with chairs and tables, then another door to reveal—my heart leaped into my throat—a bedroom.

"Our bedroom," Aedin verbalized my thoughts.

I shifted uncomfortably, becoming distinctly aware of his movements as he unclipped the sheathed dagger at his belt and placed it on the bedside table.

The room was filled with light—an airy breeze floated through open doors revealing another garden just outside.

"Mary—please get Gwyneth something suitable to wear," Aedin directed, busily unrolling a parchment scroll. "Then… we'll talk." His eyes finally lifted to mine and my gut twisted in response.

I had willingly confined myself to my room during the three-day voyage, but I supposed it was inevitable that I had to speak to my new husband.

Mary guided me to an open door, revealing a large bathtub, standing sinks, and a tiled floor. We had never had such luxuries at home.

Turning the tap of the tub, she poured in some soap as the water began to foam and the scent of lavender filled the room. She closed the door and ordered, "Undress."

The word was stated like she was accustomed to giving orders. I obeyed.

Although I was eager to take off my furs, I was reluctant to be rid of the last vestige of my former life. Gingerly, I removed the coat, neatly folding it on the sink counter.

It had taken my father half a year's wages to pay for that coat and he'd insisted that I bring it to Lailan. I'd had little else to wear that was appropriate for my new life.

I cringed—he hadn't known that I would never wear it here in this oppressive heat. Neither had I.

After removing the last layer of cotton, I sank into the lukewarm water. My hands and body were the same color as the porcelain tub, from the years of my youth spent on an island with little sun. An island with snow, rocks, and an endless frigid breeze. An island where I had left my dearest brother and friend, Ephraim, my father, and the love of my life—

Mary's hands were strong as she massaged something into my scalp. The bath water turned slightly brown—I hadn't bathed since the morning of our wedding.

She must have seen this as well, as she ordered me to dunk and then repeated the process.

"Have you been to Lailan before?" Mary asked, her voice reverberating in the small room.

"No."

"This villa has always housed the Lords of Lailan… You are lucky to be here."

Anger prickled my skin at her presumption. "Am I?"

"Yes," she replied simply, as if it was a fact. "Do you know how many Lords of Lailan there have been in the past fifty years?"

Mary's question caught me off guard. "No."

"Rinse," she commanded.

I obeyed, wincing and rubbing the soap from my eyes. When I emerged, she answered, "Twenty-six. None have survived for more than two years."

"Survived?"

"Some imprisoned, others publicly beheaded. Most died of… natural causes."

I shivered, recalling the rumors and snide remarks concerning the Lords of Lailan. Everyone grew up hearing the stories—it was a running joke. Notoriously unscrupulous and wicked, the king was quick to dispose of each lord before they had cheated him and the Empire out of too much gold.

Many would mysteriously die of the plague, a shipwreck, or bad food, with a select few removed in full view of the island as an example.

The stories had always been entertaining at parties—now they sounded cruel and ominous.

Mary stepped back and held up a towel. I exited the tub and dried myself as Mary said, "This is the fourth year of my lord's reign."

I looked at her in wordless surprise. The old steward inclined her head carefully and handed me a comb.

When my hair was brushed and my body was deemed clean, Mary dressed me in a pale green gown. The fabric was thin and nearly sheer—my arms looked comically bare and hung awkwardly at my sides.

Without the layers of fur and cotton, I felt exposed and vulnerable. I clutched at my chest, warily eying the bare skin between my breasts.

"This is the fashion on Lailan, my lady." Mary watched my reaction with faint amusement.

Despite the heat, I wanted the comforting weight of my furs. But I steeled myself as Mary opened the door and we reentered the bedroom.

Aedin sat at a desk in the antechamber, scribbling in the parchment. He looked up at me, his dark eyes widening in surprise.

"Thank you, Mary," he said stiffly as she curtsied and opened the door. In her arms were my old clothes.

"Wait—"

She stopped abruptly at the sound of my voice.

"My furs… What are you going to do with them?"

Mary looked slightly guilty, as if she had been planning to burn them. "Wash them, my lady." She cleared her throat. "They will be in your wardrobe when they are clean."

"Thank you," I muttered, relief washing through my body. I couldn't bear to part with them. Not yet.

Aedin stood as the door closed and gestured to a chair and table in our room. "Please, sit."

The breeze passing through the open doors tickled my bare skin. I crossed my arms over my chest, keenly aware of his gaze as we sat opposite a small table.

I shifted my knees to avoid his as he diplomatically folded his hands and began, "I'm sure you're enjoying this heat."

A wry grin tugged at the corners of his mouth. Was it a joke? I thinned my lips and didn't respond.

In the brief awkward silence, the chatter of birds from the garden floated through the room. Aedin sobered and looked away.

"Do you prefer Gwyneth?" he asked quietly. "I heard your father and brother call you Gwen."

"Gwen is fine," I admitted hollowly.

"Gwen," Aedin pronounced my name slowly, testing it on his tongue. "I wanted to set some ground rules to ensure that we have an… understanding. As my wife, and the Lady of Lailan, you will be required to take certain precautions."

I couldn't meet his eyes, so I watched a bead of sweat form on the tanned skin of his throat.

"Such as?" I challenged.

"Such as taking security precautions. You should not leave the villa without a guard, or myself, and limit visits to Tahuna, the main port of Lailan."

"Why?" My throat prickled as I fought to keep my voice even.

"You are the Lady of Lailan; there are political enemies or people who may try to hurt you. Lailan can be… dangerous."

"What kind of danger?" I couldn't resist—my eyes flickered to meet his cool and impassive gaze.

He shrugged. "Like I said, political enemies, rival lords… you know."

I didn't. I had grown up a shopkeeper's daughter on one of the poorest islands in the Empire. Irritation bubbled in my chest as I picked at the fabric of my dress.

"And," Aedin continued. "It would be best if you keep your emotions in check."

"What?" I snapped.

Aedin winced, as if my anger had hurt him. "I said, it would be best if you keep your emotions—"

"Incredible," I muttered.

"Hm?"

"You are *incredible*," I repeated bitterly, anger unfurling in my blood. The monstrous dislike that I had curbed and restrained for my family's sake finally roared forth. "I hardly even *know* you and you ask me to *marry* you, then bring me to this island where you lock me up in a villa—"

"I'm not locking you up," Aedin protested with a grimace.

"—And then you tell me to *keep calm*?" My voice rose to a higher pitch and nearly broke on the last words.

He was silent as he waited for me to finish, but I had nothing else to say. I swallowed a frustrated cry, wanting to smack his pained expression. As if this was painful for *him*.

Leaning forward, he placed his hands on the table. "You *need* to keep calm." Aedin's voice was low and steady. "I know this is difficult—"

I gave a short laugh.

"—But you are safe here. And you have everything you will ever need—"

"I don't understand—what do you want from me?" I cried, my fingernails biting into my palms. "Do you want me to just sit here? Bear you a dozen children? Throw tea parties?—"

"No—no." Aedin held out a placating hand. "No, I want you to be happy—"

"Well then you should have left me on Berge," I fumed. "Because I had a *life* I loved."

And a man I loved. But Daniel was a hundred miles away.

My chest throbbed as tears pricked in my eyes. I wanted to go home.

"Gwen—please." Aedin extended a hand. I eyed it with caution, inhaling sharply.

"*Please*," he repeated.

His eyes were the color of mahogany—a rich brown mingled with flecks of dark greens and blues. I hadn't noticed it before.

Guardedly, I placed my hand in his grasp.

At his touch, a stillness, like warm water, rushed through me. I felt the coolness of the breeze as it moved through the humid air, bringing the scent of flowers and seawater. And the echoing taste of honey in my mouth—

My fury retreated into an inaccessible cave. I was devoid of emotion—stale and subdued.

Aedin gave my hand a soft squeeze and then pulled his away. My fingers were cold and heavy.

"Now," he said with a sigh, brushing back his jet black hair. "In three days time we will attend a reception at the home of a local noble family to celebrate our marriage. The de Boughs are quite a handful, but I am sure you will manage. Mary will help prepare you and such."

I was only half listening—my hand continued to lay lifeless on the table and I had to make a conscious effort to put it back in my lap.

"In the meantime…" He stood and retrieved the scroll from the antechamber, placing it on the table between us. There were nearly twenty pages, both sides scribbled in ominous dark ink. Some words were crossed out, others scratched in the margins—it looked like a mess of footprints in the dust.

"It would do you well to read these papers, to understand our court. These are my notes on all of the merchants and courtiers of Lailan. The latter pages"—he touched the last ten—"are those throughout the Empire, particularly in the capital, Radiance, and within the king's palace. These, perhaps are more important, but it is less likely that you will meet them… Let's hope Lord Tours doesn't come for a visit," he added wryly.

I swallowed, but the action was difficult as I focused on the parchment with a sinking feeling in my stomach. The tightly formed letters were alien and obscure.

My father had had little time or money to teach me to read. Ephraim—being the male and heir to our tiny family—had learned, and attempted to teach me some of it, but more often we had settled for swordplay instead.

"I trust you understand the importance of this document, and that itself and the knowledge of its contents will not leave this room." Aedin confirmed my thoughts, watching me carefully.

"Yes," I rasped, my throat thick. I was too proud to admit my deficiency. All I wanted to do was curl up in the bed—*our* bed— and cry.

"Good," he said quietly, looking down at my slumped form in the chair. I avoided his gaze, staring at the swirling grains in the wood floor.

He reached out a hand, as if he might touch me again, but then stood abruptly. "I have to leave for Tahuna," he announced, grabbing the sheathed dagger from the bedside table and buckling it to his belt. "I will see you at dinner."

I didn't respond. My mind was hollow and numb.

Aedin left without another word and I was alone again.

Chapter Two

I SLEPT THE rest of the day—until the sun completed its arch through the sky and cast a golden hue over the stucco walls. When Aedin returned, Mary summoned me from the room and our first dinner together progressed silently.

We sat opposite each other at a square table in a smaller, more casual dining chamber, adjacent to the grand one. The room was like a simmering pot of water and we ate the first couple of courses without a word.

There was a trembling pit in my stomach that made it painful to speak. Eventually I tried making small talk—asking him perfunctory questions concerning his day and the weather, but his short answers made it clear there would be no conversation.

Soon, my pleasantries turned to bitter words I feared would spill out, so I tightly shut my lips. Even the sight of him eating calmly, avoiding my glance, further ignited my irritation.

Despite my anger, I couldn't find the energy to fight. The effort was exhausting, and I wanted nothing to do with him.

Once the last course was taken away, we stood simultaneously and left the table. He said nothing as we passed through the bright halls and dark atrium. The crickets provided a barrier of sound for the silence between us.

He opened the door to the antechamber for me, and I passed through to the bedroom without a word.

I went straight to the bathroom—terrified at the sight of our empty bed. My hands trembled as I unclasped my earrings, placing them in a shallow bowl by my basin of water. I washed my face, patting it dry with a towel. My actions were slow and methodical as my ears strained for any sign of noise from the bedroom. But there was none.

Finally, when I was sure that I would not be intruded upon, I took off my dress, exchanging it for a thin cotton nightgown. I swallowed for courage and entered the bedroom, my feet padding quietly against the wooden floor.

The room would have been entirely dark, save for the full moon that cast light onto the floor through the open garden door. I thought of closing it for safety but was grateful for the night breeze cooling the room. The fountain gurgled quietly outside.

As I tiptoed to the bed, I found my husband sound asleep underneath the thin blankets. His eyes were shut fast, his breathing even, and as I caught sight of him in sleep, I marveled at how human he looked. Aedin's mouth was ajar, his black hair stark against the white pillow.

He was no more terrifying than my own shadow.

When he's asleep… a dark voice muttered in the back of my head as I shook away the thoughts and walked to the other side of the bed and slipped between the thin sheets. I stifled a sigh at the soft bed then immediately felt guilty. My entire life I had shared a straw mattress with my brother, Ephraim—at least he finally had the coarse blankets to himself.

I braced my chin, letting my mind swim back to memories of my former life.

The weight of Aedin's body shifted slightly and I held my breath—waiting for the inevitable.

My thoughts raced through scenarios—a wandering graze on my thigh or an insistent hand on my breast. What would do I do if it happened?

Would I submit? Or protest? Or clumsily feign enjoyment?

But nothing came.

Aedin did not make a sound.

That night, my first night in Lailan, I slept fitfully in the humid air—my eyes too dry for tears and my mind unwillingly restless.

—

When I awoke the next morning, the sun was high and already warming my skin through the curtains. They swayed in a cool breeze, the full-length glass doors thrown open to admit the chirping of birds and the murmuring of the garden fountains.

Blinking the sleep from my eyes, I lay in bed, staring up at the light grains of the wooden ceiling. My lids were still thick and heavy, and my head ached. Neither the patterns of the wood, nor the soft swelling of the curtains soothed my mood. I felt empty.

Everything that I wished to dwell on inspired a swelling pain in my stomach. I wondered where Daniel was, remembering the pain in his face the last time we had spoken.

How had it happened so quickly? I searched my mind for an answer but found nothing I wanted—only Aedin's dark flashing eyes.

I turned to see the opposite side of the bed empty. It was as if I had slept next to a ghost—the sheets were tucked neatly, the pillow skillfully fluffed.

Unnerved, I pushed back the covers and wandered into the bathroom. My bare feet trod quietly on the cool floor, offering a relieving contrast to the stifling heat. I splashed water onto my face, my mind still groggy, as several crisp knocks sounded on the door to the bedroom.

I paused. "Yes?"

"May I enter?" Mary's voice was faint through the thick wood.

"Yes, please," I called back, eying my discarded formal gown from the previous night with reluctance. I hoped ladies ate breakfast in their nightgowns.

The door clicked open and Mary entered the bathroom without bothering to check whether I was properly dressed. "Good morning," she stated stiffly.

Without waiting for a reply, she began to pick up my crumpled dress, fussing with the creases.

"Good morning," I replied, grimacing at my reflection. There were circles under my eyes—signs of another sleepless night.

"What would you like to wear this morning?" Mary tucked the dress in the crook of her arm and began to tidy the towels of Aedin's washbasin.

"I don't know…"

"My lady, don't slur your words—it's unbecoming," Mary said shortly.

I frowned at her hypocrisy. "But you—"

"I am not the Lady of Lailan—merely an individual in the employ of a great lord. Yet even I know the proper place for grammar and courtesy."

I shook my head, patting my face dry. "I grew up a shopkeeper's daughter. My mother died at a young age… I've hardly had time for grammar or courtesy lessons. It isn't what you think… I spent my time helping my father and learning to spar with my brother—not learning etiquette or anything—"

"My lady," Mary stopped my words, staring solemnly at me with her dark brown eyes. Although a full head shorter, she appeared nearly a foot taller. "Your previous life is dead. Gone. No more pitiful glances or sighs of complaint. *You* are the Lady of Lailan. You have expectations, rules, and standards to uphold—"

"What if I don't want any of that?" I challenged, my throat prickling. I crossed my arms, awkwardly standing by the sink.

"It is not a question of desire but of action. You cannot change the facts of your situation, but you can determine the context."

Her words hit me as my fingers traced the edge of the sink, a pit forming in my stomach. It just wasn't fair—I had never been prepared for this.

But here I was. I said quietly and without hope, "What must I do?"

I was grateful that she released me from her gaze as she turned to exit the bathroom. "Begin with proper grammar. That's a good place to start."

My lips thinned at her back.

I heard her open my wardrobe and dreaded her next words. "Which gown do you prefer today?" She was relentless.

I sighed. "I do not care." Each word was laced with a formal stiffness.

She re-entered the bathroom, carefully folding a cerulean gown on the counter. "Bath." She pointed and began to pump the water.

I soon understood why she was Aedin's preferred secretary—she was a merciless perfectionist. I had to endure nearly an hour of brushes, lotions and paints all to simply appear "decent," in her words.

Remembering her admonitions, I sat in silence, not daring to complain. With a final spritz of scented oil, she deemed me suitable to be seen. And I was—my long brown hair was pulled back into an intricate style and the dress flowed free of creases.

"My lady," Mary began as we walked to the dining room, "today, I am to fetch some fabric for my lord in Tahuna. He suggested that you come as well—to choose more dress fabric."

I was about to protest that I had more dresses than I would ever need when a quiet voice stopped me. A day outside of the villa would do me, and my nerves, well.

I consented to the idea and ate a quick breakfast that had already been prepared in the small dining room. Swallowing a large mouthful of tea underneath Mary's watchful eyes—I could see she was eager for me to finish—I forced down some bread and fruit as elegantly as possible and followed her to the front.

A black, horse-drawn carriage awaited in the turnabout. With an umbrella held above my head to shield me from the sun, Mary ushered me inside. It wasn't until I was settled that I realized we weren't alone.

"My lady," two guards intoned, nodding respectfully in unison.

Their dark uniforms blended into the black satin of the carriage's interior. Marks offered a familiar grin, as the younger man—no, boy—eyed me with cautious amazement.

"Mr. Marks," I replied stiffly, self-consciously tugging at the fabric of my dress.

Marks gestured towards the boy at my side. "This is Tieren—he will be joining us today."

Tieren made some polite reply and I couldn't help but let my confusion surface as I met his hazel eyes—he was so young! He must have been at least several years my junior, his boyish face only beginning to lose its roundness.

I remembered how Daniel had trained for *years* before being selected to join Lord Tremer's guard. And even he had been the most junior among the other men.

The young guard's eyes met mine with an eager curiosity and I flushed, staring at the floor.

"How are you settling in?" Marks asked as our carriage rolled through the gates and onto the main road.

"Fine enough." I could feel the backs of my thighs already beginning to stick to my dress. "And you are happy to be back?"

"Very much so." He brushed back his pale hair, watching me with bright blue eyes.

For a moment, the only sound was that of the carriage wheels hitting dusty ground, until I asked, "How long have you been head guard, Mr. Marks?"

"Four years," he replied. "I came to Lailan about ten years ago from Acedes."

It was the neighboring island to Berge in the north—another cold environment that specialized in hunting and fishing, though not as poor. "Were you guard to Lord Stovel previously?"

"No." A humorous smile tugged at his lips at the thought. "My wife and I wanted to live someplace warmer… and Lailan's economy provided opportunity."

"Does your wife miss you, then? Since you live on the villa property?"

"She is dead, my lady," Marks said evenly.

"Oh, I'm sorry."

I didn't know what else to say. We lapsed into an awkward silence as I looked out the window. The wall of greenery was occasionally interrupted by iron gates guarding large estates or small shacks along the road.

We were jostled as the carriage encountered a bump—my leg hit the scabbard of Tieren's sword.

"Sorry, my lady," Tieren murmured, shifting away from me.

"It's fine," I said automatically, ignoring Mary's meaningful look at my slurred speech. Stifling a sigh, I tried to enjoy the bright colors and passing breeze on my face, but it wasn't calming.

Nor did it feel like home.

Fifteen minutes later, the dense vegetation of the jungle progressively transformed into townhouses of wood and stone. The carriage rolled to a stop as the dirt gave way to cobbles and the clean buildings of freshly scrubbed stones bore small windows of glass and hanging wooden signs.

I grabbed my skirts, eager to exit as soon as the stairs descended, but Marks put out a hand in my direction.

"Wait here, my lady."

He excused himself to step out of the carriage, a tall figure in black amongst the wandering ladies and men in finery. After several seconds of scanning the crowd, he lowered the steps and offered me his hand to step down. Tieren remained motionless in his seat.

Ignoring Marks' hand, I held up my chin as I shielded my eyes from the bright sun and stepped into the street.

We had stopped in a shopping section of Tahuna above the main port. It was evident, from the colorfully dressed shoppers, glass storefronts, and carriages, that this area was dedicated to the upper class of Lailan. There were no cluttered carts or street-side vendors—the cobblestones were freshly swept and suitable for the well-dressed men and women who trod upon them.

Black carriages similar to ours rattled up and down the street. I now understood why ours was plain and unadorned: it was intentional. If there were an attack, our carriage would be hard to pick out from the others.

I scolded myself for thinking of such ridiculous things. I was in no danger—yet, no longer was I a common gentleman's daughter.

"Come along." Mary's command saved me from excess worry.

With the umbrella held high above my head, she led me to the nearest shop. Its stone exterior, similar to the others on the street, was bisected with glass and wood and painted with a word I couldn't distinguish. Behind the glass, gilded pools of cloth hung from the ceiling on display.

Marks trailed wordlessly behind us as we entered the shop.

A tinkling bell announced our arrival. Without waiting to be greeted, Mary led me to the back of the shop, where a large room was scattered with couches and full-length mirrors. Curtains separated small dressing areas off to the side. Seconds later, a tall, elegant woman glided into the room.

Her silver-streaked brown hair was piled on top of her head in a way that made her height all the more intimidating. She held a grace that I could never accomplish—even at her advanced age she looked like a dancer.

Her eyes went from Mary to myself and back. She assessed me as one views a porcelain doll for cracks. "My lady." She bent into a curtsy, pronouncing her words with pride. "I am Madam Porter. Is there anything you need in particular this day?"

Unsure, I glanced at Mary, who thankfully took control. "We are in need of more black cloth for my lord, and my lady would like to browse for dress material and patterns."

Madam Porter nodded. "Of course. I will fetch the cloth and have someone present our newest shipments." With another quick curtsy, she left the room.

As I sat on one of the pale silk couches, a young girl appeared, carrying two thick books.

"My lady," she murmured with a curtsy, placing one book on the couch next to me. "Here is a sample of our cloths. And here"— she held it outwards and I took the heavy thing in my hands—"is a sample of the latest dress designs we are able to fashion."

I thanked her and handed the latter book to Mary. Hesitantly, I flipped open the first. The book was divided into shipments— from the latest to the first the shop had ever received. Each shipment, in turn, was organized by color, ranging from the purest white to the darkest blues and blacks.

The multitude of colorful squares was overwhelming and I found it very hard to choose. After a while, I settled on a lovely shade of blue, a rose-colored fabric, and a wispy yellow pattern with flowers.

When Madam Porter returned, she handed a large roll of black cloth to Mary and listened as I showed her my choices.

"Is that all?" Her nose crinkled in faint condescension.

I paused. "Yes…" It was more of a question than a statement. I had thought three would suffice.

Sensing my inadequacy, Mary added, "She will also take this one"—she pointed to a pale orange I would have never imagined myself in—"and these." This time she pointed to ten of the newest cloth shipments that I had been wary to choose. The expense of one alone had been greater than my entire wardrobe on Berge.

With a snap of her fingers, Madam Porter sent the girl to search for my choices as she briefed me on dress fashions. I listened without retaining what she was saying. Instead, I gave her the charge of choosing the designs. Madam Porter simpered, as if flattered, but I sensed an irritation at the addition of work.

The cloths arrived and I approved them all. Most were the same as the thin translucent material that clothed my body, others a fine cotton, and a few, like the rose, were a shiny silk. After my measurements were taken, Mary and I bid Madam Porter good day and left the shop. I breathed a sigh of relief as we stepped into the bright sun. In an instant, Mary shielded my face, the umbrella held proudly aloft.

I turned to her, trying to catch her eyes—to thank her in some way for saving me from further embarrassment. But she looked straight ahead, her thin mouth fixed and clenched, towing me with the shade of the umbrella down the street.

A quick glance behind us confirmed that Marks had not abandoned his post.

Mary stopped mid-stride and pulled me towards the façade of another shop. This time, jewels—long necklaces, rings, bracelets, and even tiaras—were draped on display.

"I don't believe I need—"

"Every young lady is in need of jewelry," she scolded, opening the door for me. "Especially one of your standing, my lady."

She was right—there were already several other young ladies browsing the shop. Relief washed over me as I saw their bodies were clothed in the same revealing fashion; long gowns and dresses just covering their breasts or exposing their tanned backs. Their eyes turned towards me, judging at first, then curious at Marks' trailing black shadow.

I turned away from their attention, moving towards a case as if I knew what I wanted.

Thankfully, the first case was of emeralds—stones I had always admired. I perused the selection, pausing to touch a pair of teardrop earrings. Set into a thin gold frame, the polished stones sparkled as I held them up to the light.

An unfamiliar voice broke through my thoughts. "Beautiful, are they not?"

Surprised and discomfited by the intrusion, I glanced at the woman who had spoken. She was unquestionably older—her painted lips lifted in a smile and I noted the creased corners of her eyes and mouth.

"Yes they are," I replied cautiously, taking a step back, uncomfortable at her nearness.

"My husband just bought me a pair similar to those," she chatted with a complacent ease. "Same style, but they were ruby. Of course, it took him nearly half of his year's wage to purchase them, but he said I was worth it." She gave an airy laugh.

"Oh." I was unsure how to reply. "That sounds lovely."

"They are." Her eyes twinkled, and she said with realization, "I do not think we have met—my name is Francesca de Bough. My husband, Sir Gerand de Bough, was knighted by the king himself."

Internally, I grimaced. I knew the reaction I would receive when I gave her my title. "I am Gwyneth… Aedin."

I hated saying that last name with my own.

Her murky brown eyes grew as large as cherries. "*You* are Lady Aedin?" she managed to squeak out.

Unfortunately, her voice was not quiet. Immediately, Francesca and the other shoppers dropped into bows and curtsies. I fought to keep a pleasant smile as they murmured formalities.

When Francesca rose, she faced me with incredulity. The rest of the shoppers spoke in muted whispers.

I gritted my teeth.

"My dearest apologizes. Forgive me, Lady Aedin. What a… surprise!"

She looked on the verge of groveling. I let out a short sigh, forcing a smile. "No harm was done."

"I confess, this is a pleasure!" she continued with a confident, beaming smile. "You were only married to the lord seven days ago, am I correct?"

I wondered how she knew as I placed the emerald earrings back in the case. "Yes, I was—"

"Brilliant," she crowed, "then I suppose *your* husband will have no trouble purchasing those jewels for you."

"I suppose," I agreed, looking away in embarrassment.

Francesca laughed. "You are such a pretty thing! So young! And so pale! I knew Aedin—excuse me, *Lord* Aedin—would settle for nothing less than the most beautiful girl!"

I was about to argue that I was hardly the most beautiful girl, but Francesca continued, "My husband and I are very familiar with my lord." She gave another breezy laugh. "Sometimes I forget his title—we are such good friends! Please, do us the favor of passing on our compliments when you see him next. And, of course, we are *so*, so pleased that you have deigned to allow us to host your nuptial celebrations!"

My stomach sank at the mention of the party.

"O-Of course," I stuttered. "Please excuse me, Madame de Bough, but we have an afternoon appointment and I must be getting back," I lied politely, eager to be rid of the shop and her presence.

"Of course, of course! I understand you must be getting back to the lord! He is quite a character, is he not?" The curls of her fading brown hair swung limply as she shook her head in laughter.

"That is one of many ways to describe him. Please excuse me, madame." I nodded civilly.

"Yes, yes, farewell, my lady! I look forward to seeing you soon!"

"Yes… You too."

I opened the door to the shop with a huff, not waiting for Mary. Marks allowed a smirk at me as he effortlessly matched my long strides.

"Oh shut up!" I hissed at him.

I didn't slow to wait for the umbrella. The sun scorched my skin even during that brief exposure. I headed for the nearest carriage, but then stopped in the middle of the street as I realized I couldn't distinguish ours from the others.

Marks saw my hesitation and took the lead, walking towards a carriage parked across the street in the shade. Without another word, I leaped inside.

Tieren was seated motionless as before and he grimaced empathetically, as if knowing what had passed, before shifting his gaze out the window.

Mary stepped in, closing the umbrella and shooting me a mixed look of disdain and worry. I leaned my head back against the satin wall, squeezing my eyes shut as tears threatened to fall. The carriage rocked as Marks closed the door, and I sighed in relief when I felt it roll away.

When we came to a stop in front of the villa, I exited quickly. My feet and mind were heavily numb—I strode to my room, thankful that I didn't get lost.

Once inside, I shut and locked the door, then took a deep breath and sat in a chair, tearing off my sandals and unclipping my earrings. A soft breeze blew into my room from the garden, playing with the curls of hair that had escaped my braid.

My lips trembled as I pulled each clip from my hair, trying to focus on the sound of the distant fountains. I threw the clips on the floor in frustration, and then was ashamed of my anger. I gathered them from the floor and carefully placed them in the bowl by the bathroom sink.

I stared at my reflection in the mirror, assessing myself from every angle. The same oval, plain face looked back, as if daring an emotion to surface. I hadn't changed in the seven days since I'd left home. Aside from a faint blush on my skin—likely a sun rash —and the paint on my face, I looked the exact same.

I did not feel like a lady—I did not feel of any importance at all.

Tears began to glisten. I shouldn't be crying over such a small thing—hadn't I already? Yet I couldn't fight the bitterness and humiliation that swelled in my chest. I found it hard to breathe. I walked back into our room and collapsed on the couch.

Fighting back a sob, I wished for my father and brother. For some familiarity to ground and secure me. I felt lost in this foreign world, and a burning resentment for Aedin. He had taken me from my friends, family, and *love*.

At that word, my heart ached, inspiring new tears. I sniffed, making a fist as I burrowed my head into my knees.

I hated my husband.

And I hated myself for going along with this. Though I'd had little choice, I had still allowed it to happen. Allowed myself to be convinced by the social expectations and promises. Was it worth the price my father had claimed?

A quiet knock on the door echoed through my tormenting thoughts.

Quickly, I dabbed at the tears on my cheeks, careful not to smear the powder or paint. Swallowing my grief, I called, "Come in."

The handle twisted for a moment, then I remembered I had locked it. Growling under my breath, I stood, blinking back dizziness, then unlatched the door and opened it—only to almost shut it again.

Aedin stood in the antechamber.

My breath caught in my throat as a flurry of emotions attacked me—raw pain, spite, irritation, fury. I inhaled, intending to tell him off, but he spoke first.

"May I come in?"

"It's your room as well, isn't it?" I said in a hoarse and cool voice, turning my back.

I was still shaking. I walked to the open door of the garden and sat down on the steps, folding my arms and hugging my knees into my chest.

I felt him move cautiously into the room and then towards me. He pulled up the legs of his pants before joining me on the step, clasping his hands together and staring at the nearby fountain. I was grateful for the silence.

Out of the corner of my eyes, I watched his expression—his dark irises were guarded and calm, yet there was a hint of sympathy, or weariness, about his mouth. Bronze skin gleamed in the sunlight, a hint of sweat on his brow.

Inhaling shakily, I realized that all my witty retorts and harsh words had fled, and dropped my gaze to the cool stones below my feet—small clovers of moss were growing in between the cracks.

"Gwen." Aedin's eyes flickered towards mine as lines creased his forehead. "Mary told me what happened."

"What happened?" I challenged, my voice threatening to break. "Nothing happened."

I heard him breathe slowly. "You were approached by Francesca de Bough."

"So?"

"So I understand that you were placed in an uncomfortable position."

That was an understatement. "Yes, I was."

"I am sorry."

"Sorry for what?" I fixed my jaw as my voice grew harsh. "Sorry for marrying me? For making my life some huge… formality?"

"The last one," he replied quietly. "I am not sorry for marrying you."

I picked up a small twig from the ground, snapping it in half in frustration.

Again, we lapsed into silence. I was grateful for the gurgling of the fountain and the birds' melody—they were brief distractions from the uncomfortable present.

"Aedin?" I asked quietly, still not meeting his gaze.

"Yes?" His head lifted.

"Why did you marry me?"

Aedin exhaled once more, his eyes reluctantly moving to my face. There was a momentary pause before he said slowly, "Because… I love you."

The words were foreign and hollow in his mouth.

His eyes flickered away with unease, his copper jaw fixed, and my gut told me that he was lying.

I blinked back tears that were threatening to break as I stared at him. Elbows on his knees and hands folded under his chin, Aedin looked blankly ahead—that familiar mask covering his face.

My eyes traced the black brows and slanting cheekbones, the full lips that were pressed into a neutral, straight line. I stared until tears formed again and smeared him into a blur. I turned away, shivering.

"I'm sorry that this position has made your life difficult," he admitted quietly after clearing his throat; staring straight ahead, unable to meet my eyes. "But this is your new home. You are safe here."

I didn't respond. My throat felt thick.

Aedin's hand brushed against my fingers, lifting them from my thigh, lightly placing them in his grasp.

There was an imperceptible vibration against his skin for a second and then it was gone. I blinked.

Gently, he lifted my hand to his mouth and brushed his lips against my knuckles. I trembled when I met his eyes, perturbed by the gesture.

My heart thudded as I wondered whether he *had* been telling the truth. Perhaps this was his idea of love, though it was an odd way of showing it.

Aedin placed my hand back onto my thigh then wordlessly stood, as if settling a business meeting, and left. I shivered in the warm sun, suddenly cold, staring dismally at the dazzling colors in the garden.

Chapter Three

THE CRY OF gulls echoed fiercely above as the sharp, pale light of dawn hurt his eyes. Emerging from the belly of the ship, the island of Radiance greeted him with a crisp and fresh wind.

Lord Frederick Tours disembarked with a frown marring his usually stoic face, a piece of parchment gripped in his hand. It was creased and wrinkled, nearly torn, from being read and reread over and over again. But no matter how many times he'd perused the simple lines on the page, he couldn't make sense of them. He did not understand. And that ignorance was terrifying.

Within the confines of his carriage, he stared at the velvet-lined wall with a still gaze. His vehicle did not pause at the preliminary walls surrounding the capital; nor did it stop at the palace's thick, iron gate. Tours only had to show his face to the soldiers, and they understood.

The horses' hooves clattered to a stop at the roundabout and Tours did not hesitate. Jumping down without waiting for the groom, he was pleased that his boots made little sound against the stone. His black satin cloak swirled around him as he walked soundlessly into the palace.

"My lord—" His pathetic excuse for an assistant had to run to keep up with his long strides.

"Get me the king." Tours did not slow, or bother to look at the small man he kept as a ceremonial duty. "Tell him I will be in his rooms shortly."

"But, my lord—"

"Now."

Breaking into a run, the man's mop of graying hair zipped through the crowd with noticeable urgency. Tours exhaled between gritted teeth—he wished he wasn't so conspicuous.

With two fingers, Tours reached up to unclip his cloak, folding the thick fabric over his arm. His mind raced—he tried to bring himself back to the present and watch the passing courtiers, but it was no use. He did not understand.

Why? *Why* would *he* do such a thing?

Habitually, Tours felt the crowd, but nothing responded. Everything was as it should be—he nodded at the black-clad guard standing before the door to the private residence. The pale, short-haired man inclined his head in response, disappearing back into the shadows of the massive doors. This calmed Tours, but only briefly.

His fist tightened around the parchment.

All was quiet as his boots trod across the thick, ornamental rug. Magnificent hand-carved wooden arches supported the high darkened ceiling of the presentation chamber—there were no windows here. The king's palace on Radiance was one of the most secure places in the Empire. Hanging chandeliers suspended by thick chains of steel cast the room in a soft, shadowy glow.

Tours turned a corner and saw his assistant exit the largest door at the end. He paled, bowed, and excused himself as Tours passed through to the entrance room of the king's suite.

Ignoring the curious, and irritated, glances of waiting courtiers, Tours continued through another pair of doors to the private sitting room. He could feel their silent indignation—the courtiers would have been here for hours, perhaps days, waiting to see the king.

A few couches and a thick silence, save for the sound of a ticking clock, and then Tours opened the doors to the private rooms.

A half-naked girl was pulling on a dress. The King was lazily lacing his pants, watching her with mute frustration. He saw Tours and a flash of color flooded his cheeks.

"You couldn't wait five minutes?" the king growled, shooting a look at the girl, who disappeared through the open doors.

Tours waited until they were closed, folding his arms. The parchment crunched in his grip.

"My apologizes, Your Majesty." Tours attempted a voice of sincerity, but it failed. "But recent news trumps a whore."

The king grumbled under his breath, pulling a linen shirt embroidered with gold over his large gut. "Did you not just arrive from Lailan?"

"Yes."

"And you *had* to come *straight* here?"

"Yes."

The king motioned to the couches before a smoldering fireplace, groaning as he grabbed a pair of leather boots, tucking in his pants and lacing them. His health had grown worse, Tours noted quietly as he watched. It was only a matter of time.

Tours moved towards the couches, but then decided to stand before the fire. He thought it would create a striking image for the news he was about to break.

"Your Majesty…" Tours spoke quietly, feeling the room—they were alone. He continued, "Your Majesty, Lord Aedin has taken a wife."

The old man snorted, finishing his laces and lounging against the silk brocade. "*This* is your pressing news?" He rubbed his face in fatigue and irritation. "You cannot be serious."

Tours' mouth twitched—it was not the response the report deserved.

"I have just received the news myself." He unwrinkled the paper, waving it for effect. "He was visiting Berge to conclude his tour of the other islands—as was required—met a girl there at the closing ball—not *even* a noble girl—and married her within three days of leaving." His breath caught as he laughed at the ridiculousness of it all. Aedin—*married*?

"Did you give him permission—"

"He did not ask for it."

The king scratched at the beard on his chin. He was grinning. "Hm, that is strange."

"This is *not* amusing," Tours hissed.

The king's lips attempted to straighten. "Well if he wants a girl to keep him warm at night, why is it a problem?"

"It is a problem because we don't know *why* he married her. And so quickly? You know him—he trusts no one. If he were to marry—*if*—then he would have *at least* courted her for much longer. He would have *at least* conducted a routine background search before he would even consider a spouse. He would have tested her loyalty with all sorts of challenges… *But* he *knows* that it is dangerous to marry—he *knows* we can kill him with a single word. Why would he rope a girl along with him? He has been in power for only a few years and now he believes he is invincible? Able to marry? Perhaps to even create *children* for *succession?*"

Tours paused, surprised that his breath was coming so quick. He was satisfied to see the king sober, becoming thoughtful as he watched his most loyal lord.

"Should we kill her?"

Tours threw the parchment in the fireplace and folded his arms. Destroy the evidence—that was the lesson he had been taught. But everyone already knew by now. The marriage of a lord was no light business.

"No," he sighed heavily. "No, that would be unwise."

"But if we made it look like an accident—"

"No," Tours said flatly. "Aedin would know, and it would anger him. We do not want an upset *and* irrational Aedin on our hands… Though I am at a complete loss as to why he married her. He must *at least* feel something for her. If he bound her to him, he must like the girl to some extent."

"Maybe he fell in love?"

Tours chuckled, smoothing back his dark blonde hair. "He knows better than to 'fall in love'."

The king shrugged. "I am merely supplying hypothetical answers. What do you want me to say? Maybe he was just desperate to have a woman—you know he has refused our offers of diversions in the past."

"Perhaps." Tours shifted his weight, staring thoughtfully into the fire. "But *why*?"

"Ask him yourself." The king waved his hand dismissively. "Who is the girl?"

"Gwyneth Doyle—a shopkeeper's daughter from Berge. No one of significance—not even exceptionally pretty as far as I've heard."

"He was extremely desperate then." The king rose, clapping Tours on the shoulder. "I will leave it to you."

"Will you allow me to go to Lailan?"

"No." The king shook his head. "I need you here. I dislike it when you romp off to Lailan every couple of months."

"You know I have to keep Aedin in line."

"Yes, but has he not proven himself loyal in the past four years? We have never had any reason to suspect his intentions were unfaithful."

"Until now."

"You cannot jump to conclusions." The king did not attempt to hide his weariness of the conversation.

"That is the reason I am Lord of Radiance, Director of the Rhidge, and not dead."

The king shrugged, ringing a bell. "It is in your hands, Tours. I do not care what Aedin does. As long as he continues to keep Lailan out of unscrupulous hands and gold in *my* pocket, unlike the previous lords, he can do whatever the hell he wants."

Tours' mouth thinned. There was more at stake than gold.

"Very well—leave it to me."

"Stay here for now—we have work to do with these damn advisors, and my health… Give it some time and then you may pay them a visit."

"Yes, Your Majesty."

They were silent as a servant entered, uncorking a bottle of dark red wine and pouring it into a glass decanter. The king shooed him away, helping himself to the large glass, then motioned to Tours, but the latter shook his head.

"You have never been fun." The king smacked his lips, coughing through the drink as Tours met his eyes steadily. After a moment of silence, the king looked away, as if distracted. Uneasy under Tours' predatory gaze.

"Shall I send someone to your rooms to keep you warm?" The king stood, shrugging on his fine coat, then fixing his thinning hair in a mirror.

"No thank you—I can find my own."

The king picked up the glass, motioning for Tours to exit with a polite smile. "Of course you can."

Chapter Four

THE BLACK CARRIAGE rattled into a wide turnabout, joining a crowd of identical vehicles that flooded the cobblestones.

The bright chatter was loud even from our place at the back of the line. A fountain echoed in harmony with the crickets as the soft sound of strings and drums echoed from within the mansion. Torches cast a warm glow over the crowd as they meandered inside the archways.

Laughter floated from within, hitting me with a wall of anxiety as our carriage lurched forward, nearing the carpeted path that led into the house.

I blinked back a wince, my gaze flickering to Aedin for the briefest second.

My husband, as usual, hadn't said anything. He looked pensively at the dignified estate—too thoughtful for an evening at a party. I looked at his hands, eying the brown fingers that gripped at the fabric of his pants.

It was a façade—the slouching of the broad shoulders and bored gaze. The unyielding grip of his right hand and slightest creasing between his brows—somehow I knew he was as anxious as I. Then why had we even come?

My stare was felt and Aedin met it with an impassive expression. I flushed at being caught and looked away, suddenly nervous. I still didn't understand the necessity for this party. Our marriage was not entirely a celebratory affair.

When our coach rolled to its final stop, Aedin straightened his shoulders, loosened his hands and ducked to exit. Immediately, there were stares, the other guests pausing in their conversations to gawk as the black shadow of my husband stood tall.

Trembling, I pushed up from my seat, wishing I'd thought to feign sickness to get out of this. The small steps leading to the ground felt impossibly rickety and unstable.

I tried to brace myself on the door frame but saw Aedin's hand outstretched. I eyed it as well as the crowd who had already begun to bow, realizing who I was—who *we* were. Would I risk falling in front of them by not accepting my husband's help?

Reason won, and I grasped Aedin's hand. He held mine in an iron grip, sturdily guiding me down the steps. When I was somewhat steady in my heels, I loosened my grasp.

But he held tight, entwining his fingers in mine as if it was only natural. I wanted to unwind them but forced a smile as the guests came to greet us, one by one.

They were mostly older, a collection of women and men that appeared to lead very comfortable lives. The women were painted, gilded in a mixture of silks and linen, and draped in stones ranging from diamonds to pearls. The men were larger, the buttons of their embroidered vests straining, their shoes polished enough to sparkle as brightly as the women's jewelry.

I now understood the net of pearls that Mary had tucked into my hair, the thick band of diamonds around my wrist, and the gold-and-blue silk dress that swathed my body, leaving one shoulder entirely bare. I felt like a gift or a newly prized painting, being offered and displayed.

Aedin was dressed in his usual uniform of dark pants and shirt. The only difference was the black doublet—inlaid with silver thread, stitched gracefully in patterns of vines—the traditional garb of a lord. I recalled seeing Lord Tremer wear something similar for formal celebrations on Berge. Around his neck hung a stone nearly the size of my fist that shone a soft blue in the firelight. It was the stone of our island.

But the doublet and stone did little to impress the crowds—it was the quiet civility and authority that oozed from his person that was enough to command their attention and bows. I felt insignificant next to him, even as he carefully held my hand.

I suddenly realized how young he was—over a decade younger than the men who bowed in front of him. It struck me as odd, and I was surprised I hadn't noticed it before. Most lords received their position after nearly a lifetime of service to the king. What had Aedin done to receive his lordship so young?

My husband introduced me to each person who sought our attention. He knew all their names; I forgot each one as they bowed in front of me.

Aedin didn't let go of my hand. I wanted to squirm and run back inside the carriage but forced a calm, polite expression, smiling or laughing when needed. In this manner we slowly made our way inside. I tried several times to pull my hand out of my husband's grip, but he never relented.

Finally, after an elderly couple moved to allow us room to walk through the open doors, I inclined my head towards Aedin with a civil smile, whispering, "How long are we staying?"

I didn't expect a straight answer, so I was surprised when he responded equally quietly with a charming grin, as if we were having a normal exchange. "Perhaps an hour or two. We can't escape it," he said shortly, and I knew it would be a long night.

I swallowed in understanding and studied the musicians in the corner, the row of shiny glasses filled with wine, the dozens of bouquets of flowers that perfumed the air, the shining jewels… This was all for us—and yet we were hardly the main act.

I bit back a yawn, longing for the quiet of my room and the comfort of my bed.

I wished I was in Berge where it was cold—I was still sweating and the sun had set over an hour ago. I wished for Daniel. I wished it were his hand grasping mine, his voice that tickled my ear. I clutched my husband's hand tightly, wishing he would let go and hoping he didn't mistake the squeeze for something else.

"My lord!" A loud voice brought me to the present. A short, round man came forward through the crowd, bending into a low bow. "I cannot tell you how pleased I am that you have graced us with your presence, and your beautiful wife—"

"Sir de Bough," Aedin cut him off with a tight grin, "you are too kind."

"Where is Francesca?" He whirled around as if she would appear. "She should be here! Ah, well, here, take some wine, please, please, here!"

From one of the polished tables, he handed us each a glass. I took it, a bit puzzled by the man's exuberance. As we locked eyes, a toad-like smile stretched across his face. The sweat stains under his armpits shone darkly on his red silk jacket.

I was thankful that Aedin let go of my hand to take the glass.

"Are you hungry as well? Here, try this pastry—fig and onions, absolutely delightful!" He grabbed a silver tray from a passing server, putting it in front of us. Aedin politely declined for us both.

I bent the glass towards my lips to take a sip as Sir de Bough began to rattle on about some new shipment of his—mock complaining about how rigid Aedin's rules had been to not allow all of his ships in the port—when I felt a hand stop me. I frowned as Aedin gently took the glass from my hand, nodding at Sir de Bough as if in concern.

Subtly, he switched our glasses, giving me his. I stared at him, bemused, watching as he took a sip of *my* wine, rolling it around his mouth before finally swallowing. Sir de Bough noticed nothing —he was laughing at something he himself had said.

Biting back a comment, I drank his wine.

"My lord!" Another voice drew our attention, breaking Sir de Bough off mid-sentence. I watched Francesca stride towards us, perfectly made-up from her elaborate hairstyle to the fashionable sandals clicking on the marble floor. "And my lady! How good to see you again!"

She curtsied low, before coming forward to kiss me on the cheek. I started in surprise and saw Aedin stiffen at the contact. Her perfume was strong, and I tried to smile at the welcoming gesture.

"I see Gerand has already helped you." She gestured to our glasses of wine. "I cannot tell you how pleased I am to see you here! And married!" Francesca smiled at Aedin. "What a great surprise it was, my lord, when we heard the news. I am so glad that we are finally able to celebrate it with you!"

"Your hospitality is much appreciated," my husband said solemnly, inclining his head.

"My lady." Francesca took my arm, grinning. "Have you ever met Miss Taylor? I believe she is about your age—she lives with her father not a mile from us."

"No, I do not believe I have had the pleasure." I focused on not slurring my words, as Mary had advised, and I tried to smile but understood what she was doing. I eased closer to my husband, struck with a suddenly childish fear of being forced to leave Aedin's side.

Aedin looked unwilling to let us part, but Sir de Bough's insisting laugh must have changed his mind. "We must let the women be with their own kind, my lord. They do not want the company of men."

I fought to repress a sharp retort to his statement.

Francesca shot me a beaming smile. I was at her mercy as she towed me towards an adjacent lounge where a group of women were elegantly seated, chattering away.

I looked back for a brief second but saw two men taking my spot next to Aedin. My husband looked as unenthused as ever.

Swallowing my nerves, I sat where Francesca commanded me. She handed me a tray of food and I took an item without thought, patiently nodding as she introduced the women in my vicinity (including Miss Taylor).

I held the tart in one hand, responding as an elderly matron asked me how I liked the villa. Composing a civil answer, I smiled and straightened my back as I tried to take a bite of the tart as gracefully as possible.

A black shape against the whiteness of the far wall caught my eye. I recognized Marks. What was he doing here?

My brow creased in confusion, and I was momentarily distracted from another woman's question. I placed the tart back down on the napkin in my lap, apologizing.

Again, I shot a look at Marks. He was shaking his head, his blues eyes locked on me.

I glared at him, slightly amused. Raising the tart to my lips, I saw him look pointedly at me and shake his head. He didn't want me to eat it?

I shifted my gaze to the women before me, laughing at something that had been said. Another asked a question. Yes, I lied through my teeth, I like the lord very much. No, the rooms are very simple and lovely, but elegantly so. Yes, the heat of Lailan is wonderful!

I took a bite of the tart.

Just as I had expected, Marks began making his way through the couches towards me. I tightened my lips as I watched him come to my side, leaning down to my ear.

The women looked curiously at him, giggling and whispering behind their hands. I set down my glass as I heard him say quietly, "My lady, would you please join me outside?"

I nodded in submission, eager to be relieved of the group. "Please excuse me for a moment." I stood as they all cried out for me to stay. "It will only take a moment," I promised, putting on a charming smile as I followed Marks onto the deck.

A warm breeze caressed my arms; I hadn't realized how hot it had been inside. I could barely see Marks against the blackness of the night sky. Even with the torches casting lights to illuminate the set-up of couches and tables, I strained my eyes to follow him. He stopped at the deserted railing of the balcony, turning to me angrily.

"Why would you do that?"

"Do what?" I replied innocently.

"Eat the food. It could have been poisoned!"

I looked at him dubiously. "But it wasn't."

"It very well could have been," he said bitterly, his voice low. "My lady, please understand. The only safe place in the *entire*

Empire is the villa. When you are not within its walls, precautions must be taken."

"But I drank the wine!" I objected.

"Only because my lord tested it for poisons beforehand," Marks said scathingly. "You didn't even know what you were eating!"

"Yes, it was a fig and onion tart," I replied indignantly, pleased that I'd remembered Sir de Bough's description.

"But did you sniff it for any odd smells? Taste a bit to make sure nothing foreign had laced it?" He stopped shortly. "What am I saying? You know nothing—"

"Of what?" I frowned, hating my ignorance.

"Of this!" He waved his arm around. I was surprised to hear so many words leaving his mouth—and with so much energy.

"My lady—you are a *lady* of extremely high rank. And you are married to Aedin of all lords. He is above all other lords. Do you know how many enemies he has? Do you know how many want him dead? Do you know how many would want *you* dead?"

My mouth opened and closed in shock. Heart pounding, I stared at the far, dim lights of the port. "Marks—who would want him dead?"

He looked away, as if he regretted his last words. Folding his arms, Marks looked around for a distraction, the torchlight reflecting red and gold on his pale hair.

A loud laugh from a nearby couple stiffened his shoulders and shadowed his eyes. Their chatter paused as they glanced at us in surprise, until they finally passed by.

I looked away until they were gone. When I turned eagerly back to Marks, he was pensive.

"Political enemies—do you know how many Lords of Lailan there have been in the past fifty years?" he said, after a long moment of silence.

"Yes, twenty-six," I said, recalling Mary's little history lesson the other day. I understood Marks' implication. "But he is favored by the king..." I objected, suddenly afraid. "Everyone says that Aedin is one of his most loyal servants—"

"Let's hope it remains that way." Marks shot me a look that closed the conversation.

We were quiet, until he finally pushed back from the ledge with an almost empathetic expression. "Don't let me detain you from your new friends." He paused with seriousness. "Heed my warnings. Don't eat anything, and let me get you a new glass of wine."

"Why?"

"We have been away from it." Marks quirked his lips into a sardonic smile. "Someone could have poisoned it by now."

My stomach churned in response as I followed him back into the light of the house.

The noise and heat of bodies was overwhelming as I re-entered the party. Marks disappeared into the crowd and I was left alone. I craned my head to try to spot Aedin but saw no sign of him amongst the clustered bodies of silk and linen.

Remembering my promise, I made my way back to the couches. Francesca and the other women hadn't moved. I sat down as if I hadn't left and was immediately engulfed in conversation.

Minutes later, Marks appeared by my side, a glass of wine in his hand. I took it without question, sipping the red liquid deeply, wondering if every passing guest was an enemy.

"… it is so rare to have my lord attend an event. We are so grateful to now have you in Lailan."

There was a brief pause as I realized they were looking at me, and I blinked, my gaze refocusing on the group of women. Miss Taylor smiled awkwardly—it was she who had spoken.

"Yes," I said slowly. "I… am glad to be here."

Her cheeks were freckled from the sun. She looked about my age and her loose honey-brown curls swung as she spoke. "We *never* used to see him," she said, giggling as the other women exchanged amused glances.

"Except for that festival last year," another lady piped up from a nearby settee.

"Yes, that was disappointing." Miss Taylor tilted her head. "He stayed for an *hour*—talked only to the men and then left!"

Francesca chuckled. "Incredibly frustrating. He has frustrated all of Lailan since his arrival. So young and so handsome—and giving no thought at all to the ladies."

"Even Kitra tried so hard to get his attention. Do you remember that time when she—" This incited a bout of laughter that cut off Miss Taylor's words. I didn't know what to say, my smile frozen and awkward.

"Oh dear." Francesca patted my knee. "My lady, it is all in good jest. We thought he would *never* marry—and then you came along!"

"How did you meet?" Miss Taylor bent forward eagerly. "Are you related to Lord Tremer?"

I nearly choked on my sip of wine. Related to Lord Tremer—*that* was a jest. I doubted the lord had ever known my father had existed until Aedin's proposal.

"Er, no. Not related," I offered lamely. "My father is… a merchant on Berge. He deals in the fruit industry." It was the most profitable trade on Berge, and worked for the lie. A merchant was better than a shopkeeper.

Straightening, I noted their patient and attentive gazes and realized I would have to offer more. "I met Lord Aedin at the closing ceremonial ball before the conclusion of his tour. He asked me to dance, and we had a lovely evening together." I raised my voice a pitch and forced a smile.

"What did he say? Did you sneak off at the end of the night…?" Miss Taylor's words fueled another round of giggles.

I blushed in memory. I *had* ended that evening with Daniel—sitting by the lake outside of Lord Tremer's estate. Watching the moonlight on the rippling water. Curled up together under his furs. Our bodies hot and pressed against each other. I'd had no idea the next morning would bring so much pain.

"We had a lovely discussion about Lailan." My words felt hollow as I lied. "Spoke about our lives… our love of the outdoors." I hardly remembered what Aedin had said that night, or if he had even spoken at all.

"We connected…" I offered unconvincingly, wondering if they were aware of my performance. I had never been a good liar.

I took another swig of my wine, enjoying the sweet, earthy taste on my tongue. I suddenly wanted to be very drunk.

"I do not mean to pry," Miss Taylor said sweetly. "You see—I am not married yet and am still considering suitors. So I must live through the stories of other married women."

I winced internally and offered an obligatory smile. "Not at all." I shifted in my seat. "I am happy to oblige and enjoy meeting you all."

"Lailan is small," an elderly woman croaked from the other side of Francesca. "You will see—we have known each other for *many* years and look forward to getting to know you as well. It is not often that we welcome noble men and women from other islands into our circle."

Miss Taylor nodded eagerly. "It is *so* interesting to hear the perspectives of outsiders. We rarely leave Lailan—we are so blessed by the gods with our good weather, fine shops, a *wealth* of parties and events… We rarely want for anything!"

Lailan certainly didn't feel that way to me, but I nodded obligingly. "That sounds wonderful."

"Oh, you should come!" Miss Taylor grabbed my hand, which was resting on my knee. "We're having a garden party next week. It should be lovely—"

"Yes." I didn't see a way out so replied perfunctorily. "I would love to attend."

"Oh good!" This seemed to appease her. "You may call me Andrea. I promise—we will save all of the good gossip for next week." She eyed me conspiratorially. I wasn't sure if I wanted to know.

"Lovely to chat with you, Andrea." I gently took my hand from her grip. My glass was empty. "Excuse me." I rose with some elegance and moved away from the women.

The heat from the crowded bodies in the room was overwhelming—I felt a line of sweat trickle down the back of my neck. Spying Marks in the crowd, I grabbed another glass of wine from a passing tray and made a beeline for him.

I pushed the wine into his face with a glare.

"Enjoying this?" He smirked as he took a sip of the wine.

"Completely," I replied acidly and grabbed the glass, easing towards the welcoming dark of the outdoors.

It had only been about an hour, but by now I was well recognized. I felt as though every eye was upon me. Resting my forearms against the railing, I avoided the stares of a nearby group. My face ached from smiling.

I took a large mouthful of wine, rolling it around my tongue. I had never had wine this good on Berge. We had never been able to afford it and typically drank ale or the rare diluted dredges of wine leftover from Lord Tremer's parties. I wished for a pleasant buzz to drown out my thoughts—to make me feel light and happy. But it didn't come.

A dark shape drifted slowly towards my side. I tore my eyes away from the distant lights to meet Aedin's keen stare—then quickly looked away, sipping my drink like a crutch. Even through the darkness, I was very aware of his presence and instinctively shifted away.

"I never liked these," he offered in a quiet voice.

I was thankful his eyes had moved from me and now focused on the black abyss of the night. The torchlights from the party cast sharp shadows on his handsome face.

"It sounds like you didn't attend many," I said humorlessly. "You've made enemies of all the young ladies of Lailan."

He shrugged indifferently. "I am busy."

We lapsed into silence. The breeze moved through my dress, cooling my body. I finished the glass of wine, eying the last dregs with disappointment and a sigh.

"My lord," a deep voice resonated through the darkness as a large figure bowed.

"Cabot," Aedin said tersely, turning to face him.

"I must congratulate you—along with everyone else—on your recent nuptials." The man's gaze slid up and down my body with a leering smile. "We were all quite… surprised."

"Thank you." Aedin's voice matched his cold expression. "Gwyneth, may I present Mr. Renalt Cabot. He owns one of the largest sugar plantations on Lailan."

"I also have homes on Cachelle and Tente," he added breezily, sipping his wine. "But Lailan has always captured my heart… It is a pleasure to make your acquaintance, my lady."

Cabot bowed low, the silk buttons on his colorful jacket straining with the action.

"And yours as well," I replied, watching Aedin's stiff posture. "Are you enjoying your evening?"

"Indeed, my lady. I would not have missed this for the Empire. " Cabot eyed Aedin with humor. "Domestic life suits you, my lord."

I saw a crack of bitterness in his bored mask. "So it would seem," he muttered.

"The epitome of marital bliss," Cabot crowed with delight, saluting us with his glass.

I shifted uncomfortably next to Aedin, eying the nearby courtiers who watched us with smug expressions. I felt out of place in my diamonds and silk and it appeared I wasn't alone in the thought. Everyone knew that our marriage was a joke.

My stomach sank with the realization. I wanted more wine.

"We do need to sit down, my lord, and discuss the sugar prices. If there's anything to be done—"

"Yes, please write to Mary and set up a time," Aedin cut him off brusquely. "Although it will have to be several weeks from now, or more."

"On my next trip then." Cabot seemed satisfied. "It has been a pleasure, my lady." He bowed again, turning from us with blundering grace.

As Aedin watched Cabot go, he allowed a scowl to cross his face. "I hate that man," he said quietly.

I snorted. "He thinks very highly of himself."

"Indeed," he mused, eying my empty glass of wine. "Another? Or are you ready to leave?"

"I'm ready," I said quickly and plopped the glass on the rail—not caring if it might fall.

Aedin held out his hand. I hesitated then took it.

We made our way back inside, moving through the crowd of simpering smiles and smirks with nods to their curtsies and bows.

I was grateful when we finally ducked inside the carriage and it rolled off into the darkened jungle. I had the impression that the party wouldn't have missed us if we hadn't been there anyway.

I relished in the silence—broken only by the quick sounds of the horses' hoofs trotting along the dirt path. Across from me, Aedin swayed with the movement of the carriage, looking thoughtfully out the window. His brown hands hung limply on his thighs, his face shadowed and weary in the dim light of the lamps.

After a moment's silence, summoning the courage to speak, I whispered, "You checked my wine for poisons, didn't you?"

He looked at me carefully before responding with an equally hushed voice. "Yes, I did."

"Why such fear?"

Aedin turned his face to the window again, ignoring my question.

"Marks told me something… He said that you have enemies— that some want you *dead*." I paused. "Why is that?"

He laughed lowly, rubbing his strong chin as he looked at me. "Gwen, who doesn't want the lords dead?"

"And why would they want me dead as well?"

"Because you are married to me," Aedin said slowly, as if it was obvious. "Because you are my wife, they would use you against me, perhaps. And if I lose my lordship or am assassinated… Well it's only natural that they destroy any family or relation of mine as well."

My blood ran cold at the casualness of his speech. "Then why did you *marry* me?"

Aedin opened his mouth to respond but immediately shut it. Perhaps he knew that I hadn't bought his profession of love the other day. I was glad that he didn't try another lie.

"I thought you said we were safe!"

"We are," he said shortly, his expression turning grave as he looked away. But the way he said those words did not soothe my fears—they didn't sound like a guarantee of perpetual safety.

My heart beat wildly as I stole another look at my husband— completely absorbed in the passing jungle. I didn't believe I was safe with him. Not as a lady, not as *his wife*. I couldn't stay here—caught in this mad political web that surrounded him.

But I couldn't escape.

We retired to our room that night without a word. I tried to sleep, reminding myself of the retinue of guards surrounding the villa and Aedin's bland assurances.

But my thoughts were haunted by wild imaginations as I tried to envisage a horror greater than political rivals.

Chapter Five

THE NEXT DAY I awoke, and my husband was gone. It must have been early. A soft glow of light hit the wooden floor near the window. The birds were singing their usual melody, and it echoed through the open doors to the garden.

I wondered if I should get out of bed.

A memory of my former life flittered through my mind. The first time I had met Daniel. It had been an unusually warm spring on Berge—the scent of pine had filled the air as I watched him spar with my older brother. I had been eight or nine years old.

Even at first sight, I knew it must be love—I loved the shape of his mouth and his unruly mop of auburn hair. The way his warm brown eyes flickered towards me when he noticed my presence. I had ignored Ephraim's complaints insisting that I leave as Daniel hadn't seemed to mind.

And then, when Ephraim had left, he had kissed me shyly on the cheek. And I knew I was in love—

My mouth felt parched and dry, my body numb and lifeless as I shoved the memory aside. There was a stinging in my chest. I loosened my grip on the fine cotton sheets and reality hit me in the gut.

I looked around the room—there was nothing to do. Dejected at the lack of a goal or distraction, I lay in bed for a while, listening to the birds and wishing, praying to the gods for something to change. I doubted any of them were listening to the troubles of a wealthy lady.

After a while, I decided to rise and have breakfast. I did so in my nightgown, pleased at the shocked looks I received from the servants in the dining room. They would have to adjust to my lack of formality in the early hours of the morning.

Slightly smug with myself, I sat in the adjacent smaller dining room, taking the chair that faced the ocean. A vast, blue abyss. I sighed, wishing I were on the ships going *anywhere*—even to the gates of hell—but here.

"Good morning," a servant's voice interrupted my thoughts. I looked up to see a young girl—perhaps around Tieren's years—place a napkin and utensil set in front of me. "What would you like this morning?" Her voice was soft and sweet.

"Um, bread, fruit, and some tea please," I said with some hesitancy at the unfamiliar face.

The servant inclined her head, pouring water into my glass and exiting quickly.

I frowned in puzzlement, watching her retreating form through the glass door. Where was Mary?

Bored at the lack of company, I rested my chin on my hand and watched the waves of the ocean. I wondered if this was becoming a habit—watching the ocean. There was nothing else really *to* watch, save for the unceasing activity of the port.

If I stared long enough at the miniature winding streets, would I be able to discern people, tinier than ants, as they weaved up and down the alleys and roads of Tahuna? I was thankful for the view: it was a distraction, a brief respite where I could imagine myself sailing far, far away.

But I tore my eyes away with a shudder. Was this was how I was to spend the rest of my life? Watching it pass from within the glass and stucco walls of the villa? Only venturing out for garden parties or dress shopping?

It wasn't a pleasant thought on which to dwell.

The door opened. "My lady," the young servant's voice broke through my thoughts once more. She carried a tray, setting down several plates on the table.

"Thank you," I said in the awkward silence, as the china sounded dully upon the wood.

"You're very welcome." The servant smiled shyly, her teeth dazzlingly white against her smooth, tanned skin. I suddenly had an idea.

"My lady, is there anything else I can get for you?" She held the empty tray loosely.

"Yes. Please sit down." I motioned to the chair opposite mine.

The servant froze, perhaps thinking she'd heard wrong. I said nothing for a long moment, beginning to dip my spoon into the jam, and watched as the servant eased hesitantly into the chair.

"What is your name?" I asked quietly.

"Talia, my lady," she said with uncertainty.

"Talia. And where is Mary this morning?"

"She usually helps my lord with his affairs in Tahuna on the fourth day of the week… my lady," she added quickly with a blush.

"Ah." I spread the jam over the warm toast. "And so you are assigned to me for the day?"

"N-No, my lady." Talia looked unwilling to contradict me. "I was to assist in the kitchen."

"Well I have no attendant for the day." I bit into the toast, brushing off the crumbs on the table. "Would you be able to serve that purpose?"

I knew very well that I could survive a day without the help of a servant—Mary usually left me alone save for dressing and lecturing me. But perhaps a friend or companion could be made out of Talia.

"My lady, I have other duties—"

I raised my eyebrows at her and watched as she added quickly, "But I would be able to give them to another, in order to serve you."

"Perfect." I smiled, pleased at the tiny victory.

A brief silence ensued. Talia looked uncomfortably at her folded hands and the empty tray on the ground.

"Can I get you anything else, my lady?"

"No, I am fine for now."

More silence. I chewed my toast thoughtfully—it was harder than I had thought to get her to talk.

"Do you live in Tahuna?"

"Yes, my lady."

"You don't have to use the 'my lady' nonsense unless we're in company," I pointed out gently.

Talia opened her mouth and awkwardly said, "Very well…"

"How many siblings do you have?"

"Five."

"And they are…?"

"I am the oldest, seventeen years of age, and my youngest brother is five…" Again, the pause for a "my lady," but she obeyed.

"Do you miss them?"

A flicker of a smile passed across her lovely face. "No, not really. Our house is small and I share a room with my two sisters. I see enough chaos on my days off."

"How long have you been working at the villa?"

"Only two weeks, my—" She caught herself, grinning. "I'm sorry. My father fishes and Mother sells the meat. The growing competition has been hard and so I decided to seek work at my lord's villa. He's been very generous in the past with providing work to other locals, so I came here."

"That's very kind of you to help your family." I smiled at her, sipping my tea.

She looked uncomfortable but nodded with a tight-lipped grin.

"You can call me Gwen."

It was Talia's turn to raise her eyebrows. She looked dubiously at me. "I don't think that would be proper…"

I sighed through my teeth. "Talia, about two weeks ago I was a shopkeeper's daughter who practiced swordplay with her brother and preferred rolling around in the mud and fighting rather than sitting through civility lessons. Although… my situation has changed, I have not."

I was pleased to see a brief grin flicker across Talia's face, and so I continued. "Marrying Lord Aedin has set me quite over my head. I'm still learning, but it's been lonely. I left everyone I had ever known in Berge, so I should like to gain at least one friend in this place."

Talia nodded, smiling. "Very well, Gwen." She pronounced my name like it was foreign. "What would you like to do today?"

I bit into a strawberry, a genuine smile spreading across my lips.

———

Talia proved to be exactly what I had hoped for—with enough prodding, she soon became rather open and chatty, more like a young girl of seventeen than a servant.

With Aedin and Mary in Tahuna, we took the liberty of having the villa to ourselves and walked in the gardens all afternoon simply talking. It felt so refreshing. To talk to another without the stifling fear of formalities clouding the conversation.

Talia was young, smart, and witty. I found myself laughing at her quick remarks and bantering playfully with her, sparring word for word. And thoroughly enjoying it. Growing up with a brother and father, I had had few female friends.

"Do you miss home?" she asked, lounging on the side of a fountain.

We were on the back of the property, on a terraced garden overlooking the ocean. The salty breeze messed with my hair, and I smiled with true happiness for the first time since my marriage.

"Yes," I answered honestly. "And no. I miss my brother and friends… But—to be honest—I am somewhat enjoying the warmth. Berge was constantly cold."

"That would be terrible," Talia agreed with a laugh. "I can hardly stand the nights in the winter—I was made for the heat."

I eyed her dark complexion jealously as my pale skin suffered in a pinkish hue from the heat and sun. "There is definitely still a period of adjustment."

Talia giggled, her round face breaking into a smile. "Your skin will grow darker… unless you continue turning into a tomato." She gestured to my arms.

I groaned. "I certainly don't hope for the latter. But I will continue working on it."

"Yes you will." Talia nodded. "You have time."

"Yes…" I trailed off, the familiar sinking feeling entering my stomach.

I would remain here for the rest of my life.

"What is your brother like?"

"Ephraim?" I thought with a grin. "He has a sweet heart. Always acts tough and courageous for the ladies or to impress my father, but he was always kind and sensitive with me."

"What does he do?"

"He was an apprentice to a sword craftsman, but after the marriage Aedin had promised my father to find a more 'noble' situation for him… I never found out what that was. Who knows where he is now."

"Do you write to them?"

"To my family?"

"Yes."

"No, I haven't."

"Perhaps you should!" Talia supplied, dipping her fingers in the hot water of the still, shallow fountain. Miniature, golden fish swam below the surface, darting between the leaves and plants on the surface.

"I could…" I shrugged noncommittally, feeling awkward. I quickly changed subjects, not wanting to reveal my disability. "So what's for dinner tonight?"

"Dinner!" Talia gasped, pushing up from the fountain. She looked at the sun—it hung above the shoreline and betrayed how quickly our afternoon had passed. "Gwen, I'm sorry…" She wrung her hands, coming to stand in front of me. "I need to get back—the kitchen needs me tonight and I told them—"

"Talia." I took her hand. "Don't apologize—go to your duties. Thank you for your time this afternoon… You don't know how much it meant to me."

Her large amber eyes surveyed me for a silent moment, before she gave a half-smile. "You don't have to thank me. I enjoyed it as well."

I embraced her quickly before shooing her off to the kitchen. Grinning, I folded my arms, watching the ocean with a more optimistic sight. I thanked the gods for Talia—for an afternoon of keeping me sane.

Since I had been in the sun all day, and I was sweating from nearly every pore, I returned to our rooms and eagerly drew a bath of cold water. After some time, I felt my body cool, but the sun rash remained—my skin felt hot and sensitive.

When the afternoon drifted into early evening, I left the bath and dried myself with a soft towel then dressed in the loosest cotton dress I could find, grumbling at how hard it was to find something comfortable and casual in my growing wardrobe of sheer and tightly swathed dresses. I tied the bow around my waist, forgoing any jewelry or paint, and exited my rooms for dinner.

The smell of roasted meat wafted through the halls as I made my way to the casual dining room. A familiar mess of dark hair sat in the seat across from mine. Pushing open the glass door, I graciously offered Aedin a smile and sat across from him.

"Hello," he said quietly.

"Hello," I replied, spreading the napkin in my lap.

We were quiet. I clasped my hands together, trying to ignore the jewels that sparkled on my left hand. I stared out at the darkening sea behind Aedin.

"How was your day?" he asked.

"Good." A brief pause, and then: "How was yours?"

"Good."

"Excellent," I said under my breath.

The silence grew between us. I waited awkwardly until a servant arrived to pour wine into our cups and then exited quickly.

Clearing my throat and speaking up, I commented, "I noticed Mary was absent today. Why does she accompany you on the fourth day of each week?"

"The fourth day of the week is the busiest time for merchants, and so the busiest time for us. Her extra eyes and advice is appreciated when managing the imports and exports," Aedin said brusquely, staring into his wine before taking a sip.

"What do you do every day?" I asked curiously.

Aedin leaned back in his chair with a sigh. "We record the transactions conducted by the merchants—ensure there is no illegal activity and tax the goods flowing through the port. Of course, I have assistance with the actual recording, but there are often issues, disputes, or inaccuracies that may arise, which require my presence as a mediator."

I nodded thoughtfully. "Was this your job… previously?"

His brow furrowed. "What do you mean?"

"Before you became a lord—were you a merchant? Or oversaw a business?"

He shrugged. "No."

I waited for him to elaborate, but he was silent. His eyes were cautious and guarded as his long fingers grasped the delicate stem of his glass.

I slowly rotated my glass on the table, staring at the grains of the wood.

"Is there anything… you need?" Aedin asked slowly.

"No." I managed a quick smile. "Thank you."

Another pause. "Are you enjoying the villa?"

"Yes—it's very nice," I offered.

I pressed my lips together in frustration—was there nothing more interesting to discuss?

Aedin fell silent. We avoided each other's gaze and I almost sighed in relief when the food arrived.

The moving of plates and scraping of utensils filled the uncomfortable space between us. We dined the rest of the night without talking and retired to our room shortly after. I quickly exited to the bathroom, changing slowly and only reemerging when I felt it was safe. When I opened the door, Aedin lay under the covers, fast asleep.

Grateful to avoid another embarrassing interaction, I eased under the sheets and curled on my side, staring blankly at the wall as I willed sleep to come.

Chapter Six

ROWYN MOVED WITHOUT haste, his feet trailing in the dust of the road.

The sun was set, the final rays stretching over the snow-tipped mountains and through the colored clouds. A warm shadow blanketed the valley, echoing the coming of summer. Rowyn felt alive—his lips upturned casually as he hummed a melody under his breath.

He had forgotten about the Prophet's words and was reveling in the momentary bliss of ignorance.

Behind him, the white marble walls of the Haven were cast in a wash of colors: pink, orange, blue, purple, and gray. It was a beautiful sight. During his descent he often turned around to see the shadows of the sunset reflect on the stones. The building itself was a tribute to Iselleden—a symbol of the ideals for which the island stood. A haunting tribute to the purity of the land.

It was the last that was untainted, and so would forever stand.

Few in the darkening hour trekked up the path to the hills where it lay. Rowyn was amongst the flow of people descending the dirt road into Farist, the main town. Men and women chatted quietly, laughing, a few singing, as they returned home.

He exchanged pleasant words with some and recognized most by sight. Though the green expanse of their island stretched for miles, their numbers were small—it was rare to see a strange face.

The birth, marriage, and death of each citizen was a communal affair. Every family was a tight-knit and proud group, yet in harmony with the island's common ancestral line.

Rowyn followed the main route through the brightly lit houses and taverns, where the dirt turned to cobbled stones. The air was crisp here—cool in the deepness of the valley and littered with the comforting scent of bread, ale, and cooked meat. He was tempted to stop, to grab a drink at a tavern, talk with old friends. Slowing his pace, he craned his head to scout the crowded tables of a nearby patio.

"Rowyn!"

A hand clapped him on the shoulder from behind. Rowyn turned to face his dark-haired friend and they embraced with a laugh.

"Ager." Rowyn chuckled. "It's been a long time."

"It has!" The man's clean-shaven face stretched into a smile. "You've been cooped up in the Haven for too long—do they ever let you out?"

"Only to cause trouble," he replied with a wry grin.

"Ha, that's true enough." Rowyn saw his friend's eyes shift uneasily to the buckled sword at his hip until they met his face again. "Well—do you have time for a drink?"

"No." Rowyn shook his head. "Unfortunately not. I'm having dinner with Rea and the family."

"Of course, family first." Ager folded his arms in an easy manner. "Will you stop by another time to catch up? I'm usually here after work."

"Yes, I will," Rowyn promised. "I have missed you, Cain, Melus and everyone—"

"All of them are usually here—let me know before you stop by and we'll make sure of it."

"Of course." Rowyn smiled.

"And give my love to Rea, Darius, and the children."

"I will."

They shook hands warmly, and Rowyn turned away from the welcoming light of the tavern.

Something like regret churned his stomach, but he brushed off the feeling.

Everyone was Called to their respective duty for a reason. Everyone was Called to sacrifice something. Everyone knew their Calling was best for Iselleden, no matter how grand or modest the role. Rowyn understood this, and so he would not complain.

He turned out of the town and followed another earthen trail.

The stones and buildings were again replaced with dirt and tall grass that nearly reached his knees. Trees stood like statues, silhouettes in the failing light, cows, horses, and sheep picketed in clusters beneath them—some grazing, some slumbering, and some calling out to him as he passed. The houses here were larger —no grander than those in Farist, but with more room for large families. Each was lit with a warm light that spilled onto the road, easing Rowyn's eyes as he passed through the dark.

He inhaled the crisp, wet air and walked up the steps of the last house on the right.

There was loud chatter—no, shouting—as he pulled open the oak door. High-pitched voices, giggles, and yelling.

"Stop it, Darien—no, put your sister *down* this instant! Darius —Darius?"

"What?"

"Please get them *off* of each other—"

"Darien, let your sister go—"

"I'm *hungry*, Mama—"

"Five more minutes, Darra—until Rowyn is here—"

"Look, Mama, I can *fly*!"

"Darien, this is a warning—"

Rowyn called a greeting, walking into the sitting room.

As usual, chaos had taken the children—Darien stood on a sofa, holding his younger sister by her feet as he dangled her above the rug below. The youngest child cried with laughter, gurgling in surprise as she saw her uncle.

"Darien." Rowyn rolled his eyes, taking Demi's chubby feet from his hands. "Do you *always* have to be the instigator?"

Demi swayed gleefully in his hands. "Let me go!" she yelled through laughter. "Let me go!"

"She told me to." Darien widened his green eyes in innocence, but a wicked smile came over his features. "It sounded like fun."

"Rowyn? Are you here?" Rea's voice floated from the kitchen. "Can you get them in here? Darius, *where are you?*"

"Here!" A tall man stooped under the wooden beams to enter the sitting room. He tied back his long blonde hair as he grinned at Rowyn. "How are you?"

"Fine." Rowyn gripped his hand with a smile. "And you?"

"A little overwhelmed at the moment—" He bent to take his daughter, smoothing down her dress. "Demi, why did you tell your brother to do that?"

Demi shook her short red locks, squinting at her father. "I wanted to catch myself! Darien said I could!"

"Just because Darien says something doesn't mean you should do it." Darius sent a warning look at his son. "But let's eat—where is Darra?"

"I'll find her—oh!" Rowyn's knees buckled, choking a laugh as Darien jumped atop his back. "You're getting a bit old for this," he admitted grimly as the boy grabbed his neck, entwining his legs around his uncle's waist.

"Not yet!" Darien crowed.

"Not yet—now where did Darra go?"

"I dunno—library?"

Rowyn jogged to the library with Darien giggling with delight on his back.

The eldest child sat neatly on the rug in the middle of the room, a large book poised in her lap. She looked up at them with annoyance.

"What?"

"Time for dinner." Rowyn came, bending, with Darien clinging to his back, to pick up her book. "What are you reading?"

"I found it." Darra stood defensively. "I can read whatever I want."

Rowyn raised his eyebrows at her—until he looked at the spine. He read the words, paled, and forced nonchalance. "Of course you can—" He towed Darra out by her long, red braid. "You can finish after dinner."

"Fine," she grumbled, taking back her braid and holding on to her uncle's hand.

When everyone was seated around the table, Rea breathed a sigh of relief. Darius grinned at his wife from across the table, holding out his hands as everyone grasped each other's.

Rowyn squeezed his sister's fingers, sending her an encouraging smile. Rea's tanned eyelids crinkled as she smiled. "Thank you for coming."

"Thank you for having me." His stomach grumbled as the scent of the stew before him wafted into his nostrils.

"Now—remember we practiced this," Rea said, looking at her children significantly. Darien pouted as he stared at his stew but obediently closed his eyes.

The entire table fell silent as they joined hands. Warmth spread between Rowyn's fingers as a faint humming wavered in the air around them. A thick and resounding peace settled on the inhabitants of the table as they remained quiet, their eyes closed. During these times, like usual, something shifted in Rowyn and he felt an easy coherence and joy. After several more slow breaths, Rea opened her eyes and said, "Well done," smiling at each of her children in turn.

She patted Rowyn's hand, picking up her spoon. "Well, it is good to have the family together—save Raine, of course."

"Still busy as always?" Darius asked. "Here you are, darling," he said, tearing a piece of bread for Demi.

"Yes," Rowyn admitted. "She rarely leaves the Haven." He sipped his hot stew carefully.

"She came several months ago." Rea's green eyes—identical to Rowyn's own—looked softly at her brother. "And yet it's not often enough. I miss her, and I doubt the children even remember what she looks like! She was Called to the Council when Darra was born, you know."

"I remember."

"Remind me again, when were you Called, Rowyn?" Darius asked through a mouthful of stew.

"Only ten years ago."

"But as Captain of the Guard, you're not confined to the Haven," Rea pointed out. "So you are able to visit—to have the gift of time!" She laughed.

"Sort of," Rowyn admitted, although it wasn't entirely true. Being Called to the Haven left little room for personal matters.

"I want to be Captain of the Guard!" Darien piped up, looking eagerly at his uncle. "How do I get Called?"

Darius' laugh boomed. "That is how—you are *Called*. You have no choice in the matter, Darien."

"But I want to be Captain of the Guard." His son looked disheartened, banging his spoon against his bowl. "I don't want to sell horses or plough fields."

"You will be Called to whatever best suits you," Rowyn said softly. "If you truly know that you don't belong in the fields—like your father—then you shouldn't worry, for Fate has already decided such."

"But how do I *know* that I will not end up in the fields?"

"You don't—you have to trust and have faith."

"But what if Fate is wrong?" Darien looked concerned.

"Fate is never wrong, darling." Rea brushed some stew from her son's cheek. He squirmed away. "How do you think we have functioned for all these years?"

"I dunno." He frowned into his bowl of stew, until he asked hopefully, "Can I have your sword after the next one is Called?"

"No!" Darius and Rea said at the same time. They looked at their son in dismay, and then gave uneasy smiles.

"No one is allowed to carry a sword," Darius chided his son. "You know that. Save Rowyn and the guards, of course—"

"But I want one," Darien whined. "I want to fight the evil Empire and—"

Rea looked expectantly at her brother. Rowyn coughed. "Darien, you may be Called to fight physical battles with swords, but that won't happen for some time. We do not wish to fight."

"Why?" Darien challenged. "Why can't we destroy them now?"

"Darien!" Rea scolded.

"Everyone hates them—why can't we?"

"We do not hate them," Rea said sternly. "We simply want to correct the wrongness…"

Rowyn's lips thinned. That was the sentiment everyone had been taught, but it was difficult to deny the anger towards the fallen place. Although the wars had been over five hundred years ago, the memory still felt fresh and painful for Iselleden.

Darien opened his mouth for a rebuttal, but Darius silenced him. "That will be enough about the Empire."

His son picked at his stew, staring glumly into the bowl. Darius looked at Rowyn impatiently, while Rea stuttered, "So, Demi, what were you going to show me earlier?"

The youngest daughter's round face broke into a smile. "Mama, Darien said that if I pushed at the floor when he dropped me, I wouldn't get hurt!"

"You will put a dent in the floor, Demi, if you do such a thing." Rea rolled her eyes at Darien. "*And* still hurt yourself. But I'm happy that you're practicing."

Demi opened her mouth to continue. "And I can also—"

"What is the Rhidge?" Darra interjected.

Rowyn's spoon paused halfway to his mouth. His heart stopped.

"Do not interrupt your sister, darling," Rea chastised her, but Darra was insistent.

"I was reading it in a book. It said the Rhidge is the reason the Empire is impure. What is the Rhidge?"

Darra was looking directly at her uncle.

"I have never heard of such a thing," Darius offered with a shrug. "Where did you get the book?"

Rea tried for an answer, "It must be the history book that Raine left on her last visit—I was going to return it to her—"

"Uncle?" Darra stared at him with large, emerald eyes— curious and waiting.

"This is not the time or place to speak of it," Rowyn said flatly. "You should not be reading such things, Darra."

"But I want to know—"

"No." His voice became cold. "Do not mention that name."

"If Rowyn doesn't want you to speak of it, do not, Darra," Rea advised, copying her brother's stern voice.

"I will tell you when you are older," Rowyn said gently, "but please—for me—don't say that word again."

Darra was silent, confused.

"Mama," Demi continued in the awkward pause, "I can push things. Look!"

"Not the bowl!"

When everyone was full of stew, Rea and Rowyn washed the dishes while Darius played games with the children. For an hour, they chatted by themselves, discussing Rea's children, marriage, and Rowyn's duties. He mentioned neither the visit from the Prophet nor the prophecy. Only those in the Council needed to know. Some things were better left unsaid.

Afterwards, Rowyn entertained Darra, Darien, and Demi by telling mythical stories. He avoided ones with the Empire as the antagonist—which left few options—but settled by throwing in some sword fights to appease Darien.

When the moon was high, Rowyn kissed the children and Rea goodnight and made to leave. But not without stealing into the library and taking the book first.

He read the spine again and shivered as he left the house. Why in the world would Raine have left such a book? Or even brought it to their home in the first place?

Rowyn sighed in frustration. She should have known better than to share that knowledge with those outside of the Haven.

Raine had always been difficult—intelligent and wise, but difficult. Her Calling to the Council had come as a surprise to Rowyn, who approached his duty with an unwavering commitment to tradition and loyalty. Raine always seemed to have other plans.

Despite his earlier words, an unnatural hatred and sadness filled Rowyn as he thought of the other place. The place that had ruined the beauty and killed countless of his people.

And the Rhidge.

Rowyn raised his shoulders, hugging the book to his chest, terrified to say the word aloud. The moonlight was bright and the songs of the crickets were loud in his ears, but they did not sway the growing desolation in his heart.

From the dark valley, he raised his eyes to the Haven, still and white, like a marble blanket, covering the hill. There was hope. He could feel it like a building pressure of possibility.

After five hundred years, something was going to change.

Chapter Seven

IT WAS UNFORTUNATE that I awoke early with the sun. I opened my eyes to see that the other side of the bed was empty, but the sheets were unmade. The sound of running water echoed from the bathroom door.

I winced, considering feigning sleep when Aedin emerged. His black hair was wet as he buttoned his shirt.

He caught my gaze and hesitated. "Good morning."

"Good morning," I said stiffly, pulling the sheets up to my chin.

I watched the lean muscles of his back flex under his shirt as he bent to open the wardrobe drawers, rummaging in their depths. He paused, stopping and moving to the bedside table, where a sheathed dagger sat innocently.

Aedin belted it to his waist, watching me carefully. "Will you come to breakfast?"

I supposed I had no choice.

"Yes," I replied reluctantly and pushed back the covers as he turned away to fasten the cuff of his shirt. I grabbed a gown from the wardrobe and exited quickly to the bathroom to change.

When I emerged, Aedin was gone. A dark, folded pile sat on our bed. Relief washed through my body as I touched my furs—as clean and new as the day my father had purchased them. Just as Mary had promised.

Gently, I lifted the coat and placed it in the wardrobe. I shut the doors with a heavy heart—I would likely never wear it again.

Combing my fingers through my hair, I made my way to the dining room. The morning light was gray, and the marine fog still clung to the blades of grass in the courtyard.

I relished in the cool air, biting back a yawn as I pushed open the glass door. Aedin was already seated, surrounded by a collection of parchments, drinking tea.

He paused. "Do you usually go barefoot?" Aedin's brow furrowed as he eyed my feet.

"Do you usually wear the same outfit each day?" I countered challengingly, observing his ironed black linen shirt and pants.

Aedin chuckled low under his breath. "Yes to both, I suppose."

A brief silence clouded the space between us as he returned his attention to the parchments.

I settled back in my chair, not caring for civilities—it was too early, and my mind was still foggy. Aedin sat straight-backed, his wrists on the table, hands folded, as if he had been awake for hours.

Feeling my gaze, his dark eyes flickered to mine. I shifted uncomfortably and looked at anything but him.

"Did you sleep well?"

I shrugged. "Fine." I wasn't in the mood for small talk.

Aedin paused, forgetting the parchments and watching me evenly. "Why haven't you read the scroll yet?"

The question caught me off guard. I frowned. "I have."

Aedin raised his eyebrows, surprised that I would lie to him. "No, you haven't. The scroll has remained untouched since I first gave it to you. Additionally, you would have questioned me about its contents had you read it."

"I didn't need to ask anything," I replied defensively, realizing that I was digging myself deeper and deeper into the lie. "It all made sense—you have political rivals."

"Who is Welm Charles?"

"I... don't remember."

Aedin's reply became caught in his throat as the door swung open and Talia entered, carrying a kettle of tea.

In the taut silence, she bent to pour the amber liquid into my cup. I met her gaze, and we exchanged half-smiles—I was sure she sensed she had intruded on a tense conversation.

My husband was staring straight at me as Talia refilled his cup. His dark brows were slanting—accusing. He leaned his elbow against the arm of the chair and rubbed his chin thoughtfully.

I didn't want Talia to leave. I watched her exit, hoping I might somehow communicate to her, but it was fruitless. The door swung shut, and I was trapped.

"What did you do yesterday?" Aedin demanded coldly.

I pressed my lips together tightly, unwilling to respond. Taking a deep breath, I mustered the words, "I wandered around the gardens… with Talia, the servant."

Aedin's eyes flashed as he dropped his hand and took hold of his teacup, taking a large sip. After replacing it on the saucer, he said silkily, "Gwen, I do not want you talking to her."

"Why not?" I objected with a frown.

"Because I don't trust her," Aedin hissed—his expression became dangerous, almost fearful. "There are few people I trust inside this villa: Mary and the guards."

"That's rich," I scoffed with an astounded expression. "You don't trust anyone else? Not even me?"

Something like an invisible force pushed against me as he enunciated his words quickly and in a low voice. "No, because you *lie* to me. And you seem intent on deceiving me and rebelling against everything I advise of you."

"Well perhaps you haven't made this the easiest two weeks of my life!" I felt a cry rising in my throat and fought to control it. "I don't want to read your bloody scroll or care about your political enemies—you want me to listen and obey you? How about giving me *freedom* to roam outside of this damned place and befriend whomever I please—"

"I can't do that," Aedin cut me off, his eyes flashing. "It's not safe—you'd get *killed*—"

"Well I've survived this long," I lashed back at him. "I suppose the next *years* won't be so hard—"

Aedin threw up his hands with an expression of frustration, fighting to keep his voice low. *"You don't understand.* It's dangerous! I can't just let you go romping off to Tahuna whenever you please, visiting whomever you like—"

"I don't care what you think—I just want to bloody do whatever the hell I want." I could feel a headache beginning to throb in my temple.

"You. Can't."

"Why not?"

"Because they're looking for you! You'll get killed!"

"Who's looking for me?"

Aedin stuttered, frustrated, "Political rivals… They'll jump at any chance they get—"

"Really?" I said dubiously. "The other lords, merchants, and nobles are just going to attack me in the street in broad daylight? Oh, 'That'll show Lord Aedin!'—"

"It's more complicated than that—"

"Then why not explain it?"

"I don't trust you."

"And why not?"

Aedin pressed his lips together, folding his hands. He said his words slowly, the temperature in the room decreasing to a simmer. "Because there is certain information surrounding my person and lordship that is extremely confidential and would be dangerous if it became public…"

He paused, looking at me with a meaningful gaze. "Simply admitting that is dangerous in itself. I need to—*we* must—maintain a low profile if we wish to survive."

"Survive what?"

My husband sighed, leaning back and ruffling his hair. "Each day… each month… With each passing year, I feel that something's about to break. That something will happen to… mess this all up."

There was a short pause. "Well that's a rather cynical view of the world," I commented lightly, taking a sip of my tea.

Aedin looked directly into my eyes with a serious gaze. "It's the truth. And I don't want *us* to make any mistakes to put our lives in danger. Which is why I would advise you to limit your trips outside the villa and not talk to Talia—or any other servants here."

I inhaled. "Aedin, I understand the safety of remaining inside the villa, but Talia…" I gestured helplessly to him. "I have no friends here, no one to talk to or spend time with. I do *nothing* all day. Spending the afternoon with Talia was the best thing that has happened to me since… since coming here."

Aedin was unmoved. "I told you—I don't trust her."

"Why not?" I asked with exasperation.

"Because her family in Tahuna doesn't exist and she only came here looking for work during the period when I was away—when we were in Berge."

"No." My heartbeat was loud in my throat. "She has five siblings and parents that are fish merch—"

"Gwen," Aedin said softly, "she told Mary the same story and we have investigated and… it is not so."

"So where does she stay at night? Where does she go after—"

"I had one of the guards follow her—she resides in a small inn on the outskirts of Tahuna."

My heart broke. "Then why would she lie…?"

"I believe that she works for Lord Tours, the Lord of Radiance —and the king's right hand."

"How do you know this?"

Aedin chuckled darkly, swallowing a mouthful of his tea. "Tours keeps a close eye on me. He's sent servants here before, pretending to seek work… Or courtiers requesting an appointment. Often he's sent his own guards—which is rather bold, but they hardly stay longer than a day or two—just to check in."

I shook my head in disbelief. Were all lords surveyed with such suspicion? "I still don't understand… You've been the most loyal Lord of Lailan since…"

Gazing at the table, Aedin delicately traced the fine curves of the saucer. "As I said earlier, there are certain things you don't know about my person, or my past."

I realized I wouldn't get that information out of him during the course of this breakfast. We exchanged empathetic glances, and I looked down at my lap, mustering my courage.

"Aedin, I can't read… or write."

A reluctant grin crept onto Aedin's face. "I assumed that much." The smile quickly faded. "But you didn't have to lie."

"I was—or I *am*—ashamed of it… It was something that my father never deemed necessary. Since coming here… I've been terrified that someone would find out. It makes me feel even less adequate as a lady." I released a low laugh at my honesty and my embarrassment.

"It's nothing to be ashamed of…" Aedin paused. "I couldn't read until about five years ago."

I raised my eyebrows. "Really?"

Aedin nodded, tight-lipped.

"Where… are you from?"

"What do you mean?"

"Which island were you born on? And how… did you come to your lordship?"

My husband gave a broad grin. "Those are two very different questions." He paused, sipping his tea. "I was born in a small town on Radiance. Not many people have heard of it before."

"Was your family nobility?"

"No."

"Were they wealthy?"

Again, that smile spread across his handsome face. "No."

"Well." My brow furrowed. "How then did you become a lord?"

"Well," Aedin shot back, "can I trust you?"

The door opened—Talia and another servant entered bearing trays of food. Talia smiled at me as she placed down plates of fruit, bread, and cold meats. I mustered one in response, despite the pit of sadness and loneliness in my stomach.

When they exited, Aedin raised his teacup towards me. "Congratulations."

I frowned, mimicking his motion. "For what?"

"Our first fight and resolution."

I couldn't help but smile as we clinked our cups together. For the first time, I felt a sort of unlikely camaraderie with Aedin. I watched his lips stretch into a smile as he held my eyes, the warm glow of the sunrise on his copper skin. My stomach flipped in a momentary rush of desire.

But then I thought of Daniel and felt hollow.

After our meal, Aedin and I moved slowly through the halls. "Are you leaving for Tahuna?" I asked, unsure of what I was going to do for the day.

"Yes, but first I would like to show you something." He motioned towards our rooms and I followed him inside.

Closing the door, Aedin opened the wardrobe and pulled out an empty sheet of parchment, an ink bottle, and a quill. He took a seat at the table near the garden door, beckoning for me to sit.

"Here is the alphabet." Aedin wrote out twenty-six figures in a vertical line.

"Copy each of these as many times as possible until you memorize them—it may take a while. There are other sheets in the wardrobe." He held up the quill. "You hold it like this—use these three fingers for the main support, and the other two can brace your hand against the page."

I took the quill gingerly—the object was foreign in my hands.

"You always want the point to be facing down, at an angle. When you run out of ink, just dip it into this bottle."

"Very well." I began to trace the letters on the sheet. I smiled at my characters—they looked sloppy and shaky compared to his examples.

"It will take a while," Aedin said quietly. "I'll have Mary instruct you during the day when I'm in Tahuna… That will give you something to do."

I smiled bitterly—he was smart. Learning to read and write would give me less time to spend with Talia.

"Aedin."

"Hm?" He stood.

"Are you going to dismiss Talia?"

He paused, looking at me. "You don't want me to." It was a statement.

My chest felt heavy as I sighed. "No—I understand that if she is here purely to spy on Tours' account that is an inconvenience… But how does that present a danger?"

Aedin nodded. "It would simply be a nuisance—having to be extra careful to not say anything that could be used against us. I don't like knowing that Tours has a pair of eyes and ears in my household."

"What about the other lords? Do they have spies as well?"

Aedin gave a short laugh. "Occasionally they will try—and perhaps they do and I am unaware. But by far, Tours presents the greatest danger. We've… We have a tangled past, to say the least."

"Really?" I raised my eyebrows. To have had troublesome dealings with the man second-most powerful to the king was not a pleasant revelation.

My husband grimaced and shrugged. "But as I said earlier, there's little we can do save keeping up our appearance. If things change—as they may—then we will be prepared."

I paused. "Are you… involved in illegal activities?"

"No, certainly not." Aedin's lips quirked into a grin despite the subject. "I am loyal to the king and have done nothing wrong… That, perhaps, is my only saving attribute. If I had been dishonest, I would have been killed long, long ago."

I nodded, believing that he was telling the truth. "Then… why do you think things would change? Why fear political rivals if you have the king's favor?"

"It's… complicated," he said delicately, looking at his hands, then back at me pointedly. "To get the full story will take some time."

I managed a smile, setting down the quill, surprised that we had achieved a civil and honest conversation.

Aedin nodded at me then exited our rooms. I looked at the letters on the page, marveling how these characters could form words, meanings, and identities. Listening to the birds in the garden, I delicately gripped the quill and continued to write.

Chapter Eight

"CAT. C-A-T. Write."

My wrist and hand burned as I scrawled out the word. C-A-T. C-A-T. C-A-T.

"Wife," Mary announced the next word, smiling devilishly. "Sound that one out."

"Wuh… ie… f… W-U-I—"

"No!" exclaimed Mary with unrestrained exasperation. "W-I-F-E! Wife!"

"Sorry," I muttered with annoyance as I busily pressed my quill into the paper. W-I-F-E.

Whether I liked it or not, I was a wife.

Since learning the alphabet, Mary's lessons had become an unexpectedly pleasant diversion. We had spent the last two days connecting sounds to letters and starting to form words. She was a thorough instructor—if not occasionally severe.

"Very well—that's good enough." Mary looked outside. "I believe it's time for a break."

"Thank the gods," I swore under my breath, flexing and stretching my fingers and palm. Who knew that writing was so hard?

"How do you spell 'Gwen'?" Mary asked as she shuffled the papers littered with letters that looked like chicken scratches.

I shrugged. "I don't know."

Mary looked archly at me as I shoved back my chair, stretching my arms to the high ceiling of the bedroom. "I *do not* know," I stated stiffly. "Maybe "G-W-Y-N—"

"You are spelling your full name, Gwyneth: G-W-Y-N-E-T-H." She picked up my abandoned quill and elegantly wrote my full name on a blank page. "But your preferred name," she continued, "is spelled G-W-E-N."

It looked so small and dismissive next to my full name. I made a face, but at least it looked good in her script.

She wrote other letters next to mine. A-E-D-I-N. The hardest part was connecting each letter to its sound, but I knew, from the A and E, what the word said.

"Aedin."

"Yes, my lady." Mary smiled with satisfaction and replaced the quill in the pot of ink.

"What is Aedin's first name?" The thought hadn't occurred to me till then. It was custom that the eldest man of a well-established family was addressed by their last name. Although they still held the first name they had been given at birth, it was reserved solely for family or close friends.

Mary paused. "I don't know… It's not my place."

"Yes, but you are his most trusted counsel." I paused, adding as a side with a wry smile, "You probably know more about my husband than I do!"

"Yet this I do not know." Mary curtsied, ushering me into the hall. "Would you like to take a midday meal?"

"Yes." I thought she would have known. I would have to ask Aedin.

We entered the hall and headed towards the dining room as a servant intercepted us. "My lady." He bowed and held out two envelopes.

"Thank you." I took them as he rose and left quickly. I didn't recognize any emblem on the seals—as if I would—and continued to the dining room.

I sat in the chair facing the ocean, ordered a light midday meal, and opened the first letter. Mary waited near the door, watching me.

Stupidly, I stared at the words on the page. They were still strange symbols to me, even if I recognized a few. Aedin. I caught that word, proud of this small victory.

Motioning for Mary to sit in the opposite chair, I handed her the letter. "Would you please?"

Mary nodded solemnly. "'*Lady Aedin. It was a pleasure to enjoy your company at our reception earlier this week. I hope you and your husband passed the evening in high spirits. I would like to call upon you sometime this week, or the next, if you would spare the time. I should very like for us to be friends. Please—if you find any time in your busy schedule—let me know when it would be appropriate. Many thanks and the highest blessings, Francesca de Bough.'*"

"Hm." I raised my eyebrows as Mary neatly refolded the parchment. "Well that's too many words for one small message. Do they all write like that?"

"Unfortunately, my lady." Mary smirked, unfolding the next letter. She held it up. "Shall I?"

I nodded. "Please."

"'*My lady. My name is Miss Andrea Taylor and we had met previously at the reception hosted generously by the de Bough family. As I had mentioned, I wish to extend an invitation to our garden party next week. It will be on the second day of the week—a collection of lovely women who all wish to make your acquaintance. Please write back should your schedule allow you to attend.'*"

I recalled the group of women from the party with reluctance. So my social calendar was becoming full. Yet perhaps this was the diversion I needed.

"Would you mind writing on my behalf, Mary?"

"Of course not, my lady." She graciously inclined her head. "What would you like to do?"

"Tell Miss Taylor that I will gladly accept her invitation for next week… And invite Francesca and Gerand tonight for dinner."

Mary started and opened her mouth to object. "Tonight? There is usually more time given to prepare—"

"Are we unable to prepare?"

"No," Mary admitted slowly.

"Then why the objection?"

I had never before given her a decisive order.

Mary paused, and I thought that she might reject the idea without Aedin's consent. I looked at her pointedly. "Send word to my husband and let him know that we will be having some special guests for dinner."

There was a look of incredulity on Mary's face. "You know he dislikes these people very much."

"And so do I." I folded my hands carelessly. "But should I neglect my duties as a lady and not entertain my nobles? Besides, she's eager for attention so we might as well get this over with." I motioned to her. "Get a messenger to deliver a reply to Francesca telling her of tonight."

Mary saw she had no choice. She stood and curtsied. "My lady." And exited the room.

I felt strangely satisfied with my newfound power. Chuckling under my breath, I imagined the reaction on Aedin's face when he returned home—the absolute worst end to the day.

With a future plan, I felt that my day had more purpose than usual. I bathed and dressed and had Mary paint my face with the goal of impressing the de Boughs. Although they had thrown the party, we were the rulers of Lailan.

A clever, smirking, cold face looked out at me from the mirror. I would not be intimidated or ridiculed—I was Lady Aedin.

When the sun lowered to hover above the horizon, I was ready. Standing by the front door in my silk, with paint and a smile plastered on my face, I waited.

A dark figure caught my sight and I saw Marks staring at me from his position at the front gate. His blue eyes were fixed on me in a strange expression of mixed fury and astonishment.

So he knew. I wondered if Mary had told him.

There was still no sign of Aedin.

Tossing back my long hair, I straightened my shoulders, watching as a black carriage came through the gate. They were ten minutes early. Perfect.

I fixed my smile wider as I watched Gerand and Francesca de Bough descend the carriage, looking up at the villa in amazement.

I assumed that Aedin had never condescended to invite them here.

"My lady! It is so good to see you again! My—you look more beautiful than ever!"

Francesca's voice made me hide a wince. I greeted her with as much amicability as I was able to muster as she rose from her curtsy.

"Madame de Bough! You are too kind to grace us with your presence."

"You remember my husband, my lady, Sir Gerand de Bough—knighted by the king himself!"

I remembered him all too well from the earlier party. Just as before, he wore multiple layers of silk despite the humid evening air, and I could see his pit stains already forming.

His gray hair, although thinning, was combed in the most fashionable style. "My lady." He bowed low. I wondered for what he had been knighted.

"Please." I smiled at both of them, then gestured inside. "You are welcome."

I knew that what I was doing—inviting the de Boughs over for dinner—was, in essence, rude and unkind to Aedin. But my intent was not purely to irritate him—it was my duty to entertain and build relationships with the nobles of Lailan, was it not?

It was only one dinner, I concluded, as I led them into the sitting room. And I was bored. Perhaps resorting to the de Boughs' company was a cry borne of desperation; it was better than Aedin's usual silence.

"So grand..." Gerand murmured as we passed several tapestries. "Look at this one, Francesca. Such beauty!"

"Ah yes, it looks to be the port itself! Do tell me from whom you commissioned it?"

"I confess, I do not know." I smiled apologetically. "Many of the tapestries, paintings, sculptures, and furniture here were placed by the previous lords. I do not believe Aedin did much," I lied, unsure of what Aedin might have done to the villa. But since he always seemed so consumed with work, I could have been right.

"But of course!" Francesca beamed brightly. "With all this finery, who could be able to keep track of all it?"

I fell silent, momentarily awkward and ashamed of Aedin's wealth. I stuttered to make shallow conversation.

Thankfully, we reached the sitting room and took seats on opposite couches. Gerand, upon sitting down, immediately reached for the food that covered the low table between us. I winced as the wood creaked under his weight.

A fire crackled merrily in the hearth, providing a warm smell I missed from my childhood. I glanced at the setting sun outside—it was nearly below the horizon. Aedin should have been here by now—unless he had heard of my ploy and was avoiding this event entirely?

"Where is the lord?" Francesca asked, echoing my thoughts and cheerfully biting into a piece of cheese.

"I believe he will be here soon. He spends long hours at the port." I shifted in my dress, feeling slightly uncomfortable although it suited me very nicely. Its low-cut square neckline revealed cleavage I'd thought did not exist and cinched my waist to exaggerate my slender form.

"Oh, well, we dearly miss him." Francesca made a sad face as Gerand popped grapes in his mouth. "It has been nearly a week since we last saw you both—too long! It was such a pleasure to spend time with my lord and get to know you better. He works so hard! I hope it doesn't prevent him spending time with you?"

"No, of course not," I assured her. "We make sure to set aside time for us to be together." I thought of our mute dinners with a smile.

She mistook the meaning of my smile. "Oh, and he is so handsome! I remember when my husband and I were young and in love… But that was so many years ago!"

"When were you married?" I asked, hoping to learn something from them.

"I was married to Gerand when I was eighteen." She grinned like a schoolgirl and I almost thought her to be beautiful. "My father had arranged the marriage, of course. Gerand—he was twenty-five—had just been knighted for his military services to the king, so we were a fine match!"

I forced a smile, remembering the turmoil when my father had announced my marriage. "So did you move here then?"

"Yes. Gerand's family owns the largest sugar plantation on Lailan, which he was to oversee after the passing of his father. So we settled here and have lived on Lailan ever since!" she concluded, brushing a few crumbs from her lavender silk. "And how are you finding Lailan?"

"Lovely," I said simply. "The colors and beauty are astounding —however I am still getting used to the heat after living on Berge my entire life."

Francesca smiled knowingly. "It does take some adjustment. And I hear you have a brother…?"

"Yes," I said slowly, not sure what she had heard. "His name is Ephraim—he is several years my senior."

"And historian to the king! What a great accomplishment."

This was news to me. "Ah, yes," I said slowly, "that was a recent appointment after… our marriage." I realized this had been Aedin's doing. Why had he never told me? I could hardly imagine my brother within the inner circle of the king.

"And is he engaged?" Francesca giggled slyly. "I know *quite* a few ladies who would be thrilled to have him on Lailan."

"I confess, I do not know. However, if he is *not*, I will be sure to recommend Miss Taylor," I said with a coy smile, remembering her words at the party.

"I am sure her father would be thrilled to arrange that. It is the only proper way to get married anyway," Francesca said with a sniff, as if marrying for love was a condemned practice.

Seemingly content from sampling each of the foods on the table, Gerand leaned back on the couch, draping an arm around Francesca's frail shoulders.

They both grinned at me as I fought back nausea. As silly and self-absorbed as they were, I realized they were in love. I couldn't help but imagine Daniel, sitting on this couch with me, aged, but together and in love. That was something I would never have.

Quiet footsteps echoed from the hall into the sitting room, and I watched Francesca and Gerand's eyes round. Inhaling for courage, I turned around and saw Aedin move regally towards the pair—like a king in his dark and sparse uniform.

He nodded towards me, as Francesca and Gerand stood, immediately falling into postures of submission. They exclaimed niceties as Aedin received them with a fixed, grim smile.

But he interrupted them, holding his hand out to me.

"May I have a word? Please excuse us," Aedin said politely to the de Boughs as I tightened my jaw and stood. Head held high, I followed him into the hallway, away from the curious eyes of the de Boughs.

Once we were out of earshot, he turned around and faced me. His façade dropped, a fatigued annoyance overcoming his features. "What are they doing here?" he whispered fiercely.

"I invited them for dinner," I replied coolly. "Is there something wrong?"

"Gwen." He rubbed his face. "I'm too tired for this. Why did you invite them?"

"Francesca requested a reception with me earlier today, and I thought inviting them over for dinner would be a kind gesture and fulfill my duties as a lady." I stressed these last words.

"You know that they are the most *tedious* and *ridiculous* of people on this island—"

"Yes, but they are our subjects." I paused. "They hosted the party for us."

"It was a party for their ego," Aedin muttered darkly, messing his hair.

"Look." I bravely met his eyes with a hard stare. "They're here, whether you like it or not. So just put on a good face for the next several hours, and then we can go back to our life in silence."

"We don't live a life in silence—"

"We can discuss this later." I turned from him, walking back towards the sitting room, which was flooded with light.

Aedin took several long steps and matched my strides. We re-entered the room together.

"I hope everything is well?" Francesca simpered as we sat down, opposite them on the couch.

I was about to open my mouth and reply when Aedin answered. "Of course, Madame de Bough—it was nothing of dire consequence," he replied suavely, his voice smooth and assuring, unlike anything I had ever heard before. Aedin sat close to my side.

"Oh good! I wish nothing to endanger this lovely meeting." Francesca smiled, settling deeper into her husband's embrace.

"And we as well," Aedin agreed warmly. With a casual gesture, he tossed one arm over my shoulders, mimicking the de Boughs' pose. His legs were pressed against mine as his scent— salt, leather, and a rich bitterness—invaded my senses.

I stiffened at this display, my mind racing. He had never touched me like this before. What was he doing?

Francesca must have noticed my alarmed expression because she asked, "Is there something wrong, my lady?"

I forced myself to calm—there was nothing wrong with Aedin putting his arm around me, even if it was for show. Putting on a complacent grin, I settled back further in the couch, leaning against him. "No, of course not," I reassured. "Just a passing fear of this party being broken."

We exchanged smiles, both seemingly content under our husbands' arms. Aedin's was heavy and constricting upon my shoulders.

His hand began to trace circles rhythmically, lightly on my skin. My mind felt fuzzy and my stomach clenched—what was wrong with me?

"How are the merchants, my lord?" Gerand asked cheerily, giving us a toothy grin. "I have heard that they are actually following rules of late."

Aedin laughed. "As productive as always—continually trying to find a loophole. I have been tightening the reins but that is nothing new."

"Ah, yes," Francesca commented, leaning forward, "Gerand and I were discussing that the other day. We were wondering what it was you did to gain such high favor with the king? Not that *we* need higher favor—Gerand is already good friends with his highness." She patted her husband's knee affectionately. "We had simply never seen you at court before you were appointed."

Aedin's hand stilled on my skin. "I was an ambassador for the king," he stated plainly. "I was never at court because I traveled—visiting the islands and their lords to make sure they were paying enough taxes, not taking too much from the treasury, or preventing scandals… his highness must have been impressed with my skills, for he assigned me to one of the most trying lordships." Aedin's lips tugged into a smile.

Francesca stared at him wide-eyed, nodding. "Of course, that makes complete sense—you are able to smell any illegal activities from a mile away!"

"I am flattered you think so highly of my skills, Madam de Bough." Aedin motioned to a servant, and a decanter of wine was brought.

"Oh, please." Francesca batted her eyelashes at my husband. "Call me Francesca."

Aedin nodded. "Of course."

My mind dissected this new information as Aedin's hand once more smoothed circles in my skin. Was this the truth he had been hiding? Or another lie?

Mary entered the room quietly, bowing to Aedin and myself before the de Boughs. "Dinner is served," she announced proudly, staring at me with accusing eyes. I smiled back at her as we rose.

The four of us sat at the formal dining table overlooking the pinpricks of light in the darkness that was Tahuna. Elegantly carved brass chandeliers illuminated our food and fine silverware. I had never before seen the crystal glasses or plates on which dinner was served.

Aedin sat at the head of the mahogany table, presiding over the meal with his poised smile and eloquence.

Francesca and Gerand ate it up, but it only unsettled me further. Even when I heard him laugh over some terrible story of Francesca's, the sound shattered my ears. I gritted my teeth.

Occasionally, he would reach over and touch my hand—the feeling of his skin against mine was still shocking. Every touch of his reminded me that this was *my* wish, *my* fault. By the end of dinner, I began to regret my decision. I had suffered a worthy punishment.

"Oh, my lord," Francesca exclaimed as the last course was taken away, "that was an excellent meal—the best I have had in a long time."

"I am glad you liked it," Aedin replied silkily, pouring himself more wine.

"Oh, it was delicious! So exotic! Haven't had anything like it!" Gerand exclaimed, patting his stomach.

I hadn't eaten much—my stomach being unpleasantly unsettled throughout the entire dinner.

"This has been so enjoyable," Francesca continued. "I hope that we will see more of you, my lord, and my lady more often."

"Yes, that would be lovely." Aedin looked at me, his fingers running lightly across the soft skin under my wrist. I fought to not withdraw my hand and hold his stare. "We have both enjoyed your company very much."

"Indeed," I agreed, taking a large sip of my wine to distract myself from his touch. "But it is difficult to see many friends or neighbors with our busy schedules." I glared at Aedin with knowing eyes.

"Well, you mean *my* busy schedule." Aedin chuckled darkly, looking at Gerand. He raised a glass to Aedin's words, and they exchanged laughs as my stomach dropped. "You did say the other day that you were looking for more activities to fill your time."

I wanted to scowl at him and suppressed a retort.

Francesca sat up eagerly. "I would be delighted to extend some invitations, my lady. I visit regularly with many women on the island—and I heard you are joining Miss Taylor's garden party next week!"

Aedin nodded to me. "There you go—I'm sure there will be *many* garden parties to attend with the ladies."

I shot him a momentary frown, squeezing his hand, then forced a grin. "That sounds lovely."

"Mm." Aedin winked at me. "Well, Francesca, Gerand, this has been quite a delightful evening, but I am afraid that we must retire."

Gerand stifled a yawn. "That is a good idea."

"We will call the carriage." Aedin motioned to Mary, who stood quietly in the corner. She left with a bow.

"Thank you, thank you."

After the politest goodbyes and offers again and again for social engagements, Gerand and Francesca were finally placed in their carriage and driven out of the gates.

We gave our final waves, and then we were alone. Aedin and I stood in the quiet—both reveling in the gentle sounds of the crickets.

"Well," Aedin said at last, taking my hand, "that was quite delightful—"

"Urgh, stop it." I pulled my hand away from his, turning back into the hall.

"You say we live a life of silence," Aedin sighed behind me, as if hurt. "Well, Francesca spoke of a charming solution when she boasted of months and months of garden and tea parties planned to entertain even the dullest of young ladies on Lailan—"

"Really? Do you really want to have a go?"

"About what?"

"About how you were right." I threw up my hands. "They are the most *ridiculous* people on Lailan and I never want to suffer a dinner party—or hour—with them again."

"You're forgetting one more."

"What?"

"That you don't have to spend time with people like them." Aedin's voice softened. "Gwen, you're a *lady*. You can do whatever in the gods' names you want—well, almost anything. You don't have to entertain the socialites or nobles. They can entertain themselves."

"That's not what Mary said."

"What did she say?" Aedin folded his hands behind his back as he fell into step with me.

"That it was my *duty* as Lady Aedin to be civil, to engage the populace, to set a standard—"

"Mary is generally correct, but you have no obligation to do any of those activities. The power is in your hands."

"Oh, is it?" I laughed lowly. "So when Francesca complained about how you had been neglecting them and the rest of society for the past *four* years, she simply meant it as a light jest?"

Aedin's lips thinned as he grumbled, "I understood her ulterior motive, I simply think it so *silly* and insignificant—I have other duties that trump tea parties and dinner engagements."

"Well I don't," I said bitterly. "The unfortunate reality of being a woman *and* a lady in Lailan. At least on Berge I could work in the shop or spar with Ephraim…"

He was silent as we walked towards our rooms. I remembered Daniel telling me of all the parties, engagements, and balls that Lord Tremer and his wife had hosted to entertain—and pacify— their court. And yet Aedin didn't appear dependent on the social demands of Lailan.

Despite what they thought of him, he maintained power and was able to rule with little interference. I wondered if it was because he was in the good graces of the king.

My head hung heavy—my back ached from keeping myself as straight as a stick. I was tired. Aedin took several steps ahead of me and opened the door to our antechamber. I silently thanked him and entered through and into the bedroom.

"Are you angry with my conduct?" Aedin asked as I collapsed on the sofa at the foot of our bed, unlacing my sandals.

"No—you were perfectly civil."

A moment of silence passed as Aedin sat on the bed and removed his boots. I couldn't see, but I knew that he placed them neatly under the bedside table, lined up next to each other.

"Do you really think that we live a life of silence?" Aedin asked through the thick stillness of the room.

"Since when have you ever talked to me save a rebuke or warning?" My words were tart, yet shy and mumbled. I threw my sandals on the floor.

I couldn't hear a reply, only the quiet rustle of clothing.

"What should we discuss?" he asked finally, after a long moment of silence.

"I… don't know." I shook my head, brushing off his attempts. Perhaps he didn't have normal conversations without an end goal or purpose.

I stood, leaving my sandals haphazardly on the floor and pulled out a nightdress from the wardrobe. Exiting the room, I quickly exchanged my dresses and washed my face in the basin. With a large sigh, I re-entered the room. Aedin was in bed, wordlessly folding his shirt, as I dragged my feet to the other side of the bed.

Pulling back the sheets, I slid underneath them and settled on my back but turned my head to stare at my husband as he silently watched me.

"What?"

Aedin was pensive, his eyes cast in the dark but his brow lit in the moonlight from the open door. I tried not to stare at the corded muscles lining his shoulders and chest.

He shrugged and said, "Nothing," moving to go to sleep as well.

It was then that I noticed it.

"Wait," I stopped him, sitting up. "What's that?"

"What?"

"On your shoulder."

Aedin's face fell. "Oh." He resumed his movements. "It's nothing, just a scar."

"No, wait." I reached out to grab his arm. And then I was surprised that I hadn't seen it before. Perhaps this was why he was always in bed before me. "Sit up," I ordered.

"Gwen," Aedin said stiffly, "let it go."

"Let me see."

With an angry sigh, Aedin sat up, his left hand rubbing his face, his right shoulder facing me.

I was suddenly afraid. I let go of his arm, as if burned.

Above his bicep, on the thick part where the arm met the shoulder, was a scar in the shape of an "R".

It was large—the straight back of the letter stood imposingly on the left side of his arm as the slopes of the loop and the extended tail stretched across to the right.

I wanted to touch it but was frozen in place. In the moonlight it looked silver. The scar was thick and raised, as if someone had etched the letter into his skin over and over again…

It wasn't a scar. It was a brand.

"Who did this?" I whispered.

Aedin looked down at his crossed legs—avoiding my gaze with shadowed eyes. "It doesn't matter."

"Why…" Anger, sadness, and fury swelled inside of my chest —I was at a loss for words.

"Gwen, leave it." Aedin eye's snapped to mine, his expression suddenly grave. "Do not speak of this to *anyone*. Do you understand?"

I opened my mouth, but no words came out.

"Can I trust you?"

My mouth felt dry. "Yes," I forced the words out. "Yes, you can trust me."

"Thank you," Aedin said shortly and shrugged quickly under the covers, lying on his back. The covers were pulled up to his chin, and he said nothing.

I swallowed and followed suit. But I couldn't fall asleep. In the stillness, I whispered, "Will you tell me… sometime soon?"

"Yes."

That was a promise.

"Goodnight."

"Goodnight."

Chapter Nine

TOURS NURSED THE thick, amber liquid in the glass in his right hand.

A permanent scowl of thought had crept over his features in recent days. His eyebrows were drawn together in a sharp line, wrinkling the pudgy skin that had grown accustomed to a life of luxury.

Though his face had aged through his fortieth decade, his body had preserved a merciless tightness from the endless years and hours of training. It was a well-maintained machine. Tours tapped his foot irritably, feeling every sinew of muscle in his leg as the toe of his boot clicked on the floor.

To say that he was vexed was an understatement. Tours was past the point of crossed exasperation. He had only begun to enter the furnace of the fury that simmered in his belly.

It was an angry madness of uncertainty and loathing. Tours rarely entered this state. His years of training had strengthened his mind and given him a cool demeanor that could not easily be disrupted. Very few people could upset it.

Aedin, unfortunately, was one of them.

Why, why, *why*? The word raced around his head over and over again. The spirits in his cup did little to soothe his temper.

It simply did not make any sense. Aedin was Rhidge. His actions were predictable. He had been trained. Tours even knew what Aedin would think—no, he *told* Aedin what he would think —before he thought it for himself. This was why he was lord.

The Empire needed a controlling figure in Lailan—someone who could be trusted. Albeit, to *fully* trust anyone was a mistake, but Aedin was trusted. Tours had been there since the beginning.

The letter had said that there had been a celebration for the marriage several nights ago. Tours wished the journey to Lailan was shorter—*three* days by boat—else it would have been comical to attend. To see Aedin and his new wife. He chuckled darkly at the thought and wondered if Aedin had bedded her yet.

But he was there—if not physically, then through his sources. He would find out how this girl held her new role, what Aedin said or did, and how the Lailan society dealt with their new lady. He had sources on every island—even within the king's private rooms—in order to be constantly aware and controlling.

He liked the feeling of being omnipotent. He was already powerful enough—a figure known almost as well as the king himself—yet there was always a slight chance of failure. He liked to be aware, to know the progression of the game, and play with the odds stacked decisively in his favor.

———-

"Who is he?"

"The new historian, my lord."

"No, who *is* he? What's his name?"

"I do not know, my lord."

Tours harrumphed at Kellen's words. Ignorant bastard. Did anyone know who the new boy was?

More importantly, why had Tours not been notified of his coming? He had appeared at court only two days ago.

Since returning from Lailan a few weeks ago, Tours had been swamped with information from his spies—who had slept with whom, who had insulted whom, who was acting suspicious, who was vying for power—the usual delicate morsels of gossip.

But this historian—his sudden arrival made Tours skeptical of the entire affair. The last historian had hardly done *any* work, save showing face in meetings and scribbling notes. He had disappeared to a distant town only south of the palace. Why the sudden change?

Crossing his arms, Tours frowned at the young man—no, *boy* —sitting to the right of the king, writing hurriedly on the parchment in front of him. He dipped his quill in the ink pot, nearly spilling it as he rushed to record the words.

The scene was a joke—everyone knew it. The smug faces of the advisors circling the room watched the boy with stifled amusement as the king spoke.

"And furthermore, I desire to see the forests contained with clear boundaries, so as to keep out the commoners who wander to hunt in *my* hunting grounds. If I run into another filthy peasant whilst riding, I swear, I will have your head, Sir Greymont—"

Twiddling his thumbs, Tours watched the historian. His mop of brown hair was styled most unfashionably—unkempt and damp, as if he had hastily washed and combed it minutes before the meeting. His pale round face bore signs of an attempt at a beard. The blue eyes watched everything with a childlike amazement.

He was a sheep amidst the wolves of the palace—Tour knew he would get eaten alive. How in the *world* did he gain this position?

"Also, finally, I would like to notify you all of my… condition."

Tours was now paying attention. He ceased his slouching, watching the king with expectant eyes. Could it be what they had discussed?

"The medicators say I do not have more than a year left—" The king coughed, shaking his head as he threw his handkerchief on the floor. "Disgusting. This sickness has become 'lethal', they say. *I* say that is golden shit, but there is some truth… I have begun the process of conducting my final wills before the line passes to the next heir."

That was right. Tours thought of the whore-born son of the king. But he was just a child. And Tours was the only one who knew where he was hidden.

"In order to keep the bloodline of the Empire pure, I will elect Lord Tours to mentor my son until he comes of age. Tours has proven himself completely loyal, and I trust will keep the Empire's line pure. Send word to the other lords to notify them of my decision."

There was an awkward pause.

"Send word," the king repeated gruffly, looking down at the newest member of his cabinet.

"Er—yes, yes, Your Majesty." The boy-historian looked up in brief incredulity, then wrote frantically on the parchment.

The king looked out at his advisors, irritated and amused. "That is all. Any questions?"

The silence was thick. Tours could feel the scorn from the side glances of the other men in the room. He stifled a smug smile—the cards had been played.

"Very well." The king stood and the entire room was filled with the sound of scraping chairs. Tours watched him exit into his private rooms, and for once did not follow.

Moving past Kellen, Tours weaved through the sea of grumbling advisors. They were useless—he knew who held the real information. He nodded at a guard standing against the wall. "You there—come."

The guard shifted, looking at the closed door in hesitation.

"The king is fine," he said with exasperation, beckoning the guard into a corner. He said lowly, "Do you know the new historian? Who is he?"

The guard's eyes grew wide. "Yes, my lord. His name is Ephraim… Dail, no, Doyle I think it was. He comes from Berge. It's rumored that Lord Aedin gave him this position."

"Lord Aedin?" Tours repeated dubiously.

"Yes, my lord." The man nodded, his armor clinking.

"What else?"

He shifted. "Well I know he's never set foot in the palace before. His father is no one of importance, and—that's it! I've just remembered. His sister is the girl who recently married Lord Aedin."

"Really," Tours breathed, watching the boy sprinkle sand on the parchment, then roll it messily.

"Hm." Reaching into his pocket, Tours pulled out his purse. "You've given me much to think about. Thank you for your time." He slipped three gold pieces into the soldier's palm.

"Thank you, my lord." The man beat his closed palm against his breast in respect. "I will keep an eye out for anything more."

"That's what you're here for." Tours nodded at the guard. They weren't good for anything else—they certainly weren't the ones protecting the palace and king.

From the corner of the room, Tours watched Ephraim Doyle pick up his satchel of ink and quills, the roll of parchment, and descend his raised desk. He bustled past Tours, staring at the floor as he hurried into the main hall of the palace. Moving awkwardly through the crowd, he seemed uncertain of his whereabouts.

Tours would have to get his room location. And find out more —the boy could be of some use if his sister was, indeed, the new Lady Aedin.

"My lord—my lord!"

Tours held a sigh back at his assistant's chirp. "Yes, what is it?"

"There is someone here to see you, my lord."

"Who?" he growled, moving down the thickly carpeted hall to his office. It was only a length away from the king's private rooms.

"A man from Berge. Says he wants to serve you."

"In what way?"

"He did not specify, my lord."

"So many men from Berge today…" Tours mused. He didn't wait for his assistant to pull open the door. He felt into the room— there was no danger—and stepped inside.

From a chair under the window, a young man stood, falling into a bow.

"My lord." His voice was deep, though his face was only just beginning to sharpen into manhood.

"You will excuse us." Tours motioned to his assistant, who closed the door.

Tours sat behind his desk and beckoned the youth forward with his hand. The young man sat gracefully—looking more proper than Ephraim Doyle. Tours smiled, in spite of himself, and poured two glasses of wine.

"What is your name?"

"Daniel Terrace, my lord."

"Mr. Terrace," Tours said silkily, pushing the glass forward. "What brings you here?"

"Thank you." He took the glass, eying it suspiciously before taking a tentative sip. Tours watched this appreciatively—the boy had brains.

"I am looking for a position at the palace, specifically in the court."

"Why? And why come to me, might I add?" Tours folded his arms, leaning back in his chair.

It was common for youths to come and seek their fortune—or a pretty, rich wife—at the king's court, but there was always more to the story. Tours briefly wondered if Lord Tremer—as thick as he was—had sent the man to spy on him.

"My lord recommended me." Daniel handed him a slightly crumbled piece of parchment. "I wish to—ah—begin again. To see more of the world and experience new things."

There was a note of honesty in his words. Tours watched his large, brown eyes flicker unsurely around the room.

"What was your position in Berge?"

"I was a soldier in Lord Tremer's guard, my lord."

"A steady position," Tours commented. "Why give it up?"

Daniel's broad shoulders shrugged. "Things changed, my lord. I wanted something more."

Tours watched him closely, choosing his next words carefully. "You are from Berge. Tell me—are you familiar with Gwyneth Doyle?"

There was a spark of recognition as Tours said the name. Daniel fixed his jaw, feigning a casualness. "Yes, I know of her. Berge is a small island."

"So it appears to be." Tours was satisfied. It would take some digging to get him to confess the entirety of their relationship, but he was certain this boy would be worth his time.

Tours watched him carefully, sipping his wine. The fellow was good-looking—he would most definitely be welcomed at the court. He had a soldier's build, an attractive face, albeit pale from the snowy mountains of Berge, and spoke with a steady confidence.

Yes, he would do just fine. He would need some new clothes, of course. And a haircut. But he would do fine, indeed.

Ringing the bell on his desk, Tours watched as his assistant pulled open the door, popping his head inside. "My lord?"

"As of this time, my good sir, I will not need your further assistance. Please inform the king of my decision and get out of my sight—"

"My lord?" The man nearly choked, gripping the door frame.

"Get out of my sight," Tours repeated in a growl.

The man threw the door closed. Tours could hear him running down the hall.

"Never ask me to repeat myself in rhetorical disbelief unless you are confused by my instructions," Tours said irritably, taking a swig of wine.

Daniel sat, shocked, in his chair. He shook his head, gathering himself with a smirk. "Of course, my lord—"

"A position appears to have opened up." Tours stood cheerfully. "I have no use for you as of right now—tell the chamberlain to place you in the rooms on the third floor, as per my command. And I will see you at dinner. Also"—he grimaced disdainfully—"tell him to get you some new clothes and a haircut. Cost is irrelevant—see what you can do."

"Yes, my lord!" Daniel stood, a beam stretching across his handsome face. He followed Tours out of the office, his shoulders straight and proud.

"You should go that way—" Tours pointed down the hall to the right. "Here is where I will leave you."

Daniel bowed low and left. Tours watched him go, the ghost of a satisfied smirk on his face. At least he had fixed one thing today. If he could also figure out this Ephraim Doyle situation, Tours would count the day as incredibly successful. But until then…

Tours looked up and down the hall, feeling for anyone. He was alone—the silence was thick, save for the echoes of passing courtiers in the main hall. But no one would see.

He walked five paces to his left, as if gazing at a mounted silver trio of candles. Pushing at the ornately carved wood of the wall, indistinct from the rest, Tours felt it give way. There was no sound as the section of the wall swung inward on its hinges.

Stepping into the darkness, Tours closed the hidden door and disappeared from view. The blackness was thick in the passage, but he knew his way. He lit a lamp, discarded his doublet, golden chain, and rings, and pulled on a pair of dark leather gloves.

His expression turned grim, and the recent humor and lightness of the palace were lost within the shadows of the room.

There was work to be done.

Chapter Ten

THE CHIRPING OF birds lulled me from sleep. Bright and chatting in the morning light, they called to each other from the garden. I shifted with a groan, wishing for peace. An exhaustion hung over my mind, though my body felt rested.

And then the sunlight—I winced, shutting my eyes against my pillow as I became conscious of its searing presence. Its rays were already heating the room and the foot of the bed. Untangling my feet from the blanket, I pulled them out from under the sheets, pleased at the cool breeze that tickled my toes.

I blinked the sleep from my eyes and noticed the opposite site of the bed was empty—I wasn't surprised.

I hadn't remembered falling asleep. After seeing the scar, I had stared at the ceiling, lost in terrible thoughts for some time.

Swallowing the stale taste of wine, I pushed back the covers. The wood was warm underneath my bare feet. I wondered how early it was—or was it late?

I walked on unsteady feet towards the bath, closing the door as I discarded my nightgown, then pulled water from a nearby pitcher, pouring it into the basin and splashing my face. It was lukewarm—I wished it had been colder. A numb haze hung over my mind as I patted my face dry and wrapped a towel around my body.

Pulling a dress from the wardrobe, I slipped it on in the corner of the room and buttoned the back. I didn't bother with shoes, not caring if anyone noticed, and headed to the dining room.

The halls were empty save for the distant bang of pots and audible chatter of servants from the adjacent kitchen. My bare feet were soft against the floor as I made my way towards the smaller dining room. As soon as I sat down in the wooden chair, Mary opened the glass door and greeted me with a stiff smile.

"I see that you are awake—what would you like?"

"Bread, fruit, and tea… please?"

"Of course." Mary curtsied and left.

Minutes later, she brought in the breakfast on a tray and plopped a small pile of folded papers in front of me.

"What's this?" I asked, picking up my tea and inspecting one curiously. I still couldn't make out most of the words, save for "Aedin", "Lady", and "wish".

"*These*"—Mary enunciated the word with precision—"are invitations from various young women wishing to meet with you as well."

"As well?" I recalled the dinner with the de Boughs the night before. "But all we had was dinner!"

"And so they also want your attention, my lady." Mary smirked at my aghast expression. "You give an inch, they'll take a mile."

"And do I have to meet with *all* of them?"

"Did you have to invite the de Boughs last night?"

"No," I said hesitantly. "But—"

"Use discretion," Mary stated shortly.

I pursed my lips. "Will you read them to me?"

"Of course, my lady." Mary sat with more grace than I could ever wish for and unfolded a letter. I buttered a piece of toast and prepared for the worst.

My lady, I write with extreme humbleness and servitude to request an invitation to sit for tea with you. My daughter and I seek counsel on marriage, and we wish to hear your advice…

My lady, we had met previously at the reception, though perhaps you do not remember. My name is Miss Catherine Mirelli and I would like to extend an invitation to join us at dinner next week...

My lady...

On and on, nearly half a dozen letters later, the voices of all these young women mingled together.

"And the last one..." Mary trailed off, growing silent while reading the letter to herself.

"Who is it from?"

She cleared her throat. "Kitra Devereux."

I remembered hearing Andrea Taylor mention that name at the reception. I shrugged. "And what does she want?"

Mary read the words aloud: "'*My lady, although we have not met previously, I wanted to extend a formal introduction and request a moment in your presence. My name is Kitra Devereux, and I am friends with many of those whom you have become acquainted with of late. While I enjoy their company, I hope to benefit from yours and become more familiar with you. Please write when you would be free for a light meal or afternoon tea. Yours faithfully, Kitra Devereux.*'"

She snorted, folding up the letter and tossing it on top of the others.

"What?"

"Would you like my advice?" Mary looked seriously at me.

"Of course."

"Don't become involved with Kitra Devereux."

"Why not?" I frowned over my cup of tea. "She sounds just as harmless as the rest."

"She may appear so"—Mary stood, pushing out her chair—"but she has many motives that rule her actions. Her father was a scoundrel merchant who settled in Lailan and quickly ran through his profits. It is said that she had a whore for a mother, but no one is quite sure... You would think that a young woman of her status would be trapped in the fish markets or prostitution, but she is extremely ambitious and has alleviated her situation considerably in recent years. After her father's death, she inherited some small funds, enough to purchase a modest apartment in Tahuna—but she also had much help from her... admirers."

"Admirers? Is she a famed beauty?"

"She is. One of the most beautiful women in the Empire, it has been said."

I tried to shrug it off but felt a pit of jealousy form in my stomach. "So her admirers support her."

"Yes. To put it bluntly, she is infamous as a high-class… er… woman of the night—I suppose that is the best way to describe it. *Engaging* herself with various nobles who give her gold, dresses, or jewelry in return. I suppose it helps to fund her lifestyle. She was after Aedin, you know, ever since he became lord."

"Really?" I couldn't imagine anyone attempting to seduce Aedin. That was an amusing image.

"Oh yes. An unmarried, handsome lord—who would not try to secure that? But since you have stolen her place"—Mary smiled —"perhaps she has set her sights elsewhere."

"If she lived on Radiance, she could always go after the king," I pointed out with a snort. "He throws away women as quickly as fashions change."

"But the one who bears to him a son is given whatever she needs to raise the next king," Mary reminded me. "Yes, perhaps the wife of a lord is more domestic and public, but to have the sole key to the king and kingdom inside your arms is another power within itself."

"The king is so old now I doubt he could spawn anything," I muttered into my cup.

Mary allowed herself a wry smile. "Well take that up with Kitra when you advise her the best course of action to climb the ranks. You, yourself, have some experience in that."

"Hardly," I said bitterly.

"But in all seriousness"—Mary's dark brown eyes bore into mine—"do *not* engage this woman or bring her into this house. She is trouble."

"Duly noted." I set down my teacup and bit into a piece of fruit.

"We will continue your reading lessons today, my lady," Mary said in an authoritative manner, picking up the empty tray.

"I suppose I have no choice." I gave her a half-smile.

Mary smirked back. "Not in this respect."

"What use is it to be lady," I sighed dramatically, "if I am slave your wishes?"

"Oh hush," she scolded with a hint of a playful smile. "Will you invite the de Boughs over for *another* tedious evening to repay your husband's kindness?"

"Perhaps. Or Kitra Devereux if I am feeling especially rebellious."

Mary pursed her lips. "If you do, I will call my lord back here as fast as the gods fly."

"And so we are at a stalemate." I smiled at her, biting into my toast, as she curtsied and left.

Pleased with my progressing playfulness with Mary, I finished my breakfast in a cheerful mood. Even if she was loyal to Aedin first and foremost, I felt as if I was winning favor to my side as well.

Satisfied with that thought, I stood up, drinking the last dregs of my tea, and left the room.

Passing through the sitting room, which was slowly warming from the skylights above, I stepped into the coolness of the hall— and nearly ran into Talia.

"Oh—" I refrained from using a curse word, remembering my status. Talia's eyes were wide in surprise.

"My lady." She dropped into a slight curtsy, despite the large pile of towels held in her skinny arms.

"Talia!" I tried to sound happy but failed. She must have seen the expression of shock and hesitation—we hadn't been alone or talked since Aedin had told me of her lie.

"How are you?" she asked after a brief, awkward moment of silence.

"Good, very good," I stuttered with a grin. "And you?"

"Same—very well, thank you." Talia gave a shy smile back. "You seem very happy of late."

Was I? "Well thank you." I wasn't sure if I agreed, but I was glad that I gave that appearance.

Another pause.

"Excuse me—I have been so busy." I moved past her with a forced laugh. "I must go meet Mary for my lesson."

"Have a good day," she said with another curtsy. I smiled but gave a sigh of thankful relief as I walked down the empty hall.

The rest of the day I sat in lessons with Mary. I had progressed in skill with the quill and could write characters, but it was still difficult learning to form the sounds together into coherent words. However, by the afternoon, I was able to read some simple words. We even tried reading some of the letters—but those were more challenging because of the flowery language.

Afterwards, I retired to the garden in the atrium and sat on a bench watching the gardeners weed, dig, and tend to the plants. I wanted to join, although I knew nothing of planting, and presumed Mary would give me the scolding of a lifetime for ruining my dress. I was bored. Flies buzzed around my head in the humid air as my dress stuck to the backs of my legs.

Wishing for a breeze, I wandered through the halls towards the terraced gardens overlooking the ocean. There was more movement in the air—I gratefully felt the sea breeze shift through my dress and cool my body.

A low wall extended around the perimeter of the villa property. Beyond it, there was nothing but thick trees, a wall of leaves, and the green abyss of the jungle. I followed the wall until I found a section that provided cool shade and a wide-enough view of the port.

My hand touched the cool stone as I sat—there was an odd buzzing beneath my fingertips.

I frowned, staring down at the gray, unmoving stone. It was rough and unyielding, yet there was an almost imperceptible vibration that hummed underneath my touch.

I lifted my hand, but it was still there under my body, so I sat up, moving a foot to the right, and sat down again.

It was still there.

"Good afternoon, my lady," I heard a soft voice call.

I nearly jumped—Tieren was seated on the wall just five feet below me. How had I not seen him?

"Good afternoon," I said courteously.

I thought of asking him about the odd sensation but then quickly realized he would think I was crazy. I filed it away, ignoring the feeling as I tried to enjoy the wind and shade.

"How are you?" I asked, after a moment of silence.

Tieren shifted in his seat to face me. "Well! It is a beautiful day." His smile was charming and sweet. He almost reminded me of Ephraim. "And you?"

I shrugged. "Good, I suppose. Just trying to fill my time…"

Tieren frowned. "I thought ladies were often busy with social activities and the running of the household?"

"To be quite honest, I had never *met* a lady before becoming one," I said slowly, brushing a leaf off the wall. "So I wasn't sure what to expect when I came here… I suppose I should find more social engagements and, well, Mary runs the household, and I doubt she would give that up…"

He grinned empathetically. "Mary has been in charge ever since my lord first came to Lailan. She has a unique talent for control."

I laughed. "So it would seem."

He crossed his legs and leaned back, surveying the terraces and the view.

"How long have you been with Aedin?"

"Almost two years," Tieren said thoughtfully.

"How old are you?" I asked, hoping he wouldn't be offended by my inquiry.

Tieren laughed easily, giving me a coy smile. "Old enough to protect you and my lord."

I didn't doubt his words and grinned at his playfulness.

"I am eighteen," he said proudly.

"Is that the beginning of a beard I see?"

He rubbed his chin, a blush spreading across his cheeks. "If my lord will allow me to grow it."

I rolled my eyes. "I'm sure he has more pressing things to worry about."

"Do you like Lailan, my lady?" Tieren asked, eyeing me with a keen gaze.

I sighed, watching the boats circle the harbor. The sails were a stark white against the deep sapphire of the water. "Yes... and no." I paused, pondering the level of honesty I should share.

Tieren sat quietly, waiting.

"Before coming here, I had never seen such a variety of wildlife," I said with a reluctant smile. "Berge is a rocky island there is a frigid wind that is merciless for most of the year. Even the warm seasons are generally cold. There is a perpetual layer of snow covering the tops of the mountains, dusting the hills. I was always wearing furs and multiple layers of clothing." I eyed my bare arms with a smile. "It still feels odd to not have something covering me.

"But..." I faltered, tucking a loose hair behind my ear. "I had a father and brother, whom I loved very much. It was hard to leave them—I miss them every day." As the words left my mouth, I realized I had never vocalized that particular pain. A homesickness.

"I hardly knew Lord Aedin. I still don't know him well. It has been... an adjustment, to say the least."

"I... can only imagine how difficult that must be," Tieren said quietly, looking at his hands. "I am an orphan, so my only family has really been, well... here."

"How did you manage to become a guard to a lord?" I wondered aloud. In Berge, as on most other islands, it was a coveted position that required years of training.

A wry grin broke across his face. "My lord caught me stealing and *must* have been impressed with my skills..."

I laughed incredulously. "You were rewarded for theft?"

"*Attempted* theft of some change in my lord's pocket."

I grinned at the thought of Tieren attempting to pick Aedin's pockets. "That was quite courageous of you," I commented lightly.

Tieren shrugged, looking off towards the villa. "I had nothing to lose. My lord saw I had talent and brought me here to serve him and train as a guard. It... changed my life."

I nodded, meeting his eyes with a smile. "Quite a change of fortunes."

"And you as well, my lady."

I raised my eyebrows. "I suppose," I replied and hopped off the wall. The buzzing disappeared—I had almost forgotten its presence. I frowned and touched the stones again.

"What is it?" Tieren asked, watching me.

"Nothing," I said quickly, putting on a smile and removing my hand. "Just… nothing."

Tieren observed me casually, his feet playfully hitting the wall. "Hopefully we can chat again," he said with a smile.

"I would like that." I curtsied at him and he laughed in response.

I returned to my rooms for a cool bath and remained soaking in the tub until the sun was low on the horizon. Retiring to the balcony overlooking Tahuna, I ordered some wine.

This was the life—I tried to tell myself how lucky I was, how few people would ever see this view or drink this wine. But there was an ache in my heart as I thought of Daniel. I missed the comfort of intimacy.

Aedin returned, and our dinner was as shallow and bland as ever. I acknowledged his effort to attempt conversation, but his questions were dull and could be answered shortly, and we soon lapsed into silence. It was almost more entertaining when we were fighting.

We retired to bed. I saw the scar again but said nothing. Looking at it gave me the chills, so I tried to focus my gaze elsewhere.

As I lay down in the sheets, I felt a strange weariness settle in my bones, although I had accomplished little during the day. My mind was quickly drawn into sleep and for the first time in a very long while, I dreamed.

Large raindrops fell hard upon my head in a cacophony—like a million pearls descending on a marble floor. A symphony of chaos, it drowned out all other noises.

It was incredibly cold. I shivered in the foreign, muddy courtyard, hugging a fur coat around my body. It reminded me of one I'd brought from Berge—the one I would likely never wear again.

It was a dream. I knew I was asleep, but nothing was familiar. This was a world I did not know.

I let myself take in my surroundings—the downpour of rain on the soaking courtyard and the mud sliding across the stones. Blinking droplets out of my eyes, I noticed two figures on the other side of the filthy yard. One was tall, six feet at least, while the smaller one had fallen on the ground. Curiosity overwhelming my common sense to get under shelter, I walked towards them and, from about ten feet away, watched.

They both gripped large metal swords—ostentatious ones that I knew were exceptionally heavy and only used for show. The figure on the ground appeared to be only a boy, younger than Tieren, with hair that was so filthy with mud its color was lost.

A young man, lined with muscle, stood above him, casting the boy in a dark shadow, a disappointed grimace on his face as the boy groaned in agony.

"What have I told you?" he asked quietly, yet his words could still be heard through the rain. "Why have you fallen again?"

The boy desperately attempted to push himself up, as if to prove his worthiness, but his hands slipped in the mud, causing him to sprawl pathetically back down on the ground. The sword fell out of his hand, the mud nearly concealing the silver.

As he tried to grasp the slick, wide handle, the man kicked it, sending it a good distance away from where they stood. I jumped in surprise but didn't move, transfixed by the scene in front of me. The boy's breathing came in gasps as the man brought his sword down swiftly to touch his throat.

"Answer me."

"T-To never show your enemy your pain..." the boy cried out hoarsely as the sword's tip dug underneath his chin—just enough to break the skin.

"I am your enemy and you have shown me your pain." The man turned on his heel, barking to the boy, "Get your sword."

With surprising speed, the boy leaped up and ran to grab his sword from the mud. In a half-crouched position, he faced the man's back, his face as blank as a stone.

"Now," the man began in a nonchalant voice, "show me again why we are here."

Without turning to glance at his prey, he swung his sword out behind him, nearly catching the boy in the stomach. Leaping back just in time, the boy brought his sword up to meet the man's. Neither of them made a sound or showed any sign of tiredness as they fought.

The muscles on the man's arms were large and intimidating, his actions swift as they sparred. He was the obvious better of the two, the instructor. In contrast, the boy's thin frame held little muscle, but his footwork was so fast and swift that every time it seemed he was to be overcome by his teacher's blade, he would step out of harm's way or his feeble arm would bring the sword up within seconds, enough to brush off the attack.

There was a fire in his dark eyes—something that triggered a memory, but I brushed it away, entranced by the fight in front of me.

In the pounding rain, I watched the boy begin to tire. Although he continued to hold the same stoicism as his teacher, his dancing steps could not match his opponent. Every attack he made was mercilessly beaten down; the boy began to pant, creases of worry marring his forehead. The blows became faster and heavier, almost invisible with speed, and yet the boy somehow blocked each one.

Suddenly, there was a sickening crunch, and the boy was thrown to the side, like an unwanted rag doll, near my feet. Frozen in my dream state, I could only stare down at him in mute horror as the man approached. His enormous form cast a shadow upon both of us.

The boy's face was contorted with pain, his lips pressed into an extremely thin line and eyes closed as if he was holding back a scream. His hand clutched his side, his chest moving rapidly up and down with an irregular beat.

The man exhaled in frustration as he gazed at the boy's helpless form then pressed the sword's tip to the boy's right cheek.

"Calm yourself," he commanded.

His student struggled to obey, his fingers contorting then smoothing out flat at his sides, his face going blank and loose. After a slight tremble ran through his body, the boy was so still he could have been sleeping.

The man grimaced. "But can you hold it?" he asked quietly to no one in particular, and I knew his action before it came.

Leaving the cheek, his sword's tip trailed down the boy's quivering throat and onto his ribs, which the boy had been clutching a second ago.

A choked, nightmarish scream echoed through the courtyard.

The man swiftly turned around again, raking his hand through his short hair. The boy, trembling on the ground with tears streaking through the mud on his cheeks, fought to stand. After three unsuccessful attempts, he limped to his full height, standing before the man's back once again, his head hung in shame.

"Do you know why I'm doing this?" The man turned to face the boy, his arms spread open in question. "Why I'm torturing you?"

"Because it will make me a better fighter?" The boy glanced meekly at the man's calm and waiting face. He guessed again. "So I can benefit my king by eliminating his enemies?"

"I'm talking about life, Aedin."

The sound of my husband's name sent an electric current down my spine.

The young Aedin's brow furrowed as he searched for an answer. "To never show others your feelings?"

The man's hand came up and slapped Aedin's cheek. Aedin gasped as blood lined his lips and touched his cheek tenderly.

"And have you mastered that?" the man asked sarcastically.

"No," Aedin admitted, obviously disappointed as blood ran down his chin.

"And what if I was to do this?" The man's hand moved swiftly to Aedin's injured ribs, but Aedin's face had become calm and composed, so similar to the one I knew that I nearly cried out.

To my relief, the man's hand stopped within a centimeter of his tender ribs and merely tapped them. Aedin blinked.

"Better," the man said, replacing his hands behind his back and staring down at Aedin with a strange expression.

"This isn't about… what we're doing here in this little world of ours." The man's voice lowered seriously as he looked at Aedin, as if searching for something in his expression. "This will end one day—but life will continue. I'm teaching you this because someday you will meet someone who will beat you, Aedin. Not in the sparring ring or through surprise attacks. Someone who will take everything about you and tear it apart—make your life such a crossfire that you won't know if you'll come out broken or alive. Any emotion you show, every action you commit, they'll use it against you, mentally and physically.

"That day has not yet come for me and it is yet to come for you. They could be your worst enemy or your best friend. But the thing to remember is to never, ever give up fighting until they defeat you. And when they do, it will either be your downfall or your rebirth."

They stared at each other in contemplative silence as the rain slowly lessened. "How do you know this?" Aedin asked finally.

The man's blue eyes warmed in reminiscence. "It was something my father would always say. It's stuck with me since…" His words faltered as he gazed at Aedin, and he looked away, as if avoiding a painful memory.

"Who do you believe will beat you?" Aedin questioned, a boyish eagerness glinting in his eyes.

The man stared at him, cocking his head to one side, and then replied quietly, "I believe it will be you."

Aedin raised his eyebrows, taken aback, but did not comment. I almost expected the young boy to grow into my present-day husband in front of my eyes.

"And guess who broke my father?" The man gave a short laugh.

"You?" Aedin reasoned.

The man snorted a laugh. "No, his wife."

A cry ripped from my lungs as I resurfaced.

I heard my name repeated and felt the mattress move. I didn't understand it—my heart raced as tears rolled down my cheeks and I gripped at the sheets with tight fists.

"Gwen… *Gwen!*" Aedin's voice was soothing. "Gwen, look at me." He sat above the covers, cross-legged, holding my shoulders.

"I…" The words faltered on my lips and I struggled to regain control of my breath—I tried to focus on each inhale and exhale. Loosening my grip on the sheets, I found a tingling in my fingers, like a thick blood was vibrating through my veins. My body was energized, as if it was lit with an inner fire. It was the middle of the night, but I could see the room as clear as I could in daylight.

"Gwen." Aedin's hand came to cradle my face. "Are you alright?"

I floundered, my heart pounding in my chest. "N-No. I had a dream… a horrible dream."

Aedin's face paled to an expression that reminded me of the boy in my dream. "Of what? What did you dream?"

I opened my mouth but couldn't find words, suddenly aware of my surroundings. There was something in the air, pushing against me, as if it was malleable. But nothing was there. I felt Aedin's presence—although he was only inches away—and someone else's in the garden.

Aedin took my hands in his—and the aching tingle suddenly receded. The air became air again. And my blood felt thin and weak.

The tears on my cheeks dried and I cleared my throat, finally able to meet Aedin's eyes. They were dark and empathetic.

"I'm sorry," he whispered and pulled me into his arms. I didn't resist. I closed my eyes against his warm shoulder and took long, shaky breaths. Hands ran up and down my spine—soothing and pacifying—as my heart slowed to a steady beat.

The dream was seared into my mind, like a memory from my own life.

Chapter Eleven

THE SOUND OF running water echoed from the bathroom, waking me from sleep. I squinted at the curtains, hanging pale and still in the early morning. Why in the world was I awake?

I groaned, wishing to fall back asleep, but my mind was already whirling. The dream was haunting—I was surprised that I could still recall every single detail. As if it had been real. I shivered, pulled on a robe over my nightgown and stepped onto the floor.

"Good morning," Aedin said from behind me.

I turned, startled, to see him buttoning his shirt cuff, standing by the bathroom door. His skin was freshly dried, and he appeared almost boyish with uncombed, damp hair.

"Will you come to breakfast?" His words were more of a statement than a question.

I found my voice, though it was hoarse from crying the night before. "Yes, I will."

There was an awkward moment where he paused. "Do you… need to change?"

"Do I have to?" I rubbed the sleep from my eyes.

"I suppose you don't *have* to…"

"Fine, I will."

I moved past him and opened the wardrobe, selecting a dress at random. Slipping into the bathroom, I threw it over my head and splashed some water on my face, braided my hair, and deemed myself good enough for the crack of dawn.

When I re-entered the room, Aedin was slipping something into his boots. I eyed the long dagger attached to his belt.

"Do you carry that often?"

"Hm?" He straightened and opened the door to the antechamber.

"The dagger? Do you carry that when you're in Tahuna?"

"Oh, yes. Just a precaution."

"Precaution?" I repeated skeptically. "You have guards around you all the time. Do you really need a weapon?"

"Of course." Aedin looked at me with a dumbfounded expression. "It's a precaution."

I shot him a look of incredulity but said nothing and moved into the antechamber.

As we walked silently down the hall together, I tried to piece together what had happened last night after the dream. Aedin had comforted me—I remembered crying against his shoulder as I tried to collect myself.

And then… had I fallen back asleep in his arms? My face burned as I thought of those strong, brown limbs cradling me, holding me. I must have been exhausted.

The silence continued as we entered the small dining room. Aedin opened the door for me, and I went to the chair with the view of the ocean. He sat opposite, avoiding my gaze as he folded his hands together on the table.

Thankfully, to prevent any awkwardness, Mary appeared only seconds later, taking our orders. She entered with an expression of surprise at seeing me awake this early and left quickly. I, too, could not explain it.

As soon as the glass door closed, Aedin's eyes went to my face. "How are you?"

I hesitated, suddenly suspicious. "Well?" I replied slowly.

"How do you *feel*?" Aedin was looking at me intently, as a medicator would inspect a patient. I was bemused.

"Good…?"

His lips thinned, his dark eyes drilling holes into mine. I shifted uneasily under his gaze. "Why do you ask?"

Aedin ignored my question. "Do you remember how you felt last night? Was it different from this morning?"

"I suppose," I said slowly, wracking my brain to try and remember. "Yes… Last night I felt… good… except for the crying of course; I felt very oddly… energized."

"And now?"

"I feel… normal. I… I don't know how to describe it other than 'good.' Wholesome, perhaps. Or natural and free…" I was surprised at the words coming out of my mouth. Only scraps of memories remained in which I could recall the thick, pounding, and lively sensation of my blood. It was the strangest thing.

Aedin nodded as if understanding.

"Why do you ask?"

"No reason," Aedin said quietly, looking away. "Do you remember your dream?"

"Yes. It was about you."

My husband's face paled. He choked out the word, "What?"

"You were in my dream. It was about you… Well most of it was."

Aedin opened his mouth then shut it again. "I…" he said hoarsely. "Dreams are private things… If you do not wish to share, I understand…"

I shrugged. "It was just a dream. You were fighting—no, sparring with—an older man with blue eyes who was a sort of teacher. It was raining and you were in a courtyard of mud and stone. He…" I swallowed, remembering the man's blows. "He… hurt you."

As I said those words, Aedin's gaze moved from my face to the wood of the table, and he became as still as stone, transfixed in thought.

"He taught you about overcoming your enemy… Something dramatic. And said that you would someday meet someone who will make your life a crossfire." Immediately the man's face swelled in my mind, and I remembered the words by heart. "Someone who will take everything about you and tear it apart—

make your life such a crossfire that you won't know if you'll come out broken or alive."

My last words hung motionlessly in the air as Aedin swallowed. His head seemed to hang from his shoulders as he folded his hands on the table and attempted to break out of his trance.

"But…" I said awkwardly after a moment, "it was just a dream. I don't know how I came up with something as absurd as that."

Aedin's voice was gruff when he spoke. "It's not… absurd."

"Yes, it is," I objected. "Unless you're advocating for my overactive imagination?"

A brief smile flickered onto his lips. "I would not condemn it… as long as it were grounded in some truth of reality."

"I suppose," I agreed mindlessly.

Aedin opened his mouth and inhaled as if to say something, but the glass door swung open, and his jaw shut. Mary entered carrying a tray with tea and toast.

The silence was palpable as she placed the items down and exited with a grace rivaling that of a noble. I turned to look at Aedin, but his eyes were fixed on the table once more.

I hesitated but finally said, "Were you about to say something…?"

"No." Aedin picked up his tea and took a sip.

I followed his lead and did the same.

Shortly after the meal, Aedin left for Tahuna without another word. I could see the thoughts running through his head, but there was little I could understand. Why had the dream scared him? And more importantly, why had it affected me in such a way?

I had never before felt so… alive. I mused on the recollection—nursing it to preserve the impression as best as possible. It was as if the god of life himself had breathed into my soul—there had been an immense joy I hadn't noticed the night before. Terror, but also joy. My body had breathed in time with my heart and soul. I had simply never felt that way of existing was possible… Unless I had been imaging things?

The answer was elusive. I sat on the balcony watching the sea. My hair tickled my face as I smelled the salty air.

"My lady," Mary's voice echoed through the door.

I turned from the horizon. "Yes?"

"The garden party with Miss Taylor is this afternoon. We will begin getting ready in several hours."

My stomach turned into a knot at the reminder; I chided myself for the childish anxiety. "Thank you, Mary."

"And this came for you." Mary offered me a silver plate, upon which rested a white, folded parchment bearing an unfamiliar seal.

Frowning, I took the letter from the plate. "Let's hope it's not another invitation to tea," I muttered under my breath but saw her face was strained.

"My lady, that is the king's seal," she said quietly.

"Is it?" I hadn't received any letters from the king in my lifetime. I examined the figures on the purple wax circle—a bear and an eagle, bearing teeth at each other as if about to launch into an attack. In the center, there was a crown studded with seven circular shapes that suggested precious stones.

Perhaps it was a great and terrible sign—personally, I thought it rather silly-looking.

Shrugging, I tore the wax from the paper and opened its contents. My reading had progressed and I could now make out more previously unfamiliar words. "E…ph…r…aim…" I sounded out the letters at the bottom and then suddenly realized.

"Ephraim!" I exclaimed in excitement. "By the gods, I haven't heard from my devil brother in ages! How dare he go so long without writing?"

I laughed aloud, handing the letter to Mary. "Please read it!"

"No, my lady." Mary took the letter and sat in the adjacent chair. "We shall tackle this together."

I groaned at this, eager to hear his words, but agreed.

"My dear… sis…ter," I said aloud, proud that I could recognize the beginning words.

I hope you are doing well and happy in your marriage to Lord Aedin. Neither Father nor I have heard from you directly since your departure so please write back and tell us both about your new life!

Personally, I have greatly missed your presence. The transition in my life has proved both beneficial and challenging. Lord Aedin gave me a post as historian to the king thus I am able to send letters at great speed using his symbol!

Life on the island of Radiance and at the king's palace is filled with endless parties and beautiful people, but the demands of my position are quite a bore. I suppose it's a healthy balance; to be sober as a hermit one hour, only to be drunk as a brewer the next. I am confident you would find it quite amusing to watch the crowds of revelers and wish you were here to join in the fun.

Although he was offered apartments within the palace, Father was unwilling to move from Berge. I believe he was right to reject them as he would not have enjoyed this place. He remains at home, tending to the shop, as he has done for decades. Fortunately, now he does not risk poverty (and has two less mouths to feed!).

I hope that your new life is filled with as much luxury and peace as is expected. Please send word as soon as possible. I am quite busy attending to the king and enjoying the finest wine in all of the Empire, but I will make time to hear from you, dear sister. The king seems keen to visit Lailan in the coming months, so I hope to join the party to visit you soon!

Much love from your brother,
Ephraim

Mary's brow furrowed as we completed the letter. She grew silent.

"Well!" I commented cheerfully. "We shall have to practice writing him back!"

"Yes, of course." Mary's brown eyes quickly reread the letter. "Would you mind, my lady, if I showed this letter to my lord when you are finished with it?"

"Why should he need to see it?"

"I think my lord should like to know if the king is planning to visit in the coming months," Mary stated, straightening her posture.

"Very well," I said stiffly. "I suppose I wouldn't mind."

"Thank you, my lady." She rose from her chair. "Would you mind composing a response on your own? I shall look it over for mistakes before you send it."

"Yes, I wouldn't mind…" I was taken aback by her sudden urgency. "Do you have to be somewhere?"

"Yes, my lady." Mary curtsied. "If you don't mind."

"Not at all," I said slowly. "Do what you must. But can you bring a sheet of parchment and ink?"

"Of course, my lady." Mary nodded gravely and slowly walked inside. Minutes later, a servant reappeared with the items on a try.

Brushing off the strangeness of her composure, I pulled a sheet of new parchment and dipped my quill in the ink

Dear brother,

My words looked scrawled and messy compared to his impressive, swirling letters.

I am writing to you in my own hand. Much has happened since we last spoke…

Chapter Twelve

ROWYN'S HANDS TRACED over the embossed letters on the book's spine. It was large—a mass of papers stuffed into a leather cover and messily sewn. Even the leather was poorly crafted, but that was the least of Rowyn's concerns.

Why in Fate's name had Raine left the book? The mere idea of the knowledge leaving the Haven was terrifying and astounding. Had Raine simply misjudged the extent of the history? Or intentionally—and in poor judgment—wished for Rea to know its contents?

It was a cruel story. Rowyn's lips thinned as he remembered his sorrow the first time he'd been told of the Empire's history.

The killings, the purges, and the men who had sought to destroy them. It was horrific. But it was in the past. The Empire did not seem as keen on seeking out their kind anymore. Iselleden was separate—far away and pure. The Empire was tainted, save for a few that remained. But the Rhidge had nearly corrupted them all.

He remembered the Prophet's words and said a quiet prayer that the girl would remain safe.

"Rowyn."

A quiet voice and knock on his door echoed in the bright room. Rowyn blinked away his darkened thoughts in the sunlight.

Standing, he opened the door for Celion, nodding respectfully to the guard.

"The Council is about to meet—you asked me to remind you."

"Yes, thank you. And did you speak to Raine?"

"She said she would talk with you privately after the meeting."

"Many thanks." Rowyn touched his shoulder in gratitude.

Celion gave him an encouraging smile as Rowyn's heart skipped a beat. Despite the heaviness in his heart, he mustered one in response and shrugged into the hall of the Haven.

He knew the way to the Council Room by heart—each month he walked this same path to meet with the leaders of Iselleden. The meetings were usually succinct, rarely tense, and often inspiring. Everyone in Iselleden knew their place: there was little discussion and even fewer arguments. Yet Rowyn suspected that his words might make this meeting the most controversial one to date.

Sunlight poured through the glass ceiling, warming the white stone walls and floors. The wardens thoughtfully swept errant dust and leaves, exchanging smiles with Rowyn as he passed.

As he turned a corner and stepped down into the unfiltered sun, he exited the residential and communal area of the Haven then crossed the cobblestones littered with olive trees and benches, veering towards two guards at the entrance of a wide tower. They exchanged respectful nods, and Rowyn greeted them by name—"Selena, Loran."—as he passed inside.

The ceiling hallway was clad in colored glass tiles, creating a symphony of color on the whitewashed floors and walls. Rowyn always felt like he was walking through a kaleidoscope, and the sensation never changed. Although his eyes lingered on the bright shapes and colors in wonder, he stayed the course—and soon he entered the large expanse of the Council Tower.

Pure, nearly blinding white light streamed down from the partitioned glass ceiling. Seven daises stood in a circle around the room. Even the smallest whisper became the largest echo—the room was filled with voices. Rowyn scanned the small crowd for Raine but could not find his sister.

"Rowyn!" a small wrinkled man addressed him warmly, clasping his arm and hand.

"Josiah." Rowyn inclined his head with a familiar smile. "How is the family?"

"Very well thank you." The man stretched his neck to look up at Rowyn with a twinkle in his eyes. "You know my granddaughter Terra is still looking for a husband…"

Rowyn laughed. "Josiah, you've been saying that for the last ten years—"

"I've just had a feeling, that's all." Josiah waved it away with a laugh. "But I know that's not in your plans at the moment. Are you doing well?"

"Yes and no," Rowyn sighed. "There's much I have to tell the Council."

"Well." Josiah's thick eyebrows crinkled. "I shall hope we can help you."

"I hope you can as well." Rowyn gave a half-smile. He wasn't entirely convinced—the burden was his to bear.

"But Rea and Darius are well?"

"Yes—very busy with the three children, but they're getting along well as a family."

"Very good to hear." Josiah's eyes gleamed and Rowyn knew that he was sincere.

The sound of his sister's voice set the entire room to silence. Rowyn started—he hadn't seen her come in.

"All please sit for the beginning of this meeting."

Rowyn clasped Josiah's arm as they moved to take their seats. The daises were carved into the circular wall of the Tower itself and raised nearly six feet off the ground. Rowyn looked over his shoulder to see if Josiah had made it up the steps—but the old man was already being helped by Ferra. Jumping lithely up the steps, Rowyn took his seat, thankful for the cushion to soften the hard marble.

He looked at his sister, poised in her seat, and did not understand—even after all these years—how such a beautiful creature had come into existence. Although many years her senior, he had always felt inadequate.

Raine had always retained a powerful presence, but since she had been called to become Speaker of the Council nearly eight years ago, she had only grown even more impressive. Her strawberry-blonde ringlets hung loosely, cascading down her shoulders like a river of warm gold. She wore the traditional tunic of the Haven, simple and unadorned, which hung from her broad shoulders and flickered a multitude of colors in the bright sunlight.

Feeling Rowyn's gaze, Raine turned her head and smiled at her brother, her wide emerald eyes full of warmth. It was a breathtaking smile of comfort and encouragement, but it did not ease Rowyn's fears.

Once the air was still, Raine began.

"My fellow people—we meet on this beautiful afternoon which Fate has brought us in order to discuss private matters that cannot yet be brought before the public. Rowyn, the Captain of the Guard, has expressed concerns that we must address. Yet before we begin, I ask that any other issues that need to be dealt with be brought before the Council."

Her voice echoed through the chamber for some time before the notes faded. Finally, a young woman who had only recently been Called to the Council stood and spoke.

"Council, I call upon you to address rumors that ships have been seen in the west. I do not know if these ships present any threat to us, but I have heard from fishermen in the harbor that"— she paused to swallow visibly—"many believe them to be from the Empire."

There was a stir of motion as White's words caused the Council members to lean forward, casting their eyes around to see who would respond.

Rowyn was unsurprised. He had heard such reports in weeks past and had himself gone to see the ships. It was the most contact Iselleden had had with the Empire in five hundred years. Seeing the sails on the mountaintop that day had sent a pit of fear into Rowyn's stomach. Trouble brewed on the horizon.

"Perhaps this is something that the Captain of the Guard could address?" Raine ventured, looking at her brother.

"Council." Rowyn stood with trembling knees. "These are not rumors—they are true. From the watchtowers we have seen sails. They are sails from the west, although we cannot confirm their intent."

"And do they come for us? Or merely float on the horizon?" Josiah piped up from his dais.

"Since we first saw them two weeks ago, they have come no further than the horizon. We have knowledge of a small island—a spit of rock, only several miles across—that was used as a fortress during the wars. It has been uninhabited since the wars, but now it appears that the Empire is using it. For what purpose, however, we know not."

"What if they seek peace?" White said hopefully.

"Or war," grumbled Berius.

"Or an agreement?" Raine ventured.

"All these are speculations," Rowyn concluded, "until we know more. However, it is against my advice that we should seek them out. It is possible that the Rhidge could be inhabiting the island—"

"Then let us send a large troop to finish them off!" Berius exclaimed. "We cannot continually live in fear of the Empire."

"But we do not want to incite the Empire into a full-scale attack," Josiah countered wisely. "We were fortunate enough to retain this island after the wars. I say we should not engage unless they bring the battle to us."

"But how will we be ready for an attack?" Raine spoke softly. "Our guards—no matter how valiant their hearts may be—have never seen blood nor been trained in such a manner as the Rhidge."

"The Rhidge are cursed," Pria spoke up in a loud voice. "We cannot attack them directly—they have corrupted the Gift—"

"But we use it for good," White interrupted. "Our power is stronger."

"Yes, but they are terrible and vicious," Raine said quietly, an expression of hatred marring her elegant features. "They were breed with the sole purpose of eradicating our people. They feed off fear and pervert the goodness of the Gift to create something entirely darker."

Her last words reverberated ominously in the Tower. The Council fell silent with dread and sadness.

Rowyn pushed away his feelings of despair and spoke to the quiet audience. "The reason I come before you all this afternoon is because I have heard from the Prophet…"

"Rowyn… of what are you speaking?" Raine glanced at him in surprise. The Council was silent in rapt attention.

"The Prophet has shown me the way to end the terrible deeds of the Empire and restore the Gift. To restore—no, to bring to life a *new* Empire." Rowyn nearly stuttered the words. It sounded like insanity, saying them aloud. "This is what… I was told."

"Tell us what was said," Raine said patiently.

Rowyn swallowed, his throat dry. "It was several weeks ago, before I saw the ships. I was doing my rounds and stopping by the watchtowers to inspect the guards when I saw a distant figure. I was walking down from the mountains, alone on a pass, and the Prophet called to me from a ravine. Words… echoed in my mind and they spoke of a prophecy…" He shivered remembering the gleaming opalescent eyes, void of any pupil. "Fate had told the Prophet that I was to search out a girl—no, a young woman—with the Gift whom I would train to overcome the Empire."

There was a thick, brief silence before the questions came in abundance.

"Who is the woman?" Pria asked.

"I… do not know," answered Rowyn lamely.

"How is she to be trained to end the Empire?" Berius inquired pointedly. "How can an individual, man *or* woman, overcome a vast and powerful dynasty?"

"I am unsure—"

"And how will you find this woman? If you know not her name nor what she looks like?" Josiah asked softly.

"I—"

"Is there anything we can do to prepare for her arrival?" Raine questioned.

"Nothing I can think of at this moment…" Rowyn held out his hands, tired of standing. "Look, Council, if I could please have your attention—*please.*"

The whispered conversations around the room ceased.

"Thank you." Rowyn hesitated. "What I have just told you concerning the prophecy was all that the Prophet relayed to me. I assure you—I questioned them in the same manner you just did me… because I very much want more information. But, as we have experienced before, the Prophet would only say what Fate has told them, as confusing and vexing as this puzzle may be.

"And… after some thought and consideration, I anticipate that Fate may show me through the Dreams. Although I have sixty-five years in this world, I have yet to have my Dream of the present. The Dreams came for me late—unlike most. But Fate shows us the proper things in due time. I have Dreamed of the past and future… but not the present. Although I could be mistaken, I expect that Fate will show me in this Dream all that I need to know…"

"You have great faith, Rowyn," Raine said. "Something for which we all strive."

There were murmurs of agreement around the room. The Council Tower seemed to have settled to a simmer.

"Thank you," Rowyn muttered. His words sounded loud against the marble walls.

"Council," he continued, clearing his throat, "what I suggest is that we wait. I will continue to listen and wait for a sign, but I know that all will happen in Fate's time. And the ships"—Rowyn looked at White—"I do not think they will dare to venture closer than the abandoned fortress. I will have guards mark the times that the ships appear, and we will try to find a pattern. Meanwhile, I will train my guards harder than ever to prepare for the worst. If the Rhidge come… We will be ready."

Berius nodded. "We should prepare."

"Berius speaks wisely," Josiah agreed as Pria nodded too.

"Very well." Raine nodded. "Rowyn, thank you for your cautions. We trust you will do your best in seeking out the will of

Fate. We will pray for you and the safety of Iselleden. Please, let us know if there is anything to be done."

"Thank you, Council. Just… speak of this to no one till more is revealed." Rowyn sat down, sighing in relief that it was over, though his hands still trembled against the marble arms of the chair.

Raine stood. "Is there anything else to be presented before the Council?"

No one spoke a word.

"Then let this session be closed until next month. Let no one here speak of what was heard—save considering the matters silently in our hearts."

Each leader stood and bowed in unison before making their way out of the Tower. The murmurs of conversation resumed.

Rowyn stood silently watching his sister. In response, Raine smiled sadly and inclined her head to the side.

Exhaling heavily, Rowyn followed Raine outside the Tower doors and into the piercing sunlight of midday. The chatter of birds and the humming of insects was an alien sound compared with the stark silence of the empty Council Tower.

Raine continued down a path that wound around the outside of the Haven until they were alone in a garden overlooking the valley below. A stone bench roasted underneath the hot sun, but Raine took a seat, patting the empty space beside her. She squinted in the sunlight, the freckles on her nose wrinkling as her dress swayed gently.

Rowyn sat uncomfortably in the heat and rolled up his sleeves. He shielded his eyes, resting his elbows on his knees, and looked out at the winding road that led from the Haven to the heart of Farist.

"Why did you not tell me before the meeting?" Raine asked softly, after a brief moment of silence.

Rowyn shrugged. "You were gone. I was busy watching the ships. Things came up."

"When did it happen?"

"The day before I went to visit Rea."

"How is she?"

Rowyn chuckled. "Strained with the children. But well… she misses you."

Raine nodded, looking down. "Yes, I miss her as well."

Again, silence overcame them.

Raine looked up as if to speak. "I…" She hesitated, choosing her words carefully. "Do you ever think it strange that you and I were Called to the highest roles in Iselleden… and yet Rea was Called to remain a farmer's wife and raise children."

"Which is more challenging?" Rowyn pointed out with a smile.

"Indeed," Raine said, her laughter a musical sound. Then she grew sober.

"In the stories of old… in the stories of the Empire that I have read, families rule islands and have networks of power that simply do not exist here. Why is that? If we were in the Empire, we could rule… everything."

Rowyn's emerald eyes flashed. "Do not speak like that."

His sister shifted uneasily. "Faith is a fickle thing. I don't understand why I was Called to this position when I so often question the path of Iselleden. Yet…" She plucked a strand of tall grass from below the bench. "I suppose it has worked thus far— why should it not survive?"

"Raine," Rowyn said steadily, his voice low. "You are charged with being the Speaker of the Council—the mouthpiece of our leaders. You may personally question the decisions of Fate or the Council, but you *must* maintain an appearance of tranquility. Keep your private affairs private. You must follow Fate for the Council, for Iselleden. Otherwise, are we any better than the Empire? To bend to our every whim, doubt, and desire?"

Rowyn shifted in his seat, looking directly at his sister. "Do you know why they fell? Why they became corrupted?"

Raine was silent. Her red lips were closed, her green eyes hollow. "Why?" she asked mechanically.

"Because they desired *control*. Their arrogance made them question the traditions set in place by Fate and they believed that they could do it better. They eradicated the Gift because of fear—

they sought dominance and believed that they could use it in stronger and perverted ways."

"So were they wrong?"

"Yes!" Rowyn retorted. "Look at their mere lifespan—an average man in the Empire does not live above sixty and yet Josiah survives healthily at a hundred and twenty! There is constant feuding between the lords and king, endless bribery and treachery… And then the Rhidge that spoils the goodness of the Gift. It's a dark place, Raine. And it all began when one man desired control and believed that his way trumped the natural progression established by Fate."

"I suppose you're right." Raine cast her eyes to the long grass that tickled their feet and laughed sharply. "I wanted to console *you* with your prophecy but now you have helped me! You've always been an excellent older brother."

"And you a younger sister." Rowyn gripped her warm hand, trying to give an encouraging smile.

But his heart was darkened by their words. For years on end, they had hardly spoken of the Rhidge and Empire, and now it occurred in daily conversation. He marveled at the changing tides.

"I think I will visit Rea tomorrow," Raine said thoughtfully, standing with grace.

"You will make her very happy."

Raine smiled toothlessly in response.

"Why did you leave that book at their house? I caught Darra reading it when I visited last."

She shook her head. "I must have forgotten it. I was going over the historical notes and was spending every moment in between appointments—"

"Is that really it?" Rowyn look at her dubiously.

Raine bit her lip. "I think," she began slowly, "when I started reading through the book, I thought, *Others should know this.*" She turned to him with a quizzical gaze. "Rowyn—why were we never taught about the Rhidge? Why did it have to remain a secret within the Council? All of these years?"

He didn't have an answer. He stared at his feet. "There are things we may not understand…"

"But doesn't knowledge empower? Doesn't knowledge free us from making the mistakes of our past?" Raine continued eagerly. "Why should we have to hide it? Even as hideous and shameful as it may be?"

"I don't know," Rowyn said flatly. "And we can't account for the decisions of the past."

"But we can choose how to move forward."

Rowyn shrugged. "I suppose that's the only power we do have."

They fell silent. Raine's lips moved as if to speak, and then she confessed, "I left that book intentionally. Hoping Rea would read it and understand *some* part of what we have come to know. However… I can see that was a mistake."

"It was," he said. "And unlucky that her curious daughter found it before she did," he added wryly.

Raine chuckled. "Fair enough. Did you bring it back with you?"

"Of course—it's in my rooms."

"Good. You might need it for reference if you intend to follow through with the Prophet's words."

Rowyn hadn't considered that. "Yes, I think you're right."

She bent to kiss Rowyn's cheek and then left. Her dress waved in the warm breeze as she walked on the stepping stones through the garden.

Rowyn said a silent prayer for his sister and tried to purge his mind of his own troubles. Thinking of the young woman, he wondered how their worlds would align. And if it really would— as Fate had promised—turn out for the better.

Chapter Thirteen

"… AND YOU WOULD *never* believe what happened next." Miss Andrea Taylor paused for dramatic effect. "He ate *all* of the cakes!"

There was a chorus of laughter, and even I chuckled. Andrea lovingly patted her small dog as he jumped up to lick her fingers. His nose sniffed insistently, expecting a treat.

We were seated in a semicircle facing a grand fountain. Tables burdened with sweets, salted meats, and fruit sat in the cool shade of the patio. Umbrellas sheltered us from the pounding heat of the sun, but there was little breeze as the Taylor estate sat in the thick of the jungle, away from the coast.

It was a grand house, with plentiful and spacious gardens for parties. Francesca, Catherine Mirelli, and several other women whose names I couldn't recall fanned their faces and held glasses of cold, pale wine.

Andrea appeared to enjoy holding court—she smiled at each of us in turn, ringing the bell for more wine. Her ringlets were pulled back in a sophisticated fashion, her pale dress stitched with gold flowers.

Marks watched us from the shadow of the portico, grimacing as he eased into the little shade provided by the wall. I wondered if he considered this a demotion for the day.

"Do you have any animals, my lady?" Andrea asked, easing the brown-and-white dog onto her lap.

"No," I said with a smile. "I am afraid I do not."

"My other dog—sweet Felicity—just had puppies. You are welcome to take one!"

I laughed. "No, I could not. But thank you for the offer—it is very kind." I could imagine Aedin's dismayed expression at the introduction of a puppy into the household.

A servant came and refilled my glass. The white wine was crisp and cool, tasting of tart lemon and salt on my tongue. I would have to ask Mary to stock some at the villa.

Surprisingly, I was enjoying the afternoon. The small group felt more manageable than the grand party at the de Boughs, and for all of their giggles and gossip, it was refreshing to connect.

"So what suitors have you been considering, Andrea?" I asked archly, settling into my chair.

"There are several." She grinned at me as the dog ensconced itself in her lap. "Willem Tarken—he runs a private estate that supplies fruit to the merchants in the port. He is a bit older, but—"

"But his estate is lovely," Francesca finished for her with a knowing smile.

Andrea laughed. "Exactly. And then Liam Spence—the younger brother of Alexander Spence. Sweet, but a bit dull. And Samuel Cittar—very handsome, but he seems, well…"

"A bit self-absorbed?" Catherine offered with a snigger. "I caught him eying himself in the mirror at Francesca's party."

"Exactly," Andrea sighed dramatically. "Imagine trying to have a conversation when he's admiring his reflection in a spoon!"

I giggled, shaking my head. "It cannot be that bad," I protested.

"You'll see," Andrea said pointedly. "I promise you—let us all have dinner next week and I *promise* he will mention his sword-fighting regimen or how well his clothes fit—"

"At least he would be nice to look at," Catherine countered. "We cannot all be so lucky…"

"Catherine," Francesca cooed. "Your betrothed is sweet and kind."

"He is as ugly as a rock," Catherine muttered into her wine as we burst out laughing.

"There can be other rewarding attributes," I agreed with Francesca. "If he is sweet and kind, then you will never have any arguments and you can decide everything."

"You can decide to only let him bed you in the dark." Andrea eyed her playfully as Catherine hit her arm, spilling some wine. The dog in her lap woke up with a rude expression at the intrusion.

Francesca giggled like a schoolgirl as Andrea withdrew her attack. "Well at least *you* will be having some bedding soon. It feels that I will forever be a single woman."

"You will find someone soon," I said reassuringly.

"My lady has a handsome brother." Francesca looked at me pointedly. "He is unattached, is he not?"

"Oh, please!" Andrea leaned forward. "Please tell me he's not boring."

"He is *not* boring." I glared at Francesca. "But he is on Radiance, serving as historian to the king."

"I would love Radiance!" Andrea offered with a wave of her hand, sipping her wine. "I have heard the parties are delightful. What is his name?"

There was no deterring her. "Ephraim Doyle. And," I added, grinning, "he said he might visit in the coming months. If he does, I will be sure to invite you to the villa."

"Thank you! And in the meantime, I hope every woman he meets on Radiance is an ugly bore."

"That is doubtful," Francesca chirped. "Gerand and I have been to Radiance and it is the epitome of fashion and good taste."

Andrea rolled her eyes and took another sip of her wine. "And I am stuck here. Waiting for a suitor to agree and my father to make up his mind."

"Well we are here to console you." I saluted her with my glass of wine.

"And drink with you," Catherine added, clinking her glass with mine. We grinned at each other.

"How is my lord?" Andrea asked suddenly. "How is he as a husband?"

I hesitated. "Well—"

"Oh, they are so in love!" I was grateful that Francesca cut me off. "When we dined with them last week, it was so heartwarming to see them together."

"Er—yes," I added. "It has been such a blur since our first meeting…"

"Is he kind?" Catherine asked. "He always seems so serious and grim."

I laughed, despite myself. "He *is* kind, but yes he is serious… There is a lot of work to be done managing Lailan and the ports —"

"How is he in bed?" Andrea winked at me as Catherine shot her a glare and hissed disapprovingly, "*Andrea*—she is a lady!"

"Nice," I said quickly. "Very… nice." I felt suddenly hot and uncomfortable. I hadn't kissed Aedin since our wedding ceremony.

Andrea looked disappointed. "I would hope my husband would *ravage* me in bed—kissing me softly every night—"

Catherine rolled her eyes. "You are such a romantic."

"These things take time," Francesca advised me gently as my face grew flushed. I took a large mouthful of wine, trying to ignore her words. "Gerand and I are only *just* beginning to thoroughly enjoy our time together after *years* and *years* of marriage."

Andrea crinkled her nose—likely at the thought of Francesca and Gerand together in bed. "I should hope it would not take *that* long—"

"Oh, just practice!" one of the other women interjected. "It just takes practice!"

"Practice on your own?" Andrea raised her eyebrows, unable to suppress a giggle.

The woman smirked. "*And* with your husband. Never hurts to have practice."

I thought of my nights with Daniel on Berge. My body ached for his touch—it felt like a lifetime ago. I suddenly felt tightly wound and keenly aware of the lack of intimacy in my life.

There was a lull in the conversation, and I was eager to change the subject. "Tell me—where did you get this wine, Andrea?" I held up my glass as the pale, cold liquid frosted the outside.

"It is from Tente," Andrea said, caressing her dog's ears. "It is a small vineyard on the island that only produces fifty barrels a year. I confess, I do not know the name, but my father is friends with Lady Adim and we were able to purchase a barrel last year."

"Can you please inquire regarding the name? It is wonderful." I sipped the wine appreciatively, savoring its brightness on my tongue.

"Certainly!" she said, her eyes shining. "I will also see if we could secure a barrel for you and my lord. It is in high demand— especially on Lailan when it's so hot."

"Lady Adim is so lovely," Francesca mused. "We met her when we were at Radiance *years* ago—back when her husband was still alive."

"What happened to him?" Catherine asked, her brown eyes growing wide.

Francesca shrugged. "He fell ill. Never recovered. It was such a blow to her family, but she has remained so strong and taken over his duties with ease."

Andrea nodded. "She is quite capable. Fiery and lively as well. I would never dare to double-cross her. Her children were quite energetic and demanding, from what I remember."

"How is she able to govern an island when she has children?" Catherine frowned, considering the possibility.

Andrea rolled her eyes in response. "Catherine—how quaint! Women can do many things."

"I would imagine it does detract from their upbringing," a woman next to Francesca chirped.

"Nonsense," Andrea scoffed. "There are plenty of hours in a day. Why shouldn't a woman be able to govern an island?" She looked at me as if I knew exactly what she was talking about.

I didn't, but I came to her defense regardless.

"I am sure it is difficult," I said evenly, "but she must be capable if she has survived this long."

"Unlike Lord Bennett." Catherine nodded sympathetically.

I frowned. "Who is that?"

Andrea scowled at Catherine in disapproval. "He was… a previous Lord of Lailan. About six years ago."

Francesca sighed, looking down at her hands. There was an awkward silence.

"How did he die?" I asked quietly, looking at Andrea.

She shifted in her chair, giving me an empathetic look. "He was publicly beheaded."

I couldn't contain the grimace that crossed my face. "That sounds… horrible."

"It was," Catherine said simply. Andrea gave her a look of exasperation.

"But that will *never* happen to my lord." Andrea gave a soft tinkling laugh.

"Yes, he has done *such* a good job with his duties," Francesca added enthusiastically. The other women nodded eagerly as I took a large sip of my wine. I didn't know what to say.

It struck me that Catherine and Andrea—along with the other young women on the island—had likely seen *ten* different Lords of Lailan. And the older women even more.

They shifted in their chairs, avoiding my gaze. I wondered if they had sat in circles—similar to this one—with the previous Ladies of Lailan. Perhaps they had befriended them, only to watch them executed in the name of the king, or mysteriously pass away in silence.

My heart sank as I grimly wondered if I was next.

A servant appeared at Andrea's side, bending down to whisper in her ear. She frowned, looking up at him with a start. *"Here?"* she exclaimed.

"What is it?" Catherine asked.

"Apparently Kitra Devereux is at the front, requesting an audience." Andrea's brow was furled. "I do not believe I sent her an invitation…"

"Insolent. Appearing without an invitation," someone murmured.

"Oh, what harm would it do?" Francesca's cheeks were bright from the wine.

"I do not think my father would like it…" Andrea said hesitantly. "You *know* the rumors."

"We are in good company." Catherine gestured towards me. "It cannot hurt."

"She does bring a certain *humor* to parties…" another woman said, chuckling.

I recalled Mary's words with hesitation. "It is your choice, Andrea," I said openly.

Glancing at Marks, I saw his lips tighten—he'd obviously overheard the news. He straightened his posture as beads of sweat collected on his brow.

Andrea gestured towards her servant. "Bring a chair for her. Put her over there." She pointed towards the outermost edge of the circle, next to the fountain. I was grateful I was in the middle. We fell silent as the servant walked away and exchanged meaningful glances as we waited.

Andrea stroked the dog on her lap, staring into the fountain thoughtfully. "At least we might gain a story out of this," she murmured.

There were answering smiles and chuckles as we sipped the cold wine. Minutes later, we heard the patter of heeled shoes against the stone, which turned soft against the grass.

"Miss Devereux." Andrea assumed her confidence. "What a surprise."

"It should hardly be a surprise. Where there is a party, I am obligated to attend," a low voice echoed from behind me.

A tall and slender woman made her way towards the empty chair and curtsied. "Ladies," she murmured. "*My* lady." She nodded gravely in my direction, a coy smile on her full lips.

We offered polite responses as she took a seat and I watched her with a sinking feeling. Mary had been right—she was likely the most beautiful woman in the Empire. Her pale hair was a bright gold in the sunlight, complimenting her light tan from the Lailan sun.

Kitra accepted the glass of wine from a servant with grace and poise, a ready smile on her painted lips as she gazed at our group. She regarded me with bright blue eyes and a knowing look, as if we held an inside joke.

I was simultaneously completely envious and intimidated.

"I am sorry we did not make acquaintance earlier, my lady," she addressed me without hesitation. "I was unable to attend Francesca's reception, and I have heard you have been quite busy."

"Yet now we are here." I nodded at the group. "It is a pleasure to meet you."

"Kitra," Andrea said eagerly, "you *must* tell us about your recent journey to Radiance. Did you happen to meet Lady Aedin's brother? His name is Ephraim Doyle—he is the new historian to the king."

"No, unfortunately I did not have the pleasure." She gracefully sipped her wine. "Radiance was wonderful—the gardens are lovely this time of year. The king is ill in health but still kicking," she added wryly. "Advisor Kellen asked me to dance several times in the span of one evening. I accepted once, but two more times was a bit much… Lord Tours was particularly charming—we have known each other for *years* and he is an old friend. Nevertheless, it was lovely to get away. The heat of Lailan can be particularly oppressing after a while." She sighed, her chest rising and falling with the action.

Andrea nodded, as if she understood. "That sounds delightful."

"I heard there have been changes since I was away. How is your beau, Catherine?" Kitra asked silkily, watching her with careful eyes.

"Good," she replied cautiously. "Our wedding date is set for the next month."

"If you need any advice"—she bent her head with feigned modesty—"I am happy to oblige."

Catherine's cheeks reddened as she gripped her glass, mumbling thanks.

"I did encounter an unfamiliar face in Radiance," Kitra said suddenly, as if remembering something. "A Mr. Daniel Terrace."

My stomach dropped as Andrea commented eagerly, "He sounds handsome."

Kitra's low voice echoed a laugh. "He *was*. And we had a peculiar conversation—he claimed to have an acquaintance with *you*, my lady."

The group stared in earnest at this new information. I inhaled sharply, bravely meeting her eyes with a cool gaze. "Yes, I know him from Berge," I offered slowly.

"Oh." She seemed amused by my answer. "I am sorry, I must have misunderstood. It sounded as though you both *knew* each other *well*…"

I watched Andrea's eyes grow round as I steadied my voice, my heart sinking lower in my chest. "He was a friend of my brother's… we grew up together and were good friends… I did not know he was at Radiance."

"Well you should be cheered to hear that he is the new personal assistant to Lord Tours. It is a highly coveted position, and he seems to fit in very well at the palace," Kitra said lightly.

I couldn't wrap my head around it—*Daniel* at the *palace*?

"I am glad he is improving his situation," I offered distantly, masking my face with boredom as I sipped my wine. "I thought he would serve as Lord Tremer's guard for the rest of his life."

"A guard," Andrea repeated with a wistful expression in her eyes. "*Please* introduce us should he also make it to Lailan."

I couldn't resist a smile. "I promise. But I confess we do not keep in touch, so I am unaware of his plans."

Kitra was quiet. She eyed me thoughtfully, but I averted my gaze.

It sounded as though nearly all of Radiance knew about Daniel—or, at least, he wasn't keeping our history a secret. I wondered if Kitra would continue to spread the news on Lailan and blushed at the thought of word getting back to Aedin. But he must have known…

I suddenly did not want to be there; I set down my wine and stood up. "It is getting late—I must be returning to the villa."

"Oh, not so soon!" Andrea cried, setting down her dog and coming to her feet. "Please promise you will join us at Catherine's next time."

"Just tell me when, and I will be there," I promised with a smile as she embraced me with a kiss on the cheek.

Andrea curtsied and the other women inclined their heads, murmuring, "My lady," as I caught Marks' eye. He was already easing towards the front, gesturing at a servant to bring the carriage.

Chapter Fourteen

WHEN I HAD eased myself and my dress inside, I took off my hat with a sigh of relief. The breeze flowed through the open windows as we drove towards the coast, cooling the thin layer of sweat on my neck.

Marks watched me carefully, but I avoided his eyes. I was digesting what Kitra had said—marveling at the change in Daniel's fortunes. Had he left Berge shortly after my marriage?

Envy coiled in my stomach at the thought of all the fashionable ladies of court fawning over him. I gripped my dress, glaring at the sapphire-and-diamond ring with distaste.

Was it wrong for me to hold these feelings of yearning and remorse? Even though I had only been married for some weeks, I couldn't part with the past.

I wondered if desiring him was infidelity. I wondered if Daniel was sleeping next to someone else as well. Giving them his body and his heart—or waiting and pining for me?

But he was no longer mine—I had no claim over him nor his feelings.

I wished I could tell him the reality of my situation. There had been little time to communicate after the proposal. My father knew of our involvement and had kept him away while preparing for my marriage to Aedin. He would not risk this opportunity for a love affair.

Writing a letter was a possibility, but I knew any correspondence would be tracked and read. And what would I even say?

The carriage stopped and I looked up with a start. Marks hopped out and I grasped his hand for help descending the steps then headed towards our rooms, grateful for the cool and welcoming halls of the villa.

Closing the door to our bathroom, I eased off my dress and wiped clean my face, unclipping the heavy jewels and laying them on the counter where they sparkled in the dim light.

I paused, standing naked in front of the mirror, surprised at the contrast of my tanned arms against my white stomach. I was changing—it was so gradual I hadn't noticed.

Pulling on a soft cotton dress felt like heaven after wearing a tightly fitted gown at the party. I wandered into the halls, reveling in the silence of the courtyard garden. Afternoon clouds had begun to obscure the sun, and I was thankful for the brief respite from its pounding heat.

I watched the gardeners prune the flowers, hedges, and trees, inhaling the fresh scent of earth. My feet padded quietly on the stones, and then I heard a strange noise echo through the hall. It was something reminiscent of my youth—the ring of steel upon steel.

Alarmed, I paused, like a rabbit caught in the sight of a hunter. Had anyone else noticed? Although but faint echoes, the ringing was quite audible. The gardeners calmly continued to clip away at the bushes. Were we under attack?

Heart thudding, I walked swiftly from the garden, following the noises. Servants passed by without a care—busy with their tasks. None of them reacted—or perhaps they ignored the sounds. Was I mad?

As the clanging grew louder, I heard the scratching of dirt, muffled grunts, and hurried footsteps. I followed the sounds across the garden courtyard to the guardroom and servants' quarters—I had never before explored this part of the villa.

A small flight of stairs led down from the hall to a dirt footpath. I quickened my pace as the path exited the stucco walls of the villa and emptied out to a wide circle of packed earth.

The guards outlined the outer edge of the circle—my husband stood among them, his arms folded, as he and the others watched two men fighting in the middle. I recognized one as Marks; the other I did not know.

Both men sprang forward and back with swift movements and footsteps, wielding swords with impossible speed.

Marks engaged the young man, swiping his weapon to the side as a feint blow before coming back around to twist his body and hit the other side. The ring of their thin blades clashing was piercing, and I started, taking a step back.

I felt Aedin's eyes lock on me from the opposite side of the circle. There was an energy emitting from their combat, as if the blows aimed at each other somehow sent tendril blasts of air into their surroundings. I felt my blood dance and sing, and longed to join them—

"Stop," Aedin said quietly, and the men parted.

Standing tall, their breath was controlled and even, though sweat poured down their faces. Marks wiped his palms on his pants, turning to face me. His blue eyes were lit with a spark of fire.

In unison, all the guards bowed, murmuring, "My lady."

Tieren offered a small smile in my direction.

"Gwen." Aedin held out his hand.

The circle parted and I saw I had no choice but to enter. I slowly moved past Marks and his opponent—although I gave them a wide berth, I could still smell the sweat and unsettled dust. A bird chirped nearby, breaking the sudden silence.

As I came to stand next to Aedin, I noticed that he was also covered in a light sheen of sweat.

He waved his hand. "Continue."

Marks' opponent was fast to begin. He lifted his sword and swung it towards the other man's chest.

With small steps, Marks backpedaled, before clashing again with his opponent's sword. They came close, nearly breathing on each other, their swords tight, as the opponent swung a fist aimed at Marks' cheek.

I stifled an intuitive cry as Marks staggered back, brandishing his sword to parry each blow from his opponent.

"Marks, less waving and more footwork," Aedin said above the ringing of swords.

The advice was obeyed. Marks sidestepped a strong sweep by his opponent and ducked to hit the flat of his sword against his opponent's waist.

"See? Easily done." Aedin smiled as the two disengaged and shook hands.

"Where was my fault?" Marks' opponent asked, placing his sword back in the sheath at his belt and wiping his forehead with his sleeve.

"You were too quick to assume that your strength could overcome Marks," Aedin replied. "Marks may be older—and perhaps weaker—but his footwork is what saved him. It's not about your own strength but what you assume about your opponent's strength. Save it for another time in the fight when you will need it and rely consistently on your technique. But that was well done, William."

William nodded and took the water Tieren offered him.

Aedin looked at me and then back at the guards. "Gwen, these are my guards, whom I assume you have either seen or met during your time here so far. We train together three to four times a week in engaged combat of sword, dagger, staff… among other things." He turned to me. "I doubt you have little experience in the sword, but—"

"I do," I objected quietly.

"Sorry?" Aedin looked at me in confusion.

"I do… have some experience with the sword," I said lamely, watching the guards eye me with interest. "But nothing grand," I objected, raising my voice. "My brother and I used to practice swordplay… when we avoided our lessons. He was given some proper instruction and taught me some basics…"

"Well then," Aedin said after a brief, incredulous pause, "would you like to join?"

I was taken aback by his offer. "Yes… Yes, I would."

"Here, my lady." Tieren stepped forward to offer me the handle of a sword.

Hesitantly, I took it and pulled. The blade was much lighter and longer than I had used previously. I headed towards the center of the circle, moving it through the air—it cut beautifully.

"I've never seen anything like it," I commented almost to myself.

"I had them made by an especially talented ironsmith in Tahuna." Aedin folded his hands behind his back, stepping forward to join me. "They deliver the same strength without the added weight. Although we prefer these in combat, we also use the traditional, heavier swords to train."

He stood still for a moment, looking at me with a mixed expression of puzzlement and amusement then shook his head, turning to his guards. "I suppose we're finished for the day. You're welcome to stay or free to be dismissed…"

No one moved. I suspected this was the first time they had ever seen a lady wield a sword.

"Very well." Aedin drew his own sword and turned towards me. "Now then." He gave a slow stroke to my right.

I parried him, the reverberation jarring my senses to attention. It had been a while since I had fought.

Clenching my jaw, I took a swing at Aedin, moving several steps forward. He brushed off my strokes easily, his feet dancing lightly on the dirt. Mine dragged noisily as I met his sword again, and again, gaining speed.

A part of me wished to disengage from my focus and contemplate the incredulity of the moment. This was the most fun I'd had in a month.

A gritted grin emerged on my lips as I continued, my hands sweating. I tried grabbing the hilt with two hands, but my movements became clumsy. Switching back to one hand, I swung a broad panicked stroke at Aedin's side, which he easily sidestepped to place the flat of his blade on my shoulder.

I couldn't help but emit a shaky laugh. Aedin wore a wide grin, his face half cast in brilliant sunlight. Something tugged in my stomach as his broad shoulders faced me, the collar of his shirt unbuttoned to reveal the lines of muscle beneath.

"Good start." Aedin sheathed his sword and stepped back. I forced the thought of attraction from my head, nervously wiping my palms on the skirt of my dress.

"I am quite impressed. But your handling of the sword could be greatly improved." He motioned for me to hold out the blade. "Here—you're wrapping your hand close to the hilt, which makes the sword lighter but decreases your flexibility. Instead, shift your grip down to the middle." Aedin gently pushed my fingers back. "That will give you more flexibility and range of motion. And don't hold it too tight—you want it to be fluid."

My husband touched my wrist lightly—the feeling sent a thrill straight to my core. "You'll need more wrist strength for serious combat, but for now, focus on your footwork. Pick up your feet, as if you're dancing."

I withdrew my arm with a smirk. "I chose swordplay over that activity unfortunately."

"Such a lady," Aedin muttered with a smile.

I could hear some guards coughing to disguise mumbled laughter.

"Let's try again."

For the next hour, Aedin and I sparred, exchanging blows for blows, although I remained mostly on the defensive front. His sword found an opening no matter how many different strikes I attempted. Not once did I get a chance to deal a final blow.

I was no master of the sword, but Aedin had a unique talent. Combat appeared too easy for him—it was an effortlessness of mind and body that freed his movements and made him a formidable opponent. I now understood why the guards revered him—not only was he a leader and lord in words but also in action.

Aedin disarmed me for nearly the twentieth time. I didn't bother to pick up my sword.

My feet and calves felt like metal and stuck to the ground, unwilling to move. Hands on my waist, I paused to suck in air—I was past the point of caring what the guards thought of me. Half had stayed till that moment. The other six Aedin had sent to guard the perimeter, once he realized that I meant to spar for more than a few rounds.

"Finished?" Aedin sheathed his sword, eying me with some hesitation.

I gulped air. "For now." Inhaling a long breath to relieve my lungs, I bent to pick up my sword and winced, already feeling a soreness creep into my muscles.

Tieren stepped forward quickly, taking the blade from my hands.

"Thank you." I smiled at him, brushing hair back from my face.

"My lady… you have surprising talent," Tieren commented with a blush, half looking at the ground with a boyish grin.

I gave a short laugh. "No, it's just more fun than dancing."

———

I spent a long time soaking in the tub, lying there until the hot water became cold, the dirt settled on the top and bottom of the water, and my toes and fingertips shriveled like raisins. When my muscles finally decided to obey me again, I drained the water and repeated the process.

Something like joy bubbled and unfurled like a simmering fire in my chest. I felt purpose and strength. Mingled with the adrenaline was a resolve for a new life. I no longer felt hopeless, illiterate (well, almost), and helpless. I had purpose.

Mary dressed me fussily—tying on a silk gown as if in repayment for my unladylike conduct earlier that day.

"Completely uncalled for," she grumbled under her breath as she tugged on the laces.

I bore her words with light-heartedness. "Aedin had no qualms about it." I lifted my hair, smiling at her reflection in the mirror as she clasped a jewel around my neck.

Mary sighed, but then admitted slowly, "It is important for you to *defend* yourself, but *engaging* in combat! You might soon get some scars on those hands."

I shrugged, retorting silently that I would have been rather proud of having battle scars.

The door opened and Aedin strode into the bedroom, eying Mary and her busy hands with a smirk.

"Is this what's keeping you from dinner?" He sat on the sofa at the foot of the bed, watching us as he crossed his long legs. Aedin's hair was damp, his auburn skin gleaming from the bath.

"Where did you bathe?" I returned the question.

"Well you were taking so long in our bath that I took the liberty of using the guards' quarters." My husband picked the dirt from under his short nails.

Mary raised her eyebrows but refrained from commenting. She picked up the black paint, but I shook my head. "No, please, I'm weary of paint."

I turned to Aedin. "Is it almost time?"

"It *is* time."

"Thank you, Mary." I grinned at her as she curtsied silently in response.

Aedin opened the door for me and we walked together through the silent hall. I hadn't realized how late the day had turned.

A thick, luminous sheen hung over the villa. It was the golden hour. The birds were quiet, and the sky was a brilliant orange. Color seeped into everything—the worn floor, the thick limestone arcades, the green leaves and colored flower buds.

We sat for dinner in a natural, rather than awkward, silence. A servant came and poured wine into our goblets. When he left, Aedin lifted his glass in my direction.

"To surprises."

"And joy."

We clinked our glasses together and sipped the thick red liquid.

"So," Aedin began, setting down his glass, "Mary gave me the letter Ephraim sent to you."

"Yes—she said it would interest you."

"It did indeed." My husband rubbed his chin thoughtfully, looking at the table, before he again met my gaze. "Especially his statement that the king and Lord Tours were planning to visit us in the coming months."

"I thought it said just the king."

"Where the king goes, Lord Tours often follows. And Tours is the only lord that has consistently kept a keen interest in my dealings. He has often stopped by in the past—surprise visits to keep me on my feet."

"Do we need to prepare?"

"Most definitely." Aedin raised his brows as if he found this humorous.

"Are all your illegal exportations well hidden for his next appearance?" I joked.

"I would never participate in that kind of scheme."

The humor was lost on Aedin. I sobered.

"Why do you so fear the king? And Lord Tours?"

Aedin was thoughtful for a moment. "Well," he decided, "shouldn't every mortal man fear a dominant figure?"

He had avoided the question. I took an impatient swig of my wine. "You're hiding something from them."

Aedin smiled to himself. "Doesn't every man have things to bury?"

"Not if they'll dig themselves back up."

"True." Aedin shifted uneasily, meeting my eyes. "Can you promise me something?"

I pursed my lips. "Depends on what it is."

Aedin was quiet for a moment. "If I were to ask you to leave— to leave the island for several days, or two weeks at most—would you go?"

My brow furrowed. "I thought you said that it was dangerous outside of the villa… Why would you want me to *leave* Lailan?"

"If, for example, Lord Tours were to come here, I would rather you go visit your father in Berge."

"But… why?" I asked, startled. "If a lord were to visit, wouldn't you *need* me here? To… to entertain him or host a dinner or reception?"

"Tou—Lord Tours is more of a private individual. He would not want affairs such as these." Aedin placed his hands on the table, fidgeting with his utensils. "Gwen—" He suddenly looked up and reached for my hand.

I let go of my wine glass, and hesitantly placed my hand in his. The same tremor ran through my bones as Aedin wrapped his fingers around mine, looking into my eyes.

In the fading light, I saw the dark mahogany of his irises, flecked with notes of forest green and sapphire blue. The color reminded me of the rich, dark earth on Berge. My heart lurched as his thumb ran lightly over my knuckles.

"Gwen, I have told you that I will keep you safe, and I will take that promise to my grave. I need you to trust me when I ask of you things that may sound absurd or unnecessary."

"Why should I trust you?" I swallowed nervously, feeling my heartbeat echo within the hand securely enclosed in Aedin's grasp.

"Do we have to go through this again?" His lips tugged into a small smile.

"Until my questions are answered, yes."

My husband sighed. "*Please* give me time."

"For what?"

"I need time… to put some things in order first."

It was in that moment, looking into his eyes and seeing that troubled gaze that I saw something else.

There was a slight panic—a kind of madness that shook me. A dark, pressing terror of something great. Yet that alone was what terrified me—there was something out there that my stoic, aloof, and unyielding husband feared.

"I promise," I assented with a half-smile. "But you *will* tell me soon."

The maddened panic retreated, and Aedin inclined his head, bending forward to press his lips against my hand. A wave of heat shot straight through my body.

Flustered, I immediately put my hand back in my lap when he released it. Guilt washed through me as I thought of Daniel.

But Aedin was unaware and contented with my words. The dinner arrived and we feasted with idle chat.

Chapter Fifteen

AEDIN AWOKE AND wished to fall back to sleep.

It was early—the sun had not yet risen. His mind was heavy. Even in the first hours of the morning, thoughts for the day were bombarding him with tasks unfulfilled. There was so much to be done.

Suppressing a groan, he rolled over, until he remembered he was not alone. Even many weeks later, it was still a shock.

He rubbed his face, the ring feeling cold around his finger, and watched his wife, only inches away, as she breathed, unaware of his gaze. It was one of the few times he could take the liberty— watching her without the forced calm inspired by the flash of those pale blue-gray eyes.

He wished he could lie there all morning, and then wondered what she would think of that. Despite her good-naturedness she could be so… cold. Still undecided and rebellious. Aedin tore his gaze away from her delicately closed lids and quietly pushed back the covers.

He wished for peace of mind—it did not come.

Running the cold water, he splashed some on his face and body, pleased at the rude shivers that ran through him, wakening his senses. He patted his face with a towel then walked to the wardrobe and pulled out a black linen shirt. Tugging it over his head, he grabbed his boots and sat on the sofa at the end of the bed.

The sight of Gwen tangled in the sheets, asleep, her skin illuminated by the morning light...

With ruthless efficiently, he laced his boots and put the image from his mind.

Things were not going how he'd planned. It should have been easier—this was unexpectedly hard.

Why did she dislike him? He had anticipated some aversion but had expected more gratitude. Their marriage had brought her to a social and economic status she had never dreamed of attaining and *saved* her from certain death.

But had he done something wrong? Perhaps he should have flattered or courted her, but there had been no time. Would the coming years—even *decades*—be filled with this painful awkwardness?

For once in his life, Aedin was at a loss for an answer.

Standing, he opened the wardrobe, pulling out a drawer full of embroidered shirts that Mary had purchased years ago—which he would never wear. Hands digging underneath the fine linen, he pushed at the wood, easing it back. It was a deep drawer—he had designed it as such—but in the space underneath were crammed knives, daggers, poisoned pins, and some rope he thought might one day be useful.

On top of this he had carefully replaced the roll of parchment —the years of notes on courtiers, merchants and advisors he had given Gwen to read. Of course, her illiteracy had stalled his plans, but there would, hopefully, be time enough for that. From underneath the roll he pulled two knives, two daggers, and some pins—delicately placing the latter in a velvet case.

Aedin began to methodically strap concealed daggers to his calves, the knives to his inner forearms, and placed the pins in an inside pocket he'd stitched into all of his shirts. He stretched—as usual the weapons did not hinder any movement.

Satisfied, he strapped the final dagger to his hip—the only one visible for all of Lailan to see. Aedin touched the handle, comforted by its presence. Old habits died hard.

He paused, thinking of the other knife under his pillow, the daggers sheathed beneath the bed and behind the headboard. Would she notice? The bed was big enough that Gwen would likely remain on her side, but if she were to slip her hand underneath his pillow…

Aedin shook off the worries and exited the room, though reluctant to separate himself from her.

The halls were quiet, save for the cooks bustling in the kitchen, preparing the daily meals, and he passed few servants. Mary would not be up for another half hour.

Aedin moved past the sitting and dining rooms, the public baths on the other side of the atrium, the sleeping quarters for the servants, and descended the steps into the garden. He entered the circle of packed earth, stretching his hands up to the pale morning sky then bending down to touch his boots.

It was a routine he repeated almost daily. Stretch every part of the body. Then reaccustom his hand to the swords, knives, daggers, and pins. Practice throwing them at the wooden target near the fountain. Move through the motions of weaponless self-defense.

Then the guards would wake, and Aedin would leave for Tahuna to monitor those miserable, insatiable merchants. When he returned, he would train the guards, run through exercises with them in case of an attack—

"My lord."

Aedin had felt him before he'd entered the circle. "Marks." His eyes remained closed as he tested himself to find the weapons strapped against his body without sight.

"You're early."

He felt Marks move towards him, pausing to his left. Aedin smiled in satisfaction—the guard was learning to move as soundlessly as he.

Opening his eyes, Aedin twirled the dagger in his hand. "I have a long day ahead."

Marks nodded, running through his own set of stretches, his arms swaying as he bent to touch the ground.

"How is she?"

Aedin made a face as he swung his dagger and was glad Marks couldn't see. "The same. Bitter and confused. Not much has changed."

Marks eased into a straight posture. He paused and then said with a smile, "She quite startled the guards."

Aedin snorted. "She startled me."

"I thought you knew."

"No." Aedin shook his head, holding the dagger loosely by the hilt and aiming it at the target. "No. I've since learned that although I know much about her, I know just as little as anyone else."

Marks emitted a short laugh. "You can't truly know a person until you're stuck married to them."

"Those are the truest words I've heard this morning." Aedin hurtled the dagger towards the target. He winced as it thudded an inch outside the center.

"Can I ask something?" Marks twisted his back.

"Yes."

"Have you told her?" He paused. "Anything?"

"No, it's not time. At least not yet."

"I felt her, Aedin, when she came upon us sparring. She's like a lit cannon about to ignite."

He frowned, digging the heel of his boot into the dirt. "But if she knew then she would insist on learning *everything* and practicing…"

"So it's better to just wait and see when it erupts?" Marks challenged, pulling out his own dagger from his belt.

"It's not that unpredictable."

"But it's just as dangerous."

Aedin grinned. "Perhaps even more so than a lit cannon."

Marks didn't smile at the joke. "At the Taylor estate, last week, Kitra was there."

Aedin raised his eyebrows.

"She had returned from Radiance—in bed with Tours again." Marks threw his dagger at the target—it landed in the center with a satisfying thump.

Aedin retrieved both blades and stepped back. "Her bark is worse than her bite," he said quietly.

"She seemed intent on Gwen—Tours must be asking questions… Have you heard of a Daniel Terrace?"

The name inspired a foul taste in Aedin's mouth and he grimaced, remembering the furious expression on the handsome soldier's face the day of their wedding. "Yes, I know about him."

"He is Tours' new personal assistant."

Aedin swore under his breath as he flung the dagger into the target. It settled in the middle, but he didn't feel any better. He ran a hand through his hair in frustration—this was not good news.

"Anything else?" Aedin asked succinctly, watching Marks as he eyed the target and landed his dagger next to Aedin's.

"You already know they might visit." Marks shrugged. "I wouldn't be surprised if Tours brings Daniel with him."

"Yes, he enjoys that sort of thing," Aedin said with acidity.

Tours took pleasure in playing with his food before devouring it whole.

Marks was silent, as if debating whether to speak. "They were… attached… you know."

"Yes, I know."

"No, I mean… I suspect it was deeper than you think."

"Why do you say that?" Aedin forced a look of cool detachment as his heart thudded in his chest.

Marks shrugged. "I saw her respond to Kitra's questions… she was evasive, and then completely silent in the carriage. I think they were in love."

Love.

It was like a painful knife twisting inside his stomach. He would have preferred Marks to have disemboweled him right there.

Aedin forcefully removed the daggers from the target, tossing one to the guard. Grabbing the hilt, he attacked with a swing, which Marks parried easily. Aedin wished to remove the quietly sympathetic expression on his guard's face.

They trained lightly for half an hour until the sun broke the horizon. Putting away his dagger, Aedin noted the brightened sky and motioned to Marks. They headed to the front and entered the waiting carriage. A small basket of fruit and bread sat on the empty seat, and they ate as the horses broke into a steady trot.

Marks and Aedin both scanned the passing jungle, but all was quiet and still—there was only the callings of birds and shifting of animals as they passed.

"When d'you think he'll come for his little visit?" Marks broke the silence, his eyes still fixed on the tropical wilderness as it slowly made way for houses.

Aedin shrugged. "Perhaps we'll start to worry by next month, but we should prepare soon. Tours must be anxious to return since he knows little of Gwen and hasn't seen me since the marriage."

"And the king hasn't said anything?"

Aedin shook his head, pulling at the buttoned collar of his shirt. By the gods, he swore silently, it was already hot!

"They're plotting something," Marks grumbled, his blue eyes darkening. "I can feel it."

"Yes… they are." Aedin shifted uneasily in his seat. "But *we* also have a plan, and if we execute it properly, then we should be able to slip through their fingers." He paused. "You have sent the guards to repair and attend to the post since we last spoke, I presume?"

"I sent William and David this morning. They will report back later this afternoon."

"Good."

They fell into a natural silence as the carriage rumbled down the cobblestones of Tahuna's main street.

Past Lords of Lailan had placed their offices on the upper side of this street—a way to literally look down upon the governed and situate themselves comfortably within the social class they dominated. Despite the call of tradition, Aedin would have none of that.

Within the first months of his lordship, he had quickly purchased several houses on the harbor. They were situated at the lowest end of the main street and intersected perpendicularly with the dirt trails that circumnavigated the entire island. It reeked of fish, salt, and whatever rotten cargo had been discarded into the bay that week. But it had drastically changed the nature of the relationship between the Lord of Lailan and the merchants.

While in the past, lords had been pleased to raise taxes from their distant offices on the main street, Aedin had lowered them and focused on reducing fraud and increasing trade. He had taken up public works, such as the widening of the harbor to allow more ships, the building of docks and warehouses, and supplying jobs to those who were willing (and able) to cart, count, or aide the merchants in their business.

With the decrease in taxes on the harboring of ships, warehouses, and goods, the number of merchants doing business in Lailan had nearly doubled. Although Lailan was situated on the eastern-most corner of the Empire, its tropical climate and booming economy was enough to attract merchants from throughout the seven islands.

The opportunity of profits and the demand for its supply was worth the business trip. Which meant even more profits for Lailan itself and the king.

Although Aedin interacted directly with the merchants and assisted in the execution of decisions, negotiation of deals, or feuds, he was never alone. Of the three houses he had purchased to serve at his headquarters, two were empty. The guards who were scheduled to protect Aedin that day were situated within the residences on either side of his primary office.

Occasionally, Tours' men would visit them, and during those times there ensued an uneasy truce. It was understood that there would be no violence between the lords' men.

As long as Aedin was faithful, no harm would come to his guards, or those within the villa. As long as he complied with the wishes of Lord Tours and pleased his king, his reign as Lord of Lailan was secure.

As long as Aedin was faithful.

Aedin pursed his lips as the carriage rolled to a stop. In front of his office—crammed in the crowds of people and blocking nearly half the street—stood a bright red, yellow, and white carriage led by five horses. As the steps of their carriage were drawn down, Aedin and Marks exchanged an exasperated look.

Marks exited first, scanning and making a path through the crowd. Tieren appeared out of the mass and assisted, following Aedin as Marks led the trio into the building.

The aging wooden panels were painted an off-white color to dress up the ramshackle interior. They had sanded the floors and imported carpets from Cachelle—a large island south of Radiance—and Acedes, which specialized in textiles.

Old portraits of the past Lords of Lailan that Aedin had refused to keep in the villa hung on the otherwise unadorned walls. Aedin's feet were nearly silent on the soft carpet.

Renalt Cabot looked up with a start as he saw his lord stride into the room.

"My lord." He set down the glass paperweight from Aedin's desk.

"Mr. Cabot." Aedin nodded at Tieren as he bowed and exited.

Marks positioned himself in the corner of the room, watching Cabot with a fixed gaze.

Aedin sat in the dark leather chair behind his desk and pulled out a piece of parchment and quill. "What constitutes this pleasure?"

"It has been a while since the de Bough's party."

"It has," he agreed shortly. "What do you want?"

"You have avoided my appointment requests."

"I have been busy," Aedin said distantly. "But we are here now."

"Well, you know I hold a large position within the sugar market." Cabot sat with attempted grace on the edge of his chair, his hands gripping the armrests and his silk buttons straining.

"That I do." Aedin put on a disinterested expression and dipped his quill in the ink, poised and waiting.

"Then you very well know that I am extremely displeased with your recent gift to the king when we are in the midst of a shortage," Cabot hissed, his thick eyes narrowing.

Aedin sighed, pausing to look Cabot directly in the eye. "How else should I honor my king, other than by sending him an extremely coveted good?"

"We all know that you are *extremely* fond of the king," Cabot muttered, settling back in the chair and smoothing his thin, brown hair back from his forehead. "But this places the shortage back even *more*. And I only received payment for the sugar at bottom market price! Prices are skyrocketing and all of my merchants would pay top price for one pound. But you had to go and give it to the king. Especially during a generally unprofitable year."

"Then you will simply have to tell your merchants that this was an unsuccessful year." Seeing no point in recording the exchange, Aedin set the quill in the ink pot and leaned back. "Is there anything else I can help you with?"

Cabot grimaced. "You will not even offer me a drink?"

"At this hour?" Aedin raised his eyebrows, then nodded to Marks. The guard exited, leaving the door open.

"Welm Charles, you know, has been extremely dissatisfied with your handling of the tobacco fertilizer."

"So you wish to gossip." Aedin gave Cabot a tight smile.

"No, I simply wish to relay helpful information."

"Thank you, but I would rather not receive your help."

Marks returned, placing a small glass of a thick amber liquid in front of Cabot.

"Thank you, my good sir." Cabot took the glass in his meaty fingers, sipping it delicately and looking uncharacteristically pensive. "For four years, Lord Aedin, you have rejected my advice and advances to aide you. Why?"

Aedin exhaled. "Because you do not wish to *aide* me for the betterment of my rule and island but to control me for your own good."

"That hurts." Cabot made a face. "But is not everyone out for their own betterment? What else is life than to succeed in small battles that win a larger victory of status, power, and longevity?"

"I do not desire to delve into our philosophical differences this morning," Aedin said tartly. "If you wish to tell me something, then say it and be gone."

"Charles is dissatisfied that you levied an import fee on fertilizer from Cachelle. You know his brother-in-law owns that company and has been badly hurt by our switch to local fertilizer."

"That, again, is a philosophical difference."

"And I have also heard—well, you do not engage in gossip."

"No, I do not. Thank you for your consideration."

"Even if it concerns your wife?"

Aedin's fingers stilled into a formal clasp. "That would depend"—he chose his words carefully—"on whether there was any merit to the rumor."

Cabot smirked. "Some, perhaps, are not merely rumors. Everyone knows you gave the young Mr. Doyle the position of historian because you had recently married his sister."

Aedin shrugged "I do not deny it. I do have some say in political appointments."

"But—I am not sure whether you have ears inside Radiance or not—but I had heard that *another* man from Berge recently gained a position of very high power. Lord Tours' new assistant—have you heard of him? Everyone at Radiance is quite taken with him."

Aedin gritted his teeth. This was the second time this morning he would have to hear his name. "Daniel Terrace?" he offered casually.

Cabot paused disappointedly, setting down his drink. "It sounds like you *do* have some ears on the ground."

Aedin shrugged again. "Gossip travels fast."

"*News* travels fast," Cabot corrected him. "There doesn't appear to be any errors in the information." He finished his drink with a satisfied sound.

"It was in the past," Aedin said evenly with a bored expression. "We are looking towards the future."

Cabot snorted. "Well then—I suppose you have no need of me."

"No," Aedin agreed. "But thank you for your time."

He stood and half-bowed but stopped. "You know," he said with a thoughtful gaze, "ever since your recent nuptials, many have felt that you are unraveling. You do realize that we feared you because you seemed impervious to everything. But now? Now there is a weakness."

"I would remind you that you are speaking to your lord." Aedin growled softly, placing one hand on the knife strapped to the underside of his desk.

"Pardon, my lord." Cabot sketched a bow and left the room.

Aedin forced his fist to unclench as he let out a ragged sigh. Hopefully Cabot had not set a precedent for the rest of the day's visits.

"My lord." Tieren popped his head around the door frame.

"Yes?" Aedin's voice was unintentionally curt.

"There is a merchant here who wishes to speak to you."

Aedin waved his hand, sending death glares at his desk. He was tired of hearing about Daniel Terrace—or any *other* previous lovers of Gwen he might had missed. It was just talk—there was little harm to it. The only harm was Daniel giving information about Gwen to Tours, but that was outside of Aedin's control. Radiance was at least three days away, and yet it had never felt so close.

"My lord." A merchant gripping his hat between his hands slunk into the room. His beard was thick and his eyes cautious—almost fearful.

Aedin motioned at the seat opposite him. "Please."

"Thank you, my lord." The man sat on the edge of his seat in deference—quite the opposite from its former inhabitant.

"What is your name?"

"Frewin Turner, my lord."

"Mr. Turner, you wished to speak to me," Aedin prompted, folding his hands together on the desk, attempting to free his mind from Gwen.

"Yes, my lord." His husky voice matched his unshaven face and crinkled, tanned eyes. "I… I didn't want to come to you several weeks ago when the issue arose but since having investigated… I find I must be the first to tell you."

Aedin's brow furrowed, but he was silent.

"My lord…" Turner's mouth was large and his gap teeth were white against the darkness of his skin. "I'm in command of two vessels that ship cargo regularly to Tente. About four weeks ago—when there was that great storm off the southern coast of Lailan, one of our vessels—which was captained by a younger man whom I had recently hired to expand my business—was set off course… I don't know if they have sunk or are simply lost in the east, but I have heard reports from others who saw this the ship on the eastern horizon after the storm… I fear I have lost my vessel, crew, *and* an entire shipment of tobacco."

He was nearly in tears by the end of his muttered speech.

Aedin was silent, pensive.

"I-I…" Turner paused to breathe deeply and collect himself. "I have searched the eastern sea as far as I have dared to go and seen no sign of shipwreck. It is my fear that they are lost… in the east." He paused. "I… I don't know if you listen to the myths of the east —"

"I am aware of them," Aedin said shortly. "Yet, Mr. Turner, what do you wish for me to do to aide you in this catastrophe?"

"My lord, I did not expect—"

"Then what did you expect after telling me this tale of your misfortunes?"

Turner was silent. "To notify you…" he mumbled, "of the potentially unaccounted-for ledger… I cannot pay for the lease on the lost ship and crew…"

"And since you have been upfront with your situation, I will loan you enough money to replace the ship you have lost." Aedin reached for a blank parchment and scribbled the note legibly. "I expect you to return the money to me within two years—at one percent interest—and supply your own crew in the meantime."

"My lord…" Turner was breathless. "You are serious?"

"I take care of those who do honest business in my name." Aedin handed him the note with a nod. "Thank you for notifying me of the lost ship—I will make sure to keep a lookout in case it ever returns."

Turner shook his head sadly as he stood. "Not from the east— nothing ever returns from there."

He bowed low and exited.

Chapter Sixteen

TIME PASSED, AND one day I woke up and realized I had been married for nearly four months.

My life had grown into a steady rhythm of normalcy, interspersed with occasional moments of joy. I had gained a small social circle—primarily Andrea and Catherine—and enjoyed their friendships, the diversions of parties and teas. Occasionally, Talia and I would still talk, but I was hesitant since Aedin's warning, and other parts of my life took precedent.

The highlight of my days was sparring with the guards several times a week—or more, when Mary could not distract me with other tasks. My body had grown stronger, and I appreciated the mental stimulation of combat.

Aedin and I remained distant. He had become withdrawn in recent weeks—leaving the villa at odd hours and occasionally not appearing for dinner. I was persistent in my questioning but unsuccessful.

It felt defeating to continually ask, and so at some point I stopped. We continued existing in an aloof silence as I endeavored to fill my days with distractions, friends, and duties.

As I continued my reading and writing lessons, I began to delve into some of Aedin's notes on the parchment scrolls he'd given me all those months ago. I could discern most of the words and names, but I still didn't fully comprehend the exercise.

The scribbles were haphazard—random bits of information that made little sense. I didn't recognize any names from my small social circle, save for Kitra Devereux's. Next to it, Aedin had written *"Involved with Tours since 511. Cabot, Kellen, and Charles are clients. No gift."*

The summer mornings had grown hot even in the early hours, and I found it hard to sleep under the blankets, yet even harder to sleep without their comforting weight.

Aedin was already gone when I rose with the echoes of fountains and early birds chirping in the garden. I felt oddly alone and paused with my feet on the cool wood of the floor.

For some reason, I thought of Daniel, but found that the name that had once held such resonance and depth had become hollow. The pain was lessening. Resolutely I stood and rang for Mary.

The morning ritual passed easily—bath, dressing, breakfast, wandering around the gardens. Andrea came over for tea and we chatted eagerly about her upcoming wedding to Liam Spence. Her father had finally set the match and she was thrilled to be joining the ranks of married women. We conversed with ease, trading witty remarks, until it was time for her to leave for her dress fitting.

When midday came, I was already itching to spar. I sat on the balcony, reading a book to help the time pass quickly. Even in the shade, the wind was warm, and the air felt overwhelming. I shifted uncomfortably, feeling the sweat on my back.

Mary came through the open doors with a curtsy and sat across from me, setting a sheet of parchment and a quill upon the table.

"I thought we might as well do another lesson," she announced.

I groaned. "I would rather not. Look"—I held up my book—"I am reading."

"You have been making significant progress…" she admitted slowly.

I gave a short smile. "So that merits a rest."

Mary stiffened. "Do you have an alternative suggestion?"

I cocked my head in thought. "How about… Tell me a story?"

"A story?" Mary replied dubiously, looking at me as if I had shrunk in years.

"Yes." I snapped my book shut, looking at her expectantly.

Mary considered the request with the proper thoughtfulness. She opened her mouth moments later, as if to say something, but resolutely closed it. "Do you…" she began hesitantly. "Do you know the myths of the Empire?"

I shrugged. "Some."

"The stories of creation? It is a common tale on Lailan."

I shook my head.

Mary sat again in a momentary silence before she began. The afternoon sun cast her graying hair in a halo of light. Her eyes were shadowed.

"They say that in the beginning there was nothingness. And then chaos. And out of the chaos came water and fire. The water settled down into the deep as the fire arched above it and drew colors. It formed the sky and painted each morning and night with its power.

"From the water came Fate. It is not a being, like you and I, but a rhythmic motion, which unifies and spreads harmony through all that it touches. From the depths of the deep blue, Fate raised mountains of solid earth and thus land was formed.

"Fate, being the incarnation of coherence itself, raised eight islands—"

"Eight?" I interrupted.

Mary eyed me with an annoyed gaze. "Are you interrupting my story?"

"No." I shot her a quick smile.

She continued after a brief pause. "Fate raised eight islands from the blue. It called them all by name and littered them with birds and beasts and creatures of the sea. And then Fate drew a glass of water from the deep and formed it into a woman.

"Now, the woman grew strong and tall and wise, but she was lonely. She asked Fate for a companion. So, as the sun came over the horizon, Fate reached into the sky and pulled out a string of colors and fire. It formed this into a man, and the woman was pleased, for the man was also strong and tall and wise.

"Yet, like the fire of the sun, he was more rash, decisive, and fierce, whereas the woman was calm and thoughtful within her power. Together, however, the man and woman spent many days in joy. As they made the first love, the fire of the sky burned brightly as the waves undulated over the sea.

"Fate was pleased with Its work, but It could not stay among them for long. Fate knew that the man and woman could not survive without Its presence, so It put them both to sleep. That day, Fate took a piece of the heaven above and mixed it with the crystal-clear water. Then, It took a piece of Itself and placed It into the glass of mixed elements—the mixture shone with the power of a thousand suns. It would have burned the eyes of the creations if they had been awake. As they slept, Fate opened the stomachs of both the woman and man and poured half of the mixture into each creation.

"When the creations awoke, they found that they had great power because Fate had put a piece of Itself inside them. Their sight became sharper, their minds quicker, their feet swifter… Even the scents of the islands became more distinct. They could talk to each other from miles away! Yet for all of these benefits, the woman and man found that they had also inherited a piece of the mind of Fate. They understood the concepts of evil and good. And they soon began to choose freely for themselves.

"As they begat children and their children grew, and their children's children grew, the presence that Fate had placed in their blood never left them. Sometimes it was weaker, sometimes stronger. But each one had inherited the same knowledge, the same presence… the same coherence.

"Thus the islands were slowly populated and the water and the fire continued to reign. And after hundreds of years, when the bodies of the first man and woman crumbled into the dust, the children of Fate continued—some in the fires of chaos, others continuing in the harmony of the water."

Mary became quiet, and the world around me stirred again into motion.

I sat in silence, my book abandoned on my lap. "That… was beautiful."

Mary was motionless. Her lips pursed, she stared at the table in a trance. With a sudden movement, she stood. "I must leave—"

"My lady." The glass door opened to reveal a manservant. He bowed low. "You asked me to notify you when my lord returned —"

"Yes." I said eagerly, nodding to Mary. "Thank you... for that story."

"It... is the story we tell our children on Lailan, my lady," she said with a curtsy. "It is... a story." She watched me carefully for a brief moment before gathering the parchments and quill and turning back inside.

I frowned at her odd formality—it was quite unlike the stories I had been told as a child. But I couldn't dwell on it for long—it was time to train with the guards.

Rushing to my rooms, I pulled on my boots. Aedin had given me some proper footwear for sparring, and I wore them with pride as I headed to the guards' quarters. The singing of the birds felt in time with my steps—joy whirred in my chest as I descended along the dirt path.

The guards nodded politely at me as I joined them in the circle. We started with stretches—I winced as I lunged, my sore calves protesting at the movement. It was hard to stretch in a dress and I eyed their loose pants enviously.

Aedin's soft voice greeted us as he joined the circle. "Good afternoon."

We nodded in response as I fell in line with the rest of the guards, thrilled that I had finally earned my part in this routine. It felt so natural to be among them and included in the practice.

"Gwen—Tieren." He gestured towards us, and we grinned at each other.

We partnered off in a section of the circle and spun our daggers for the beginning movements. Our friendship had grown, as we were often put together for combat. He was the least advanced of the guards, although his lanky frame still outmatched my amateur skill.

Our feet danced in the dust as we exchanged blows.

A few tendrils from my braid floated into my face, obscuring my view. I ignored them and feinted a blow, only to attack from the other side, placing the broad edge of my blade against Tieren's arm.

"Well done," he said, nodding, then practiced the parry motion again on his own.

I stepped back for a moment, relishing in the moment with a smile. "One for four?"

Tieren rolled his eyes. "Can't get enough." He lunged towards me and I deflected his blow with a wave of my dagger.

My body hummed with excitement at my improved ability. I took confident strokes and eagerly batted away his offense. The muscles of my arms gleamed in the sunlight as my core tightened like a spring. I felt I could have continued all afternoon.

Tieren's skill outpaced mine, and he easily won two additional rounds, but I clinched the last, patting his waist with a friendly smile.

"We can call it even." Tieren frowned, and I gave a smug smile in return. He straightened as Aedin approached.

"Has Gwen beaten you again?" He raised an eyebrow as Tieren made a face.

"Well we weren't *really* sparring—"

I scoffed. "But we *were*—"

"Let's have a go." Aedin pulled out his sword, looking at me.

"I *did* beat him," I added under my breath, exchanging my dagger for a long sword.

Tieren suppressed a laugh as he stepped aside. I shot him a glare that quickly turned to a smile as I held up my blade.

Aedin started with slow movements that I easily deflected and returned, and we fell into a rhythm. I focused on my breath, on the pace of my steps, as we continued trading blow for blow.

My blood ran with a thrilling sensation as I felt myself grow stronger. I realized I could anticipate Aedin's steps before he moved. My lungs felt light and my feet were quiet.

I shoved Aedin's sword back from my face with all the strength I could muster. It worked—my arms tingled with adrenaline as I watched him take a step back with surprise.

I stepped lightly to the side, our eyes locked as our feet made circles around the dirt.

Aedin waved his sword with show, a slow grin spreading across his face.

"You love this, don't you?" I commented.

"Love what?"

"A good fight."

"Always. It's addicting."

He moved to my left—my weak side—and swept the flat of his sword towards my open waist. I turned, bringing my blade perpendicular to defend the opening.

We exchanged continuous blows—his growing harder, forcing my feet to move and compensate for my lesser strength. I felt the other guards pause in their sparring, watching us as we battled.

I returned his strength, drawing upon some unknown well as I increased my power. The clang of steel rang noisily in my ears, beating in time with my heart.

Through the motions, I noticed his expression change to one of concentration. Sweat glistened on his brow as he fought to return the same force. I felt a pressure pushing against me and I forced against it, stepping forward resolutely.

I saw his next move and found an opening—taking it.

Aedin turned in the last second and placed the flat of his sword against my thigh with a thick and resounding tap.

My left hand brushed back the loose hairs from my sweaty forehead, and I forced my breath to calm as my heart raced.

Aedin was no longer smiling. "We're done."

I frowned. "What?"

He turned away from me, handing his sword to Marks. "Continue training—I'll stop by later—"

"Why?" I scowled at his back. "We've only just started."

"We're done."

"No, I'm not." My grip tightened on my sword, my blood pounding in my ears.

"Gwen." Aedin met my eyes. "Give me your sword."

"No."

"*Gwen*—"

I swung at his side, intending to give him a tap on the shoulder. Aedin turned swiftly, grabbing a knife from the sleeve of his shirt, and parried the blow. "Stop it."

His eyes were dark and threatening. I watched a line of sweat descend from his neck down into his collar.

I couldn't resist. I advanced, marveling at how he beat down my advances with a knife only a quarter the size of my sword. My chest hummed with energy as I smiled, dancing in the dirt. The sword sang as it met Aedin's knife again and again.

"Gwen, please—" He held up an empty hand. "*Stop.*"

"Are you afraid I might beat you?" I asked coyly, offering him a simpering smile.

"No—"

"Then let's continue—"

"We have to stop—*Gwen*—"

Aedin wasn't happy. His forehead was creased in concern as he continued to bat down my offensives, his footwork quick, and I realized he was trying to avoid me rather than engage.

"Fight me." I grew angry as he disengaged another blow, stepping aside and holding up his hands.

"Gwen—"

"Why won't you fight me?"

I swung my sword with a sudden ferocity that surprised him. As the metal clashed together, Aedin's grip loosened. He tossed the knife aside instead of trying to regain his hold.

Aedin's knees were bent in anticipation, but his hands were empty as he faced me. "We *need* to stop," he stressed.

Frustrated, I drew up my sword, intending to throw it aside, when I was hit with a wave of air.

My sword was flung out of my hands; I tripped backwards, losing my step. The metal landed with a clatter as my body hit the dirt with a sickening thud.

I gasped for air as the breath left my lungs.

Immediately, Aedin was bent over me, eying me cautiously. "Gwen?"

Staring up at the bright blue sky, I struggled to inhale and coughed, curling to my side as I panted and fought to draw in air.

I felt a hand touch my side sympathetically. My blood ran cold, and I was suddenly tired.

Fighting nausea, I struggled to stand, ignoring Aedin's extended hand, and blinked at the circle of guards who watched me without sound.

There were expressions of disbelief, incredulity… and fear.

"Gwen, let's go." Aedin grabbed my arm and led me outside the circle. I frowned—my feet felt like stones.

"What happened…"

"You tripped and fell. Probably hit your head. You'll be fine," Aedin said shortly, forcing me up the steps and into the hall.

Whether I wanted to or not, I slumped against him as I struggled to regain control over my body. It took several minutes before the pain in my lungs subsided. Although my limbs were left cold, my mind was fuming.

Aedin led me to our rooms and turned on the water for a bath. I eyed it warily, kicking off my boots, which had left small clumps of dirt on the wooden floor, then sat on the edge of the tub, scooping up some water and drinking it from my hands.

My mind was still fuzzy as I tried to replay that moment. I had tripped, but something had pushed me back—

"Do you need my help?" Aedin stood in the doorway, watching me.

I sighed, standing with effort and closed the door in his face, then untied my dress, throwing it on the floor, and sank into the bath water.

Seconds later, I saw the shadow of Aedin's boots move from the door.

I turned the handle of the tap with my toes, ceasing the flow of water. It suddenly became quiet, save for the occasional drip from the tap.

Examining my hands, I found them red and sore—I had been gripping the handle hard. Everything down to my ankles ached as I sank underwater. A foul mood clouded my thoughts, leaving me sulky and bitter. I had been having such a good day.

My throat felt tight; I wanted to cry or scream in frustration, but no sound came out. I had felt so good—so powerful. I had almost beaten Aedin. What had happened?

The dripping of water from the tap echoed throughout the small room.

I emerged when the water became cold, drying and wrapping myself with a towel. When I exited the bathroom, I started in surprise—Aedin was sitting on the couch, looking at me.

I cursed. "How long have you been…?"

He didn't answer and I didn't care. I went to the wardrobe, grabbed a dress, and re-entered the bathroom to change.

Picking up my boots, I opened the door and ungraciously threw them outside then sat fuming on the steps to the garden, working a comb through my hair. I winced as I struggled to pull the tangles loose and glowered at the bright flowers.

Aedin took a seat next to me. I eased away from him, avoiding touching his knee with mine.

"I'm… sorry," he said slowly.

I laughed out loud. We had been here before.

"You're sorry?" I challenged, shaking my head. "It's incredible. The *one* thing I look forward to—you *know* how much I enjoy training. And you had to ruin it."

Aedin's didn't protest or defend himself. His lips were set in a tight line as he avoided my gaze. "I'm sorry, but I can't train you."

"Unbelievable," I muttered.

"If you had stopped when I told you to—"

"Does it bother you that I'm good at it?" I blurted, brandishing the comb at his chest. "That maybe—just *maybe*—I could beat you at something?"

"No, that's not the point—"

"Well then perhaps *enlighten* me and we can come to a civil resolution. Because you are *infuriating*." I couldn't keep the malice from my words. My blood pounded in my veins and I felt a fight rise in my chest.

Aedin shook his head, squinting at the dirt. His hands were balled into fists and his tanned face was taut.

He looked at me suddenly, as if I had opened a wound. "Did you love him?"

The question caught me off guard. "What are you talking about?"

"Daniel Terrace. Did you love him?"

I cried in frustration, "What does that have to do with anything?"

"Everything. Did you love him?"

I stood, the teeth of the comb biting into my palm. "*Yes,* Aedin," I hissed. "I did love him. He was the love of my life and you took him away from me. We were engaged and would have married if…"

Aedin rose to his full height, staring down at me with his impenetrable gaze. A powerful pressure shoved into my skin, biting and unforgiving, as he snapped, "If *what?*"

I looked into his dark eyes, my jaw clenched and body rigid. "I hate you," I said quietly.

Not waiting to see his reaction, I went inside and threw the comb on the floor. My body was shaking with anger and despair —my hands wanted to rip something apart.

I slipped into my sandals and grabbed a hat. I needed to get away.

My footsteps clicked on the stone floor as I exited our rooms and headed towards the front courtyard. A great fire stirred in my belly—I felt something might erupt inside of me and I fought to control my breath.

Eyes brimming with tears, I suppressed them from falling as I spied a manservant. "Get a carriage," I demanded.

He started at my appearance and bowed quickly before running towards the gatehouse.

Hugging my chest, I gripped my arms tightly. I spied a dark figure watching me from the shadow of a column and ignored the prying eyes of the guard. Tapping my feet impatiently, I forced my gaze to the wooden beams of the ceiling. It wasn't comforting.

Where was the carriage?

I didn't know where I would go—maybe the Taylor estate. Maybe Tahuna to catch a ship to Berge. I didn't care—I needed to leave the villa.

I cursed audibly—this was taking too long. Gripping my hat, I walked towards the gatehouse, ignoring the scorching heat of the sun on my skin.

My steps crunched through the gravel as I muttered darkly under my breath. Tieren ambled into view and gave me a half-hearted wave.

"Don't—" I snarled, pointing at him.

"My lady—"

"Get the carriage."

"You cannot leave the villa like this."

"Like what?" I shouted, my fury rising. Rage pulsed through my veins.

Tieren took a step back, his face pained and cautious. "My lady, *please*."

"Not you too!" I cried, tears threatening to break. "Just let me go."

"We can't—" Tieren looked upset. "Listen—"

"Come with me then," I challenged. "We're leaving."

I moved around him and headed for the gate. I didn't need a horse and carriage to leave the villa. I only needed to exit the gates.

"Gwen," Aedin's voice echoed fiercely behind me.

I ignored him, picking up my dress and pace as I neared the wrought-iron gate and low stone walls.

"Gwen, please stop—"

"Leave me alone!" I shouted, my fingernails biting into my palms through the fabric of the dress.

"*Stop!*" Aedin yelled, and I suddenly stopped.

My heart beat wildly in my chest as I looked around. I noted Tieren's empathic expression as he watched from the gatehouse.

Aedin's footsteps grew closer and I realized my feet were fixed in place—I couldn't move.

A rough hand grabbed my arm in a tight squeeze. Aedin's eyes were cold, furious, and burning with flecks of mahogany.

There was a violent force radiating from his body as I stood frozen to the ground, struggling against the waves of pressure that bound me.

I was instantly afraid—a rabbit caught in a snare.

My breath slowed as I felt the anger leak out of my body. I watched him in the motionless silence as a wetness began to spread across my cheeks.

His fierce expression softened in disbelief, but his grip did not falter. Inhaling shakily, I cleared my throat and found I was unable to speak.

"We will go inside," Aedin stated quietly. "Do you understand?"

The wave of power subsided in my body and I found my voice. "Yes," I rasped. I shifted my weight and awkwardly regained my movement.

Aedin loosened his grip on my arm, and I shook him off. Looking down, I saw an angry red mark where his hand had been and bit back a cry.

I brought my hand up and slapped his cheek.

The sudden movement surprised us both. Aedin looked away, moving his jaw and closing his eyes.

"Don't *ever* touch me like that again," I hissed. "Do you understand?"

Aedin opened his eyes and stared at me, stupefied. I breathed air into my chest then turned and went inside.

I did not hear him follow.

Chapter Seventeen

AEDIN AND I didn't speak for several days.

An ominous cloud hung over the villa—even Mary had grown quiet and cautious. Aedin rose and left in the early hours of the morning. We dined on separate schedules and I didn't seek to train with the guards. Only at night did we sleep in the same bed, leaving ample room between us.

We avoided eyes and kept to ourselves. It was like living with a ghost.

During idle hours, I replayed the fight in my head, dissecting the events. There were some things that I didn't understand. I was certain that I had been pushed and *then* tripped. Pushed by the wind? I wasn't large nor tall, but it seemed odd that a simple gust could knock me that hard.

And even though I had hit my head, I hadn't imagined my restricted movement after Aedin had shouted. Perhaps it had been an instinctual reaction—I had frozen at the rage in his voice.

I had been afraid—and I had never before feared him in that way.

As I'd lain in bed that first night, the back of my head slightly sore, I'd wondered if I had imagined it all. Perhaps it had all been a terrible dream, a chain of horrible coincidences, and I would wake up and find none of it had happened.

But when I'd risen the next morning and touched the tender flesh of my arm, I'd remembered it had been real.

I pondered the afternoon—over and over again—and was frightened of the things I couldn't explain.

Later that week, I was situated in a circle at the home of the newly wedded Catherine. Her husband, Joshua Dagny, would reappear every half hour—fluttering about to make small talk or ask us if we required anything. His brown hair was thinning and his nose looked rather large and out of place, but he was kind and soft-spoken and clearly thought the world of our friend.

Catherine smiled sweetly, batting him away as he emerged for a third time.

Andrea was amused, grinning over the rim of her wine glass at his retreating form. "Is he a servant? Or a merchant? I must have forgotten."

Catherine kicked her foot against Andrea's legs, eying her with a playful glare. "He is just thrilled that we are able to host you here."

"It is a lovely space," I commented. With multiple stories, the home sat on the fashionable sector of the main street. It was on the smaller side, but the garden terrace on the roof fit our trio perfectly. We had an unobstructed view of the ships milling in the port, accompanied by the fresh smell of seawater.

"Thank you." Catherine reached over and grasped my hand. "It means a lot that you came."

I smiled back. "Of course! I have to crowd all of our visits into a year before this one is born."

Catherine rubbed her stomach. "It will take up my time, but I could never give up your companionships."

"Well we are never far," Andrea said warmly. "Liam's estate is just a fifteen-minute drive from here. So you will have no excuse to be rid of me."

I was grateful for our tight group. It felt relaxing to be in their presence—without being judged or chastised. There was a privacy and freedom in the company of close friends, even though Marks still haunted our visits. He would situate himself in a corner, watching us from an appropriate distance and with a careful gaze. Andrea had begun to refer to him as our "fourth companion."

"Nor me," I said archly. "There is little else to do in the villa."

Catherine made a sympathetic face as Andrea eyed me eagerly. "Gwen." She lowered her voice. "I heard something the other day—when I was having tea at Madame Fraser's. I heard that you *hit* Lord Aedin."

Catherine gasped, looking at me in horror. Andrea's expression was quite the opposite—thoroughly delighted at the gossip.

I rolled my eyes. "How in the Empire…"

"News travels fast. All it takes is one servant… or our fourth companion"—she nodded towards Marks—"to loosen their tongue in Tahuna."

I saw Marks shake his head with an expression of obvious distaste, as I emitted a bitter laugh. "I am certain it was not one of the guards… a servant more likely." I sobered, watching the ocean waves ripple in the wind, and sipped my wine.

"Why would you hit your husband?" Catherine whispered, looking back briefly to see if hers would appear.

"I did not *hit* him," I protested. "I… slapped him." I felt guilty saying the words, although the action had felt right at the time.

"Incredible." Andrea shook her head. "A woman—taking charge. I love it."

"It wasn't like that—"

"What did he do?" Catherine asked in dismay.

"Was he unfaithful?" Andrea's eyes glinted.

"No—"

"Did he hurt you?"

"Well, not really." I looked at my arm—the bruise had mostly faded, although my flesh was still tender.

"Not really?" Andrea repeated dubiously. "I never thought my lord to be violent—"

"He is not violent," I said with a grimace—this was getting out of hand. "He is a good man—we just have our… differences."

Andrea's brow furled in confusion as Catherine's expression turned worried. "How bad could the differences be…?" she mused, certainly thinking of her own relationship.

"Catherine—this will never happen to you," I stated plainly. "Trust me—you and Joshua are too in love… You would never lay a hand on each other."

"And you are not in love," Andrea finished quietly, watching me thoughtfully.

I opened my mouth to reply but had nothing to say. Flustered, I sipped some wine, avoiding their eyes. "I do not feel that I know what love is," I said slowly.

We grew silent, listening to the cries of the gulls and the gurgle of the nearby fountain.

Andrea smiled down at her feet. "What is love? I am not sure I understand it either."

"Surely we know what love is," Catherine protested. "It is a feeling of affection and mutual goodwill… It—it can be a romantic feeling, but it can also be a feeling of attachment and camaraderie."

Andrea snorted at her words. "Camaraderie. We then certainly love each other."

"Yes, we do," Catherine replied indignantly, pleased to make sense of something. "It may not be a romantic love, but there are different forms of love."

"I thought I was in love once," I said softly, remembering Daniel with a smile. "But perhaps it was more of a youthful lust. Or an imagination of love."

"It is easy to imagine love—it is the easiest thing in the world," Andrea said, chortling. "You just conjure up some warm and pleasant feelings and tell yourself that they are the most perfect partner for you. The harder part—or at least this is what I *suppose*—is acting out those feelings so that they reflect in your reality. So those sentiments can withstand the obstacles of our everyday lives."

I pressed my lips together as I listened. "I think you're right," I admitted quietly.

"Of course I'm right—I'm always right." Andrea waved her hand at me. "How do you not know this by now?"

Catherine settled back into her chair, sipping her wine pensively. "If Joshua and I act as though we love each other, I suppose that would help…"

"It's not always about you, Catherine," Andrea chided with a gentle smile.

"I just want to make sure I am doing everything *right*," she objected looking at me knowingly, "so that we do not have any… you know…"

"Fights?" I suggested with a raised eyebrow.

"Not that you and my lord fight," Catherine added quickly.

I gave a low laugh. "We certainly do…"

"Perhaps the post-marital sweetness is wearing thin," Andrea counseled.

"There was never any—" I stopped myself, realizing I had never told anyone this before. A heavy weight rested upon my breast as I tried to continue with a lie. "We did… enjoy each other… And I think we can still enjoy each other's company… But it will take a trying effort."

Andrea gestured towards Catherine's small, swollen belly. "Catherine is trying and she has only been married for several months. What have you been you doing?"

I started, realizing that Andrea had noticed. It was common for newly wed women to soon become pregnant—the thought hadn't crossed my mind. Perhaps it was a signal that something was wrong, or perhaps that something was wrong with *me*. Perhaps all of Lailan suspected as such, except for me.

Catherine saved me. "Andrea," she scolded, "you cannot *let* that be an indicator. Not all women have fertility."

I blushed. "It's fine, Catherine—"

Andrea gave a half grimace. "Again, I have not filtered my speech. I apologize, my lady."

"Andrea—please." I gave her an encouraging smile. "I always appreciate your unfettered opinions. They have kept me entertained all these months, and I should hope that they also entertain your future husband."

"I do hope he knows what he's getting into," Catherine said nervously.

Andrea hushed her, pouring more wine. "There is nothing like a surprise."

When Joshua returned to check on our party, I realized we had been sitting for several hours. Our fourth companion looked stiff and uncomfortable, so I bid my friends goodbye and we settled in the carriage. The sun was beginning to set above the horizon—it would be a beautiful sunset.

I looked at Marks watching the passing jungle through the window. His brow was etched with a perpetual line of worry—I wondered if it could grow any deeper. His blue eyes met mine as we exchanged sympathetic glances and I looked down at my hands, unsure of what to say.

"I'm sorry you have to… sit through our idle chatter," I managed. "I'm sure it's quite a bore and you would prefer to be somewhere else."

Marks shrugged. "I am protecting you, my lady. I don't care what you discuss."

I was glad to hear it, although I wasn't sure if I believed him. His first allegiance was to Aedin, and I assumed he was informing him if we discussed anything relevant.

"Please don't tell… Aedin," I said quickly. "About what we discussed today."

Marks was quiet, before he looked at me blankly and said, "What did you discuss?"

I forced a shaky smile and braced myself as the carriage rolled through the gates of the villa.

"Thank you," I said softly, following him down the steps.

"My pleasure." Marks nodded gravely, leaving me at the front. I wanted to follow him to the guards' quarters—they were likely finishing training at this hour—but instead I walked to our rooms and took off my hat.

Pulling open the door to the bedroom, I nearly swore in surprise. Aedin sat on our bed, quill in hand as he scribbled notes on a parchment. He looked up, unperturbed.

After a moment of awkward silence, I found my voice. "Hello."

"Hello," he responded, bending again to the parchment.

I wondered if he was writing about how much he hated his wife.

Hanging my hat in the wardrobe, I thumbed through my dresses until I found a light cotton one then exited to the bathroom to change. I splashed water on my face, thinking of Andrea's words. I shook my head.

It was ridiculous, but what if she was right?

Pausing to look in the mirror, I steeled my nerves resolutely.

When I re-entered the bedroom, I walked slowly to the bed and sat at the foot, staring at Aedin. The sounds of the garden wafted through the open doors as his quill scratched noisily against the page. I thought he might ignore me and braced myself to walk away.

After a long moment, he returned the quill to the ink pot and place the parchment on the side table.

He met my eyes with an expressionless mask. "Yes?"

"I'm sorry I slapped you," I offered gently.

Aedin's face softened slightly, but his eyes remained guarded. "I'm sorry I hurt you."

My heart beat in my throat. I shifted forward and reached for his hand. As I brushed the firm knuckles with my fingertips, he opened his hand in response, entwining it with mine. I felt the calluses on the ridge of his palm and the pads of his fingers.

Our eyes met and I saw flecks of mahogany, green, cobalt, silver—a multitude of colors in the dark. His hand was warm and slightly coarse when it lifted to touch my chin.

Daniel flickered through my mind, but I forced him out. I could no longer live in the past.

I wanted to laugh at the absurdity as I instinctively leaned forward and met his lips. Inhaling a shaky breath, I tasted the salt and sweetness of his skin. His mouth was warm and inviting, and I felt his hand reach up to run through my hair.

My skin prickled with chills as I wrapped my arms around his neck, pulling him closer. I didn't know what I'd expected, but not *this*.

Aedin's hands ran down my back as we kissed, and our breath became fast and light. His tongue pressed through my lips and I opened them eagerly as a rush of heat descended through my body.

I wanted him. Like I had never wanted anyone before.

It was overwhelming—the feeling of his lips crushed against mine and mingled with the intoxicating masculine scent.

The energy and power of an invisible, gleaming thread drawing me towards him, pulling us together.

Pulling us to the mattress.

And his hands on my waist, just below my chest.

There was a sudden hunger, an urgency, as I gripped his biceps and he bent his lips to my neck—

A hollow knock echoed through the room.

Aedin froze, his lips suspended above the curve of my neck as my heart beat wildly in my chest, his breath hot on my skin. Slowly, he removed his arms and rose, avoiding my eyes.

I blushed and smoothed my hair, walking towards the welcoming breeze of the garden doors; the pounding of my blood reduced to a simmer.

I heard the door open and the exchange of murmured words. It shut again shortly after and I turned to face him. He walked unhurriedly towards me, staring at a letter in his hand.

"What is it?" I whispered.

He didn't respond, frowning as he read the words on the page.

I waited, watching the early evening light flicker across his creased brow. Gazing at the firm lines of his body, the same thrumming of desire began to swell. I wanted to feel his hands on my skin again, his lips on mine—

Finally, he looked up. "Lord Tours has boarded a ship in Radiance and is on his way to Lailan." Aedin's mouth was set in a hard line as he watched me with those keen dark eyes.

A hollowness descended in my chest, suddenly curbing the mood.

"Well." I swallowed, mustering my courage and remembering our conversation. "I can leave—as you wish—and set sail for Berge at first light tomorrow morning—"

"Your brother and father are on the passenger list," Aedin continued slowly, "as well as Daniel Terrace."

My mouth felt dry. I tried to contain my expression as emotions flickered through me at his words—joy, eagerness, anxiety, and unease. Ephraim and my father—*here*? It felt impossible, and yet I had wished for their presence since leaving Berge. And Daniel…

Aedin observed my reaction, waiting.

"Then I will stay…" I said haltingly, not sure how to respond.

Aedin balled up the letter in his fist, staring wide-eyed into the distance. Avoiding my gaze.

Cold gripped my chest in a tight fist.

"Aedin." I moved towards him, reaching for his arm, as he turned on his heel. "Aedin, *please*—what do you want me to do?"

He turned abruptly, regarding me with a harried expression as he held up his hands. "Nothing… Just let me think."

"About what?"

"There are some things I have to… do." I saw his mind racing as he struggled to speak, his body edging away from mine. "Just stay here… do nothing."

"Can I help—"

My husband left, the sound of the closing door echoing painfully through the room.

Chapter Eighteen

"ROWYN."

His name echoed in the silence of the night.

Rowyn woke with a start, seconds before insistent knocks reverberated on the door. He had been flying—he had dreamed of soaring over the mountains, heading west across the wide sea until he'd reached an island in the Empire—Lailan.

Scenes streaked across his mind revealed in flashes of color: the silver edge of a sword, the black cloth of a tunic, a thick, green wall of jungle. A thundering and indistinguishable voice muttered words that resounded in the cavern of his mind. Rage, fear, and grief.

Unfamiliar eyes haunted his waking gaze: pale blue-gray.

Shivering in the warm night, Rowyn pushed back the covers and stepped onto the wooden floor.

Firelight flooded into his room as he opened the door. Selena's face was white, her eyes wide.

"I ran as fast as I could," she whispered, her lips trembling. "Rowyn, there is a ship from the Empire in the western inlet."

It took some seconds for the words to sink in. Rowyn blinked. "A ship from the Empire?"

"Come," Selena ordered, gesturing with her hand to where an open flame spiraled into the air, illuminating the night. "You are needed. We have remained hidden—they think the island is uninhabited. There are about fifty men with cargo aboard. It appears to be a merchant's vessel—no sign of weapons, but we aren't certain."

Rowyn's body threw itself into action. He grabbed his tunic as his mind raced. "They could be the Rhidge."

"They do not appear aggressive."

"No, but they could be deceiving us."

Rowyn hastily laced and tied his boots then pulled his sword from the wall and latched it around his waist. "Take me to them."

It was a two-hour run to the western mountains. Their feet were light upon the grass, which was damp with dew. The full moon shone brightly and illuminated the entire path. Rowyn watched the sleeping valley pass below, thinking of Rea, Darius, and the children.

Marveling at the stark contrast of their lives, he fingered the steel at his hip. The sword sang lightly as it bounced in its sheath. It had never seen blood—perhaps tonight that would change.

They were nearly silent as they ran together—only the whispering of the grass betrayed their presence.

Selena slowed to a quick walk. Rowyn's lungs burned—it had been some time since he'd run at such speed. He felt his blood quicken, his fingers tingling as Selena motioned for silence. Their steps paused as the other guards emerged onto the path.

The moon was now partially hidden by the peaks of the mountain. Shards of darkness blanketed the path in between beams of light. They greeted each other with wordless nods as they stood in the dark.

Fear clouded Celion's bright blue eyes. Rowyn met his gaze—the eyes he had loved for so many years—as his gut twisted in knots.

He could die—they could all die tonight.

Pointing to the west, Selena gestured for Rowyn to take her position. He stepped forward—beyond the curtain of a large tree—and saw the ship.

It was from the Empire—the white sails bore a familiar seal he recalled from ancient manuscripts. Even in the dark, Rowyn could discern a purple insignia underneath a white gull.

Slightly relieved to not see the infamous "R" of which he'd read, he wondered from which island the vessel had come. They didn't appear aggressive—the men mulled about on the beach in small groups. Some sat by a fire, keeping watch, while others slept.

The boat creaked in the small waves—abandoned on the beach. Rowyn saw the cracked hull and discarded sails and understood: they were shipwrecked.

"What will you do?" the familiar voice whispered just near his ear.

Rowyn's heart thudded in his chest as he turned to see the cloaked face. The Prophet.

"Prophet."

Perhaps it was an apparition, or a passing dream, but the others had disappeared into the dark. They were alone.

The moonlight vanished along with everything in his sight, save for the thick, shrouded cloak covering the body. A thousand colors soaked the fabric, swirling endlessly, seeming to simultaneously absorb and discharge all the light in the world. Nausea roiled in his stomach at the infinite spinning colors as Rowyn forced himself to stare into the darkened face beneath the cowl.

"No, they are not Rhidge," the Prophet said slowly—a thick, dark grimace beneath the gleaming opalescent eyes. "But they are Empire."

"What shall I do?" Rowyn searched the nearly invisible face for any sign or answer. He felt his heart might vacate his chest as he fought to control his breath. An eternity seemed to pass in silence.

"Kill them."

The words were loud in his head.

"Rowyn!... Rowyn," Selena's voice echoed in the background. "*Rowyn!*"

As he blinked, the moonlight returned to the land. Gone was the hooded face and cloak that stole his breath.

He could smell the fear—the rich tang of blood about to be spilled.

Selena's eyes were wide as she gasped, "Rowyn, what will we do?"

Drawing his sword, Rowyn watched the moonlight flicker on the silver steel.

In its spotless reflection, he saw the blue-gray eyes from his dream.

His pulse quickened and he felt the Gift thicken his blood and lighten his mind. Turning to the others, he motioned with his sword.

"It is tonight that we will spill the first drop of blood… The first drop to end the hundreds of years of bloodshed." Rowyn watched his guards as they hesitantly drew their swords.

"Be quick and merciful. It is the way of Fate. Leave none alive."

Rowyn turned on his heel, making his way down the covered path to the beach.

His sword sang that night as that first blood spilled on the sand. Muffled cries filled the beach, the ocean waves crashing relentlessly.

They piled the bodies, wrapping them in the sails with their emblem, and burned them on a pillar of fire that glowed brightly of gold, green, red, and blue.

Near dawn, when it was over, all that remained upon the spotless shore was the carcass of a stripped and broken ship and a pile of rubble and charred bones. Rowyn left someone to deposit the burned remains out at sea—even then they were too close for comfort.

Chapter Nineteen

AEDIN DID NOT come back that night. I dined alone, waiting for his familiar shadow, sipping my wine slowly and taking my time.

Even after I'd finished and settled in our rooms, I curled underneath the sheets alone and listened to the wind echo through the curtains, wondering where he was. When my eyes burned from fatigue and I could no longer keep them open, I finally fell asleep.

When I awoke, he wasn't there.

Mary found me the next morning at the breakfast table, sipping my tea and rubbing sleep from my eyes. "Good, you're here."

"That makes one of us," I muttered.

Mary ignored my comment. "We need to start preparing for the reception."

"What reception?"

"When Lord Tours and his party arrive."

Of course—my mind felt numb and heavy. "Yes—"

"I have your friends on the list—Mr. and Madame Dagny as well as Miss Taylor and her fiancé, Mr. Spence—" She inspected her parchment, running her finger down the names. "Unfortunately, Kitra Devereux has *also* been invited, at the request of Lord Tours, but I suppose one night can't hurt. We have the de Boughs, Cabots, Steeles… the usual names, *and,*" she added with emphasis, "your brother and father, Ephraim and Gregory Doyle. Is there anyone you might also suggest?"

Mary looked up at me when I didn't respond.

I fingered the small handle of my teacup, saying quietly, "Where is Aedin?"

"My lady," Mary said lowly, eying me sympathetically, "he is *very* busy preparing for Lord Tours' visit—"

"But where is he? Why didn't he return last night?"

She hesitated and I realized she knew. "He was in Tahuna last night—finalizing some reports—"

"Don't lie to me," I said scathingly.

She avoided my glare and continued steadily. "Your brother and father have the option of staying at the villa. Would you want that?"

"Of course." I frowned. "Why wouldn't they? They have to stay here."

Mary made a note on the paper and didn't respond.

"Is the king coming as well?" I asked, remembering Ephraim's letter.

"No," Mary said evenly. "His health prohibits him from traveling at the moment."

I shrugged—I had no desire to meet the king anyway. "When does the party arrive?"

Mary lifted her eyes, counting in her head. "We received word regarding their departure yesterday—the note was sent on the fastest ship that can sail here from Radiance… I believe they might arrive tomorrow."

Tomorrow. My heart leaped in excitement and fear as I clutched my teacup, gazing into the waves. I missed my family dearly but also dreaded the reception of Lord Tours and the possible sight of Daniel.

"The reception will take place in two days' time. I have ordered a new gown for the event, which should arrive tomorrow morning. Is there anything else you need, my lady?" Mary sat upright with her signature patience and tactfulness.

"No," I said shortly.

She hesitated, as if wanting to say something. I avoided her gaze, fuming silently.

Mary stood with grace. "My lady," she murmured with a curtsy and left me alone.

I felt hollow. The ocean did little to soothe and distract my mind. Thoughts and scenarios ran through my head as I imagined having my family at the villa, the reception, the meetings and teas…

Draining my cup, I set it down and left the table. I needed to do something. I thought about going to the circle and training with the guards but remembered Aedin's words. Dejected, I made my way back to our rooms.

Turning the corner in the hallway, I saw a familiar dark figure—Aedin was speaking to Marks in hushed tones.

The harshness of their whispers carried through the halls and I realized they were arguing.

Aedin stopped abruptly, meeting my eyes. My heart jumped into my throat as I held his stare, glaring at him.

"Where have you *been*?" I hissed, advancing towards them.

Marks said something to Aedin and clapped him on the shoulder, then nodded in my direction before leaving us alone in the hall. Aedin eyed me carefully.

"Where did you go—"

"Come inside." Aedin marched down the hall to our bedroom door, ushering me through. I followed obediently, closing the door to the antechamber as Aedin went to the garden and shut the doors. The room became eerily quiet without the sounds of the birds and fountain.

He drew the curtains and sat down at the table with a sigh, rubbing his face. The sunlight that poured into the room was muted and it suddenly felt cold.

I sat across from him. "Aedin—*what* is going on—"

"I need to tell you something."

My breath caught in my throat. I watched him evenly. "What do you mean?"

"I mean… what I am about to tell you may sound absurd or unbelievable, but it is the truth." Aedin observed me with a serious gaze. "And what I am about to tell you *cannot* leave this room—under any circumstances. Not even in jest, or gossip, or if you are threatened…"

I flinched at the last word but remained silent, watching him restlessly, only daring to breathe, as I realized this was the moment I'd waited for since we'd come to Lailan.

Aedin exhaled noisily, tracing the grains of the wood with his finger. He emitted a harsh laugh, leaning back with a groan. "Why am I so frightened?"

"Frightened?" I frowned at his choice of word.

He licked his lips, looking away. "I am afraid—" Aedin broke off with a nervous exhalation of air, like a desperate laugh. "For some reason, I have this fear that you will… hate me."

"Why?"

There was a moment when our eyes met and something became understood. The truth was ugly. Aedin nodded and looked at the floor for a moment before bravely meeting my eyes.

"There are some people in this world who are given a rare gift. When the Empire was young—no, before there even *was* an Empire—eight islands existed in harmony. Acedes, Radiance, Cachelle, Berge, Lailan, Tente, Avellian… and an eighth. I don't know its name, but it is said that all of the islands were ruled independently and enacted judiciously with each other.

"The people back then, some thousand years ago… most of them had what is called "the Gift." It is a kind of power—like ordinary street magic, but real and possessing. They are still alive today, but they have nearly all retreated to the eighth island, which resides far off in the east. But… there are some of us who still exist here, within the Empire."

He met my gaze knowingly. I stared at him mindlessly until something clicked.

I choked out the word on unsteady lips. "Us…?"

"Gwen, I have the Gift… and so do you."

"No." I shook my head, my stomach dropping at his serious expression. This must be a jest. "No, I am not 'magical' in *any* sense…"

"Don't think of it as magic—I'm sorry, that is the wrong word." He rubbed his face. "It's a power—a gift of life that enhances… your capabilities." Aedin straightened, leaning towards me. "You have the Gift, and you have one of the strongest Gifts I have felt in my entire life."

My heart nearly leaped out of my chest. "But how do you know? You can *feel* it?"

"You've felt mine. You've felt Marks', Tieren's, the guards', Mary's too possibly… It's like a force that projects from your body —an indescribable atmosphere that presses outwards and often feels like the wind."

I thought immediately of the wall of air that had thrown me to the ground and frozen my body. "I suppose…" I swallowed. "But I still don't understand…"

"The Gift often first manifests itself through highly charged emotional situations. Whether joy, fear, or anger… It is often incited by extremes when you don't know how to control it."

I remembered the feeling in my blood, and his desperate attempt to cool me whenever I was angry. "But… what does it do?"

"The Gift *is* a gift—it is a power bestowed upon us as a means of controlling our surroundings and using our bodies to produce seemingly extraordinary things. It also raises our general senses— such as hearing, seeing, or tasting—to a remarkable level."

Aedin rested his forearms on the table and opened up his palm.

A blue flame unfurled itself from the center of his hand.

I started, leaning back in fear, and then forward in amazement. It was the color of the ocean—deep blues and greens intermingled with tinges of gold and red. Hesitantly, I reached out my hand—it was warm.

"Unbelievable…" I murmured.

Aedin's full lips tugged upwards in a slight smile as our eyes met. He slowly closed his palm, and the light went out. The room was cast once more in the dull sunlight and silence.

"But…" I trailed off, still bemused, "my hearing hasn't been particularly good nor my sight any different—"

"That will come with time as you learn to control it. The Gift also sends Dreams—knowledge of the past, present, and future."

My brow furrowed. "Do you mean like prophecies?"

"Prophecies are predictions—the Dreams are glimpses of realities… You saw my past," he reminded me gently.

Despair washed over me as I remembered his pained, young face in the mud. "That was true?" I whispered.

Aedin nodded wordlessly. I reached out and grabbed his hand, comforted by the warmth of his skin, then inhaled shakily as I met his eyes. "And you have… also had these dreams?"

"Yes," he said. "I have Dreamed of the past and future… but not yet the present."

"Why not?"

Aedin shrugged. "The Dreams are one of the things we don't fully understand about the Gift. Although there are some irregularities between how the Gift can manifest itself in each individual, the Dreams seem to be consistent in their appearance and inconsistent in regards to timing. I have known some Gifted to have all of their Dreams by the time they are eighteen—yet for others it takes longer."

My mind stumbled over this new information, but I recalled his earlier words. "You said that the guards and Mary also have… the Gift."

"Yes."

"Who else knows of this?"

Aedin removed his hand from mine and leaned back, folding his arms. "This is where our situation becomes a bit complicated. I will answer your question, but you have to know the history… A long time ago, before there was even a king, the ruler of Radiance, a lord by the name of Rhidge, decided that those with the Gift were dangerous and malevolent. He amassed a large following of hostile, like-minded people who began a purge of all those with the Gift.

"It was a bloody genocide that spread through the islands. Although the Gifted, individually, were physically more powerful than their opponents, Lord Rhidge had created a campaign of fear and propaganda that was spreading unrest and gaining many followers. And after years of bloodshed, they had arrived at a battle stalemate… when Lord Rhidge had an idea that changed the course of history.

"They—the followers of Lord Rhidge—began taking children and youths who were Gifted. They were easier to find than the adults—most of them were even unaware of their power or how to control it. Extreme emotions"—he gave me a bitter grin—"that expel unwanted forces of power is the most common sign. Very easy to detect. Lord Rhidge figured that if educated in warfare and brainwashed to serve the newly forged Empire, the young Gifted would grow into an invaluable army ready to remove other Gifted, as well as political opposition… He was right."

Aedin became silent—his face was shadowed. I stayed quiet as his eyes flickered to mine.

"Lailan became the last bastion for the Gifted. A terrible war was fought on these shores before they retreated to the eighth island. Perhaps the Empire was weary of war after nearly a decade of fighting, but Lord Rhidge was content to let them stay and inhabit the eastern island. The Gifted were afraid—they did not seek retribution or any counter-attacks—and have since remained there.

"Lord Rhidge soon crowned himself king and upon his death he passed the throne to his bastard son. That is why the tradition has held that kings never take a wife. To share political power with anyone else would be dangerous. The eighth island was removed from the collective memory of the Empire and faded into obscurity, the east becoming synonymous with the threat of the unknown.

"The men *and* women Gifted whom Lord Rhidge trained to serve and fight for him were turned into a secretive group and given his own name: the Rhidge. They survive even today.

"The Rhidge is an extensive network of Gifted spies and assassins that are loyal to the king and protect the Empire but are under the direction of the Lord of Radiance—who is currently Lord Tours. No one—except for the king and the Lord of Radiance—knows about the Rhidge. And though the king is aware of the Rhidge, he is not Gifted and does not know of the Gift's existence.

"The Lord of Radiance is typically Rhidge *himself* and chosen by the previous Director of the Rhidge to take over the lordship upon their death. Therefore the Lord of Radiance is typically a powerful position—perhaps even more powerful than the king himself.

"Of course, rumors circulate and stories have arisen regarding the Rhidge, but no one is ever quite sure of the full scope of their power. The Rhidge heavily protects its identity and continues to seek out Gifted within the Empire to either dispatch or recruit them. Yes, there are some Gifted who still linger—many in Lailan, in fact. And then there are the rare cases when someone will be born with the Gift, even if they have little to no family history of the power."

He looked at me meaningfully.

I remembered the "R" on his shoulder and a shiver ran down my spine. "Are you… part of this?" I whispered, unable to contain an expression of horror as his words sank in.

Aedin gave me a melancholy smile as he continued. "I grew up in Radiance, in a small town not too far from the palace. I doubt it even exists now—I believe it was swallowed up by the growing capital years ago. My mother was Gifted, as was my father, but he had a less powerful one than her. However, it was enough to produce me—a son with more power than both of them combined. I remember little of my childhood else that it was happy and quiet. The only vivid memory I can recall is when the Rhidge… caught me.

"I was eleven and I remember being extremely happy that day, though why I can't recall." Aedin glanced at me with a humorless smile. "I was running down into the village when a tall man started following me. I remember slipping into an alley to avoid him, to find that he was there was well.

"He glanced down at me—he was terrifying. I wanted to run but was rooted to the spot. He said nothing to me—just stared with an unknown coldness. After he left, I was scared… That night I was kidnapped, and my father and mother were murdered.

"I spent the next fifteen years in the Rhidge: brainwashed to love and serve the king, tortured till I was unconscious, taught to fight and kill, to never show pain or emotions—they were considered irrelevant and weak… For all that time spent in a secluded wing of the palace, I don't recall much of it. Because I was caught at such a young age, I was easier to mold than some of the other… participants. However, that changed when I met a man named Jon.

"At the Rhidge," Aedin continued, meeting my eyes, "they try to limit contact between trainees for fear of a rebellion or plot. It was normal to talk during meals—to forbid all social contact was unrealistic. But befriending another was unusual, and even looked down upon. You see, everyone at the Rhidge was plotting against one another. You were more likely to gain favor—more likely to survive—if you successfully attacked another. They praised the element of surprise—if you succeeded, you would immediately be placed higher in rank, given more bonuses or privileges.

"That was why I, like all the others, did not seek friendship. Social contact perhaps, but friendship? The idea was a death sentence. With friends come expectations and unspoken rules. Why should you sacrifice your life for another when you, yourself, were struggling to stay alive? It was incredibly foolish to befriend someone in the Rhidge; they would end up using it against you.

"Jon's arrival changed my life. He was caught when he was twenty—older than usual, and much less malleable, but still useful. He was built powerfully—tall and brawny. But he was also strong-willed, and less willing to give in to the indoctrination of the Rhidge. Despite how reticent I was to his kindness and attention at the time, he persisted, and we became allies of a sort, perhaps even friends, though we never admitted it.

"We trained together and Jon filled me with ideas, hope, stories of the outside world—he was always a dreamer, always saying it was possible to escape or even go back to a normal life. Yet I was more realistic… I had seen failed escape attempts and knew that no one survived the Rhidge. After your service, after they are finished using you to assassinate or spy on political enemies, or capture other Gifted… you are killed. That is why the Rhidge is so well kept a secret—there is no way out.

"But Jon was the light during those years. He taught me… to hope. I had long abandoned hope of a 'normal life,' of living in the outside world… Jon influenced me to be more humane and compassionate, not the ruthless animal the Rhidge teaches you to be. He even fell in love with another trainee. Her name was—is Rebecca.

"Years passed and I became the best prodigy the Rhidge had ever seen. Not only was I powerful with the Gift, skilled with the sword, and flawless in my training, I was also loyal. For all they knew, I loved the king and would do anything—kill anyone—to please him.

"And I had hidden myself well… Upon Jon's urging, I had lied to the Rhidge about the Dreams. Perhaps that was why they felt so secure in me, because they thought they knew my fate and could control me.

"When I was twenty-six, Lord Tours told me to assassinate the Lord of Lailan." Aedin opened up his palms, looking at me. "And I did. But then he surprised me—Tours let me become lord. Because Lailan is such a prosperous island, the king had always had trouble controlling the lords he sent to govern. They would cheat, take more than their allotted share of the taxes—it was a nightmare to keep them in line.

"Convinced of my dedication to the king and the Rhidge, I was given the lordship. Tours, who had recently been promoted to Director of the Rhidge and the Lord of Radiance at that time, considered it a test. I suspect he wanted to see if it was possible to assimilate us back into society, without letting the secret of the Rhidge be known. After all, if I failed, they could easily dispose of me.

"But it was terrifying, being placed back in the normal world —living in a *villa* instead of a fortress. Everything—from the gardens to the sky—was terrifying. For years, all I had known were the palace walls, and suddenly I was free? Supposed to act normal?

"I tried and failed miserably. I nearly killed some of my servants for walking too close to me—I was paranoid as hell, hardly ate the first month for fear of food poisoning. I locked myself in this room, putting the Gift and physical barriers all around that door. I hardly left, only venturing out for meals and business meetings, to appear normal. For over half a year I struggled in a madness.

"And then Jon's service to the Rhidge was coming to an end.

"The Rhidge had no more use for him and he was old, about thirty years of age, and failing each test they sent him. I wondered at this though, because he had always been the fiercest fighter… I supposed that he had finally become suicidal—that he had purposely failed the tests the Rhidge presented.

"I wondered how Rebecca would survive without him—he had kept her in spirits as he did with me. Helping her when she was wounded, being a constant, positive presence… I don't know what inspired them, because it was clear stupidity, but together, Jon and Rebecca decided to escape the Rhidge—and succeeded. Don't ask me how they did it—it still puzzles me today how they managed to outsmart the guards and the Gift barriers.

"They stowed away on a ship to Lailan, and I hid them on my island. They lived in the villa for several days until they found passage to an abandoned island outside of the Empire. It had been used as a fortress during the wars but is now deserted and unused. They are still there today—they are the ones to whom we will flee in case… of anything. But their escape made me consider the possibility: if I could help them evade the Rhidge, I could help others as well.

"I approached Tours with the proposition of having a dozen guards—Gifted guards—who would help to guard myself and the villa. I offered the incentive of turning them over to the Rhidge when they were needed. I had considered doing this without the detection of Tours but realized that the extensive Rhidge network would eventually find out if I was saving and hiding other Gifted.

"At the time, the Rhidge wing of the palace was becoming crowded, and Tours was having trouble containing and training all of the new inductees. He considered it a 'waste' to kill Gifted simply because they couldn't bring them into the Rhidge, so I thought that my solution presented another way in without burdening the current system."

He broke off, suddenly aware of his words, his dark eyes shadowed. "Please"—Aedin's voice was low—"do not think ill of me. This idea—having the Gifted guards—would only have worked if I made Tours some sort of promise, or offered a favor in return. Otherwise, they would have been slaughtered."

Wordlessly, I nodded. "I…" I found my words. "I understand the predicament, but…"

"Yes." Aedin shifted uncomfortably. "I gave them the choice of a slow or a quick death. But the slow choice also offered the possibility—albeit a slim one—of escape.

"I went into Tahuna, searching for those who had the Gift. It wasn't too hard, and quickly I found Tieren, Marks and the others. I offered them jobs as guards but also temporary protection. To the girls I found, I offered them posts as servants—to have women guarding the villa was suspicious to those outside the Rhidge. Some of them, like Mary, in full control of their Gift, even came to me, seeking protection from the Rhidge."

"Is Talia…?" I asked.

"No, she is not," he answered quickly before pausing. "And then I saw you, at the closing ball on Berge. And I suddenly understood…" Aedin trailed off then reached for my hand, entwining his fingers with mine. I relished the feeling.

"My Dream of the future happened when I was eighteen. And in it, I saw you," Aedin explained quietly, his fingers tracing the curves of my knuckles.

"At the time, the idea seemed ridiculous—imprisoned in the Rhidge and never thinking of the outside world. I thought it was a mistake. But it gave me hope—and kept me alive during some especially hard times, knowing that you were out there, somewhere.

"So, all those years later, when I saw you in Lord Tremer's estate and felt your power, I knew what I had to do." Aedin met my eyes, warming my hands in his. "I married you, Gwen, not simply because it was destined to be, but because I did not want…

what had been done to me in the Rhidge to happen to you. I was incredibly selfish in my reasons. And I could *not* let the Rhidge find you."

I swallowed, remembering the intensity of the moment we had first locked eyes across the crowd. Aedin had been protecting me all along.

"How… how did I survive all this time?" I wondered aloud to him. "With my Gift… you said that it's powerful. Why did someone else not notice?"

Aedin nodded. "When I first felt your power I was stunned. When I realized that you didn't even know of your Gift, I was even more bewildered. That night at the ball, I followed you, terrified that another would feel your power as I did.

"You have to understand: only a Gifted can sense another's Gift. And even then, it is a subtle thing. Unless their emotions are at a high, it can be difficult to detect. You have been incredibly lucky: Berge hasn't often been a harbor for the Gifted, thus it's not as frequented by the Rhidge, and your powers have only just begun to reveal their full strength."

He laughed bitterly. "Your first weeks at Lailan, I thought you might run me over. Your power rolled off you in such waves that it was almost painful to be in the same room as you."

My mouth fixed in a line as a blush rose in my cheeks, embarrassed at my anger. "You didn't exactly make it easy," I protested with a grin.

"No," he agreed, watching our hands with a grim smile. "I probably would have acted the same if someone had kidnapped me to live with them for the rest of my life."

I tried to laugh but no sound came out. I felt incredibly weak, my shoulders sagging wearily as I considered the weight of my husband's story.

Aedin continued, and I listened eagerly—it was a rarity to hear him speak this much. "I thought that marrying you would keep you safe, that it would draw you away from the detection of the Rhidge." His voice turned somber. "When I received the news yesterday, I… regretted not telling you everything. Despite my 'loyalty,' Tours has kept a close eye upon me and required that I request his permission for most decisions… And I did not ask for his consent when I proposed to you.

"Tours does not know that you have the Gift," Aedin said quietly. "He is likely confused as to why I have married you—especially without seeking his permission—and suspects something. This is why it is of vital importance that you keep your emotions in check. You will need to be at the reception—I cannot hide you—so I beg of you to not do anything rash. I will be with you the entire night. Since you have survived twenty-five years without detection, I hope that one more week will suffice."

He paused, watching my face, and said in earnest, "Gwen—I am telling you all this because I need you to understand that *we*—the both of us—are on the verge of life or death. If you are found to be Gifted, then Tours will have your shoulder scarred with the same 'R' and send you on the fastest ship to Radiance. And I, undoubtedly, will be killed… I don't know how to make this point any clearer, that your life is hanging in the balance and there is only so much that *I* can do to save you now."

Aedin's expression was pleading and desperate. I gripped his hands, saying slowly. "I understand… Thank you, Aedin, for all that you have done."

Releasing a heavy sigh, he lifted my knuckles to his lips and set down our hands. "If it comes to it—and we need to escape—I have prepared a boat on the eastern shore of the island. We will sail to the fortress and leave Lailan."

A knot formed in my stomach. "It won't come to that…"

"I can't promise that," Aedin said flatly. He hesitated. "But I do know… that we *will* leave Lailan. Eventually."

My brow furrowed. "What do you mean?"

"My Dream—all those years ago—my Dream of the future was in a foreign place. A place I didn't recognize. And we are not there… yet," he said slowly.

"What else did you see?"

Aedin's dark eyes avoided mine. "I'll tell you another time. I think that is enough for one day." He patted my hand, wincing as he stood. "I have given you a lot to digest."

"Indeed." I remained sitting, watching him as he twisted into a stretch. "Is there anything else I can do? To avoid detection?" I suddenly grew worried, thinking of the reception and events of the upcoming week.

My husband considered my words silently for a moment. "Other than remaining calm and aloof, there is little you *can* do. I suppose we will have to rely on your luck a little longer... Don't sword fight." His eyes twinkled.

That was why he'd wanted to stop sparring. I pursed my lips delicately. "For now..." I agreed.

"For now," Aedin consented with a smile. He held out his hand; I took it and rose to my feet. My nose was only inches from his—I smelled sea salt on his skin.

"So your brother and father are staying with us." Aedin gradually ran his hands up my arms. Warmth shot through my body at his touch.

"Yes," I flustered, hesitantly placing my arms around his waist. My actions felt clumsy and shy—I was still becoming accustomed to desiring Aedin. His back was tight and lean under my grip. I could feel my heart beating in my throat as I forced myself to look into his dark eyes.

They were smiling.

"Mm." He bent his head to kiss my cheek. My skin tingled and my blood quickened. There was a force emitting from Aedin's body that was drawing me in—I turned my head to meet his lips as joy thrummed in my chest.

We kissed me softly and I reveled in the sensation. A deep, aching desire rose in my body as I was enveloped in his arms. Pressing my chest against his, I came up for air as he whispered in my ear, "I have to go."

"No." I nuzzled his cheek, feeling the pleasant sharpness of stubble.

"I'm sorry." His eyes were pained as his fingers traced the line of my jaw. "But I have to prepare the guards, run through plans..."

I hesitated but dropped my hands as the dizzy pleasure faded. "If you must," I admitted reluctantly.

Aedin pressed his lips to my forehead. "Do you trust me?"

"Yes," I replied, and realized it was true. "And thank you… for trusting me."

"I do." Aedin regarded me seriously, his fingers dropping to my arms. "I'm sorry I kept you in the dark for so long. I did what I thought was best at the time."

In response, I wrapped my arms around his waist again and pressed my cheek to his collarbone. My husband's arms encircled my body as we stood in a silent embrace. The sounds from the garden were muted through the closed doors as I held him and he discharged a long breath.

As if a weight had finally been lifted from his shoulders.

"Thank you… for everything," I whispered, hoping the simple words were enough to convey the magnitude of the sentiment.

The muscles of Aedin's arms tightened in response

My heart leaped with joy, even though we were on the verge of darkness.

Chapter Twenty

WE SLEPT CURLED in each other's arms.

Aedin returned when the moon was high—the thin sliver of light barely illuminating the dark. I felt him move under the sheets, wrapping me in his arms. His breath was warm on the back of my neck as his body pressed against mine. A thrill of pleasure washed through the fog of sleep, and I rested soundly.

When I awoke in the early hours of the morning, he was still there.

I fidgeted, moving my numb hand from its awkward position and turned over. Aedin's eyes flickered open at my movement and watched me. I lightly touched his forearm, which was draped over my waist, eying the "R" with a wary gaze.

"The 'R' stands for Rhidge?" I asked, my voice soft.

He nodded wordlessly.

I nestled my nose against his and pressed my lips to his cheek. His arms tightened, pulling me close—then his lips met mine. There was a soft humming as his hand stroked the length of my back. A thrill of desire unfurled in my chest—gentle and eager—as our mouths moved together.

We paused; I watched his eyes carefully. "Did it hurt?" I whispered.

Aedin pressed his lips together, moving his face to the crook of my neck. "At first… yes. After some time… no."

I touched the soft curves of his ear, savoring the feeling of his breath on my skin. We were quiet and the birds sang in the gray light of the morning. I stared at the scar—the skin was silver and puckered.

As my fingers moved towards it, Aedin grimaced and withdrew his arm, shying away from my touch.

I froze, my hand in mid-air, as he shifted and pushed back the covers. The warmth of his body suddenly gone.

"I'm sorry," I murmured, watching him pause.

In the morning light, I became aware of the thin silver scars lining his back. They flexed in time with his breath, chronicling a past darker than my imagination.

Aedin turned to look at me humorlessly. "Do you know why it's silver? They reopen the wound every year—on the anniversary of your capture—with the Gift. They use a dagger, lined with the Gift, and—"

"I didn't know…"

He deflated, looking away. "I know."

I scooted up to lean against the headboard, eying him cautiously and folding my hands diplomatically. "Although you've told me your story, you have to understand that there are still many things I will not comprehend. With time, however, I hope that will change, but we have only just begun to be honest with each other…"

He considered this for a moment, then released a sigh and leaned back to kiss me tenderly. "You're right."

I smiled as he rose from the bed and grabbed his shirt from the wardrobe. He buttoned the cuffs, watching me with a smirk. "Are you staying in bed all morning?"

I shrugged. "Maybe I'll sleep through the day." I carelessly rearranged the sheets and snuggled deeper into my pillow.

"Your brother and father will be arriving." Aedin looked at me knowingly, exiting towards the bathroom. I heard the sound of running water.

"Already?" I yawned. "It's so early!"

"The ship arrived late last night," Aedin's voice echoed from the bathroom. "They'll likely debark soon."

"What will you do?" I grumbled at getting out of bed, pushing back the sheets and stepping onto the cool floor.

"I'm meeting Tours in Tahuna to run through some business." Aedin emerged, drying his face and hair with a towel. "He might insist on dining together—I'm not sure. You will stay here to entertain your father and brother."

"But what if the Rhidge come here?" I crossed my arms, leaning against the wall.

"He doesn't usually travel with more than three. Two of them are already outside."

"What?" Something dropped in my chest.

Aedin shrugged. "They know to stay on the edges of the property. The guards are already watching them."

I frowned, uneasy at this truce. "So you're not concerned?"

"I'm always concerned," Aedin corrected. "It's just a matter of allocating my concern."

He gently gripped my shoulders, looking me in the eyes. "Just *please* stay calm—don't do anything brash—and act normal."

I scoffed. "Hidden assassins, extraordinary powers—how do I act normal?"

"You'll find a way." Aedin kissed me briefly on the lips.

He left shortly after—I heard the carriage exit the gates as I drew a bath. Mary arrived and helped me dress in the pale orange gown we'd purchased months ago. I was skeptical as I shrugged on the cloth but realized the color suited my newly tanned skin.

Sitting patiently, I watched her in the mirror as she braided my hair and painted my face. Her eyes met mine briefly in the mirror before returning to her work. I tried focusing on her form to sense anything—but there was nothing. I wondered in the stillness of the morning.

"Aedin told me," I said quietly, my words echoing through the bathroom.

Mary raised her eyebrows, saying nothing.

"He told me… about you as well."

"My lady, please lift up your chin," Mary directed.

I obeyed, making a face as she powdered my neck. I couldn't resist. "How long—"

"My lady," she said firmly with her brush mid-air, "we *do not* discuss such things openly."

I deflated my posture, dejected, as she continued her work. Minutes passed, before she added in a low voice, "But I am glad that he told you."

"Yes," I admitted, watching my face in the mirror. "I am glad as well."

Mary snapped shut the case of paint—the signal that we were done. I stood with a grateful sigh, awkwardly grimacing at the sight of my painted eyes and red lips.

"You know, it's only Ephraim and my father," I pointed out. "I hardly need to dress for them."

"You are the Lady of Lailan and will be receiving company." Mary eyed me wisely. "Of course you need to dress accordingly."

I rolled my eyes, picking up my skirts, and headed to the dining room where I ate a quick breakfast, sipping my tea impatiently as I watched the ships in the harbor.

There was an unusually large vessel anchored just outside the mouth of the port. The sails were emblazoned with a purple insignia—although it was hard to discern the shapes from this distance, I knew what they meant. I had seen the same symbols on the wax seal of Ephraim's letter.

I watched as smaller boats moved back and forth between the port and the ship. Like ants trailing to and from their queen. I imagined Aedin on one of them—resolute and stern as he approached his greatest fear.

My stomach turned as I was reminded of Daniel. He would be on board. It felt so unimaginable—having him here in Lailan. I wondered if he had changed.

I looked down at the silk of my dress and the jewels around my wrist—*I* certainly had changed.

And yet, I worried that seeing him would inspire the old affections I'd held for so many years. Daniel had been my first love and, until now, the only man with whom I had shared a bed. Perhaps it wasn't possible to completely ignore that my heart had been so accustomed to desiring him.

Although I now felt a strong affection for my husband.

A wave of heat flashed through me as I thought of Aedin's touch and I blushed, finding it incredible that I longed for the man I had resented for so many months.

Perhaps Andrea had been right—or was I just desperately longing for an intimacy I had lost?

"My lady," a manservant interrupted my thoughts. "Your guests are at the front."

Grinning in anticipation, I abandoned the remains of my breakfast and walked quickly to the front of the villa. The halls echoed with the sounds of horses and familiar voices. I nearly wept with gladness at the sight of a hunched, old man looking very out of place in the surrounding luxury.

"Father!"

Abandoning all civilities, I ran into his arms. His deep, coarse laugh brought tears to my eyes.

"Gwen! My Gwen… It's been a long time."

The familiar scent of sea salt and smoke was embedded in his furs and leather. It felt so good to be held.

When I pulled away, I saw my father's blue-gray eyes fill with tears. This was the longest I had ever been away from family. And what a relief it was to be reunited.

A thick, leathery hand caressed my cheek. "I've missed you."

I grasped his hand and kissed it. "And I you."

"Gwen?" another voice echoed, descending from the carriage. Through the beaming sunlight stepped a young man—nearly unrecognizable beneath the newly grown beard that decorated his chin.

"Ephraim?" I laughed incredulously. "Have you grown?"

He scooped me up and swung me around like a child—I shrieked with laughter, chiding him as he set me down.

"Look at this!" I petted his face with a giggle. "I didn't know it was even possible."

"Nor did I," Ephraim admitted with a wry grin, his blue eyes twinkling.

"You must come inside! How was your journey?" I studied both of them, sweating in their thick clothing.

"Father has had enough of boats." Ephraim eyed me with humor. "When I learned of the trip, I asked the king for permission to join and bring him along. I bought him passage to Radiance, and he joined us on the ship with Lord Tours' entourage."

"The constant swaying," Father growled. "I've had enough of boats for the rest of the year."

"Well you can stay with us for as long as you please," I said affectionately.

"You're lucky they didn't put you on a rowboat with all of your grumbling," Ephraim said, chortling. "The ship was magnificent—certainly the nicest I've ever sailed. We should journey with a lord more often."

"Well we only received word two days ago that you were arriving soon," I said. "And we are thrilled to have you stay with us."

"This place is beautiful," Ephraim murmured, suddenly aware of his surroundings.

"Come!"

We left their belongings with the manservant as I led them through the halls. They were slow, almost respectful, as they watched the passing courtyard garden through the arches.

The breeze exhaled through the hall, ruffling the furs on my father's shoulders. He raised his head to smell the air. "Flowers," he said, shaking his head with incredulity. "This must be paradise."

"It is quite nice," I said lightly. "We are very fortunate."

I led them to the sitting rooms and through to the balcony. They stared wordlessly for a moment at the view—my father carefully removed his furs and folded them onto a nearby chair. "You can see the ships…" he started, his eyes wide as he regarded the expansive sea. The rough linen of his simple shirt looked coarse and out of place.

"It's absolutely gorgeous here," Ephraim exclaimed, standing at the railing, then winced, pulling at the collar of his purple doublet. "Except for this heat." I noticed it bore the same insignia as the ship and the wax seal—the sign of the king.

I smirked. "You look dressed for a winter storm."

"And you look like you're wearing a nightgown," Ephraim countered with a wicked grin.

I shrugged. "This is the fashion on Lailan. It's much easier to breathe in sleeveless gowns than all that velvet and furs."

Ephraim laughed. "Yes, Lord Aedin certainly looked more comfortable than Lord Tours this morning."

"You saw Aedin?" I paused, frowning.

"Yeah." Father cleared his throat. "We saw him briefly as we were leaving the ship to come here. He gave us his carriage. Such kindness."

I smiled—of course Aedin would have offered.

And yet, I couldn't picture him socializing with my family. Granted, my brother was now initiated to the higher ranks of society in Radiance, but my father? I eyed his clothes and weathered face with an unfamiliar kind of pity and embarrassment. A shopkeeper from Berge socializing with the Lord of Lailan?

He had brought his finest furs, but they were a far cry from the opulent luxury that Ephraim and I had become accustomed to. The distinction of class had never been clearer—my father looked out of place in the villa. He watched everything with a sense of wonder and fragility.

Servants arrived bearing trays of wine and food. I felt a brief flash of shame as my father thanked them profusely, looking with childish admiration at the delicacies set before us. Subtly, I turned my gaze to Ephraim—we exchanged knowing glances.

"So how is Lord Aedin as a husband?" Ephraim asked loudly, directing the conversation away from the praises and thanks of our father. "You look well fed and cared for—glad to see he hasn't been starving you."

I glared at him. "Perhaps I have put on a bit of weight..."

"Oh hush, Gwen." Father eagerly tore a piece of bread, handing it to me. "You look beautiful."

"Thanks, but I just ate." I scowled at Ephraim's cheeky expression. "Lord Aedin has been very generous... I have want for nothing."

"That is a grand statement," muttered Ephraim with a wry grin.

Father didn't hear. He was delightfully spreading olive paste onto his bread and sampling the selection of cheeses. "My children have risen so highly," he said absent-mindedly. "Gwen, what d'you do, as a lady?"

I emitted a short laugh. "Well, other than eating, I have learned to read and write. I meet with friends for tea and parties occasionally; I spend time in the garden…" I paused. "And occasionally Aedin will let me spar with the guards."

Ephraim nearly spat out his wine. "He lets you *spar* with his guards?"

"Yes." I straightened defensively. "I might even be able to disarm you now."

My brother puffed up his chest. "Well we might have to settle this dispute later…"

"Swordplay ain't for women." Father eyed me warningly. "He shouldn't let you spar. What if you hurt yourself?"

"I won't hurt myself, Father," I sighed with exasperation. "Besides, it's the only physical activity available to me—I can't very well take a stroll around Tahuna."

"Why not?" Ephraim sipped his wine delicately, watching me with curiosity.

I shrugged. "Political enemies might try to hurt me… The island isn't the safest."

Father nodded. "Lailan has always been a lawless place—so much money and greed. It's good you watch out for yourself."

Ephraim snorted. "Lailan is the safest it's been since Lord Aedin took control—I've seen the reports. There's no reason you shouldn't be able to stroll outside those gates."

I ignored his words, eager to change subjects. "How is palace life, Ephraim?"

"Good." Ephraim set down his glass and reached for some bread. "Life in the palace is a constant delight, though occasionally stifling. Everyone has a connection to one another—it's like living in Berge but twice the size and with better wine."

"Any women?" I asked with a coy smile.

Ephraim made a sheepish face as Father spoke up, "Tell Gwen about Hollyn Litany."

"It's nothing," Ephraim protested, tearing off some bread.

"He's been courting her for the past month." Father's eyes twinkled. "Her father works for the Lord of Acedes."

"Oh really?" I gave Ephraim a wink and smile. "When shall the wedding be?"

Ephraim glowered. "Oh stuff it."

"Watch out—I'm a lady now." I pointed my finger at him dangerously. "I could have you beheaded."

"I'd disarm you first."

"I'd like to see you try!" I shot a challenging grin as he stuck out his tongue. I had missed my brother.

Ephraim let out a sound of satisfaction as he swallowed the bread. "This is delicious."

"And yes, you *are* welcome to eat all of our food," I said tartly, pouring myself a glass of wine.

"I'm sure you have enough." He winked at me, raising his glass. "To Lailan! Besides the heat—and our damned furs—this place is a haven in the Empire."

I grinned, clinking my glass with his.

We spent the rest of the morning and afternoon on the balcony, chatting away about inconsequential matters and catching up after months of being apart. It was refreshing to be amongst my blood—to be with others who had known me all my life. There was nothing to pretend—simply laughter, petty arguments, and conversation.

When they were full of food and wine, I gave them a tour of the villa and walked them through the gardens. As I showed them their rooms, my father touched the bed linen with wide eyes, and laughed at the indoor bathrooms. "Ye can't piss outside…"

Ephraim rolled his eyes and ambled into his room, easily situating himself.

I took the opportunity of being alone to freshen up. Wiping the sweat from the back of my neck, I opened the door to our bedroom and flinched in surprise.

Talia stood in the room, hastily stuffing closed the drawers of our wardrobe. She eyed me with surprise before bending quickly into a curtsy.

"What are you doing?" My voice was hollow.

"I was organizing my lord's drawers—" Her voice was steady and quick as she forced a smile. "Mary asked me to do it—there was quite a mess."

I wasn't sure how to respond. I recalled Aedin's words with a sinking feeling. "Are you spying on us?"

"What?" Her brown eyes were round—she laughed. "No. Why would I ever…?"

"Aedin told me about your family," I said quietly. "They don't exist."

Talia looked at me carefully. "I don't know what you mean," she said, and moved to leave.

"Talia—" I stopped her. She turned abruptly, her hand on the handle of the door to the antechamber. "Aedin is a good man," I said softly. "I don't know what you've been told… but I thought you should know."

Talia avoided my eyes and left. I heard her footsteps hurry down the hall as I sighed and closed the door.

I went to the wardrobe and dug through the drawers, finding the finely stitched shirts that Aedin never wore, the carefully folded black pants—and then my fingers pushed against the bottom and I felt something move. I lifted the lip of the drawer bottom and saw the gleam of steel neatly arranged in velvet.

I exhaled noisily and replaced the drawer bottom. I wasn't surprised. And then I remembered—I dug through my rows of hanging dresses, pressing against the space behind them. There was no familiar crunch of paper—the parchment scroll was gone.

Cursing audibly, I considered running after Talia—confronting her in the hall. I needed to alert Mary—or Aedin, whenever he returned. Perhaps I should investigate in the servant's quarters and steal it back—

I forced the panic from my mind and slowly closed the wardrobe doors. There was really nothing I could do—the parchment was gone. Getting into an altercation with Talia was the last thing I should do when the Rhidge were just outside. I only hoped that whatever was in it wasn't incriminating enough to get Aedin killed.

Going into the bathroom, I wet a towel and dabbed water on my face, trying not to smear the paint, then brushed back some hair that had loosened from my braid. I tried to smile at my reflection in the mirror. Everything would be fine—I couldn't let this ruin the day with Ephraim and my father.

When I exited to the hall, I didn't see Talia. A buzz of activity from passing servants preparing for the reception echoed through the halls and I spied a familiar form slouched against a column, basking in the garden sun.

I sat next to Ephraim on the bench and leaned back. He opened an eye lazily. "How do you get anything done here?"

"We don't usually start drinking so early," I said with a wry smile.

He grunted in response, closing his eyes again. The purple doublet was gone and he wore a fine linen shirt, the collar outlined in gold thread. Sweat glimmered on the pale skin of his throat.

"Is Father still resting?"

"Yes—I think he might have fallen asleep." Ephraim opened his eyes with a frown. "I probably could as well… Did you have anything planned for this afternoon?"

I shrugged and replied, "No. I thought you might want to rest before dinner and recover from your travels. The reception is tomorrow—we'll need to be on our best behavior."

"Indeed," A smile flickered across his lips and he scratched his short beard, staring at the dirt. "It's incredible to think how things have changed," he said pensively.

"I was thinking that earlier this morning."

He grinned carefully. "It's easy to be reminded with Father's presence… And it's funny how it was his decision to move forward with the match, and yet he has benefited from it least."

"It was never for him," I counseled softly. "It was for us. For our family."

Ephraim shrugged. "It's a shame. You know Lord Aedin offered him a position as an advisor under Lord Tremer?"

"No, I didn't know."

"Could you imagine?" He shook his head with a laugh. "An advisor to Lord Tremer. But Father declined—he only wanted to keep his shop."

"He is a simple man."

"No truer words have been spoken." Ephraim fell silent. Birdsong echoed through the wall of greenery surrounding us, accompanied by the trickle of the fountains.

"But you *are* doing well?" My brother eyed me seriously.

I fixed my lips, turning my gaze to the narrow leaves of grass beneath our feet. "It was trying—difficult, you could even say—at first. Lord Aedin is not the warmest individual." A brief sardonic smile tugged at my lips. "I was homesick and lonely. But it has been getting better… I have made friends, and Aedin and I… we are beginning to enjoy each other more."

Ephraim nodded, his face downcast. "I was so angry when he proposed," he confessed quietly.

"What?" I looked at him, aghast.

"I… didn't like the idea of you being married off to someone who had only met you for five minutes." He gave a harsh laugh, ruffling his hair. "Even if he *was* a lord. You and Daniel were attached at the hip, and I knew how heartbreaking that would be for you."

This was news to me. "I… I thought you completely agreed with Father—"

"No one could deny it was a good match for our family." Ephraim picked at a nearby plant. "But I argued with him in private—I didn't think it was right…"

"Ephraim." I touched his hand, leaning my head against his shoulder.

"I lost the argument—of course." He patted my hand. "But I feel more… at ease knowing that it all turned out for the better."

I remembered Aedin's words yesterday. "It did… and I am happy here."

As the words left my mouth, I realized they were true.

We sat in the garden and didn't speak for some time. His pale skin was flushed and I smiled at the memory of when my skin had also been pale and unaccustomed to the sun.

Among the music of the garden, we heard the ringing of steel on steel. Ephraim squinted in concentration. "Is that…"

"It's the guards," I advised. "They train every day around this time."

Ephraim looked at me in wry anticipation. "Well?"

"What?" I frowned.

"Why aren't you joining?"

I rolled my eyes. "Look at me." I gestured at my gown. "Not today—I can't."

"I can't believe he allows you," Ephraim muttered, shaking his head. "Only *you* would insist on continuing your training in sword fighting."

"*That* was hardly training." I nudged him. "It was playing with *you!*"

"I'll have you know that I've disarmed some very good men at the palace." Ephraim's brows lowered and as he looked at me, I laughed.

He stood suddenly—holding out his hand. "Let's go."

"You don't mean…" I looked at him dubiously.

"*Yes.*" Ephraim grabbed my hand assertively. "Let's go. There's little else to do here other than drink *more* wine."

"We shouldn't," I protested, reluctantly picking up my feet.

"Oh, come now." He eyed me playfully. "We won't get your gown dirty."

I swallowed a biting reply and forced myself to smile. "We can just watch." I walked him to the guards' quarters and down the path as the sound of their swords clashing grew louder.

It stopped seconds before we entered the circle. Tieren and William stood in mid-stride, watching us carefully. Ephraim grinned boyishly—I wondered how much wine he'd drunk.

"My lady," they said in unison and bowed.

"Tieren, William—this is my brother, Ephraim."

Tieren sheathed his sword and stepped forward to bow. "It is a pleasure to meet you, Ephraim." His brown eyes smiled warmly as William stood back, eying us with silent suspicion and doubt.

"Er—pleased to meet you." Ephraim ignored William, addressing Tieren. "Please, continue. We only came for diversion."

"Of course." Tieren grinned, carefully watching me. I was grateful he didn't offer me the sword.

He re-entered the circle and addressed William, holding out his blade. William met him with quick movements, disarming him within seconds.

Ephraim flinched at the intensity of their maneuvers but watched the scene with an indulgent smile. I looked around the property and saw the figure of a distant guard at the edge of the boundary watching us from afar, but no one else. It felt too deserted and quiet, and I wondered if the rest of the guards were in Tahuna with Aedin.

I forced myself to watch Tieren and William with an expression of bored detachment—although I wished to tear off my gown, throw on my boots, and join them. The dirt curled around their feet in the afternoon breeze, as they engaged again and again.

William clearly had the upper hand—although he was nearly a full head shorter, his feet moved effortlessly as he avoided Tieren's sword. His opponent's tall and lanky frame quickly grew tired, and Tieren was disarmed yet again.

"You need to move your feet," William said in his usual quiet voice.

Tieren shot an expression of exasperation at me as I stifled a laugh.

"Yes," he said to William, sobering as he faced him yet again. His thin arm held out the sword, and seconds later it was on the ground. Tieren cursed as Ephraim let out a slow clap.

"Incredible." He shook his head. "Where did you learn that?"

William paid no attention to Ephraim, watching Tieren wince as he picked up his sword. I grimaced as Ephraim coughed awkwardly.

Tieren faced William with reluctance, and then turned to Ephraim. "Would you care to try?"

"Yes!" Ephraim stepped forward as I said, "No—"

I withered under William's glare. "We have no time for games," he objected almost inaudibly as Tieren handed his sword to Ephraim with a grin—pleased at the prospect of rest.

Ephraim gripped the hilt with relish, waving the sword in the air. It reminded me of the comical move that Aedin had performed when we'd sparred last week.

I winced, looking at Tieren meaningfully. "Please don't kill my brother," I hissed at him.

"I won't—but I'm not sure about William," Tieren said easily, standing next to me. I hit him in the arm.

"Where is everyone?" I whispered as William watched Ephraim with a dull expression.

"Here." Tieren frowned at me. "Where did you think?"

I bit my lip. "Who is with Aedin?"

"No one—he went to the port alone."

"But Lord Tours—"

"It's usually best that he goes alone when meeting publicly with Tours. We need to stay here with you." He gave me a significant look.

I crossed my arms. Aedin could handle himself, but I hated the thought of him facing Tours and the Rhidge alone. "Do you know when he returns?" I asked finally.

Tieren shook his head, wincing as he watched Ephraim finally raise his sword to face William. "He's holding the hilt wrong—"

We made a face as William disarmed Ephraim within two seconds. Ephraim's brow furrowed as he bent to pick up his sword, bending at the knees in an athletic posture. William was impassive and relaxed.

Ephraim swung again—William casually side-stepped the stroke and placed the flat of his blade against Ephraim's waist. My brother ran his hand through his dark hair, shaking his head.

"Nice… effort," I offered lamely and Tieren choked back a laugh.

Ephraim ignored me and turned to face William again. This time, he didn't make any movements. They stood in the circle, watching each other as the breeze ruffled through their hair. I held my breath, wondering if anything was going to happen.

William finally sprung forward, and Ephraim batted away his sword, moving to the left. Then he backpedaled, circling William as he waited for the next blow. "That's one way to do it," Tieren muttered under his breath.

Ephraim's sword was outstretched and resting in the air. William feinted forward, making my brother stumble as he spun towards the right and tapped Ephraim's shoulder with his blade.

William exchanged a look with Tieren, who sighed. "Fine." He stepped forward, taking William's blade. William retreated to my side as Tieren took his place back in the circle across from Ephraim.

"I'm not worthy of the effort?" Ephraim asked Tieren teasingly.

Tieren grinned. "You'll have a better match against me." They began exchanging blows, slowly gaining rhythm.

I sighed, easing back further into the shade. William raised his eyebrows at me. "We might be here a while," I grumbled to him under my breath.

They sparred together in longer bouts. Tieren was more willing to give Ephraim a chance—leaving him openings and slowing his speed to match my brother's.

If Ephraim noticed, he didn't comment. But I saw the look of satisfaction on his face as he embraced the challenge of his opponent. I eventually sat on the ground and watched them from the dirt, becoming tired as the sun moved through the sky.

Long past the point at which I thought they would grow tired, I sighed and eased myself to my feet. My back felt tight after sitting on the ground. I moved my shoulders, wishing for release.

William suddenly looked at me with wide eyes.

I frowned, opening my mouth to ask what was wrong when Tieren also stopped, stepping away from my brother. He squinted at the villa, immediately tensing.

"My lady—" William began but was interrupted by the sound of a carriage rolling through the gates.

Relief washed over my face. "Has my lord returned?"

William grabbed my arm, putting his face close to mine. I saw fear in his brown eyes—he was frightened. "Stay. Calm," he hissed.

I pulled my arm away, unsettled by his words. Ephraim looked at William with apprehension. "Is everything alright?"

"Quite—" I was flustered at his immediate reaction but smiled playfully at my brother. "I think we have watched you spar long enough…"

"Yes," Tieren agreed quickly, sheathing his sword.

He held out his hand for Ephraim's blade, but Ephraim protested, "One more go!"

I looked at Tieren sympathetically. "I'm sure Tieren has had a long day—"

The echo of voices drifted through the halls. William was anxious, leaning on the balls of his feet, easing closer to my side.

"*One* more—" Ephraim held up his sword with a smile. "I insist." His enthusiasm reminded me of myself when I'd sparred with Aedin.

I saw the conflict in Tieren's face. He quickly unsheathed his sword and stepped forward, catching Ephraim off guard. Batting down Ephraim's attack, Tieren twisted my brother's sword with his own—whereupon Ephraim lost his grip and it clattered to the ground.

Tieren smirked. "There you go."

The voices grew louder—I didn't recognize them. I thought I heard my husband but wasn't sure.

Ephraim gingerly picked up his sword, tossing it to Tieren with a grumble, then wiped his forehead on his sleeve. "Please tell me *you* haven't disarmed him."

"What if I have?" I lifted my chin and gave a challenging smile. Ephraim snorted, throwing an arm around my shoulder; I cringed and wrinkled my nose at his ripe stench.

Footsteps sounded on the path as three men arrived at the circle.

Aedin squinted under the sun, the silver vines on his ceremonial doublet glittering. He stood next to an older man in a matching doublet with a thickly ornate chain bearing a dark purple, almost red, jewel. The color of blood. I stiffened in understanding, but they were not alone.

My heart thudded in my chest.

Next to them stood a tall handsome man with a sharp chin and brown eyes.

"My lords," Ephraim said in surprise, recovering himself before I had a chance to react. He removed his arm from my shoulder as he bowed in respect.

"Lady Aedin," Tours announced with satisfaction.

His face was younger than I had envisioned; his dark blonde hair was slicked back fashionably and his body bore few signs of advanced age. He was wearing a strange smile of satisfaction—his eyes were locked on my face, something like hunger alight in them.

Ever polite, Aedin held out his hand with an impassive expression. "Gwen, may I present Lord Tours of Radiance."

My mouth turned dry with fear. I forced a smile and summoned my courage, addressing Tours with a curtsy. "You have come so far—it is a pleasure to finally make your acquaintance."

Tours smirked. "We could not rest until we had made *your* acquaintance, my lady. We had heard so much about you—and I also understand that you know my assistant, Daniel Terrace."

I locked eyes with Daniel, shoving down any panic and putting on an impartial smile. "Yes, we have been acquainted," I said lightly.

Ephraim cleared his throat, stepping forward gallantly and extending his hand. "Glad to see you made it off the ship, Daniel."

Daniel's hair was longer than I remembered—his cheeks were clean-shaven and he smiled as if he wished he was elsewhere. "Yes—it is good to be on land again, Ephraim… Pleasure to see you again, my lady." He bowed in my direction.

Hearing the familiar voice sent hundreds of painfully sweet memories running through my mind. It was like hearing a much-loved song after years of its absence. Nearly every note was as I had remembered.

Daniel's eyes met mine with a keen and persistent stare, and I looked away.

I assessed Tours evenly—he could not have been more than twenty years Aedin's senior, and like Aedin, he was fit and confident. Yet where I had come to trust Aedin's disposition of serene composure, the same feeling did not exist with Tours.

Looking into Tours' wolfish gaze, I became aware of a vicious and lethal terror. On the surface, his thick mustache and sharp blue eyes were fashionable and attractive. But underneath there was a suggestion of something malicious and dark. A hairline crack that threatened to burst.

I finally understood what it was to look into the eyes of a Rhidge.

"It looks like you all were having a bit of fun," Tours observed lightly. "Nothing like a good spar."

"My brother was testing his skills with the sword, my lord," I responded with ease, smiling as if unperturbed. "Our guards were giving him a good bout of exercise."

Aedin moved slowly to stand by my side, his hands folded naturally behind his back. William edged away to make room, watching us with a stoic mask.

"It was a long journey—exercise sounds like a lovely idea," Tours agreed, placing his hand on the sword hanging from his side. "Did you have any success?" he addressed Ephraim.

"Unfortunately not, my lord." Ephraim grimaced. "I'm afraid that I might be out of shape..."

Tours gave a short laugh. "All that time spent sitting on the king's stool can make one slow." He turned to Daniel. "You were a guard for Lord Tremer—I hope that you are keeping up your skills."

"Yes, my lord," Daniel said with a gracious nod. "Whenever I have the time."

Tours eyed the scene with an amused look. "Well this could be very entertaining. Daniel, I suggest that you spar with Lord

Aedin. Did you know that he is skilled in the art of sword fighting?"

I felt Aedin stiffen. "Lord Tours, that is not necessary—"

"I insist," Tours said with the utmost grace as he withdrew his sword from his belt. It freed itself with a slick sound.

"Perhaps we should go inside and take some wine," I blurted quickly.

Daniel's eyes caught mine as he took the hilt. "I would be honored, my lord."

My stomach clenched at the look on Daniel's face. Eager bitterness to inflict pain.

He faced my husband with a galant bow. Aedin hadn't moved from my side.

My heart beat in my throat as I watched him appraise Daniel with resignation. As if he had been caught avoiding a dreaded chore.

Tours stared at Aedin in the tense silence—a challenge. My husband released a bitter sigh as he unsheathed the dagger from his belt and walked into the circle.

Ephraim grimaced, sauntering back to stand with me as we watched Daniel join my husband on the dirt. "This could end badly," he muttered to me.

I wasn't sure if he meant for Aedin or Daniel.

Daniel regarded Aedin's dagger with a smirk. He thought he had the upper hand.

Although comfortably ensconced in Palace life, it appeared that Daniel *had* been keeping up his training. His burly form towered several inches over Aedin as he stood confidently on strong thick legs.

Aedin seemed unconcerned—a bit bored and impatient—as he flipped the dagger in his hand. Despite knowing the hours he spent training with the guards, I couldn't conceal the flash of worry across my face.

I glanced at Tours. He moved forward, observing me coolly and crossing his arms. "Shall you place a bet?"

"No," I declined, demurely lowering my eyes.

"Your husband is quite proficient—I would bet on him," he advised loud enough for Daniel to hear.

I blushed, setting my lips and watching them. Aedin and Daniel stood alone in the circle—Daniel lifted his sword aloft while Aedin loosely held his dagger at his waist.

"Are you ready, my lord?" Daniel asked politely.

Aedin shifted his feet, his blade steady and waiting. "Yes."

Daniel moved first, stepping forward to issue a blow with impeccable technique, but Aedin tread back lightly, batting down the sword with a swipe of his dagger.

A frown formed on Daniel's face as Aedin moved from him and did not re-engage. He walked away, dagger at his side, waiting.

Bemused, Daniel stepped forward again, sword out, as Aedin sidestepped and, again, beat down his attack. The metal clanged noisily and Daniel almost dropped his sword at the strength of the hit.

Tours was grinning with pure joy.

Aedin watched Daniel regroup in silence, his face impassive.

After a brief, tense moment, Aedin feinted to the right—Daniel took the bait. With a block that seemed almost clumsy, Daniel's sword grazed the short length of the dagger with a horrid screeching noise. I noticed the quiet smile on my husband's face as he gave another feint, this time to the left.

I frowned—he was *playing* with Daniel.

The latter, however, did not seem to notice. Daniel wiped away the thin layer of sweat that had accumulated on his temple, his eager brown eyes focused on his opponent. His powerful legs weren't able to keep up with the agile steps of my husband.

Tieren and William watched smugly as Aedin graciously exchanged multiple blows, falling into the rhythm of traditional sparring. When they came close, Aedin let his dagger cleanly slice through the sleeve of Daniel's doublet without drawing blood.

I winced as Tours chuckled. "Play nice, Aedin," he crooned. "I do not want to have to find a new assistant."

Daniel zealously thrusted his sword in his opponent's direction. It did little to change the direction of the fight—Aedin parried his attempts with ease.

His skillful steps and light breath looked stark in contrast to Daniel's slow, heavy movements. Aedin twisted the dagger easily in his hand, patient as he waited for the next move and regarded Daniel with a soft, mocking smile.

In a fury of frustration, Daniel attacked, but each blow was parried and deflected. There was a moment when I thought Aedin had made a mistake—but he slipped beside Daniel's outstretched sword and placed the flat of his dagger at Daniel's throat.

Daniel froze at the touch of the metal and then sagged to catch his breath.

Aedin stepped back with a courteous nod and replaced the dagger at his waist. He looked at Tours, his expression suddenly cold. "Shall we move inside?"

Tours' mouth twitched. "Thank you for that performance." He bowed at Aedin as my husband extended his hand to me. I walked quickly to take it, looking back to see Ephraim clapping Daniel on the shoulder as we left the circle.

Aedin gripped me tightly, allowing his bored mask to drop and reveal a look of frustration and annoyance as we ascended the steps. "Completely unnecessary," he muttered under his breath.

"You are a dear friend, allowing me that *one* pleasure." Tours' voice echoed in the passage as he followed us into the hall. "So restrained and polite—you could have killed him within a second."

My husband did not respond to the bait, and I kept silent, focusing my breath on every step and enjoying the cool stillness of the hall.

We gathered on the balcony for wine and idle chat. My father joined us, and shortly after Tours and Daniel left for a dinner with Cabot.

It was a relief to see them go—I had restrained my speech and was uncomfortable with the presence of them both. Daniel kept trying to catch my gaze as Tours baited me into another uncomfortable discussion. Even Aedin visibly loosened as they exited the courtyard and were seated in their carriages.

"I'm sorry," he murmured as we ambled slowly back to dine with Ephraim and my father.

I touched his arm, not knowing what to say.

"He loves to provoke things." Aedin gave an exasperated sigh, running his hand through his hair. "And insisted on coming after the meeting. I just didn't see a way to prevent it…"

When I was silent, Aedin stopped in his tracks, watching me with guarded eyes. "Are you angry with me?"

"No," I said, taking his hand. "It wasn't your fault."

He grimaced and I kissed his cheek. "I didn't want to spar with Daniel," he protested quietly.

I couldn't help but emit a low laugh. "I *know* you didn't."

Aedin's hand came up to brush my cheek. He eyed me carefully and asked, "You don't… Do you still care for him?"

If I had said no, I would have been lying.

The knot in my stomach twisted as I fought to choose words that would console him or clarify my reality. It felt impossible to never feel something for Daniel, though his presence in my mind was slowly diminishing in significance.

And yet, the past days had revealed a future I had never considered. With a deep attachment for a man that had gambled the securities of his life on the chance to save me. On an island that we ruled in peace and prosperity.

And in a home I was growing to love.

Though the risk of discovery and ruin was great, a resounding calm had finally settled in my bones. I knew my place in this world and I knew that I would continue on this path with Aedin beside me.

Finally, I stared into Aedin's eyes and whispered, "You are my future."

He slowly bent his head and kissed me in the middle of the hallway.

Chapter Twenty-One

A COLD SWEAT covered Tours' body as his eyes snapped open.

The room rocked imperceptibly with the harbor waves as his blood ran thick and wild, moonlight shining through the glass. His forehead was damp, his arms sticky, caught underneath the thick sheets.

Heart pounding, Tours sat up, dabbing at his cheek with the sleeve of his nightshirt. It didn't help. Cursing the heat, Tours swung his legs over and sat up, pouring himself a glass of water.

The faces echoed in his mind as he calmed his breath. He had Dreamed—this had been the second one in the past year.

The first time had been well over a decade ago, when he had Dreamed of becoming Director. It would have been the natural progression regardless, but the Dream had solidified his promising future in the Rhidge.

And the second—his Dream of the present—had been a crucial key to securing their last line of defense. Without it, Aedin would have had a chance for escape should he ever flee. But now… now they were prepared.

Tours was not a man to dismiss a sequence of events, especially pivotal events such as the Dreams. They were not inconsequential. They meant something. The Gift was never random.

Something was about to happen.

Tours considered his Dream of the past. It had disturbed him.

He had been in an unfamiliar place—no, it had been Lailan, but it was a vastly different Lailan than he now knew. The houses had been smaller, the clothes a bit more rural and rugged, and there had been fire everywhere.

Flames that leaked onto the docks, swallowed the houses and fields, bringing a terrible scent. Burning flesh, hair, sugar cane, wood… It had been a scene of chaos—men and women with swords butchering nearly everyone in their path.

At the shore had stood a tall man—the fire reflecting in his unfeeling eyes. Tours had watched as he carelessly drew an "R" in the sand with his foot. Something had triggered in the back of Tours' mind as the scene unfolded—this man was Lord Rhidge.

Tours was not a man to be put off by senseless brutality—often he was the perpetrator of such actions. To be Director of the Rhidge was to bear responsibility for the upholding of terror and strength amongst their numbers.

Yet even something inside of him had quaked at the scene within his Dream.

Usually, the bloody work of the Rhidge was performed in silence, in secret. Quiet assassinations of unruly council members —the occasional poisoning of a dishonest lord. The drowning of a Gifted woman as she attempted to escape. They were singular works of murder—never more than a few at a time. They wanted no witnesses—the Rhidge never left a trace.

But the events within the Dream had the opposite intent. Lord Rhidge had wanted to create a scene of mass confusion and physical violence. He had not taken the route of subtlety but aimed for panic and horror.

The violence Tours had witnessed in the Dream—although it had occurred centuries ago—sent a stroke of terror tingling down his spine, mingling emotions of disgust and respect directed towards the shadow of Lord Rhidge as Tours contemplated the memory. He had commanded and established an ingeniously horrific solution to establishing control of the Empire… but at such a price.

Tours watched the moon from the small window with a rare, quiet thoughtfulness. He wondered whether his mark on the Rhidge would glorify himself for decades to come—or would he simply fade into oblivion like the hundreds who had died nameless for the cause?

There was no family name to succeed him—no familiar companions, for those were too dangerous to keep. After his death —or when he was too old to perform his duties and "relinquished honorably"—another would take his place. Just as had occurred for centuries upon centuries.

Yet he considered these ideas with an impartial efficiency. There were still things to be done—his life was merely a side note in the larger journey towards power and domination. The power and domination of the Rhidge and the Empire. There was nothing else to be accomplished.

Knowing that the day ahead would be long and arduous, he considered falling back asleep but instead found it more necessary to compile a list of all that should be done. The reception would be quite revealing—Tours traced the lip of the glass in his hand. Despite all that he had heard and seen concerning Gwyneth Aedin, he knew that there was still something missing. There was something that did not connect Aedin's intent and with his actions. Even after meeting her at the villa, Tours was still plagued with this absence.

What was it? Why had Aedin married her?

Tours had posed that question to Aedin yesterday morning, when they had sat alone in the dining room of the ship, the sun rising steadily above the horizon.

Aedin had shrugged. "I love her."

Tours had responded with a ridiculing laugh. "One sight of her face and you were sold?"

"You could put it that way, yes."

There had been something unmoved in Aedin's face as he'd stared at Tours. A kind of defiance… and Tours had grown angry.

"The king and I were not pleased to hear that you had done this without our knowledge."

"What did it matter? Her family is of no consequence."

"You are Rhidge—your priorities are to your king and empire," Tours had growled. "I do not want a Rhidge with divided priorities."

"My priorities are in alignment with that of the Rhidge."

"Then if I asked you to dispose of her, would you obey me?"

Tours had folded his hands, watching Aedin from across the table.

The latter had fiddled with his fingers as he attempted not to break Tours' gaze.

"She is not Gifted."

"I don't bloody well care what's in her veins. If I asked you to dispose of her, would you obey?"

A thick, strong silence had ensued, before Aedin responded quietly, "Yes."

Tours did not believe him. Aedin had been putting on an act ever since he'd dared to bring that girl into the villa. The king didn't buy it either, but as long as he was receiving his quarterly payments of gold he saw no reason to get rid of a trusted lord.

But Tours knew that the stakes were higher than the gold in the king's pocket. And the king was a fool. He was growing old and irrelevant and would soon die of the sickness that had plagued him for years.

Tours forced himself to put away his doubts about Aedin and focused on the day to come.

When the sun rose, he called Bela to his room. She entered quietly and shut the door, assessing him with pitiless brown eyes.

Tours twirled a dagger in his hand, mindlessly spinning it as he watched her stand in the corner.

"Tell me," he commanded.

"There are twelve guards, no more," she began in a low voice. "All are Gifted. Six walk the perimeter changing watch every five hours. Three are stationed throughout the villa, two at the gates, and one in the garden outside of their rooms."

Tours nodded, digesting this information. "And has Aedin strayed off course?"

"No, he has either been with you or in the villa."

"And what of Lady Aedin?"

"She spent yesterday with her father and brother—remaining inside the villa at all times."

"Anything to report?"

"Nothing." Her short black hair swung as she shook her head. "She is… unremarkable."

The dagger in Tours' hand became still. "Are you sure?" he asked.

"Yes," Bela replied, confidently lifting her chin.

Tours pursed his lips in frustration. There had to be something. "Very well. I want you all surrounding the perimeter throughout the night. We expect there to be about a hundred persons in total—primarily socialites or nobles from Lailan. Some of our people will be in attendance. They can be an extra pair of eyes inside the reception."

Bela inclined her head in understanding.

"Aedin should not leave the villa for any reason tonight. I want you *all* to keep an eye on him." Tours pointed his finger at her. "He may be Rhidge but never assume—always doubt. I want to know his every move for the rest of the week. Notify me immediately if he leaves."

"Yes, Director."

Tours thoughtfully smoothed his mustache. "Did you watch the two guards as they sparred yesterday?"

"Yes, I did." She shifted her weight, fidgeting under his gaze.

"What did you think?"

"Tieren is weak. William has potential."

"It may be time to finally claim our reward," Tours said softly.

"Only a few are worthy of our attention." Bela's hand brushed the hilt of the sword at her hip. "Most are disposable."

"They are well trained," Tours suggested.

"Their temperament is not suitable for the Rhidge," Bela said brusquely. "They are soft and old."

Tours sighed. "It is just such a waste…"

"If they are useless to us, they are better off dead."

"You are right," Tours conceded. "I've always admired your ruthless practicality."

Bela did not smile. Her mouth was set in a firm line as she watched him. "Was there anything else?"

"No." Tours waved his hand as she exited furtively.

He gazed out the small window at the port of Tahuna, watching the line of ships docked at the harbor. The water sparkled under the morning sun. Wishing for fresh air, Tours sheathed his dagger and left the room.

Emerging from the belly of the ship, he found the top deck busy with activity. Rowboats were hoisted on pulleys, disembarking passengers from the port. A line of people waited to refill the boats. He spied a familiar mess of brown hair, itching in the queue to return to land.

Tours clapped Daniel on the shoulder. "Where are you off to?"

Daniel winced at his touch. "I need a drink."

"Ah." Tours grinned. "I can help with that."

With a hand on his shoulder, Tours steered him out of the line and towards a chair on the deck. Daniel sat reluctantly, looking out at the waves with a slightly nauseous expression.

Tours pulled a flask from the pocket of his pants, uncorking the bottle and handing it to him. "Drink up."

Daniel sniffed. "What is it?"

"Does it matter?"

He shrugged and took a swig, his face puckering as the alcohol slid down his throat. "I was h-hoping for more of an a-ale," Daniel said, coughing.

"This gets the job done quicker." Tours took back the flask and swallowed a mouthful for himself. He relished in the sharp bite of the liquid.

Daniel suppressed another cough, an expression of anxiety crossing his face. "I've been thinking about tonight, and I'm not sure if you need me there…"

"Of course I do." Tours looked at him incredulously. "You are my assistant. I thought you would enjoy the trip and the Berge reunion—you seemed to have gotten on well with Ephraim and Doyle on the ship."

"They are old friends," Daniel protested, "but Gwen—"

"*Lady* Aedin," Tours corrected with a knowing smirk.

"Lady Aedin," Daniel said the words while staring bitterly at the empty horizon. "It is still strange to see her after all these months… and married."

Tours watched Daniel's expression with satisfaction. He enjoyed seeing the gradual wave of emotions escalate, threatening to crash. His performance at the sparring match yesterday had been dismal, and he was sure the boy's confidence had been shaken.

If Tours had to admit it, he was dragging the boy along simply for the humor of watching Gwyneth Aedin ridiculed by the presence of an ex-lover. Perhaps it would disturb Aedin, or force something from Gwyneth's past to come to light.

"You have had women since her—what is she compared to all the beauties in Radiance?" Tours said lightly, folding his hands.

Daniel's lips screwed into a painful grimace. "She's different. She wasn't just for a night or two."

"Women are all the same." Tours patted Daniel on the shoulder in mock affection. "If you do not use them, they will use you. Look at you! Whining like a boy still pining for his first love. If she had truly loved you, she would have stayed with you."

"She didn't have a choice," Daniel protested weakly, shading his eyes from the sun.

"There is always choice," Tours corrected firmly. "And Gwyneth Aedin made hers. And it was a foolish one, if you ask me."

Daniel looked up, confused. "She married a lord—"

"She married into a lifetime of domestic servitude and possible early death. The lordship of Lailan is constantly changing hands—what's to say that she lasts the year?"

"You mean…" His young assistant's face paled. "You don't mean—"

"It is our little secret." Tours grinned, his blue eyes soft and dangerous. "The king is not satisfied with Lord Aedin's performance. If he goes, then she is bound to follow."

It was the threat that always hung over Aedin's head, but Daniel took the words as truth and looked troubled.

"I don't *want* her to die, even if she has hurt me…"

"No, no." Tours made a face of concern. "Nor do *I*, for that matter. But it would be best if it came from you, possibly, to advise her to control her husband. Lord Aedin is a dangerous man—he is selfish and crooked. And even though you have *every* right to hurt or deceive her, just as she has done to you, I know you care about her… You are needed there tonight."

Daniel stood up with grim resolution, brushing back his hair in the wind.

"That's a good lad." Tours patted his back and handed him the flask. "One final drop?"

Daniel took the flask and threw back the drink.

Tours was satisfied to see it went down smoothly this time.

Chapter Twenty-Two

"THERE WILL BE nearly a hundred here tonight, don't you think?"

"I hope not," I admitted to Ephraim, biting into my toast.

The next morning, we ate breakfast on the balcony—a rare occurrence. Even more unusual, Aedin had joined us. He sat beside me, our knees touching as we watched the sea sparkle in the morning light.

"It will, unfortunately, be a grand affair," Aedin said with a heavy sigh. "I have never been one for large gatherings such as these, but they are necessary on occasion."

"I find them delightful," my father spoke up, sipping his tea. "All the beauty, the gowns and doublets, an' finery—"

"And the food and drink," Ephraim added quickly. "That's the best part."

"I would have thought that you had drunk your fill last night." I quirked my eyebrows at Ephraim. "The stewards told me this morning that our stocks are unfortunately low for tonight."

"Ha." Ephraim shot me a quick glare.

"We ordered extra barrels for tonight in anticipation of your attendance," Aedin said, his face expressionless. I coughed a laugh as Ephraim looked incredulously at my husband.

"I didn't mean to give the impression—"

"It was a joke, Ephraim," I clarified, sneaking a look at Aedin. A small grin twitched on the corners of his mouth.

"And how are you feeling this morning?" I looked pointedly at my brother.

He grimaced, rolling his shoulders. "To tell the truth—a bit sore…"

"You should train more." I buttered another slice of toast. "The palace has made you soft."

Ephraim looked offended. "It's not *me*—it's your guards." He brandished his fork at Aedin. "They are too good with the sword."

"Too good," Aedin repeated, raising his eyebrows.

"Yes," Ephraim insisted. "Did *you* train them? Yesterday with Daniel…" He eyed me cautiously. "Well it was a bit of an embarrassment for our dear Daniel."

"It was," I agreed with a wince.

Aedin shrugged, sipping his tea. "He has skill, but he relies too much on appearance. It doesn't matter what you look like when you spar—only that you can wield a sword."

Ephraim chortled through his salted meat.

The cry of gulls echoed from the harbor. I shooed away a small bird that was lurking under my chair, pecking at the crumbs from my toast.

Following Aedin's gaze, I watched Tours' ship in the distance. A shiver ran down my spine as I thought of his ruthless gaze. Aedin's hand came to mine as he looked away and down again at his meal.

"Is there anythin' to be done today to prepare?" my father asked, looking expectantly at my husband. "Can we help in any way?"

"Thank you, Doyle, but the servants, Gwen, and I have everything prepared for the evening," Aedin said kindly. "You and Ephraim may do as you please. Perhaps Ephraim can continue his training this morning."

Ephraim shook his head vigorously. "I would rather read a book with a glass of wine."

"Then you are welcome to do so." Aedin waved his hand graciously.

After we finished eating, Ephraim and my father went to tour the gardens. Aedin walked beside me as we strolled down the halls.

"Will you go into Tahuna today?"

He shook his head. "No, we covered nearly everything yesterday." Aedin paused, his brow furrowing. "He is concerned and suspicious... I would like you to avoid interacting with him as much as possible."

"Still?" My lips twisted in worry.

Aedin did not respond until a passing servant was out of earshot. "He has been continually hounding me as to why I married you. I've tried to pass it off as a hopeless love, but he can see through the lie..."

I tried to lighten the mood. "You're not hopelessly in love with me?"

Aedin's stride faltered, realizing the implication of his words. "I didn't mean for it to sound as if I don't care about you..."

"I know," I reassured him, taking his hand. "Don't worry, I'm not hopelessly in love with you either."

Aedin admitted a small grin, pressing his lips to my hand as we neared the guards' quarters.

"I have to tell you," I said, lowering my voice. "I found Talia in our rooms yesterday—she was rummaging in the wardrobe. Your scroll is gone."

Aedin absorbed this information with a reluctant sigh. "That is... unfortunate news."

"I'm sorry." I squeezed his hand, looking guiltily at the stone floor. "It was for my sake that you didn't dismiss her earlier."

"Well." Aedin emitted a dark chuckle. "It is a loss, but the notes are the least incriminating evidence at this point." He gave me a meaningful look.

"Isn't there anything we can do to convince Tours otherwise?"

"No." Aedin gave me a sideways glance. "The only thing we *can* do is maintain an image of composure and loyalty. If we deprive Tours of a reason to kill us, then he has to let us alone."

I considered his words in silence, until a thought suddenly occurred. "Aedin, we can't keep this up forever."

Aedin's head hung heavy as he admitted thickly, "I know."

"What will we do when the time comes?"

Aedin paused before the door to the guards' quarters and looked at me with finality. "We will head east."

He pushed open the door and all the guards stood to attention. I surveyed their faces—behind their masks of courage there was anxiety and fear. Aedin strolled into the room with an infectious confidence, clasping his hands behind his back as he regarded the men before him.

"Tonight we will have some challenges before us," he began. "As you have felt and seen, three Rhidge have set up camp on our perimeters. They are undoubtedly watching and listening—keep a closed mouth and open ears. There is no reason why they should kill or capture you—unless they kill or capture myself and Gwen… then you should worry."

Tieren's face broke into a brief, grim smile. Our eyes met, and he sobered.

"I want you all to know…" Aedin paused, his eyes running over his men. "I want you to know how much confidence I place in each and every one of you. And I thank you for the trust you have placed in me. I hope I will not fail you. If anything happens tonight that is a cause for concern, Gwen and I will be taking the boat on the eastern shore of the island. If we leave, help to defend the servants and your own lives… But death is better than what awaits you in the Rhidge.

"Marks, I want you in charge of the guards this evening—I will unfortunately be tied up with Tours and my duties as a lord. Alert Gwen or myself if the Rhidge draw nearer or they grow in number. Tours has given us permission to be visible and on duty tonight, so do not bother with secrecy."

Aedin looked at me. "Gwen, do you have anything to add?"

All eyes shifted towards me as my mouth ran dry. "Yes," I said rather hesitantly. "I would like to reiterate our sincere gratitude. I have greatly appreciated all that you have done for myself and Aedin… Thank you."

There was a brief murmur of response from the guards before Aedin nodded to them and they dispersed. Hand in hand, my husband and I returned to the brightness of the hall and closed the door.

———

Hours later, I was bathed, dressed, and painted for the evening. Aedin was conferring with Mary. The kitchen was clouded with steam, the cooks yelling commands that could be heard even in the dining room.

The halls of the villa were decorated with flowers, elegant drapes, lit torches, and crystal chandeliers that hung from the ceiling. It was all quite ostentatious.

My father and I sat on the balcony, nursing a bottle of wine as we relished the last moments of calm before the storm.

"Your mum would be so proud," Father said quietly, his pale eyes staring at the ocean as the sun sank down towards the horizon.

My glass stopped halfway to my lips. "Thank you, Father," I managed to say.

I was surprised—he hardly mentioned my mother out of the pain of loss. She'd died when I was very young—although I could recall glimpses of her face, she was more of a ghost to me than the memory Ephraim and Father held.

"I remember the day she died." Father's gnarled hands swirled his wine. "The fishermen came to say that she'd drowned —they'd found her body the next morning." He shook his head. "The gods only know what she was doing out on a boat that early in the morning. Such a tragedy."

His face struck me more than his words. There were pangs of loneliness and regret etched in the lines on his face. I reached out to squeeze the hand that trembled on his thigh.

"You have Ephraim and me..." I tried to sound hopeful or soothing.

My father nodded, blinking back tears as he looked at me. "Yeah... Yeah I do... But there is nothing like losing your other half. Life is much lonelier now, without a partner to spend it with."

His eyes turned to me with a sudden urgency. "Don't lose him. Trust me, Gwen. Don't lose him."

"I won't, Father," I said with solemnity, the significance of his words beating into my breast.

"Ready, I see," Ephraim's chipper voice interrupted us.

I withdrew my hand from Father, but Ephraim saw the glassy look in his eyes and made a face.

"He's been talking about Mum, hasn't he?" he muttered as he sat next to me on the couch.

I nodded, my lips thinning in sadness.

"He's been doing that lately when he drinks," Ephraim said under his breath, pouring himself a glass, "ever since you left." He raised his voice. "Father, shall we toast to a night full of mischief, revelry, and amusing diplomacy?"

My father's expression brightened slightly as he raised his glass and drank deeply. The wine passed through my lips with a pleasurable sensation. It was rich, bitter like dark honey, and satisfying.

"Your outfit is quite fine." I gestured towards Ephraim's dark purple doublet, which was lined in golden brocade.

He shifted uneasily under the tight fabric. "I think the last historian was a bit smaller."

"Or you've been indulging too much."

"At the palace? Never. We are all somber as hermits." Ephraim smiled cheekily through his beard.

"That is amusing," Aedin stated as he strolled through the door, joining us on the balcony.

"My lord." Father reached for an empty glass, "Wine?"

"Yes, please—I can do it." Aedin, thankfully, took the glass from my father's shaking hands and emptied the bottle. "Perhaps another." He gestured to a servant inside the door.

"Well, you look more noble than I," Ephraim commented, smirking at Aedin's outfit.

It did look a bit ridiculous—he wore his usual ceremonial black doublet outlined in silver vines, but his arms were ensnared in the most fashionable puffy sleeves. Around his neck hung a thick silver chain bearing the large, light blue stone of Lailan.

Aedin took a large swig from his glass. "I stopped Mary at the pants, or else I wouldn't have been able to walk." He motioned towards Ephraim's legs, which were tightly swathed in a velvet-like cloth. "It's a death trap, honestly."

Ephraim nodded. "You'd better watch out—you could kill someone with that stone around your neck."

"Perhaps I—" Aedin looked at me and stopped the retort from exiting his mouth. He glanced behind him, fidgeting. "The first guests should be arriving within the hour. Gwen, are you ready?"

"Shall we be at the front to welcome everyone?"

"Afraid so." Aedin gave an unsympathetic look. "But just for the first part." He paused. "You look quite lovely."

Color rose into my cheeks at Aedin's words. "Thank you," I said, meeting his eyes with a smile. Mary had dressed me in a pale cerulean silk dress that tied with a large bow around my waist. The thin straps bared my shoulders and back and the silk cascaded down my hips to form a grand train that, thankfully, wasn't unmanageable. The whole outfit, including the paint and the diamond hairpins, made me feel the significance of my position.

"You look like a lady." Ephraim smiled at me. "Quite suited to this lifestyle."

I gave a short laugh. "At least it hasn't gone all to my head just yet."

"Yet," Ephraim added in agreement.

———

Only a short time later, Aedin and I stood at the front of the villa, watching as each carriage queued to allow its inhabitants to disembark. I knew most and greeted each with the same civil smile and nod as they curtsied and bowed before us.

It was just as I had anticipated—guests had come adorned in their best silks, jewels, and smiles. Francesca and Gerand de Bough simpered and beamed under the torchlight. I greeted Andrea and Catherine with warm embraces, as Aedin smiled thinly at some of the merchants from Tahuna. After nearly an hour, my face felt frozen in a placid smile and my feet ached from standing.

The sound from inside the villa was unlike anything I had heard before in its tranquil halls. A cacophony of chatter, laughter, clinking of glass, and the steps of heeled feet. I turned to see Tieren and William surveying the crowd with contrasted expressions of solemnity and anxiety. They were still; like two columns paired on either side of the entryway.

Feeling Aedin's hand on the small of my back, I turned towards the front, where a large black carriage had ground to a halt.

A footman dressed in purple velvet pulled down the steps and Tours disembarked.

Behind him, descending from the carriage in a similarly graceful fashion, was Daniel. His long hair was freshly washed, and he was clothed in a fine tunic of green silk. My breath caught as I saw his familiar lithe form straighten before us, his eyes immediately fixed on my gown and face.

"It has been too long." Tours grinned at Aedin as Daniel bowed, murmuring, "My lord… my lady."

"Lord Tours." Aedin bowed low and inclined his head politely at Daniel, "Mr. Terrace."

"Lady Aedin—you look ravishing." Tours reached out a hand. Tentatively, I placed mine in his and he bent to kiss it. I noticed Aedin tense out of the corner of my eye. "Your beauty has not faded since yesterday."

"You are too kind, my lord." I curtsied as he released me. Attempting to force all insecurities from my mind, I shoved a civil smile on my face.

"Would you care for a drink?" Aedin said shortly, gesturing into the halls where servants wandered with trays of food and wine.

"Would you mind escorting me inside?" Tours countered, staring wolfishly at Aedin. My husband ducked his head in acknowledgement and the two picked up wine glasses and disappeared into the hall.

My heart thudding ominously, I turned back to Daniel, who stood awkwardly on the steps.

"Please." I moved to the side. "Come in."

"Thank you." Daniel wandered into the hall, picking up a glass of wine from the tray. He handed one to me, and I thanked him.

Quietly, I gave my glass to Tieren, who took a quick sip, before returning it with a nod. Daniel watched this in quizzical silence.

"How are you?" he asked after a long pause. I realized that we had hardly spoken to each other directly since becoming reacquainted.

"Fine, thank you." I swirled the wine around my glass. Its color was reminiscent of the stone around Tours' neck. "How is working for Lord Tours?"

Daniel paused, considering his answer. "Engaging and challenging. But beneficial."

"Beneficial?"

"Well, socially. He basically runs the palace. I would not be surprised if he supersedes the king."

"That would be treason," I said slowly. "The king is only superseded by his son."

Daniel shrugged. "Just an observation. Tours is a man who gets what he wants."

"But he is loyal to the king."

Daniel gave me a sidelong look of condescension. "Each man is loyal only to himself."

"To a certain extent," I acquiesced after a pause.

He scanned the crowd. "This is a lovely party. It is kind of you and Lord Aedin to have opened your home for this affair."

"Thank you," I scoffed, "but I think we had little choice in the matter."

"Gwen—" Daniel stopped, regarding me with hesitation. "I mean, my lady, I wanted to warn you…"

"Of what?" I lowered my voice as we walked to a quieter part of the hall.

"Lord Tours," Daniel began, fidgeting with his glass, "he is… not pleased with Aedin and suspects his disloyalty to the king."

"Disloyalty?" I repeated dubiously. "In what way?"

"He hasn't spoken of any specifics to me personally, but I'm sure he has his reasons. If Aedin is suspected of treason and removed, then you are certain to follow…"

"I understand that perfectly," I said slowly, watching Daniel, surprised of his concern. "But Lord Aedin is innocent. I know many have slandered his name, but they are false rumors. I appreciate your concern… but we are completely loyal to the king and the Empire."

Something like relief washed over Daniel's expression. "That is good to hear. I wouldn't want you to…"

"Die?" I suggested.

Daniel gave a half-smile, changing the subject. "It's refreshing to see Ephraim so often, now that he's working as the king's historian."

"Yes, he finds the work challenging, I think."

"I also hear that he is courting—"

"Hollyn Litany, yes."

There was a brief pause where neither of us knew what to say. Unfortunately, we were saved by an intrusion.

"I see, my lady, you have found your old friend."

Kitra Devereux emerged from the crowd in the inner courtyard to curtsy before me. Her pale hair curled down her back as her wide lips simpered.

"Miss Devereux." I nodded to her. "I believe you remember Mr. Daniel Terrace."

"Indeed. It is a pleasure again." Daniel bowed low.

"Please excuse me." I left them abruptly and quickened my steps towards the crowd of people, hoping to find better company and eager to escape the demons of my past.

"My lady." An arm snaked around my waist as I passed by.

"Oh hush," I said lowly, sighing in relief as I caught my brother's eyes. "You saw?"

"Oh yes." He raised his eyebrows. "How was it?"

"Awkward." I shook my head. "After all this time."

"I'm sure."

Sipping my wine, I asked, "Have you seen Aedin?"

"Over there." Ephraim gestured with his glass to a corner of the large courtyard where Aedin was standing with Tours and an unknown merchant. The trio looked serious and deep in discussion. Tours looked up suddenly, catching my eye before I turned away.

"That looks even more awkward," I muttered to Ephraim. "When will this *end*?"

"Just relax!" Ephraim clinked his glass against mine. "Have another drink. Festivities should be light-hearted and amusing."

"Why do they never turn out that way?" I protested, taking a large gulp of wine.

We meandered further inside, where I gratefully found Catherine and Andrea seated on the couches with a large group of women. Meeting my eye, Andrea scooted to the side and patted the seat beside her.

"There you are." She shot me an annoyed look. "That we should come to *your* house and not talk to you at all!"

I rested my head on her shoulder. "I am tired of parties."

Catherine looked concerned "But we have only just arrived."

"Chin up," Andrea ordered. "What happened?"

"Do you remember Daniel Terrace?" I said in a low voice as they leaned forward eagerly.

Andrea's hand flew to her mouth. "Not *here*?"

"I left him chatting with Kitra." I drank my wine with a tragic expression as Catherine giggled.

Andrea groaned. "But I am now *engaged*… Please tell me he is not as handsome as you remember?"

I gave her a sidelong glance that said otherwise and she pouted.

"Girls… my lady." Francesca eased into the circle, perching herself on a small strip of the couch. "Are you aware that a certain *gentleman* is here?" She eyed me knowingly.

I shot her a withering look. "Daniel Terrace?" I said plainly.

"Yes, we know," Andrea added shortly.

Francesca looked disappointed but quickly recovered. "He is quite handsome, is he not?" She motioned to a nearby group.

Daniel stood chatting with a merchant, his chiseled face soft in the candlelight.

I sighed. "So the word appears to be spreading."

Andrea eyed him with frustration and turned back to me. "Well at least you had good taste."

"He has been eying you for quite some time." Francesca winked at me.

"We exchanged words earlier but have not really spoken since… my marriage," I admitted. "It was quite an abrupt goodbye."

"I can imagine," murmured Francesca. "I had an old beau before Gerand. Lovely man—and we… kept in touch during the first years of my marriage." She gave us a knowing gaze.

Andrea giggled. "You did not!" she exclaimed, as Catherine looked aghast.

"We all do." Francesca waved her hand around the room. "Men have their secrets—why can we women not also keep some for ourselves?"

"Yes, why not," Andrea mused, watching me. Daniel caught my gaze mid-conversation with an older gentlemen. We both blushed.

"I would… never…" I said haltingly.

"Oh, we all begin marriage with such high and lofty ideals." Francesca grinned conspiratorially. "But when reality sets in, it can be difficult to choose which ones to hold on to. It is not such a bad thing to have a distraction, but do not let it deter you from your ultimate goal. Once I had children, I gave it all up and focused on raising them and supporting Gerand. It brought us closer, you know."

I nodded. "I can imagine that… as well as the opposite."

She laughed heartily. "I suppose that is a possibility as well."

Catherine gave us a look of disapproval. "But honoring the ideals of a marriage is a true and noble aspiration. Otherwise, there is no need for the institution."

Andrea snorted. "Marriage is a business contract. *That's* the only reason it exists." Andrea pointed at Catherine's swollen stomach as she covered her bump protectively.

"I should like to take a lover," Andrea sighed. "Francesca—do you know of any men who might oblige?"

"You're not even married!" Catherine hissed. "Perhaps you might not need one!"

"It doesn't hurt to explore the market," Andrea said impartially, taking a drink from her glass.

Daniel's conversation ended and I watched him moved towards us. He leaned over the couches with a warm smile. "My lady—would you care for more wine?"

I realized my glass was empty. Andrea's face held a flirtatious grin as she extended her hand. "I do not believe we have been introduced."

"Excuse my manners." I collected myself. "Mr. Terrace—this is Miss Andrea Taylor, Madame Catherine Dagny and Madame Francesca de Bough. Ladies, this is Mr. Daniel Terrace."

Francesca and Andrea simpered as Catherine bowed her head respectfully. Wanting to prevent any further gossip from spreading, I saw my chance to redirect.

"Excuse me," I said to the group. Francesca inclined her head with a suggestive smile as Andrea sent me a teasing wink.

We moved through the crowd towards the balcony—I grabbed a fresh glass of wine and handed it to the guard by the door (it was given back)—then found a quiet space against the railing. I was grateful for a break from the pressing heat of the sitting room. The night breeze pleasantly moved through my dress—cooling my body.

"Your friends are lovely." Daniel leaned against the railing, looking at me and raising his wine glass.

I smiled. "We have become quite close. It took a while, but I'm grateful to have them."

"You seem accustomed to this life."

"For the most part," I admitted. "I had never envisioned myself as a lady… that has taken some getting used to. The rules, the household, the parties… Even all the chatting and socializing can become tiresome."

He paused. "Well don't let me disturb you—"

"As long as you don't bore me with useless gossip, you're welcome to stay. Everyone here knows about us anyway." I cast a sidelong glance at a nearby couple who were speaking in hushed tones, looking conspicuously at us.

"I see some things are no different from the palace." Daniel gave a humorless smile. "It's funny how growing up on Berge, I thought the world was so big and grand. Now I realize that it's incredibly small."

"I also shared that sentiment," I confessed, fingering the stem of my wine glass. "I used to dream about leaving Berge and exploring the islands. I thought the world would be more interesting. And yet when the time came to leave—I didn't want to go…"

Daniel grimaced. "That was hard, you know." He paused. "It was hard…"

"It was hard for me too," I said truthfully, holding his gaze. "I was sure—for so many years!—that we were going to marry each other… Start a life together… To have that ripped away so abruptly… It hurt."

Daniel gently took my hand, entwining our fingers together. His skin was warm and inviting, and I allowed myself a couple of seconds to enjoy the feeling, inhaling his familiar scent. This was the moment I had fantasized about for so many months—to leave Aedin and return to the comfort of my old love.

I pulled my hand away. "I can't…" I said softly.

Grimacing, Daniel took a sip of his wine and looked away. "I still care for you, you know."

I pressed my lips together, unsure of what to say.

"Sure, there have been other women to distract me in Radiance, but they aren't you. We had a *connection*, Gwen—"

"We grew up together. We had known each other for years—"

"And we *knew* each other. We knew our families; we knew our friends. Remember when we used to go out to the lake at night? Share secrets and—"

"Yes, but—"

"I *loved* you," Daniel whispered fiercely, his brown eyes flashing with regret. "I didn't think I could love anyone or anything as passionately as I loved you."

In the brief silence that fell between us, my heart thudded in time with the sounds that drifted from the party. I watched the hands that had held my body, the mouth I had kissed, and the eyes I had loved so dearly in my youth. The crickets chirped from the dark jungle below as I struggled to mourn for what I had lost.

But I no longer grieved for the past.

Daniel turned away with a frustrated sigh. "I just don't understand why you didn't put up more of a fight..."

"What?" My voice became sharp. "I didn't put up a *fight*? How can you think that?"

"Well you didn't try to escape, you didn't write to me, you didn't send *word*—"

"I didn't even know how to *read* until recently," I pointed out through gritted teeth.

"You have servants—"

"Who watch my every move!"

"You just went through with it, boarded a ship, and *left*."

"It was an arranged marriage, Daniel." I forced myself to keep my voice calm and my emotions in check. "I had little say in the matter."

"Well *I* would have—"

"You would have had me escape? We would have run off to Acedes and eloped?" I faced him squarely. "Could you *imagine* the shame and disappointment for my family? After a lord had proposed? We would have been dishonored—Ephraim would certainly *never* have become historian to the king—"

"But we were in love. We had something—"

"We faced the reality of the situation," I said shortly, cutting him off. "Things changed."

Daniel was quiet for a moment. His brown eyes met mine with a foreign hardness. "You've changed," he said simply.

I lifted my chin, eying him with all of the self-assurance of my position that I could muster. "Yes," I agreed coolly, "I have."

Daniel shook his head and stared into the darkness. I opened my mouth to form some words that could console him—perhaps ease his suffering—but none came to mind.

The realization came crashing down as I regarded his bitterness with distant restraint—I didn't owe him anything.

I turned and left, ignoring the stares from the adjacent couple. They bowed as I passed.

Making a beeline for Tieren, I drained my glass of wine and grabbed another one, handing it to him.

"Rough night?" He eyed me empathetically as he took a delicate sip.

"You have no idea," I muttered under my breath—then realized he'd probably heard. I blushed, took the wine back, and re-entered the party.

Though we had left nearly all the doors in the villa open to the night breeze, the humidity overwhelmed me as soon as I stepped inside. Wandering through the crowd, I felt a hand on the small of my back. I looked up at Aedin's warm face in the candlelight and my heart skipped a beat.

"Yes?"

"Nothing." He studied me for a moment, his dark brow furrowed, then bent down to kiss my cheek. "You look beautiful."

"Thank you." I warmed at his touch. Offering a smile and putting my hand on his arm, I suddenly laughed. "This shirt…"

"Is completely ridiculous, I know," Aedin growled under his breath. "It's amazing how little choice we have in some matters."

The statement sobered me as we shared a knowing look.

"How are you faring?" I asked, reaching for his fingers.

Our hands intertwined as Aedin lightly thumbed the soft skin of my wrist. I shivered in desire. "As good as can be expected," he muttered. "And you?"

My lips tugged into a rueful grin. "I had an… unfortunate conversation with Daniel."

"Oh?" He smirked, raising his eyebrows.

"Yes," I said slowly. "I had to inform him that our… situation had changed."

"Ah," Aedin sighed. "It seems his trip has been *full* of disappointment—"

I batted his arm with my hand as he chuckled darkly, taking it and planting a kiss on my knuckles.

A wave of heat rushed through my body as I met his familiar eyes. Surrounded by the crowd of courtiers and merchants, it was like no one else was there. My body craved his touch and I desperately wanted to kiss him, then disappear to our room—

"What are you thinking?" Aedin asked as his hand touched my exposed back, slowly stroking the skin with his fingertips.

Beneath the buzz of conversation and clinking of glasses, I purred, "I wish we were the only ones here."

My breath caught as his fingers reached lower, to the edge of my dress. "That would be ideal," he breathed, bending to press his lips against the soft skin beneath my ear. I trembled, my breasts aching in response.

A large solid object hit my back.

"My lady," Ephraim drawled as his arm dropped heavily over my shoulders.

The heat in my body suddenly fled. I glared at him. "You're drunk," I hissed.

Aedin eyed my brother with an expression of wary frustration mingled with humor. "Are you well, Ephraim?" he asked stiffly, his hand leaving my back.

"You know"—Ephraim squinted accusingly at my husband—"I didn't like you at first… But now—" He hiccuped with a smile. "*Now* I think I like you—"

"Ephraim, *now* is not the time!" I snapped, a mortified blush spreading across my cheeks.

A smile tugged at my husband's lips. "I'm glad you finally approve of me, Ephraim."

"You're my br-brother—" He struggled with the word as I rolled my eyes.

"Get a grip," I ordered, gently prying the wine glass from his fingers. "And go away."

"I love you." Ephraim's bloodshot eyes gazed tenderly at me. "You're my only sister—"

"Yes, I'm your only sister," I said impatiently as Aedin stifled a chuckle. "Now will you *please* leave?"

"Let's go sit down, Ephraim." Aedin eased the arm from around my shoulders and took the weight of my incoherent brother. I grimaced in remorse as the desire in my body and was replaced by pure humiliation.

"I'm so sorry," I muttered to Aedin, awkwardly holding two glasses of wine.

"It's not your fault—we ordered too much wine." He shot me a cheeky grin as I mustered one in response. "I'll set him on the couches."

"Thank you." I watched as my husband awkwardly guided Ephraim through the crowd, catching his lean form as he stumbled. Cursing Ephraim under my breath, I caught the eye of a passing servant and set down his nearly empty glass of wine.

I strolled towards the garden, seeking some peace and quiet among the thinned crowds and the fountains in the grass. The hanging lamps swayed softly, lighting the hallways as the night breeze moved through the villa. Soft laughter and voices echoed from the garden.

In a corner, I noticed Tours. Men surrounded him—like bees buzzing around a flower—soaking in his words and straightening their shoulders.

I slunk through the crowd, hoping to avoid his gaze, when his eyes snapped to mine. He said something with finality, patted one of the men on the back, left the circle, and ducked into an adjacent hall.

My stomach dropped—it was the servants' quarters.

I glanced back in the main hall—Aedin was unaware and lost in conversation with a merchant. Should I tell him?

Looking back towards the corner where Tours had disappeared, I clutched my glass of wine with resolve. I had no reason to be afraid—in fact, I should have felt something like outrage at a foreigner snooping around *my* domain. This was my villa, after all.

Inhaling for courage, I peered into the adjacent hallway— dimmed by a single torchlight. Tours was nowhere in sight.

Throwing back my shoulders, I stepped into the dark. Echoes of laughter and firelight floated in from the main courtyard, softening as I walked further from the party.

I knew little of this part of the villa—it was where the servants slept, but, unlike the guardroom, I had not visited their quarters. The small passage weaved to the right before it emptied out onto an open garden. I heard quiet voices, nearly indistinguishable from the gurgling fountain, emerging from the night.

"I found this in their rooms… Although I don't know its purpose."

"Well done," Tours responded in a brisk and satisfied voice. "Have you discovered anything else?"

"She misses her family, my lord," a quiet, familiar voice said. "But Lord Aedin has warned her of me—I am sure of it—as we have not spoken in weeks."

"Nothing unusual then? Anything of her past?" Tours' voice was laced with disappointment.

"I-I can't think of anything, my lord," Talia stuttered through her whisper. "Except she and Lord Aedin didn't get along at first, but they seem to have grown closer—"

"What gave you that impression?"

"She hated him her first month or so here… Only recently have they appeared closer—perhaps in love…"

"Did she give you any reason as to why she hated him?"

"It was an arranged marriage, I think, my lord. And she had loved Daniel."

"Is she close to anyone else here?"

"Perhaps Mary, the head steward, as she is always with Lord Aedin."

"Where is she?"

I took a step closer as Tours' voice was nearly a whisper.

"She is not here tonight—"

There was a sudden silence as my breath caught in my throat.

Fear coursed through my veins as the voices instantly disappeared and a dark silhouette appeared in the archway.

My heart leaped, and I felt something like adrenaline—a thickening of my blood and lightening in my body.

In the dim light, Tours' expression quickly turned from one of satisfaction at catching me eavesdropping to surprise and astonishment. My heartbeat thundered through my ears as he reached out a hand, his eyes large and expression stunned.

Stumbling, I stepped backwards, feeling for the wall as a strange vertigo rushed through my vision.

The glass slipped from my shaking hands—I heard distantly the crunch of each particle under my sandal.

There was an unfamiliar pressure, a force exerting from Tours' body—I thought it strange that I hadn't noticed it before. In the back of my mind, I felt a distant presence, and then another, and many more, in the garden and outside. It was as if a dozen invisible persons had suddenly been revealed to another sense— yet they were all out of my sight.

The shock on Tours' face quickly turned to hunger and amusement as he took another step closer, watching my trembling form.

"Well this changes everything," he murmured with a wolfish grin. "The last piece of the puzzle…"

A familiar presence gripped my arms, pulling me back. "You will not touch her," Aedin commanded.

"You dared to hide this from me?" Tours hissed, looking at my husband in amazement. "How long did you think it would last? She has the most powerful Gift I have ever felt—"

"She will stay here." He grabbed my shoulder, and suddenly I felt the spark in my body wane and decrease to a simmer.

Shakily, I gripped his arm, fighting to remain standing.

Tours shook his head incredulously. "Aedin, she belongs to the Rhidge."

"No," Aedin said quietly. "She will stay here."

Tours stepped closer. "You dare to disobey me?"

There was a short silence. I fought to control my bated breath.

"Yes," Aedin declared with finality before he turned and ushered me into the hall.

The sounds of the party hit me with a wall of noise—it was all too loud. A richness continued to pump through my blood as I stumbled and tripped on the stones, losing a sandal. As Aedin caught me, he whispered, "Keep moving. Just keep moving."

Unsteadily, I kicked off the other sandal as we walked quickly through the maze of people, Aedin guiding me towards our room. His face was pale, his mouth set in a thick line of anxiety and fear.

Opening the door, Aedin all but pushed me through the antechamber and into our bedroom, shutting it with finality, cutting off all sounds of merriment. He ran his hands along the door handle and I felt that same power exert from his body. He was using the Gift.

"Get changed," he ordered. "We're leaving."

Chapter Twenty-Three

"AEDIN—"

He didn't respond to her protests. His body had hurled itself into a mode of efficiency sparked by terror.

Throwing open the wardrobe doors, Aedin pulled out the drawers, tossing their fineries on the floor and opening the hidden compartments beneath. He grabbed the pins, two daggers, some rope, and pulled a long sword from behind the hanging tunics. Reaching into the lowest drawer, he threw down a pair of black pants and matching shirt at Gwen's feet.

"Put these on," he instructed.

"Aedin."

"What?"

Her face was white. "I'm sorry. I—"

Aedin held a finger to his lips. "Watch what you say. They are just outside."

Gwen inhaled shakily, untying the bow from her waist with quick fingers.

Aedin grabbed her boots—he had planned for this moment for the last four months. Placing them at Gwen's feet, he helped her out of her dress, trying not to stare at the curve of her naked shoulders in the moonlight.

She buttoned the shirt and tucked it into the pants, tightening the tie around her slender waist. It was jarring to see her in his outfit. The uniform that he'd worn nearly his entire life. The sight was haunting, but there were no other alternatives.

As she hastily finished braiding her hair, Aedin handed her a small dagger. "Here." He tucked it into her belt. "Just in case."

Gwen nodded mutely, watching him with a solemn gaze. "Aedin," she said quietly.

"Yes?"

"I want you to know…" She paused, fidgeting with the handle of her dagger.

"Gwen, we don't have much time." Aedin fearfully looked back at the door, half expecting Tours to burst through at any moment.

"I know." She inhaled. "Which is why I want to thank you for everything you've done for me. And I… I hope we…"

"We *will* survive." Aedin gripped her shoulders gently, pressing his lips to her forehead. "Be silent, be swift, and be ruthless—we have nothing to lose. If anything happens—if we get separated—follow the eastern stars. There is a boat on the shore of a small cove. Take that and sail east."

She nodded in agreement, her mouth twisted with anxiety.

"First"—Aedin bent down—"give me your boot."

Frowning, Gwen obliged, placing her boot on Aedin's palm. He ran his hand along the bottom, creating a thin layer of force with the Gift, like a thick coating of velvet on the sole.

"This will help mute any noise." Aedin let go and repeated the process with her other boot, then ministered to his own.

When he'd finished, he reached for Gwen and, hand in hand, they left the bedroom through the garden door.

The echoes of laughter and music floated from the villa halls into the darkened garden. Fountains babbled softly in the night. They marched silently across the gravel, like dark ghosts in the light of the crescent moon.

Aedin felt them everywhere—his skin crawled with the sensation of the Gift. He counted silently to himself: twelve guards in the villa, two Rhidge by the back balcony, one up front, two others in the jungle… and Tours.

A darkened shadow lingered near the villa gates. Carriages sat empty, littered along the driveway, their horses staring blankly ahead. Aedin dropped Gwen's hand, beckoning her to stay close.

Her Gift pulsated like an invisible light beside him as his stomach dropped. In that moment, Aedin wondered if Tours had been right. This was pure stupidity. How had he ever presumed to succeed? And stay alive?

Forcing away the haunting doubts, Aedin strode confidently towards the villa gates.

"Going somewhere?" called a soft voice from the darkness.

Aedin pushed Gwen behind him as he threw out his hand towards Tours.

A blast of air hurtled towards his stationary form. The shock of the blow reverberated through the night—Tours took a step back, his eyes wide.

"Gwen—the horses—" Aedin barely had time to speak before Tours responded with his own power. Aedin threw up his hands, propelling the force backwards, then grabbed his sword, advancing with one hand outstretched.

Gwen ran to the nearest carriage, pulling out her dagger and cutting through the harnesses of the horses. They whinnied in protest at the sounds of combat—it was a grand and powerful crackling, like the popping of logs on a fire. She pulled herself atop the animal, feeling the reverberations through her bones as they flung the Gift back and forth.

Tours' dagger hit Aedin's sword with a screeching noise—by now all the Rhidge would be on their way. Aedin swung his weapon in a feint to the left and struck to the opposite side, but his opponent wasn't deceived.

Shooting out his hand, Tours pushed Aedin, nearly knocking him off his feet. The blow hit his gut—he stumbled backwards, catching a foothold and slicing his knife across Tours' midsection.

A hair away from his skin, the silver ripped through the fabric.

"Aedin—" Marks' breathless voice resounded from behind, his blonde hair sticking to his forehead.

Grabbing the horses' reins in one hand, Marks pulled out his knife with the other, throwing it in Tours' direction. Tours quickly threw up his hand, defecting the strike with a pulse of the Gift—the knife clattered uselessly to the ground.

"Take Gwen and go!" Aedin commanded, throwing back another attack from Tours.

"No—" Gwen protested, but Marks had already obeyed.

He swung himself onto the other horse, urging them towards the gate. Gwen grabbed the horse's mane, throwing a panicked look back at Aedin as they galloped down the road.

More shadows emerged—vibrations creeping on the edge of his mind as Aedin felt numerous Gifted join the fray. Tieren ran forward, pushing a large force towards Tours and another Rhidge behind him, as William and the other guards entered the fight.

Sweat beaded Aedin's brow in the humid night air. He saw the feral faces of the Rhidge appear like ghosts in the moonlight as his stomach dropped. The lightning fast blows, the merciless flinging of power—had he done all that was possible to prepare them for this moment?

Tours read the dread on his face. "They can't… win," he spat with a malicious grin in between blows.

Aedin ducked a high knife stroke aimed at his neck and quickly returned it with a punch. The Gift connected with Tours' midsection with a satisfying grunt.

Though he longed to stay and fight till the bloody end there was little time—he had to act quickly.

Shoving Tours to the right, Aedin saw his chance and took it—he ran.

A knife whistled by his left ear as he shot off into the darkness, heart pounding.

Leaving the main road, he plunged into the jungle—trees tearing at his clothes, his feet unsteady from the Gift exerting from his soles. The stone of Lailan beat against his breast—he tore the chain from round his neck and tossed it into the forest.

Aedin counted—there were two behind him. One was Tours, the other unknown.

Blood pumping, he fought to keep silent as he ran through the twisted trees and rocks of the forest. Even in the thin moonlight, and with his eyesight enhanced by the Gift, he could hardly see—

he stumbled over a small boulder, forcing his lips shut as a curse rose in his throat.

He didn't want to die this way—running from his enemies. But he continued—losing track of time—silently wishing that he had trained more for this moment. Chest stinging with pain, he forced his legs to pump with each step.

Aedin looked up to see the eastern stars gleam overhead as the tall trees began to thin. He could still feel them behind—he heard Tours breathing loudly through the sounds of the night.

Another object whistled through the black and Aedin ducked as a knife sailed overhead, embedding itself into the tree in front of him.

"Run, rabbit, *run!*" he heard Tours yell gleefully, not far in the darkness. "We will always find you!"

The echoing words cut into Aedin's gut.

After fifteen years, this was how it would end.

He followed the sloping ground—he was getting closer. In the distance, he could feel two familiar presences—Gwen and Marks. Relief washed over him—they had made it.

Sliding on the debris of the jungle floor, Aedin tried to slow his feet as the ground grew steeper and steeper. The Rhidge behind him felt closer.

Panicked, he threw out a hand behind him, pushing his power towards his pursuers. He missed. Aedin continued sliding and running, his feet hitting more stone than earth.

For a second, he lifted his eyes from the stone underfoot and glanced forward—the beach was just ahead. Waves crashed against the sand.

In the dim moonlight, Aedin could see Marks in the shore break, the ocean soaking his legs. He held a rope attached to a small sailboat that bobbed in the surf—Gwen was perched on the bow, watching the forest expectantly.

It was the final push.

Aedin broke through the maze of boulders along the edge of the beach and sprinted across the sand.

"Go!" he shouted at Marks, waving wildly.

Marks dropped the rope and ran towards him—directing his power against the Rhidge behind Aedin.

The ship jerked unsteadily in the waves, threatening to beach. Aedin threw out his hands to the boat, feeling his last bit of energy drain.

The sails puffed as if a sudden gust of wind had exhaled from the west—Aedin shot past Marks and leaped into the waves, grabbing the trailing rope and pulling himself into the boat.

"Give me your hand!"

"What?"

Panting, Aedin grabbed Gwen's hand, using her Gift to further propel the sails. The wood groaned in the break of the waves, gaining speed as it breached one after another.

"Marks!" Gwen screamed at the dark form ashore. "Marks! Aedin, we have to—"

"DUCK." Aedin forced Gwen's head down as a knife came soaring through the air. It streaked above, tearing through the sail with a horrid noise.

"We can't leave him—" Her voice was hoarse, "Aedin, we can't—"

She fell silent as they watched the two dark shadows overtake the third on the shore. The forms grew distant, the roar of the water overtaking their hearing.

Aedin's blood pounded in his ears; his breath became light and slow.

Looking down, he saw the knuckles of their tightly intertwined hands were white. The gold of their rings shone silver in the muted moonlight.

Aedin silently wondered why there were eight hands, until he realized his vision was swimming—nausea and exhaustion rising up to claim him. His grip slipped, and he distantly heard Gwen calling his name as his head fell hard against the wood of the boat.

Before there was the obscurity of darkness, all Aedin could see were the stars.

Chapter Twenty-Four

"YOU DID WELL, you know."

Raine's words fell softly from her lips—like the dripping of salt into a wound. Rowyn winced.

"Whether I did *well* or not is irrelevant," he grumbled, entwining his fingers in his lap. "We killed innocent people, Raine. Why would the Prophet want such a thing?"

"You do not know if they were innocent."

"They were not Rhidge."

"No, but they were Empire, which is just as tainted."

"Is it?" Rowyn met his sister's vivid green eyes. "Is it really? They screamed just as any man—Gifted or not—would have done… Their blood was just as red."

Raine placed a hand on Rowyn's forearm, but he brushed her off and wiped the beads of sweat from his forehead.

They sat in the sun in the garden, just as they had done numerous times before. Nothing in Iselleden had changed—the birds chirped, the insects buzzed, and the smell of fresh herbs and flowers bloomed around them. Yet Rowyn felt sick.

Blood now tainted their shores.

He swallowed, shading his eyes. "I hear them, Raine… At night. Their cries—the smell of burned flesh…"

Rowyn shifted in his seat and heard a high note ding as metal clattered against the stone bench—an uncomfortable reminder of the sword at his hip. After that night, he had cleaned the weapon thoroughly. He would have left it in his room—stowed it away in a corner—if it had not been his duty to wear it constantly.

"Rowyn, this too shall pass." Raine tucked a strawberry-blonde lock behind a delicate ear. "You cannot hold their memory in your mind forever. The tides are shifting—time is moving quickly. You must be ready—more acts such as these may be required."

"The Prophet has cursed me with this burden. Fate, perhaps, wants me to suffer."

His sister made a clucking noise, as if reprimanding a child. "Fate never *wants* suffering—it allows it to exist."

"But why does it exist?" Rowyn's voice was a low and strangled cry. "Why did we cut and burn their bodies? Why are we on the precipice of another war? More blood will be shed—I know that for a fact."

"But it may not be by your hand."

"Who else's?"

Raine was silent. Rowyn's eyes flashed and he shook his head.

"I need some space." He stood abruptly.

His sister did not respond. Her head was still, her chin raised in thought, staring at the valley below. Rowyn paused, as if waiting for her to say something.

Only the reddish golden hair on her head shifted in the light breeze—her emerald eyes were cool and detached. Rowyn turned away.

He released a large exhalation of breath from his cheeks and attempted to unclench his jaw before he meandered the familiar route back to his quarters, in no rush to arrive at the silence of the apartment.

Passing the guards at the door to the residence, Rowyn nodded at their familiar faces. Their smiles were hesitant and wavering—nothing had been the same since that night.

They had not trained since—Rowyn didn't know when he would bring them together again. It was a moment, perhaps, that they all wanted to forget. There was no going back.

In the cool stone hallways of the Haven, Rowyn saw the flash of blue-gray eyes behind his waking gaze. He prayed to Fate that he would never have to spill another drop of blood again.

When Rowyn arrived back at the door to his apartment, he could not bring himself to go inside. There was nothing for him there.

His feet continued. He followed the winding halls and surfaced from its depths. Today, the Haven did not feel like a refuge.

The summer air was fresh—the smell of damp grass and wet dirt filled his nostrils as he strode down the road to Farist. He walked on the edge of the wide path to circumvent others as they passed and was thankful not to see many faces.

His heart was low—he avoided their eyes.

They didn't know the terror that had reached their shores. Rowyn felt as though he had failed the generations of Gifted that had guided Iselleden through peace and prosperity—that the ship from the Empire had been his fault.

Wondering if he was being punished for an unknown transgression, Rowyn watched the dirt from the road cover his boots with a fine layer of dust. He stared at the ground, remembering bitterly when he too had been free of the burden of bloodshed. The burden of responsibility.

If the Empire were to attack at this very moment, it would be *him* that had to answer the call, muster his men and women and bring them to slaughter. He knew they would not survive—their lack of experience and guileless nature barely made them opponents. The only advantage they'd had over the shipwrecked merchants was the element of surprise and the power of their Gift.

"Rowyn!" A voice broke through his musings.

Rowyn looked up, seeing Ager only several paces ahead. He realized he'd arrived in the valley—the Haven was behind him on the hill.

"Hello." Rowyn attempted to relax his face and smile, but it felt strained.

"My old friend." Ager grinned crookedly, clapping Rowyn on the back. "How are you? How are things at the Haven?"

"Fine," Rowyn lied easily. "And you? How is the family?"

"Excellent, thank you." He ran a large calloused hand through his thick hair. "My daughter, Alea, is almost two. Cerce is with child again."

"Congratulations." Rowyn meant it sincerely.

"Where are you headed?"

Rowyn paused. "I don't know. Perhaps Rea's… I more just wanted to clear my head."

Ager nodded. "Well I'm heading to the Wheatsheaf with Cain and Melus if you'd like to join us."

Rowyn considered this, wondering if a distraction was the best option. "That sounds excellent. I haven't seen anyone for quite some time."

"We thought you'd fallen off the island."

Rowyn gave a short laugh. "Sometimes I don't think that would be an entirely bad thing."

Ager paused, watching as the swarm of people gently fanned into the town. The road was widening, cobblestones taking the place of dirt and large houses, and shops for fields. "I heard of something that happened 'bout a fortnight ago." He lowered his voice. "A band of men from the Empire came… Is it true?"

Cocking his head to the side, Rowyn replied in the same tone. "Not entirely. They were from the Empire, but they were shipwrecked merchants."

"What happened?" There was a slightly panicked look in Ager's eyes. Although most of Iselleden did not know the extent of the cursed Empire, they knew enough to fear the place.

"We burned their bodies and cargo."

Ager nodded, relief washing over his face. "Then we must celebrate."

Rowyn nodded numbly—he needed a drink.

They ducked into a leaning wooden building that bore the testament of time. A sign with crackling paint still proclaimed "Wheatsheaf" and swung whenever the door was opened. It was said that if the sign fell on your held as you entered the door, it signified good luck (and a free drink).

But that didn't happen this time.

Inside the smoky atmosphere, men and women sat huddled around tables lit with candles, chatting cheerfully or laughing. It was mostly the farming crowd—gathering after a long day of planting to eat, drink, and chat. Rowyn scanned the crowd—he recognized perhaps one or two faces, but the rest were strangers. Ager steered him over to a table in the back.

"Cain, Melus!" Rowyn shook hands with both men.

They greeted him with surprise. "Rowyn!"

Cain tugged at his thick beard, eying his attire. "Now, you didn't have to go through all that trouble to meet us for drinks."

Melus snickered as Ager protested, "I met him on the road from the Haven and asked him to join." He shoved his coat onto the empty chair and shouldered his way through the crowd towards the bar.

"What's that?" Melus jabbed a finger at the sheathed sword on Rowyn's hip.

Cain whistled as Rowyn unbuckled the belt and shoved it under the table, sitting down. "It's nothing."

"That's a sword! My friend Blain has one of those—says he only uses it for training." Cain eyed it eagerly.

"Blain is a good man," Rowyn said in reply.

"Do you use it to chop your vegetables?" Melus asked, staring blankly at Rowyn, who was unsure how to answer.

"You idiot, they use it to kill people." Cain rolled his eyes. "In the Empire, everyone has a sword. Here, there's no need."

"Then why's he got one?" Melus pointed a finger at Rowyn. His face was tanned and weathered, his fingers slightly twisted from a farming accident.

"Because he's Captain of the Guard!" Cain exclaimed, raising both his hands for effect.

Rowyn groaned. "Can we please forget that title for the night? I need a drink."

Melus stared at Rowyn in awe, until Rowyn shot him a quick glare, then looked pointedly at Cain. "The last time I saw you, you abandoned your cow in the middle of a field to run after a girl. How are things?"

Cain laughed, remembering. "Well, as it turned out, I lost the cow but got the girl, and we're having a daughter together."

"You know it's a daughter?"

"I had a Dream," Cain said, shrugging confidently. "And then we'll have a son in another year or two."

"And you, Melus?" Rowyn looked pointedly at him. "What have you been up to?"

"Well." Melus scratched the side of his face. "I bought another cow." His mind had been slow since he'd fallen off a wagon as a child.

"Congratulations to you and the cow."

"Why thank you." Melus accepted Rowyn's good wishes graciously as Cain rolled his eyes again.

"Four pints," Ager announced, his wide berth pushing Rowyn aside as he placed the drinks on the table.

"But we haven't even finished ours yet," Melus protested.

"Drink up," Cain advised, swallowing what remained of his previous ale with a satisfied sound.

Ager nodded and took a deep sip. Rowyn eyed the drink with some reservation—he'd become so accustomed to the wine and rich spirits of the Haven that he'd forgotten how to enjoy the common brew.

"Just put it in your mouth—don't hesitate," Cain demanded after a large burp.

"Did you say that to your wife last night?" Ager asked politely.

Melus burst out laughing as Rowyn spit out part of his drink. A large belly laugh filled his spirits as he watched Cain's expression of disbelief. It quickly broke into a boyish grin.

"Yeah, and then right after, we got more action in one night than you've had in a week."

Ager shook his head. "Piss off," he retorted.

"What 'bout you?" Cain gestured towards Rowyn with his new mug. "You got a girl?"

"No." Rowyn shook his head and looked away, thinking of Celion.

"Are you allowed to 'get' girls?" Ager enunciated comically.

Rowyn shrugged evasively. "Not sure; haven't tried. My time is limited… No, it would be unwise to get involved."

"Well you're not gettin' any younger," Cain pointed out.

"Thank you for that observation, Cain," Rowyn said tartly. He was just over sixty-five—most men by now would have established a family and a career. Rowyn served as a rare exception and devoted himself to his island alone.

"Nothing to worry 'bout," Melus piped up. "Women are overrated."

"That's because you only have cattle. You can't exactly tell a cow to put it in their mouth."

"True…" Melus said hesitantly, looking around the room as if searching for something.

Ager changed the subject. "Well I'm glad to see you looking well. It's easy for friendships to become locational."

"Yes," Rowyn admitted. "And I'm sorry for hiding out in the Haven. You know how private it all becomes."

Ager shrugged. "You have a difficult Calling. Not everyone can be a farmer." He gave a lopsided grin, which Rowyn returned.

They finished their drinks quickly and ordered another round. It wasn't till the third or fourth that they began to feel a bit more cheerful and tingly. Rowyn's blood thickened as the Gift mingled with the ale. His head was pleasantly buzzed and he laughed until his face hurt.

Finally, he stumbled out of the Wheatsheaf, grasping the hands of his friends in farewell before he made his way to Rea's. It was closer than the trudge back up to the Haven and Rowyn was reluctant to return to the emptiness of his apartment. The route was habitual—Rowyn hardly had to think as his feet wandered down the rows of corn, the distant sounds of cows and horses mingled with the crickets' nightly song.

A crescent moon faintly bathed the path in silver. Just outside of Rea's house, his feet stopped, and he watched the light and warm windows with some trepidation.

He was alone. And he could hear them inside—the distant chatter of the children before bed, Rea's soft voice singing a familiar song.

Rowyn's knees bent, and he sank into the earth, his head bowed.

Something like despair washed over his body, and he began to cry, praying fervently that something would change. He grieved for the families of the merchants he'd slaughtered, for his sisters, his guards, the Council, his friends, and Iselleden, letting his bitter tears fall into the dust before he wiped them away, standing, wobbly, with shaky resolve.

Something had to change.

Chapter Twenty-Five

THE SEA SPARKLED in the palm of his hand. It was the symbolic stone of Lailan—just slightly more beautiful than the diamonds the guests had donned the night before.

Tours closed his fist around the rock that had hung from Aedin's neck. They had found it when retracing their steps for any clues the morning after. Other than traces of blood and errant knives, the stone had been the only thing left from Aedin's escape.

He took a sip of wine, lounging on the balcony of the villa with a mixture of excitement, bitterness, and satisfaction. In his hand was a quill, and on the table, a sheet of parchment.

Delicately dipping the quill in ink, Tours set the point to the surface.

Your Majesty,

As you might have heard by the time this letter reaches you, we had an unfortunate reception at the villa. As confirmation of my suspicions, Lord Aedin and his wife have left Lailan—they have given up the lordship and betrayed your person. We will hunt for them and have confidence we will succeed.

I have drafted the enclosed announcement that denounces them as traitors and pronounces them dead. I would suggest appointing Renalt Cabot to the lordship—if you would bestow your blessing. He is eager to serve you well.

Tours folded the parchment into eighths, and then handed it to a nearby attendant.

"Be sure the king receives this soon. Send your fastest ship."

As the boy ran away, Tours turned to face his companion, who sat across from him with a white-knuckled grip on his glass of wine.

"Cheer up, dear chap," Tours sighed with exasperation. "You did your part—there is nothing to regret."

Daniel made no sign of acknowledgement. "Do we know…?"

Tours shrugged, lying easily. "They could be shipwrecked in the middle of the sea for all we know."

Wincing, Daniel took a long sip of his wine.

There was a brief silence before Daniel asked quietly, "You did not… Did you… *kill* them?"

Tours gave a loud bark of laughter. "*Kill* them? Oh, gods, no. That would be treason, killing another lord. No, Daniel, you mistake me. I detest Lord Aedin, but, like so many people we detest in this world, we *need* him alive… Both of them," Tours added as an afterthought, remembering the waves of power he'd felt from Gwyneth Aedin. He shook his head in mute disbelief—it was still incredible—no, amazing—that she should exist without the Rhidge knowing.

"You did not enjoy yourself last night?" Tours asked cheerfully. "Kitra seemed very interested in getting to know you better."

His companion was not humored. Daniel muttered something that sounded like an excuse and pushed back from the table, exiting the balcony.

Tours exhaled loudly, not attempting to conceal his vexation. It was like playing governess to a five-year-old boy.

"My lord." Bela's voice came from behind.

Tours did not turn his gaze from the sea. "Yes?"

"They are ready."

Downing the final droplets of wine, Tours stood and followed the Rhidge. They passed through the dining room, the sitting room, and entered the main courtyard of the villa.

The silence was deadly—a stark contrast to the night before. In the garden courtyard stood all the servants and guards they'd been able to find. Of course, it was only natural that some had run off when they'd heard the commotion the night before, but the Rhidge would find them eventually. They always did.

Yet it was the guards—the ones Aedin had promised him—that captured Tours' interest. He had obviously instructed them well—there was no other explanation as to how they had given the Rhidge a nearly fair fight the night before.

They stood in a line, their faces grim, some with unmasked fear, as they watched Tours approach. He immediately recognized the tall, oldest-looking one with the blonde hair—the one that had aided Gwen's escape.

"You." Tours beckoned him forward.

The man complied, watching Tours with a wary yet still gaze.

"What is your name?"

"Colin Marks." His mouth moved with some difficulty as his lips and cheeks were bruised and still tinged with blood.

"Marks," Tours repeated, looking out at those before him. "Last night, Marks fought against the Lord of Radiance in order to help his master and wife escape the Empire and commit treason." He paused. "Is that so?"

"Yes, my lord."

"The penalty for treason is death," Tours announced in a calm voice that echoed through the arches in the courtyard.

"However, I am willing to offer a sort of compromise. Whoever has private information concerning Lord or Lady Aedin, step forward now and your life will be spared."

None of the guards moved.

The servants milled restlessly, looking at one another and speaking in hushed voices. Several stepped forward, raising their hands.

"Please follow this woman,"—Tours nodded to Bela on his right—"who will take you to a place where you can speak privately."

Their feet padded against the floor of the halls like the echoes of betrayal. The guards watched with slitted eyes.

"And so you will slaughter us all?" one of them asked loudly.

"Oh no." Tours shook his head. "There is always room for compromise. Join us, give us your *Gift*, and we will together fight for king and empire."

Tours turned to Marks, pulling out his sword. "Kneel," he commanded.

Marks did so.

"Yet there is not compromise for all." Tours gazed down at Marks with something like regret. He would have made a fine addition to the Rhidge.

But not all could be trusted.

With a sweeping arch, Tours' blade split the guard's head from his body.

A servant shrieked in terrified surprise. The only other sounds in the courtyard were the gurgling of the fountains and the thud of a head falling to the ground.

The blood on the blade was thick and gleaming in the morning light. With relish he watched the expressions on the guards' faces —hopelessness, fear, anger, and terror. Success was sweet.

"Would anyone care to step forward and offer their services to our cause?"

There was no sound. Until the one who had spoken stepped towards Tours. His expression was fierce, determined.

He kneeled on the ground beside Marks' body, offering his neck.

"To die a free man is better than a lifetime in captivity of the Rh—"

Tours' blade swung with the utmost precision.

Chapter Twenty-Six

THE SMELL OF salt filled the air.

My head knocked against something hard, waking me from sleep. Grimacing, I opened my eyes, but immediately shut them again as they met a bright, clear sky.

I touched my face with a groan and flinched as sharp pains ignited where my hands had pressed. The muscles of my hips and thighs were sore and aching as I shifted on the hard floor. Reminding myself never to horseback ride again, I shakily sat up.

I attempted to maintain my sanity and briefly wondered if I was still dreaming: all around me was a cerulean sea, speckled with whitecap waves.

"Aedin," I muttered, as the night before came drifting back into my memory.

I didn't have to look far—he lay silent only two feet away, his body swaying with the rolling waves, head resting easily against the brim of the boat. His condition had been impossible to assess in the faint moonlight, but now I saw his face was slightly bloodied, his clothes torn in numerous places.

"Aedin." I switched my position to crawl towards him and shook his boot. "Aedin," I said, louder.

My heart leaped in my throat: was he dead?

Gingerly, I moved to crouch over his legs, reaching with one hand for his neck. It was difficult to maintain balance with the rocking boat—as the vessel swayed dangerously to one side, I threw myself to the other, straddling Aedin's knees. Yet I succeeded in placing my fingers on his neck for five seconds—there was the pulse of life.

"Aedin," I repeated louder, gripping his cheek.

No movement.

I crawled back to the bow of the boat, grabbing a bucket that lay in a pile of other useful tools—a thick rope, a large jug of water, a sack of what appeared to be food, a sharp knife, a compass, and another satchel of indistinguishable instruments. I tied the rope to the handle of the bucket and dipped it overboard to fill it with seawater. Pulling the bucket up, I scrambled back towards Aedin, holding it carefully.

"Aedin," I shouted half-heartedly.

No response.

Gritting my teeth, I dumped the water over my husband's head.

Aedin shouted in surprise at the sudden cold, his eyes snapping open. He rubbed his face, pushing back his sopping dark hair, then looked at me in astonishment.

"Gwen," he gasped, gazing down at the jagged holes in his shirt and pants, and then at the endless sea. To my amazement, a small smile flickered onto his lips and he emitted a low chuckle.

"What?" I asked, tossing the bucket back towards the bow.

"We did it," Aedin stated plainly, shaking his head. His voice was hoarse. "We left…"

I tried to smile, but it faltered. "Aedin… We left Marks on the beach… And the guards…"

He sobered, staring at the waves. The dripping water from his clothes was audible even through the chatting of the waves. "Yes, I know."

"What about the servants? Mary?"

Aedin shook his head. "I don't know. Mary was in Tahuna for the night—I'm sure she escaped somehow, but the others?" He paused, looking down at his legs. "I… feel terrible for what I asked of them, and yet… they knew the risks. They chose to pledge their lives to me—to us…"

I bit my lip. "I hope Father and Ephraim are not…"

"No." Aedin shook his head. "They are not Gifted. They will endure nothing save for some questioning." He paused, squinting into the sun. "It's late morning… By now, Tours might have sent a ship to look for us. We need to head east to the fortress—hand me that compass, will you?"

I reached backwards and grabbed the compass from the pile—it was unusually heavy. Handing it to Aedin, I watched him study it, his expression concerned.

"We're a bit too far south," he declared. He eased himself onto his knees, wincing in pain.

"Are you hurt?"

He shook his head with a grimace. "No. Just out of shape."

Careful not to rock the boat, he reached for the sail line and pulled it to one side, hooking it onto the railing.

"When did you learn how to sail?" I watched him curiously.

"Less than a year ago." Aedin said with a humorless smile. "Since instigating this plan—I'd thought it would be useful to learn."

"Very useful," I agreed. "It's quite hard to run away on an island."

Aedin remained silent. He sat back, watching the sail and judging the compass again. Seemingly satisfied, he craned his head to look behind me. "Could you please pass that pack? The one on the right."

"This one?" I grabbed the bulky satchel.

"Yes." Aedin reached out his hand.

I struggled to lift it but finally succeeded. Numerous items banged together within the depths, and I wondered what was inside.

Aedin sat the pack in his lap, opening up the lip and rummaging within. He pulled out a small tin of ointment, some identical black shirts and pants, a packet of leaves, a small bottle of something clear, and a swath of clean linen.

When he shrugged off his shirt, I winced at the sight of the dark red scrapes and purple bruising on his skin.

Aedin smiled grimly, looking down at himself. "The Gift isn't entirely invisible," he mused.

"That's from the Gift?" I gestured to the particularly largely bruised area on his right shoulder—a sickly yellow and purple backdrop to the "R" that marred his skin.

"If it hits you directly, yes. If you think about it, pushing like that with the Gift is just forcing a wave of power—or air—towards another. Although it's invisible, its effects are still punishing to the body if you can't stop the blow."

He took a wad of ointment from the tin and began spreading it on the scratches. "Here." He offered me some.

I scooped some onto my fingertips and prodded gently around my face and my arms, applying where I found some grazes.

"How did you manage with Marks?" Aedin asked, continuing to attend to his wounds.

I paused, remembering. "Fine enough. We took the main road until he led us to a small sandy path that wove through the forest and led out onto the beach. They weren't on horseback and weren't able to keep us with us for long."

Aedin nodded approvingly.

"When we arrived, the boat was on the sand, so Marks used his power to ease it into the waves. He made me get in as he waited on shore..."

"Good man," he admitted gruffly, rubbing the ointment on a particularly long scrape on his forearm.

I sat in silence, watching him for some time. There were few passing birds, but they were high overhead. For as far as I could see, we were absolutely alone. It was a simultaneously terrifying and freeing thought.

"How far? How long?" I asked quietly.

Aedin made a face, closing the ointment tin and pulling a fresh shirt from the pack. "Perhaps four, maybe five days?"

"Days?" I repeated dumbfounded.

My husband nodded, unfolding his tattered shirt and tying it to the side of the boat.

"Well." I swallowed. "This certainly isn't the villa..." I eyed the boat—it was hardly fifteen feet long and five feet wide. The wood was worn and weathered; a small river trickled down the belly from the bucket of water I'd used to wake up Aedin. Where would we sleep? We could hardly even stand without hitting the sail or risk falling overboard.

"It is a bit of a demotion," Aedin admitted.

"Do you really think that Tours is coming after us?"

Aedin twisted his lips. "I'm not aware of whether or not he knows of the fortress—it's a possibility. I only found it after discovering those maps in the villa with Jon and Rebecca. At the time, I hadn't even known that there was any land past Lailan in the east…"

"Is it likely that we meet other Gifted? Those from the eighth island?"

He shrugged. "I don't know. I hope not."

"Why?"

"I would think that after the massacre they would not treat individuals from the Empire kindly… Gifted or not."

"But Jon and Rebecca will," I added with hopefulness.

"Yes," Aedin agreed with a smile. "Yes, they will." He stretched his arms above his head, wincing. "It will be good to be with them again—I am old and out of shape. Perhaps we will be able to do some training."

"Old," I snorted. "You're hardly thirty."

"I am thirty," Aedin corrected. "But I *feel* so much older…"

"I feel as if a lifetime has passed since I married you." I gave him a half-smile.

Aedin looked at me curiously. "Yes, it has felt that way. You really have grown."

I was satisfied by his assessment and stretched out my toes on the wooden belly of the boat, looking around.

"I might be able to get used to this…"

"Yes, get comfortable." Aedin crossed his legs in front of him. "We finally have time to talk."

"About what?"

He gave a sweeping sign with his hand. "Anything you wish."

"That helps to narrow down a subject," I said, smirking, then paused, remembering something. "Aedin, remember the night you told me about the Gift? About everything?"

"Yes."

"You said that you had Dreamed of the past but didn't tell me what it was about..." I trailed off, hoping he would take the suggestion.

"Ah." Aedin looked at the floor with hesitation. "Yes, I will tell you, but I have to preface and tell you that it concerns you."

I frowned in surprise. "Very well."

"Well not *you* exactly," Aedin continued slowly. "But ... your mother."

I waited in silence with rapt attention.

"When I was in the Rhidge, I had my Dream of the future, which was of you. Years later, when I became the Lord of Lailan, I Dreamed of the past. I suppose there is no other way to tell you of the vision than to recite what I saw and then conclude with my analysis...

"I saw Tours on the island of Berge. It was a cold night—like many I'm sure you were used to. In my Dream I was like a bird—my sight was above a dark and lonely harbor. All was still, save for one boat that was setting out from the rocks and into the sea. As my vision grew clearer, I saw it was a woman—alone—pale and dressed in furs and traveling clothes.

"There were several areas of storage on the boat—it looked like there was a lower deck—yet I thought nothing of this until I saw one of the deck doors open and Tours appeared. He had been hiding beneath, and the woman looked just as surprised to see him as I was.

"There was little discussion between the two of them—Tours said something that I didn't catch, and then grabbed her and pushed her in the water. He used one of the oars to push her down and I watched until the harbor water became still once more."

The boat rocked continually but I focused only on my husband's words. My mouth was dry—I tried to swallow. "How did you know that it was...?"

"Your mother?" Aedin paused, considering my words. "I didn't understand the Dream at the time, although I knew that it would never come without significance. I thought the importance of it would be to show Tours' past activity or Berge.

"But when I came to Berge for the tour and saw you for the first time, I was immediately reminded of that Dream. You look very much like her... Even from afar, I saw the resemblance. When I felt your Gift and came to learn more about yourself and your family, I knew that my Dream had to have been about your mother... Which meant that she was Gifted."

Before I opened my mouth to ask, Aedin continued gently, "I know this because it was a murder, and it was done by a Rhidge. If she had drowned accidentally, there would have been nothing to it. But Tours' involvement suggests that she was attempting to escape from Berge. She likely knew she was being watched—and with two children and a husband, she probably deemed it best to leave, to draw attention away from her family, and escape.

"Tours, or another Rhidge, then most likely watched you and Ephraim as children to see if either of you developed any signs of the Gift. Ephraim did not, but your Gift obviously did develop some time later—late enough that the Rhidge had already lost interest in your family..."

As my husband's words faltered, I turned my gaze to the sea instead of his face and tried to locate the source of the dull pain inside me, almost wishing it would broil into a more passionate loss—but the truth remained a small answer to the riddle of the past, nothing more.

My mother—murdered. It was strange to swallow. The ache I felt from the truth was more for my father's pain at losing a beloved wife rather than consolation for losing a hardly remembered mother.

"Are you alright?"

The breeze made me shiver. I faced Aedin with a resolute grimace. "Yes," I said truthfully. "I am, but it pains me to learn the truth for my father's sake. He loved her greatly."

Aedin nodded pensively. "I'm sorry."

I shook my head. "It's not your fault."

He didn't protest—merely stared at the grain of the wood beneath us.

Returning my gaze to the endless waves, I quietly wondered what the future would hold—marveling in regret at our change of fortunes.

———

Days passed, though it felt like weeks.

The sea, and the occasional passing gulls, became our constant companions. The ceaseless rocking that plagued me the first day became a lullaby; the white-capped blue and emerald waves a desert of movement. I saw animals I had never known to exist, floating warily in their home, suspicious of our intrusion.

At night, sometimes the wind would cease and the world would become a pool of stars. Aedin and I huddled together on the bow, cramped and aching from the unyielding wood, covered by a single blanket.

We rationed food to avoid starvation but hardly enough to fill our bellies. The first couple of days, my stomached cramped and growled angrily. Soon enough, it shrunk to a miserable size. We occasionally talked through the days and nights, but the silences were long and grateful.

Both of us, I expect, had quite a lot to digest. For Aedin, these were his first days of freedom from a life of captivity. For myself, I had a new power to comprehend and a new life of uncertainty. A life as an exile from all I had known.

Aedin was anxious about using the Gift even in the middle of the sea. Day and night, he would pause to scan the western horizon, waiting for the shadow of a ship to appear. But none did —it appeared that we were totally alone. Nevertheless, he feared using large amounts of power and settled in teaching me how to make a flame appear in my hand.

"Locate the Gift," Aedin said quietly. "It's in your blood, so it's not far, but it helps to imagine a physical place, like your heart or head. Find that spot, that reserve, and direct it to your palm."

I struggled with this for nearly our entire journey. There were times when I felt my palm grow warm, but my surprise scared it away. It was entirely mental discipline. By the end of our voyage, I was able to produce wisps of color in my palm, but nothing as bright and blue and powerful as what I'd seen Aedin create.

Around midday on the fourth day, I spotted the faint outline of a small outcropping of rocks on the horizon. When the sun was low in the horizon, the outline became an island, hardly five miles long. It was covered in trees, rocks, and silence.

We brought out the oars and paddled closer, then dragged the boat ashore to sit atop a cluster of rocks surrounded by trees. The sturdy boots that had provided me support on Lailan were now far from their original state. Wet and soggy, I could feel every single rock as we trudged further inland. The only thing that held me up was Aedin's tight grip on my hand. I was extremely thankful for it.

We must have been a comical sight—bruised, scraped, and drenched in a mixture of sweat, seawater, and blood, our lack of sleep obvious from the dark circles beneath our eyes. I hadn't been in a worse state in my entire life.

We walked steadily, almost ceremonially, towards the center of the island. I heard brief bird calls, as if they were announcing our presence, but no other life was visible. Trudging through the brush, trees, and boulders, I stumbled, attempting to avoid a particularly thorny-looking plant. But it caught my heel and I felt blood run down my ankle.

Without stopping, Aedin leaped into a thick wall of brush, towing me along with him. I cursed in pain as twigs chafed against my shins and knees. "Can we please slow down?" I cried, unable to resist voicing my thoughts.

"Yes—sorry," Aedin muttered distractedly, scanning the maze of trees, rocks, and brush with his quick dark eyes.

To my relief, we finally found a sign of life—behind a thicket of trees, we were greeted by a medium-sized stone wall.

"Finally." I could hear the gladness in Aedin's voice as he gracefully leaped on top, pausing to offer me his hand.

As I climbed up to join him, I felt an odd sensation—the stones were warm, despite the thick layer of fog and dew that hung over the island. Underneath me, they vibrated with an inner power—I recognized the sensation.

"Aedin," I said softly as we jumped down and resumed our course.

"Hm?"

"Did you feel… the wall?"

"Yes."

Relief sounded throughout my voice. "Was that… the Gift?"

"Yes, it was."

"Why would the wall have the Gift?"

He looked amused as he glanced at me. "Can you guess?"

I thought for a second. "It can be used as a guarding device?"

"Yes. It's a very simple technique, leaving a trace of your power, which simply warns the owner if anyone comes into contact with it. Jon and Rebecca now know of our arrival."

"Oh." I couldn't help but fantasize a steaming bath and a grand dinner, then immediately felt guilty—I shouldn't expect such luxuries. We were on an island of exiles—their hospitality would be limited.

"Here we are," Aedin announced, the relief evident in his voice. Lifting my gaze, I found it odd that I hadn't previously noticed the building in front of me.

The fortress fulfilled all of my expectations. Easily three times the height of our villa, it was built of impenetrable-looking stone with great weathered walls that gave it a guarded, haunting expression. Arrow slits in lieu of windows revealed at least four or five stories. We stood below an ascending dirt path that led to fortified double doors.

There was such a silence and no hint of smoke or light, I wondered if Jon and Rebecca were still alive at all. Maybe Aedin had been mistaken?

Wordlessly, Aedin began on the path towards the door. When we reached it, two torches in the archway sprang awake with flame. I jumped as warmth encircled us—my toes and fingers gratefully accepting the comfort. The flame was similar to the one

Aedin had produced in the villa—and the one I had attempted—a spiraling mixture of blues, greens, and red.

Aedin didn't bother to knock on the door, and I couldn't help but question if we would be greeted at all. We both held our breath for some time, standing in front of the door, until a loud rumbling sounded from within.

Seconds later, the doors opened outwards. We stepped backwards to allow room as a tall, looming man stood in the crack, eying us with surprise.

"By the gods… Aedin?" the man said in amazement as my memory was instantly triggered.

I drew a sharp breath. It was the man from my Dream. But he had aged—his full head of straw-blonde hair was thinning, his clean-shaven face now dressed in a full beard.

He popped his head further outside, looking behind us. "Is it…?"

"It's just us. We haven't been followed."

Jon looked visibly relieved. He hesitated and then attempted a smile. "Come inside—let me have a better look at you."

Inside, hanging lamps along the ceiling brightly lit the entry hall. Their warmth heated my bones—I wanted to sigh as my shivering subsided.

"Jon." I was surprised to hear the notes of camaraderie and relief in Aedin's voice. "I'm afraid I have a favor to ask of you."

Jon caught him in a one-armed hug, nearly dwarfing my husband given the contrast in their heights. "Well if you came all this way to ask it, I guess I have no choice but to accept. Does it have to do with this pretty lady?" He threw a muscled arm over my shoulder as well—I sank beneath the weight of it.

"Yes." Aedin eyed my reaction with an amused smile.

Jon cheered. "I would love to help! Do you know how long it's been since I've seen another woman besides my wife? As much as I love her, there's only so much I can take of one person." Jon's laughter echoed throughout the hall. "Rebecca! You won't believe what the ocean dragged in!"

From around the corner came a woman of Aedin's height with dark, coffee-colored skin and eyes to match. Her graceful steps and athletic physique suggested a coil about to spring as she moved towards us, one hand resting over a small bulge in her stomach.

"Aedin!" Rebecca cried with joy. She quickened her steps and enveloped him in a fierce hug.

"Easy!" Jon barked good-naturedly. "You're carrying my child!"

Rebecca ignored him, stepping back to look at Aedin with her hands on his shoulders. "You're alive! We heard the most terrible things and were so worried—"

"You two knew?" Aedin's forehead creased in confusion. "But I thought—"

"That we were cut off from all communication?" Jon grimaced. "How do you think we survived without knowing any gossip?"

Aedin frowned. "But it's dangerous to have a correspondent— you could have been tracked."

Jon rolled his eyes. "You were always a killjoy. Let them come —we're bored over here."

"Hiding wasn't as fun as he expected it to be." Rebecca shrugged, smiling.

"Well it looks like you two weren't entirely bored out of your minds." Aedin gestured towards Rebecca. "You're with child!"

Rebecca blushed as Jon threw an arm around her. "Of course! We grew bored of training and decided to try something else. You, on the other hand"—Jon's gaze moved towards me—"have not explained *her*."

"This is my wife… Gwyneth Doyle." Aedin's voice warmed as he introduced me.

There was a short pause. "Your *wife*?" Jon's face twisted in a mixture of surprise and disbelief.

Rebecca swatted him in the chest as she stepped in front of him to hug me. She smelled of the earth, spices, and warmth—a comforting mixture.

"It's lovely to meet you." She smiled, the corners of her dark brown eyes crinkling. "And I'm sure you are much prettier under all that grime and sweat."

With one arm around me in a mother-like embrace, she turned back to her husband. "Jon, get Aedin some food and drink. I think there's still some supper left in the pot. I will draw a bath for Gwyneth—you poor thing!" She squeezed my shoulders and led me down the hall, leaving Jon and Aedin to exit in the other direction.

"Thank you… so much," I mumbled as I stumbled wearily.

"It's not a problem at all—I would want the same if I'd been chased by the Rhidge." Rebecca smiled, rubbing my shoulders, then paused, lowering her voice. "How in the world did you both escape?"

I shook my head in wonder. "Aedin had planned it for months. He'd prepared a boat on the eastern shore of Lailan for us to escape if Tours discovered my Gift…"

She stopped in her tracks. "Your…?" Rebecca repeated slowly, and then eyed me with thorough inspection. "Yes… I can see that. How could I have missed it?"

I shivered. "That appears to be a common theme."

"How did you meet Aedin?" Rebecca wondered aloud, but then stopped. "No, I'm sorry." She steered me further down the corridor. "Bath first, story later."

I gave a weak laugh.

We turned into a room off the main corridor, and as the hall grew dark, Rebecca lit a flame in her hand. Opening the creaking door, she gave me a cautious smile. "Well it isn't the villa on Lailan…"

The room was dark, quiet, and slightly stuffy—the only opening was an arrow slit on the far side of the room. A small hay mattress lay in the corner, covered by coarse linen. At the opposite end of the room was a faucet sticking up from the ground over a large, rough stone basin.

"You have running water?" I wondered aloud.

"Hardly." Rebecca's mouth twisted. "We found a large reservoir in one of the towers where the previous inhabitants would store rainwater. It wasn't the cleanest, after sitting for so long, but now that we use it regularly, it's been a godsend. Still, we ration just in case."

She twisted the tap and water began spilling out. "It's not hot…" Rebecca paused, looking up at me. "If we had anticipated your arrival…" she began with a short laugh.

"It's fine." I dipped my hands in the water, eager for any sort of washing.

"I'll get some towels and a change of clothes… Unless you have any?"

I shook my head.

"Right, of course." She gave a small nod and left.

Stripping off the shirt and pants that had clothed my body for the past four days was an exhilarating moment. I couldn't wait for the bath to fill and crouched in the tub as the water licked my shins. It was cold. I shivered, wishing for warmth.

As I watched the water flow from the tap, I wondered if the Gift would be useful. Closing my eyes and grasping the faucet, I focused on an invisible source and pulled, willing the heat to come—as if praying to the gods.

There was a slight vibration, briefly numbing my hands, and then a connection within my body and mind—a sudden coherence and clarity. The water grew lukewarm as it poured out of the tap.

I felt—and heard—footsteps in the corridor.

Rebecca.

Like a bloodhound gaining the scent of its prey, I suddenly knew her movements and felt her enter the room. My eyes were closed, but I could tell she was behind me—I felt her fear, her mouth moving wordlessly as she tried to make words—

"Well…" She stuttered into silence.

Opening my eyes, I turned to see her face had paled. Why was there fear?

Suddenly remembering the bundle in her hands, Rebecca kneeled at the foot of the tub to place a linen rag and a homespun shirt and pants on the stone floor.

"I made these for myself but I think they'll fit you, even if they are a little big…"

"Thank you," I said with a gentle smile. I could feel the water in my bath growing warmer by the minute.

Rebecca hesitated, balancing on her heel. "How long… do you and Aedin expect to stay?"

I shrugged. "I'm not sure what he had in mind. Perhaps for quite a while."

She nodded vigorously. "Of course. And you are both most welcome. It's just… not safe…"

The water had risen to my stomach. Conscious not to use too much, I turned off the tap. My body relaxed in the shallow warmth, but a warning rose in my mind. "What do you mean?"

She backtracked. "Well, of course, it's *safe* in a sense—we're outside the Empire, but you're never *truly* safe, you must understand. They're looking for you—they might have traced you here—"

"But there is nowhere else to go."

"No…" Rebecca said haltingly. "Not within the Empire." She straightened. "I'll leave you to it—please join us in the kitchen when you're finished," she said and left the room in a hurry.

Considering her words, I sank deeper into the tub, my knees curling to the side in an attempt to submerge myself as much as possible. She was right—we would never be safe inside the Empire, even here on this forgotten spit of land.

I reflected on what Aedin had told me of the eighth island. Was it a terrible idea to seek refuge? Why had Jon and Rebecca not sought safety there? Why remain here?

I cupped some water in my hand and splashed my face, trying to rub away all of my anxieties, the dirt, and the fear.

"Will we ever be safe?" I asked myself quietly, staring at the bottom of the tub and listening to the droplets of water from my face echo onto the surface.

There was no answer.

Chapter Twenty-Seven

"HERE SHE IS!" a booming voice cried as I neared the kitchen.

I pushed open the thick wooden door, which squeaked on its hinges as I entered to see Jon, Rebecca, and Aedin seated around a worn pine table. The room was enveloped in a comforting smell of food, a haze of warmth emitting from the nearby fireplace. I sniffed with happiness as Aedin lazily drew out a chair for me with a foot.

"How was the bath?" he asked.

"Excellent." I turned to see Rebecca busily rise to take away Jon and Aedin's empty bowls. "Many thanks," I said to her back.

"Don't worry yourself with thanks." Rebecca turned to shoot me a quick smile. "You deserved it."

"Indeed," Jon's low, powerful voice rumbled. "An encounter with Tours followed by a nice little fight with the Rhidge, stranded on a sailboat with *this* man for four days." He jerked his thumb at Aedin and winked conspiratorially at me. "Gods above, you deserve a pint of the finest ale!"

Aedin raised his eyebrows. "You have such a thing?"

"Nah." Jon shook his head sadly. "We, unfortunately, are quite sober here."

"What a rough life."

"It is." Jon shrugged. "But we knew not to expect such luxuries. That's why we decided to try something a little different."

Rebecca placed a bowl of stew before me and a clumsily carved wooden spoon as Jon grabbed her stomach. She squeaked, pushing away from him, but he persisted, and she settled on his knees, wrapping her arms around his shoulders.

"*Now* will you explain?" Jon looked knowingly at Aedin.

My husband sighed. "Fine." He sent a meaningful glance in my direction. "Would you like to tell the story?"

I paused, about to swallow a mouthful of stew. "Of what?"

"How we… met."

I snorted. "It wasn't exactly a meeting as much as an arranged marriage."

Rebecca raised her eyebrows. "Was it Tours?"

Aedin shook his head, a sly grin coming across his face. "Quite the opposite in fact."

"Well then—tell!" Jon boomed impatiently.

Aedin and I looked at each other as I motioned to him. "You're the one who proposed."

"True." He smirked. "I was conducting a tour of the islands when I came to Berge. There was a bit of a formal outdoor ceremony where the populace gathered to watch as myself and the lord shook hands, exchanged gifts, made speeches, etcetera. And I…" Aedin paused, looking at me. "I remember looking into the crowd and seeing Gwen—we locked eyes and… Well, I remembered the past and future Dreams I'd had concerning her— they came rushing back in an instant where I was momentarily stunned. And then I felt a flash of her power—the Gift. And I was terrified."

I also recalled that moment.

While I had been preoccupied with exchanging flirtatious glances with Daniel, who had been standing guard adjacent to his lord, I had met Aedin's eyes. I remembered how he had stared at me, appearing lost, even as the Lord Tremer asked him to stand and speak—there had been a moment's hesitation as he'd appeared to wake from a dream. My heart had pounded, my blood thickening, and I'd shrunk back into the crowd to avoid his gaze.

"I—" Aedin broke off, his finger tracing the wooden knots of the table as he laughed grimly. "This sounds ridiculous, but I knew I had to marry her. It all made sense in that moment. I understood that she was my future and I had to marry her to protect her Gift—protect her from the Rhidge. We attended a ceremonial ball where I asked her to dance, and later that night I followed her—"

Jon interrupted with a snort and a dry, "How romantic."

"… and found her name and the information concerning her family, and I made a proposal to her father the next day. The day after, we were married in Berge and then sailed to Lailan."

Rebecca watched my face as Jon placed a finger on his chin, making a thoughtful noise.

"Well," she observed, shifting comfortably in her husband's arms, "that's quite a story."

Aedin leaned back in his chair, ruffling his hair conspiratorially. "Yes—and I'm sure Gwen would have her own side to tell."

They all looked at me. "Hardly much different in factual events," I pointed out. "But I did dislike you for quite a while—"

Jon let loose a belly laugh. "Of course."

"But much has changed," I continued. "I can now see the reasoning behind your actions."

"Always reasoning," Jon repeated. "What were your Dreams, Aedin? You most certainly wouldn't have told them about Gwen when you were in the Rhidge."

"No, I lied to them on that front," Aedin said, nodding, "but… I will only say that they concerned her."

"Has the present one happened yet?" Rebecca asked quietly.

Aedin was silent as he thought. "No… No, I don't believe so."

Rebecca and Jon exchanged thoughtful glances as I finished the last bites of my stew. My stomach expanded with warmth, I settled back into my chair, listening to the crackling of the hearth.

"And you don't know how long you will stay," Jon said.

My husband turned his gaze to mine. "No… My plan never extended that far and we… haven't discussed that yet. I suppose there's nowhere else to go."

Rebecca opened her mouth, but Jon cut her off. "No, there is nowhere else that's safe. Stay here as long as you like!" He waved his hand in offering. "Perhaps we could even do some training in the morning. See if your *lordship* has covered you in rust."

Aedin inclined his head. "Many thanks to you both—we are truly appreciative." He stretched his arms above his head. "I believe we both need to retire. It's been quite the journey."

"Of course." Rebecca stood with grace. "Would you like me to draw some water, Aedin?"

"No, thank you." Aedin pushed back his chair and I followed suit. "I think I'll save a bath for another time."

"Well, I've set a mattress of straw and some blankets in the room—please let us know if you need anything else." She gave a wavering smile.

"Thank you," we both repeated as Jon bid us a loud, "Good evening!"

———

I tried lighting a flame in my palm as Aedin shut the door to our room, sealing the frame with the Gift.

"What's that for?" I glared at my palm, but no flame appeared. Giving up, I moved to find a candle in the corner and lit it with a match.

"Precaution," Aedin said distractedly. He stood facing the door for some moments, then turned towards me, seeming dissatisfied and anxious.

I curled up on the bed of straw as he pushed down on the pump, wetting his face and hands.

"What's wrong?" I whispered.

He took one of the towels from the floor and wiped his face with a shrug. "It's… just a feeling."

"A feeling that…?"

"Something's wrong." He sat beside me, pulling off his boots.

I sighed in irritation. "Will I have to ask a hundred times? *What* is wrong?"

Aedin held up a hand, freezing. His head cocked up to the slitted window above our mattress, where the dark pines obscured a quarter moon. I pricked my ears but heard nothing. A few moments passed in bated breath, until Aedin shook his head, unfurling the blankets.

"Was this here when you came to bathe?"

"What? The mattress?"

"Yes."

"Yes, it was."

My husband frowned as I made room for him on the mattress and we settled down together to lie face to face.

"I wonder if they were waiting for us… If they knew we were coming."

"Jon said they'd received some communication—"

"Merchants would never come this way unless they had a prior deal. I assisted Jon and Rebecca to escape here—I know they had no other contact save myself."

"But it's been, what, several years since then? Perhaps they developed one?"

"On an island such as this? That would have only happened accidentally—if a ship had become stranded here—and that seems improbable."

"Maybe Jon or Rebecca Dreamed and knew the timing," I offered.

Aedin pursed his lips, unconvinced. "Maybe…"

"Why are we arguing about this?" I whispered fiercely, knots suddenly forming in my stomach.

"There's something strange about this—this… situation." Aedin fought out the words.

"Do you think they're in communication with… the Rhidge? With Tours?" I asked quietly, watching his dark eyes offer confirmation.

Aedin exhaled sharply and pulled me close, his brow pressing against mine. "That is my fear," he admitted in a whisper. "But I don't understand *why* or *how*… I *helped* them escape!"

"You helped them escape the Rhidge?"

"No—I helped them escape…" His words faltered as the cogs of his mind began to turn. Aedin said slowly, "I helped them escape from Lailan. I don't know how they escaped from the Rhidge… How *did* they leave the Rhidge?"

"Perhaps they…" I trailed off as our eyes met, and we both knew the answer.

"It's only a guess, Aedin. We can keep a look out and stay sharp."

He nodded distractedly, his hands tracing the length of my arm and shoulder.

"You won't sleep tonight," I ventured.

Aedin emitted a harsh, short laugh. "No… not with this on my mind."

"Let it be." I smoothed the wrinkles on his forehead with my hand, my lips bending to meet his, soft and warm. I marveled at the spark as I kissed him—only months ago I would never have enjoyed it.

"That's an easy way to forget," he commented lightly, his hand roving down my back, pulling my hips towards his.

"And the best way." I leaned over him to blow out the candle before falling back into his arms.

———

A loud pounding echoed on the door.

I shot up with a start, rubbing my face as I blinked into consciousness. The light coming in the small window was hardly light at all—a muted bluish gray, blurring with the black outline of trees. I felt something move next to me—Aedin, his eyes wide, one hand underneath my shoulder, the other clutching a knife.

He cleared his throat, calling with a clear voice, "Yes?"

"You two decent?"

Aedin and I looked at each other, frowns breaking into momentary grins at our fully clothed bodies.

"Give us a minute," I called back as Aedin dropped his head back into the crook of my neck with a loud exhalation.

"Jon, go away."

"We have training to do—"

"Go back to sleep!"

"You're a lazy bastard!"

"Give us an hour."

"Fine." The voice behind the door was clipped. "Meet me in the kitchen." Some grumbled threats followed but I couldn't discern the words.

I pressed my lips into Aedin's hair, stifling a laugh. "Was he always this bad?"

"Always."

Grinning, I curled back into Aedin's body heat and melted. He tucked the knife back under the pile of straw above our heads.

"Do you always hide weapons near you when you sleep?" I asked casually as his hand traced my cheek, chin, lips, and nose.

"Hm, yes," Aedin responded softly. "Old habits die hard." He smiled toothlessly.

"Why? Did the Rh—they attack you at night?"

A shadow flickered across his face. "Yes," he whispered, his eyes falling to my lips. "There were surprise attacks at every hour of the day and night—just to keep us on our toes. It became… like a game. I was always prepared."

Sadly, I cupped his cheek, forcing his eyes to mine. "It is no more," I said with quiet ferocity.

He gave a low, dark chuckle. "I wish I could believe that…"

"Why not?"

"The Rhidge, Tours… even…" He licked his lips, struggling with the words. "I… As long as they exist—as long as *we* exist—there will always be pursuit, and pain, and the fear of being *caught*…"

My brow furrowed with anxiety. He was right. There was no way to escape this.

And a part of me still wished that I had never left Berge, never met Aedin. I would have lived a life of simplicity, illiteracy, and ignorance. Perhaps I would have even been murdered or kidnapped by the Rhidge in my sleep. And yet even then…

"Aedin," I murmured. "And yet there is no place in this world where I would rather be—than here, with you, on this spit of land being chased by the demons of hell."

He closed his eyes briefly, serenity softening his face. "Ciaran," he whispered. "My name is Ciaran… Ciaran Aedin. Though I haven't used it for a long time."

"Ciaran," I repeated with a smile.

"Gwen," he whispered, bending his head and touching his lips to mine.

I reveled in the electricity, pulling him on top of me as our tongues intertwined and our mouths moved in unison. Hands tangled in my hair, fingertips brushing my scalp, and I gasped in pleasure as his mouth descended to my neck, my body arching in response.

Gripping his shirt, I pulled the tails out of his pants and forced them up. With a soft laugh, he drew back, watching me with playful eyes.

Sitting up, his weight on top of me, Aedin tugged the shirt off his head and tossed it onto the floor.

We watched each other for a brief moment—my eyes traced the scars littering his chest, now illuminated by the pale light of dawn. In a swift movement, he placed his elbows on either side of my face, drawing close.

"You know," he began, shaking his head, "I can't believe I'm saying this—but the last thing we need is you with child."

"I don't care," I said simply, my body flushed with excitement.

Burning from my fingers to my groin, I lifted my head towards his, pulling his face close to mine as I inhaled his sweet, salty taste.

Aedin's hips pressed against mine and I felt a hardness between us. My hands wandered in his hair and down his back as his mouth moved to my shoulders and breasts, pulling back the fabric of my shirt. Hips lifting in response, I exhaled in delight, unable to suppress a broad smile as my eyes gazed unseeingly at the ceiling.

"Mm," I heard him mumble against the soft skin of my breast. He hadn't shaved since Lailan and the growing hair on his cheeks tickled my skin. I looked down to see him watching me with an amused gaze. His fingers grazed my nipple as I spread my legs, wrapping them around him.

"What?" I giggled, unable to fight the blush rising to my cheeks.

"Why haven't we done this before?" Aedin shook his head in amazement. "Have we just been complete idiots all this time?"

"Yes," I gasped as he sucked lightly on my skin. "Yes, I think so..."

"Well." He kissed my breast briefly before pushing back down my shirt. "I'd love to continue, but—"

I groaned in fury, trying to pull him back on top of me. "Aedin!"

Neatly freeing himself from my legs and settling on his side, Aedin laid a placating hand on my midsection. "I know." He pulled me towards him, placing his knee in between my legs. "I know."

"You're a horrible person," I muttered, closing my eyes as I pressed my forehead against his in frustration, our heartbeats echoing in the space between.

"I know." I could hear the traces of humor in his voice.

"Mmpf," I grumbled. The steady fever of desire slowly drained from my body, though his hands still wandered my skin, tickling and igniting.

"We can't, Gwen... Not yet..." He groaned. "The risks would be..."

I nodded in short, jerking movements, in painful acknowledgement that he was right. To conceive a child when the Rhidge was nipping at our heels was a horrible thought. It would be poor judgment to do such a thing. And unfair to the child.

Our child.

"Someday though..." I said quietly, my body stirring as his hand ran up my waist, under my shirt.

"Hm?"

"Someday, we might—" I was distracted by the pleasant sensation as his fingers explored my skin. "We might..."

"Yes," he whispered against my throat, "we might."

——

An hour later, Aedin and I dressed. He donned his typical outfit of black that I now understood to be the customary uniform of the Rhidge.

"Why do you still wear it?"

"Hm?" He tucked the tails of his shirt into his pants.

"That outfit," I specified. "I saw Tours' men—the Rhidge—wearing something similar."

"Oh." He looked down self-consciously. "It's just the most comfortable and easy material to move in. The black wasn't ideal for Lailan," he added sheepishly, "but I was already accustomed to it."

I nodded as I straightened Rebecca's handmade shirt and looked for my boots.

"Oh, you might need this—" Aedin tossed a pile of black cloth in my direction.

"What is it?" I caught it, unraveling the package.

Aedin shrugged. "The same uniform. I had extras made for you—just in case."

The black shirt and pants were made of a thin and breathable yet tightly woven material. It stretched slightly when I pulled and I recognized it as the cloth Mary had ordered all those months ago. The same cloth I had worn the night we escaped.

Aedin placed my boots at my feet to complete the ensemble.

"You don't have to wear them…" he began hesitantly.

"No, I want to." Eager to wear anything but dresses and bodices, I shrugged off Rebecca's shirt and tugged the black one over my head, securing several buttons down my chest, then exchanged the pants, tucking in the tails of the shirt.

There was a cord embedded in the waist of the pants that prevented them from falling. I tied the strip of fabric, pleased to see them fit snugly against my waist.

Aedin watched me with a wary gaze.

"What?" I asked.

He gave a half shrug, averting his eyes. "Nothing. It's just strange to see you… in that."

"Well I like it." I twisted my arms and hips, feeling like a child freed from the constraints of formal attire.

"Good." He forced a smile.

We made our way into the kitchen where Jon sat with an earthen mug of hot water. He looked up as we entered, shaking his head. "Thought you two would never leave that room."

Aedin cuffed him on the side of the head, sitting down next to him. "Thank you for the mattress," he said politely.

"Yeah." Jon rubbed his neck. "Don't bother giving it back—you can keep it."

"So—what's the training?" I leaned against the back of Aedin's chair, looking pointedly at Jon.

"Nice outfit you got there." Jon nodded towards my attire. His own was a combination of similar pants, dirtied from years of wear, and a homespun shirt that had been repaired in several places.

"Thank you," I said with pride.

"You're training with us then?"

"If you'll let me."

"It's not a matter of whether *I'd* let you," Jon said, watching Aedin carefully.

Aedin looked at me with finality. "It's your choice."

"You've already been training me," I pointed out.

"Swordplay is only one facet of training." Aedin shifted in his seat. "At least if Jon and I are thinking of the same thing…"

"Physical, mental, and emotional obstacles combined with challenging the power of one's Gift?" Jon said lightly, with raised brows.

"Yes." Aedin smirked. "Then we are on the same page."

"Where's Rebecca? Will she join us?" I asked, moving as Aedin scooted his chair back.

"She's outside collecting herbs and nuts," Jon said dismissively. "Here, follow me—I want to show you both something."

Jon led us to the second floor of the fortress—through the hallway and up a steep, wide staircase. The entire second floor, he explained, used to be an extensive guardroom, filled with almost every type of weapon known to the Empire.

The silence in the great room was filled with Jon's lighthearted words and the cooing of pigeons echoing from the rafter.

"It was a great find," Jon said cheerfully as he picked up an ax from the wall, swinging it around good-naturedly. I took several steps back. Aedin grinned at my cautiousness.

"Of course, Rebecca and I fixed the place up and transformed it into an even better training room. We stitched some mats and found some weights, fixed up some dummies, and organized the weapons…" Jon looked around the wide, stone room with pride. "I've been keeping this place in shape and it's working well for me… You, on the other hand"—he swung the ax around to point it at Aedin; the latter didn't even blink as the point tapped his chest —"have some catching up to do."

Jon motioned towards me with the ax. "And you have some learning to do."

And with that, we lapsed into the most physically challenging activities that I had ever done in my life. Simple things like crunching my arms and legs together while lying down sent spasms through my abdominal muscles, while lunging midway through a walk tore at my thighs.

Countless exercises that I would never have been able to accomplish in a dress had me sweating profusely at the end of a mere half hour. How long could I last? My stomach felt as though it was slowly edging towards my throat with each push-up, crunch, and squat we performed…

Clutching my sides, I lay on a stuffed mat, staring at the stone ceiling as I gasped for air.

Wordlessly, Aedin came into view and handed me a pitcher of water. I stared hungrily at it but couldn't make myself sit up to reach it.

As if reading my mind, he held out his hand, pulling me up into a sitting position. I gauged his mood as I drank. By the cool set of his lips and the faint crease between his brows, I could see he was concerned. About my well-being no doubt.

As I gulped down more water, I noted that he was barely sweating and grimaced jealously—I'd been naïve to think that the training wouldn't be this bad.

Aedin opened his mouth as if to say something, but I stopped him. "I'm fine," I said, putting down the pitcher and wiping my wet hair back from my forehead, retying it with twine.

He smiled softly. "I was going to advise you not to drink a lot of water. You'll regret it later."

I rolled my eyes. "How comforting. I think I'll be regretting a lot of things tomorrow."

He feigned confusion. "You want to give up?"

"No!" I said, scowling as I folded my legs underneath me.

He shot me a quiet smile. "Good," he said softly.

Jon re-entered the room. "Stand up!" he barked. "Break time's over."

Aedin held out his hand again to help me stand; I took it. We walked over to where Jon stood in the middle of the room with a set of stuffed dummies.

"Now"—Jon patted a dummy—"this is the enemy. And you're going to give him a rough day."

Without any warning, Jon swung his fist into the dummy's face, causing the thing to nearly fall to the ground. I stood dumbfounded at the power of the strike.

"I've packed the bottom with a mixture of water and sand so it should hold, no matter how hard you hit it." Jon winked at me. "And the dummy itself is some tightly packed straw so it's rather similar to human flesh. Aedin"—he pointed his thumb at another dummy—"that one's yours. Enjoy. My lady"—he gave a good-humored bow—"this is yours."

Warily, I stood in front of the dummy, wiping sweat off my brow.

"Now, make a fist," Jon instructed, showing his own. "Like this, yes. But let your thumb naturally curl over the others—it wants to go there. Okay, now angle your fist so your pointer finger is slightly forward. Not the finger itself, just the wrist—there! Like that!" He grinned at my fist. "Now keep it nice and tight—not too tight, just comfy. And stand like this—" Jon faced the dummy with his knees slightly bent, fists at his waist.

I mimicked his stance, feeling incredibly foolish.

"Now let one loose!"

Obeying, I swung my arm to meet the side of the dummy.

"Ouch!" I stepped back, losing my stance, as my hand bounced harmlessly off the thing. Out of the corner of my eye, I saw Aedin pause in his mock battle to glance my way.

Ignoring his stare, I resumed the stance and hit the dummy harder. I disregarded the pain that shot through my knuckles. That soon diminished as I continued the movement and focused on the precision of the action itself.

I thought of Tours—of his leering, malicious gaze—and imagined his features on the dummy, an unfamiliar sensation bubbling in the pit of my stomach.

A sickeningly sweet sensation—revenge.

He had killed my mother and exiled us from our home. He would continue to hunt us as long as we existed. The thought was haunting, and my actions felt redemptive.

After twenty or so repetitions, Jon called a halt, complimenting my technique and (albeit meager) power. We paused for a break.

I rested my hands on my waist as I watched Aedin battle his dummy. His strikes made mine look pathetic—quick, merciless, and powerful, they sent the stuffed thing nearly on its back every time. I frowned—when I'd hit it, the dummy had barely moved.

Jon sighed reminiscently. "He was always the best."

"But it was you who taught him, right?"

"Some things." Jon smiled at the compliment. "Among many others."

"You were his first friend."

Jon nodded pensively. "Yes… That was a long time ago." He turned back to the dummy. "Give me twenty more punches."

Obeying, I resumed. "I… had a Dream… about you," I said between punches.

To my surprise, Jon laughed. "Oh, the Dreams. I was in one?"

I couldn't resist a smile in response. "Yes. You were…
teaching… Aedin… to fight… in a courtyard… when it was…
raining."

"Rest," Jon commanded, and I let my shoulders slump. "Stand
up straight." He took my small shoulders in his muscled hands
and pushed them back—I winced. "Better. Hm… It was raining,
you said? I think I remember that. I'm surprised you saw that
particular one."

"Why?"

"The Dreams are never random—they always have a purpose.
Like when I was feeling especially suicidal during the Rhidge, I
had a Dream about Rebecca. It gave me hope, in a way, that I had
a future outside of the Rhidge. Rebecca, likewise, Dreamed of us
escaping, right after we realized that the Rhidge was going to
dispose of me." His eyes twinkled. "So you must have been
feeling something at that time to make you have that dream of
Aedin's past."

I opened my mouth to guess, but Jon shook his head. "You
don't have to tell me. In fact, it's usually better to not tell anyone
—that can usually lead to them being used against you."

I frowned. "How so?"

Jon shrugged. "Well if I'd told the Rhidge, at the time, that I
had a Dream of getting married to another assassin, they would
have killed me and Rebecca on the spot. That was why the Rhidge
required you to tell them of the Dreams; it helped them to keep a
hold on us."

He moved from the dummy, gesturing me forward. "Now,
give me twenty push-ups!"

I stifled a groan as I hit the floor.

After the sparring session with the dummies, we broke for a
simple midday meal that Rebecca had prepared for us.

"So how was it?" she asked as we sat down around the simple
wooden table.

I grimaced as I sat down, my thighs aching with the effort. My
stomach grumbled hungrily as I dug into the cold meat and
cheese on the table. The food was nothing like what I'd eaten on
Lailan—it was rich and wild, similar to what I'd grown up with

on Berge. In lieu of fresh fruits and vegetables, it was a spread of salted meats, breads, and cheeses.

"It was alright—not too bad." I rubbed my stomach where my abdominal muscles still ached from use. "I'll be sore tomorrow."

Rebecca laughed, tying her hair back. "I remember when I was sore—it's the worst and the best feeling in the world."

I frowned as I popped a piece of cheese in my mouth. "Best?"

She nodded, still smiling as she sat down. "It's the feeling of pride that follows—that you've accomplished something most people haven't. It's the one thing that makes you want to go back and endure it all again."

I glanced at Jon and Aedin, who nodded simultaneously in agreement, their mouths full.

"Definitely," Jon agreed, between mouthfuls. "You hit the nail on the head."

Grinning affectionately, Rebecca punched him lightly in the shoulder as she refilled her goblet.

After the meal, we returned to the training room, but this time to focus on the Gift. I was grateful that we weren't going to do any more physical training, already exhausted from the simple exercises this morning.

Jon and I sat cross-legged across from each other on a mat, only an iron weight between us. Aedin hadn't joined us (after taking Jon's blunt hint that he wasn't needed) and instead opted to help Rebecca with the chores.

"Now the Gift." Jon rubbed his beard absentmindedly. "What do you know about it?"

I shrugged. "Nothing really. I know when my emotions are at extremes I can exert a kind of… pressure?"

"Yes, that is a definite indicator, as are many other things. But what do you know of how the Gift works?"

"Nothing," I confessed.

"Alright." Jon rubbed his hands together. "Then we'll start with the basics. Now, the Gift is essentially a force that pulses from our bodies—residing specifically in our blood—that has the ability to affect things outside the body. While a normal, non-Gifted person would not be able to move this weight without touching it, a Gifted could easily use their Gift to move it without any physical contact."

And, turning his gaze to the weight, I watched the dumbbell rise several inches off the ground, before landing with a clumsy *plop* back down on the mat.

"Why is it invisible?" I asked.

Jon shrugged. "Why is the wind invisible? It's one of the many things that we may never know. Now, because it runs in the blood —and your blood runs throughout you from head to toe—it makes sense that your Gift can be exerted from your body as a whole. You could kick somebody with your Gift and still knock them over. However, like doing most tasks, it's only natural that we exert it using our hands. Later, we'll teach you to use your mind so no appendages are required."

Jon reached out to me. "Here, take my hand."

It was large, calloused, and warm, and engulfed mine as I placed it in his. There was an almost imperceptible vibration coming from his hand, like a thin layer hovering over his skin. "Do you feel that?" he asked.

"Yes," I said, nodding; I recognized it from the wall and Aedin's hand.

He wrapped his hand around mine. "Now, the trick is controlling it, getting it to come out from your blood and move, or affect, the things around you. Right now, I'm drawing it out. However, usually, you aren't able to feel the Gift from simply touching people's skin unless they are consciously using it. Only extreme emotions extract it without your knowing or simply a lack of control. Now—think of a spool of thread inside your mind."

I frowned at him. "And?"

"Close your eyes," he instructed with a smile. "And just relax."

Loosening my jaw, I closed my eyes and tried to unwind. I pictured a spool of thread—white thread—that existed somewhere in my consciousness. It sat stubbornly silent and did not move.

"Now," Jon said, "take the loose end of the thread."

It took a couple of seconds to find it amidst the smooth curves of the spool. I tugged at the end and eased it towards me, and the spool slowly began to unwind.

The room was silent beyond my own breathing. In the darkness of my mind, the thread continued to uncoil itself and my hands became warm. It was very similar to what I'd felt with Aedin on the boat and I shivered, worrying what would happen when the spool ran out.

"Open your eyes," Jon commanded.

I flickered them open to see the weight floating about chest height. The thread continued to run through my mind, my hand stretched out towards the metal.

"Now, lower it…"

As the weight lowered, I felt the thread loosen.

"And stop it…"

The weight stopped; the thread tightened again but continued at a slower pace.

"And let go…"

As the weight dropped to the ground, the thread snapped. It was like a brief muscle spasm, causing my hand to jerk backwards.

I frowned. "Interesting…"

"Definitely. However, you'll get used to it. The first times, it's shocking, but after…" He shrugged. "I hardly notice it now."

I nodded, rubbing my suddenly cold hands. "Is someone able to control my Gift while touching me?" I asked curiously, remembering the times Aedin had touched me and I had felt my power withdraw.

Jon paused for a moment. "It's hard to do," he admitted, scratching his chin. "But it is possible. If there's some connection between individuals who are Gifted, they can influence each other's power. I think it depends on the relationship and the level of their power. But there aren't many who can affect your Gift simply by touching you."

I flexed my fingers, wondering when I would reach that point.

"Now." Jon grinned easily. "Let's try it again."

And we repeated the exercise several times over, until I was familiar with the thread and where to direct it. My mind ached from the effort, but I felt a renewed strength that was beginning to grow.

——

The next days passed in the same fashion—working out in the morning, a break for midday meal, and then lessons with the Gift before dinner.

Jon began each day by waking up Aedin and me with a knife at our throats. I continually failed this test, until Jon taught me how to leave my Gift, weaving a web across the door or a trip line on the floor, to signal me to wake.

And by the end of the week, I was able to flicker my eyes open before the knife met my throat—but I was slow to grab the knife I'd hidden and always lost in the end.

Aedin was rarely surprised—and if he was, he never showed it. Each morning—no matter how silent Jon was—Aedin was ready. Once, he was already dressed as Jon opened the door to "wake him up gently."

"He must have set a barrier somewhere," Jon muttered darkly under his breath as we made our way to the kitchen.

I didn't miss Aedin's smug look in response.

But it wasn't only during these sessions that I saw this side of my husband—I had plenty of time to study him when we began using daggers.

"The knife"—Jon held up a kitchen knife which looked like the one Rebecca used for cutting meat—"and the dagger"—he lifted a small blade, barely a foot long—"are two weapons which the assassin relies on to kill his prey."

Aedin folded his arms, objecting, "I thought you were preaching defense."

"I'm getting to that," Jon snapped good-naturedly. "Relax. Here." He tossed the dagger at me.

Fear flashed through me as I watched it rise in the air, floating towards me. I stepped back, letting it clatter to the ground, my teeth gritted nervously.

Jon, to my relief, rolled his eyes. "You were supposed to catch it. Pick it up—it doesn't bite."

I obeyed, gingerly holding the handle.

"Anyway." Jon cleared his throat as he eyed my hesitant grip. "Despite the dagger being one of the assassin's best tools, it is also an excellent defense mechanism. It's small enough to fit into a large pocket or belt, yet deadly sharp. If you know how to wield this, you can defend yourself from almost anything.

"Such as"—Jon beckoned towards Aedin—"a physical attack."

As I realized what they were doing, I backed up. Aedin leaped towards Jon in an exaggerated punch as the latter dodged it, pressing the blunt side of his blade to Aedin's stomach.

"Close combat." Jon pulled another knife out of his pocket and threw it at Aedin, who caught it easily. Similar to the first scenario, Aedin attempted to attack Jon with the weapon, but he parried the blow easily. I winced at the sound of screeching metal.

"A sword attack." Aedin pulled a sword from a nearby rack and swung it towards Jon, who slipped between the long strokes to place his knife at Aedin's throat.

"Or even a long range attack." Nodding towards Aedin, Jon gestured for him to back up—they ended up on opposite sides of the room. Aedin threw the knife he was holding, with blinding speed, towards Jon, who batted it away with his own weapon.

"See?" They came to stand before me, shrugging as if they practiced this sequence every day. "It's very effective," Jon continued looking at me pointedly.

I gave him a doubtful look—there was no way I would ever be able to protect myself from any of those things with a dagger.

"Anyway, we'll start with the basics." Jon gestured to the knife Aedin had thrown. "Rebecca and I designed all of the knives in the house to be not only household utensils but balanced enough to throw."

"You designed them?" I wrinkled my brow in confusion.

"We took the kitchen knives we found and welded some scrap metal to them." He picked up the knife, showing it to me. "We did a good job—the hilt looks almost normal, but, as you can see, it isn't perfect."

When I inspected the hilt, I noticed a discoloration between the sides, as well as a slight bumpiness of crude craftsmanship.

"Useful," I commented.

"Definitely." Jon shrugged. "Always be prepared—if this place is attacked, we designed almost everything to be used as a weapon."

I raised my eyebrows. "Will we be attacked?"

"It's unlikely." I detected the attempted light tone. "But the Rhidge *is* looking for you—and us. You never know." He shook his head, as if brushing away the thought. "Back to the knives. You hold them, and daggers, in a similar grip. Like this. Unless you're throwing them, but that'll come later."

And for the next several hours, we practiced defensive moves with the knife and dagger. Every so often, I would switch knife and dagger, but the technique was the same. By the end of the session, my hand was aching and my hair stuck to my sweaty forehead.

After the final exercise, Rebecca entered the room, wiping her hands on her apron as she came to stand by me.

"How is it?" she asked with a grin, gesturing to the knife in my hand.

"Good." I attempted a smile but failed. All I wanted to do was drop the knife, eat dinner, and then sleep.

Rebecca laughed at my attempted nonchalance. "It's hard, I know, but you'll improve. Already you've come so far!"

Jon and Aedin finished their moves and came to stand by us. Jon agreed whole-heartedly. "She most definitely has!"

"Thanks," I said with a shrug, meeting his bright blue eyes. "I can definitely *feel* the results, but I've yet to see them."

"So." Jon gestured towards Aedin. "Care for a spar?"

"Only if you want to be beaten." Aedin cocked his head at Jon.

"We'll see about that…" Jon trailed off suggestively, raising an eyebrow and backing towards the cleared area in the center of the room.

Aedin grinned, like a child about to play, and turned to me. "Knife?"

"Of course." I reached out, unsure whether to hand it to him hilt first.

Thankfully, he read my indecision and clasped the blade gently, tossing it up to grab the hilt, then tucking it in the sleeve of his shirt, nodding in thanks before joining Jon in the center.

"Rules," Jon stated as he twisted the dagger in his hand. "Knives, daggers, and physical contact only. No Gift. And no going within ten feet of my pregnant wife."

"I could beat either of you in this condition," Rebecca called, narrowing her eyes at them.

"Of course, but we wouldn't risk it," Jon added hastily, attempting a grin.

"You just wait until after this child—your ego is going to be beaten down so hard…" Rebecca's mouth twitched into a smile, despite her glare.

"I can wait till that day." Jon smiled innocently, adding quickly, "Because it'll never come. Anyway… Agreed?"

"Yes." Aedin nodded, spinning the dagger in his hand.

"Ready?" Jon flourished his knife in mock technique, reminiscent of how Ephraim and I used to play. "Set—"

I barely saw the first strike—it was too fast and almost escaped my notice—but I knew it was Aedin. Jon, however, appeared to have no trouble blocking it, slashing his knife at Aedin's dagger, blocking it down.

The metal sang as it met and I winced, glancing at Rebecca, who hadn't flinched. Her expression was almost amused as she studied them with her quick, brown eyes.

A quick feint was returned from Jon. My husband didn't fall for it, and instead took the brief opening to slash at Jon's unprotected side. The latter, sensing his opponent's actions, quickly brought the knife around to block it in the nick of time.

Blows continued from both Aedin and Jon, their eyes never straying from the other, their feet hardly making a sound as they danced around the clearing. It was unnerving to watch them in such a deadly exchange—several times I would gasp as I thought a hit had been made, until they spun back around, unharmed.

The longer the fight lasted, the more powerful became the blows; they took each opportunity to strike as if it was their last. I flinched as Jon suffered an especially hard blow, his arm falling with the knife. Yet it didn't seem to shake him, as he returned an equally forceful strike to Aedin.

The dagger fell out of Aedin's hand.

I watched it clatter to the floor, but Aedin didn't waste a second on his loss—efficiently, he pulled my knife out of his sleeve, slashing it across Jon's mid-section and missing him by an inch. The dagger lay forgotten on the floor as the men continued their fight.

It ended only a few minutes later, in a fashion as I had seen before. Slipping through Jon's defenses, twirling towards him, Aedin placed the flat of the knife at Jon's throat. They paused for a second, both letting their breath come easy, until Jon laughed.

Smiling, Aedin released Jon and stepped back, then clasped him by the hand. Still coughing a laugh, Jon pulled him into a bear-like hug, shaking his head.

"You were always good at that move—and I was never good at defending it." Jon ran a hand through his thinning hair, eying Aedin as a father would proudly gaze at his son. "You've been training." He narrowed his eyes in suspicion.

Aedin shrugged, picking up the dagger. "Here and there." He pocketed it, handing the knife to Jon.

Jon accepted it, throwing an arm around my husband as they came towards us. "What happened?" he asked.

"You mean the dagger?"

"Yes."

"I dropped it," Aedin said, shrugging as if it wasn't important. "Slippery handle, your powerful blow. And I knew I had another —it wasn't much of a loss."

"True," Rebecca muttered, a smile warming her face. "So," She turned to her husband. "Was that satisfying? To have spent the past years pent up with only *me* beating you—was it a nice change?"

In response, Jon threw a sweaty arm around Rebecca, pulling her close as she, giggling, attempted to spin away. "Not at all—I dearly miss you beating me. Aedin could never replace you." He shot a wicked grin in our direction.

Rebecca patted his chest. "Dinner won't be ready for a while… Jon, could you help me in the kitchen for a minute?"

"Does it involve a pint of ale?"

"Only in your dreams."

Jon shrugged at us, letting Rebecca tug him out of the practice room.

Aedin pulled the dagger out of his pocket and began weaving it skillfully in between his fingers. When they had disappeared through the doorway, he looked at me and motioned towards the other door. "Care for a walk?"

"My lord," I acquiesced with a curtsy as Aedin rolled his eyes. He held out his hand and a flame emerged, illuminating the darkness of the stairwell.

We descended the back stairs—down several flights—until we reached a rickety door. After several attempts, Aedin shouldered it open to reveal the cool mossy ground.

"Did you know this was here?" I asked curiously.

I heard the ruffled squawk of a pigeon as we emerged—it eyed us cautiously before hopping into the dark stairwell.

He shook his head and closed his hand. "No."

The birds' song announced the end of the day. The light through the trees was cooling and I could feel the thick layer of marine fog begin to creep into my bones.

We picked our way slowly through the tree roots and rocks. I projected my Gift—curious as to whether this might be a test. But there was nothing—just the quiet whisper of the waves on the rocky shore.

"Are you enjoying being with Jon and Rebecca again?"

Aedin looked back at me. "Yes…" he answered but without finality.

We were silent. A low stone wall appeared before us and, as we stepped over it again, I suddenly realized where we were going.

Carefully avoiding the thorny bushes, we made our way towards the shore. The trees stopped to reveal the endless horizon, and I felt my breath come easy. Our boat was still there—tucked at the end of the little cove and stuck amongst the rocks. I was grateful that the tide hadn't swept it away.

Aedin went to the boat, checking the ropes and sail, examining the hull with his keen eyes while I sat nearby, watching the dark rocks change color as the water washed over them. A small crab came out from under one and sat at the shoreline, clicking his claws in preparation for a meal. At the sound of Aedin's footsteps, he quickly retreated under cover.

"Well?" I asked.

Aedin sat next to me, resting his forearms on his knees. "Everything looks fine. We should repair the tear on that sail soon."

"Do we need to leave?"

He didn't look at me. "I don't know. I feel… powerless here." He lowered his voice. "I don't know *if* or even *how* they're communicating with the outside world. Whether it's the Rhidge or passing merchants… This could all be one giant misunderstanding…"

Aedin picked up a rock and threw it into the water. His lips were pressed into a thin line.

"It could be," I admitted. "But it could also have been planned. Something you—perhaps—never thought possible…"

Aedin nodded in agreement, but then shook his head. "I just don't understand… after all these *years*. And from the one man I trusted—that I even considered a *friend*… It just doesn't fit."

"Maybe there's something we're missing. Maybe Tours has something to hold against them…"

"You know"—Aedin gave a short laugh—"it took me a long time to actually trust Jon. And when I did, he made me believe in honor. In standing up for abstract convictions that *he* convinced me were true. It was such a foreign concept… but it proved a healthier way to live." He paused. "Maybe he wasn't any better than the rest of them… Just had better words."

I didn't know what to say. I placed my hand on his forearm, and he grasped it.

"What will we do?" I asked quietly, after a moment of silence.

Aedin sighed. "*If* our suspicions are correct, then we can't stay here for long. We continue training—you especially"—he looked at me meaningfully—"and wait and see. We need to watch the shoreline every morning and evening—in case of ships. If they come from the west, then we need to leave."

"And if they come from the east?"

"Well," he admitted with a wry smile, "we should probably also leave."

"And go where?"

Neither of us knew the answer.

Chapter Twenty-Eight

EPHRAIM SHOULDERED HIS bag and left the chamber with his head down.

He avoided the steady gaze of Lord Tours and the stares of all the advisors. The king was the only one that didn't seem to care—he took a swig of his wine and gingerly lifted himself from his chair. There was a buzz of chatter, but Ephraim didn't pause to listen. He turned the corner and walked quickly to his rooms.

Since the reception at the villa on Lailan, his life had turned upside down.

It hadn't taken long for rumors to spread—even in the early hours of the next morning—that horrible things had happened. He hadn't heard the sharp ring of swords or the quick fight that had ensued—he'd been lounging in a corner of their sitting room, his head pleasantly buzzed from wine.

It was only later—when he couldn't find either Gwen or Lord Aedin to say goodnight—that he'd found it odd. And even stranger when he arose the next morning to find Tours, but no trace of his sister or her husband.

Tours had clapped him on the back, ushering him inside the dining room, advising softly, "We need to make an announcement in the name of the king…"

His mind was numb.

They were dead.

Murdered in the name of political disobedience—or "executed in the name of justice" as Tours had so succinctly put it.

Ephraim had left the villa and boarded the ship back to Radiance in a fog. His father had learned of the announcement only hours after they had left port and had retreated to their rooms in silence. Ephraim had thought he might sleep on deck that night, rather than face the desolate sorrow of a man who had lost his daughter.

When they arrived at Radiance after a miserable three day journey, he had urged his father to stay with him at the palace. At least they would be together—would be able to console each other.

But Doyle had looked at him sadly, patted his shoulder, and mumbled something about keeping up the shop. Ephraim had nodded, forcing a tight smile, and disembarked the ship. It was not how they'd expected their trip to end.

A small part of him had been ripped away. His little sister— dead. And at the beginning of such a promising life. He'd allowed himself to cry in his rooms, but after a while, a solid numbness had descended over his mind. There were no more tears—he was exhausted from the pain.

Occasionally he would wonder what Lord Aedin had done to incur such wrath. Perhaps he had run an illegal business—or had failed to pay the appropriate amount of taxes. But he struggled to relate any nefarious actions to the man he'd met. Aedin had known the stakes of his lordship—but perhaps he hadn't cared. And so, in brief fits of pain, Ephraim felt anger and hatred towards Aedin—and then a helpless sadness at the futility of it all.

They were gone.

"I'm sorry—"

Someone knocked him in the shoulder as he made his way through the crowded hall. Startled, Ephraim broke from his thoughts to look up and saw a familiar face. "Daniel," he said quietly, looking down again.

"Ah." Daniel's face twisted into a combination of awkwardness and grief. "Hello, Ephraim."

"Hello."

There was an unpleasant lull despite the buzz of the hall.

"I have to—er—go," Daniel said lamely, nervously edging around Ephraim. "Busy day…"

"Yes." Ephraim nodded. "Of course." And he moved away from Daniel. They went in opposite directions.

Ephraim didn't release his breath until he closed the door to his rooms.

With a thud, he threw his pack on the chair and moved to the basin, splashing water on his face then staring at his reflection. Bloodshot eyes rested under a tanned and wrinkled brow. He laughed darkly, remembering how he'd looked forward to getting a tan while in Lailan. Now he couldn't care less.

There was a quiet knock on the door.

Ephraim fought to keep his hands from shaking as he walked to open it.

Hollyn stood outside, peering anxiously into the room. His heart sank at the sight of her.

"Hello," she said quietly.

"Hello."

"I heard the cabinet meeting had ended…" She paused. "Did you want to join me for dinner?"

"No, thank you."

Hollyn's brow creased in worry. "Ephraim, you haven't appeared for dinner since returning to court. It's been over a week!"

"I'm not hungry," he said shortly.

"I'm sure you are." Hollyn leaned around him, her gaze lingering on a pile of dishes in the corner. She wrinkled her nose. "Why don't we go outside for some fresh air?"

"No."

"I insist."

"I just don't…"

"I *insist*." She eyed him with a hard gaze. "I know this must be hard"—she lowered her voice—"but you've *got* to pull through. You can't let them win."

Her words sparked something in Ephraim. He looked at her curiously.

"What do you mean?"

She threw up her hands. "You can't let them see that you're *suffering*. Although it's heartbreaking, your sister and Lord Ae—"

"Don't speak his name," Ephraim growled.

"*They* are considered political traitors. You don't want to appear to sympathize with them—do you?"

"But I do. I sympathize with my innocent sister—"

"It doesn't matter what *you* think," Hollyn cut him off. "It's what *the king* thinks—and he has branded them such."

Ephraim was quiet. His heartbeat slowed as her words sank in. "She was innocent," he protested quietly.

"I know." Hollyn's green eyes were kind and sad.

It wasn't fair. Gwen had married Aedin at their insistence—and paid the price for her obedience. He should have pushed back more when his father had made the decision. Ephraim hated himself almost as much as he hated the injustice of it all.

But there was nothing to be done. They were gone.

His grip on the door loosened and he stepped outside. "Let's walk."

Hollyn forced herself not to smile at this victory. "Yes—let's."

They walked down the hall, following its curve to the lower floor. There was a thick crowd milling about the entry rooms. Ephraim avoided looking towards the posted announcements on the wall as they steered towards the gardens. If he had, he would have seen their names written in black ink across the large declaration on the middle right.

Nausea struck him, and he walked a bit faster.

Hollyn lifted her skirts and quickened her pace to keep up.

As their feet touched the grass, Ephraim felt a weight lift from his chest. He self-consciously brushed back his hair, wishing he'd combed it before leaving his rooms.

Hollyn didn't seem to mind—she tucked her arm in the crook of his as they milled about the gardens.

"Why do people *stare*?" Ephraim muttered darkly, glaring at a passing couple who eyed him carefully.

"Gossip," Hollyn said simply. "It will pass… It always does."

The fact didn't make him feel any better. But as they walked, Ephraim gratefully soaked up the sight of the clear blue sky and the scent of pine. Something loosened in his chest.

He felt Hollyn's fingers on his forearm and the sun on his face, and released a heavy sigh.

Hollyn didn't say anything. He thought back to how they'd first met and how he had admired her carefully chosen words. She didn't prattle and rarely gossiped. She was careful, practical, and kind.

"Thank you," Ephraim said quietly after several minutes of silence. He looked down at the grass.

"Hm?" Hollyn turned towards him.

Ephraim was about to repeat himself when he caught her wry smile and grinned. "You heard me…"

"I did," she said succinctly. "Now if we can only get you to eat."

Ephraim's stomach growled in response. "I wouldn't mind dinner later…"

Hollyn smiled smugly in response, looking out at the line of trees.

They walked in silence, listening to the branches sway in the breeze as the passing courtiers around them chatted gaily.

"I wish… I could have met her," Hollyn said haltingly.

Ephraim looked down as his boots crunched through the grass. "You would have liked her," he admitted quietly. "Growing up, she was my best friend."

Hollyn squeezed his arm in response.

"She was very competitive, in a peculiar way." Ephraim gave Hollyn a brief smile. "She would only pursue what she thought was worth pursuing but gave it her whole heart. It was difficult for her to be married to Lord Aedin—she was never given a choice. But I think she made the best of it eventually…"

Hollyn's eyes were wide with memory. "That announcement took the palace by storm… Why *did* Lord Aedin marry her?"

Ephraim shook his head. "You know… I never quite understood why a man with such power and influence chose to marry a shopkeeper's daughter he'd only met for one evening. I wondered if he was desperate—or perhaps cruel—but he never appeared vicious or unfair. I was skeptical and expressed my doubts to my father, but in the end… it was an offer we couldn't refuse." He said the last words with a mocking grin.

"Perhaps he loved her." Hollyn shifted her eyes to his.

He shrugged, kicking at a fallen branch as his lungs tightened at the painful memory.

Whether Lord Aedin had at the time of the proposal was irrelevant—Ephraim had seen the answer in Lailan. Aedin had loved her.

Ephraim pressed his lips together and didn't respond.

"How were things… when I was gone?" he asked, wishing to change the subject.

Hollyn sighed. "I have been attending to the king's rooms as of late."

Ephraim stiffened. "Why the change?"

"Priscilla was sent back to Acedes, and the king seemed to think I did a fine job with her, so he asked me to assist him."

Ephraim recalled the voluptuous young girl that had enjoyed the king's attention for almost a year. "Why was she sent back?" he wondered aloud.

Hollyn shrugged. "I think he tired of her."

"Has he…?" Ephraim looked at Hollyn meaningfully.

"No, certainly not," Hollyn said quickly, a blush staining her cheeks. "I don't think I am pretty enough for him."

"That's not true," Ephraim said darkly under his breath, but he was satisfied. "You are pretty."

A soft smile crept over Hollyn's freckled face as she moved closer to his side. "Thank you," she murmured, then paused. "It is interesting seeing how the king runs his household. I'm working with that older gentleman—you know, the one who always looks like he smells something bad."

Ephraim gave a short laugh. "Yes, I've seen him."

"Well Mr. Fray is much less disciplined than you would *think* given the scope of his role. He often takes long naps in the middle of the day and we are hardly *ever* on schedule—" She shook her head, her blonde curls bouncing in the sunlight.

"Madness," Ephraim commented wryly.

"It is truly incredible. I suggested that we might tailor the schedule to account for potential delays—to avoid the crowds of advisors and courtiers that just accumulate in that hall outside of his rooms—and he said no!" Hollyn exclaimed. "Some of them sit there for *days*! And then Lord Tours just waltzes through the door whenever he wishes—no appointment required—"

"He is the Lord of Radiance," Ephraim pointed out.

"I don't care if he's Lord of the *Empire*," Hollyn fumed. "It's distracting to the king and unfair to those who have made appointments and have to *wait* for a meeting that might never happen! And yet he is given full access to the king and will often ask us to remove or add appointments from his schedule at his pleasure. Occasionally, he will take the king's meetings himself! And he visits *every* day…"

"I am tired of Lord Tours," he muttered with a grim expression.

"I am as well!" Hollyn exclaimed loudly but then realized the connection and softened her voice. "Yes—of course you are."

Ephraim pushed away the memory of the lord's grimly triumphant face that morning in the villa. The soft enunciated words Ephraim had been forced to commit to parchment.

He wondered if Lord Tours had planned it all along—perhaps the purpose of the visit *was* to murder them. No, he corrected himself quickly, that was absurd. What a cruel and evil thought.

They entered a clearing to find tables laden with glasses of wine, fruit, and sweets. People were throwing balls on the lawn in a game to knock down wooden pins. Cheers erupted when a lady's ball dispatched all six, and Ephraim felt his spirits lift. No one stared, given the distractions surrounding them.

Hollyn led them towards the wine table and handed him a glass. Ephraim grabbed a small cake and stuffed it in his mouth. It felt good to eat something sweet.

She raised her glass at him with a small smile and Ephraim's heart leaped in his throat. He studied the freckles on her nose and her small red lips and wished he could kiss her in front of everyone.

Clinking their glasses together, the pair stood idly by, watching the game progress. Even though he had been at the palace for almost half a year, Ephraim was still unfamiliar with most of its inhabitants. They changed regularly—unknown individuals coming from their islands to seek political assistance, positions, or meetings. It was a rotating circle of fashion, politics, and greed.

The palace itself often felt like one long, unending reception. Wine was served nearly every hour of the day—meals were long and the food was rich. Coming from Berge, Ephraim had thoroughly enjoyed the scene when he had first arrived, watching the collection of courtiers, lords, and nobles with awe and interest and dining at the formal hall almost every evening.

Returning after Lailan, Ephraim had felt completely different. He'd watched the strange faces and high fashion with fatigue and had only strayed out of his rooms for meetings. He wondered if he would ever be able to properly enjoy the palace again.

Sipping his wine, Ephraim felt the alcohol enter his blood with satisfaction. Perhaps he only needed another drink—to help calm his thoughts and numb the pain.

"There's nothing worse than a political cheat," a loud voice said nearby. "Especially the likes of Aedin—he got what he deserved. Thinking he could swindle the king out of his profits."

Ephraim's head whipped around. They were standing about twenty paces away—their voices echoing across the lawn.

A group of young men in fine doublets—and among them a familiar mop of brown hair.

"You slept with her, didn't you?"

"I got what I needed at the time." Daniel's wry delivery elicited laughter from the group.

"No—don't—" Hollyn gripped Ephraim's arm as she noticed his face turn red and his body stiffen. "*Ignore* them."

"How was it to sleep with a lady? I don't think many ever get that chance—"

"Oh, you know. Quite *boring* if I'm being honest. Not a lot of creativity—"

Roars of laughter cut through Ephraim's stomach. He pulled his arm away.

"Well Aedin wasn't much fun either. One look could kill an *entire* party—"

"It nearly did. The event was dreadfully bo—"

Daniel's words cut off as Ephraim grabbed him from behind and threw his fist at his face. Catcalls mingled with boos, and laughter surrounded them as Ephraim threw Daniel to the ground and continued pounding with his fists.

Flecks of blood splattered into his vision. He felt sharp retaliatory blows to his cheekbones and arms elicit satisfying pain.

In the distance, he could hear Hollyn screaming his name.

Chapter Twenty-Nine

TOGETHER WE GATHERED the sail and carried it back to the fortress. Aedin plopped it down on the hearth floor in the kitchen where Rebecca was chopping vegetables.

"I'm sorry—can I help you?" She nudged the sail with her foot. "What is this doing in my kitchen?"

"There's a tear in the sail," Aedin responded succinctly. "Do you have any needle and thread?"

Setting down her knife, Rebecca wiped her hands on her pants. "There should be one around here…" She rummaged through a few drawers before pulling out some black thread and a bone needle. "Made it myself," she said proudly. "Treat it well."

"Well done."

Rebecca punched him lightly in the arm and resumed her spot at the table. I took the other chair—grateful to sit after the long day.

Aedin chose a spot by the fire, took the sail carefully in his arms, pulled the thread taut, and began to sew.

"Do you need any help?" I asked Rebecca.

She shook her head. "Almost done—just need to put this in the pot."

The cast-iron pot was simmering softly over the fire—wafting a warm and comforting smell through the kitchen. We sat in silence for several minutes as I stared at the fire and Aedin's deft fingers moving back and forth.

"Did you like Lailan?" Rebecca asked suddenly.

I was surprised by the question. "Yes," I offered. "It took some adjusting after the cold of Berge… but I ultimately grew to love it."

She smiled fondly at the carrots she was chopping. "I was born in Tahuna."

"Really?" I leaned forward.

"Yes." Rebecca eased herself out of her chair, hand on her belly, then grabbed the cutting board and slid the vegetables into the pot. The charcoal hissed as drops of broth splattered into the flames.

"When did you… leave?"

"That's a nice way to put it." Rebecca gave a short laugh, setting the cutting board back on the table and taking a seat. She looked at me thoughtfully. "I think I was about sixteen—no, seventeen—when I was found by the Rhidge."

I grew silent and looked away. Aedin said nothing, the crackling of the fire the only sound. The candles on the table illuminated Rebecca's soft, round face and straight nose. She struck me as suddenly beautiful, even though evidence of mental and physical weight dragged her down.

Folding and unfolding her hands on the table, she spoke again. "Throughout my childhood, I knew I was different—I could perform tricks, persuade people, other little things that none of the children my age could accomplish. When I was fourteen, I began noticing more signs. I Dreamed of the past and was able to wield an invisible pressure when my emotions were at extremes.

"Soon enough my mother noticed—she was Gifted and knew the signs. My mother also knew of the Rhidge—or at least the legend of them. It was a commonly told story growing up on Lailan, nothing to be taken too seriously, but nonetheless feared.

"Years later, my father died of a plague that swept the port, and my mother felt it was time to leave. We were at the market buying supplies for the journey when I got into an argument with a friend. I… can't even recall what it was about now, but I became angry. I used my Gift to push her, and I remember my mother becoming furious and taking us back home. As we hurried through the streets, we were followed by a woman in black. She saw where we lived—and though we tried to leave that night, we were stopped.

"That was when the Rhidge found me."

She paused, watching my expression, and said softly, "You look… worried."

I forced a smile. "I'm sorry… It's just… I'm surprised you're telling me this. I waited a long time for Aedin to tell me anything —I'm honored that you willingly choose to share it."

Rebecca laughed genuinely. "Please, it is a sad story, but it has a happy ending. Naming our fears is often the best way of conquering them. And… everyone handles their experiences differently."

In the open pause, we both glanced at Aedin. He ignored us— pensively watching the needle weaving through the sail.

"Anyway." She settled back in her chair. "When the Rhidge capture you, they drug you. Flussidik is what I think it's called— you'll have to ask Jon—it knocks you out for about twelve hours depending on the dosage. However, when you wake up, your muscles are unable to move—as if they've been liquidized. You're able to breathe, but you can move nothing else.

"With this drug, the Rhidge trains you to react quickly once you regain consciousness. Despite the slowness of your mind and muscles, they force you to rid yourself of the symptoms as fast as possible. The first time you're drugged—after you're captured— they use you as training for their students, having younger trainees come and practice their brutality on you. It is… not pleasant.

"It was Jon who was chosen to… do this to me. I remember waking up from the drug and staring up at him—his light blue eyes gazing down at me. He looked horrified. When his teacher told him to hit me or use his knife, he refused. He'd taken a step away from me, terrified and angry, shaking his head.

"Then his teacher punished him—beating Jon in front of *my* eyes. It was one of the worst days of my life, watching someone so good being hurt so mercilessly… After he was finished with Jon, he came to me and did the same, forcing Jon to watch. That didn't hurt as much though."

Rebecca paused, clearing her throat before she continued. "I spent the next nine years of my life in the Rhidge, undergoing similar circumstances, trials, lessons, which have all now morphed into one long moment. My first week, after that episode, I sought out Jon, though I was too afraid to talk to him. I thought he would hate me for the punishment he'd received on my behalf. It took me a long time to muster up my courage, but before I could make a move, Jon approached *me*, whispering quietly in my ear that we were being watched and must be subtle.

"From then on, we alternated seating during meals, passed each other occasionally in the halls, but would only talk every other time. We created methods of communication and other patterns through which I grew more and more attached to Jon in the midst of the cruel chaos. I hardly ever talked to Aedin," she admitted with a rueful smile. "I thought he didn't like me—didn't like how Jon was taking chances, risking his façade of loyalty by contacting me, keeping me sane. It was only later that I found out Aedin was afraid—he talked to no one but Jon.

"Throughout all this, I couldn't help but wonder at Jon's motive. From the first time we met—when he refused to hurt me —he always kept a special eye on me. Several times after training, when I was wounded, I would find him waiting in my room to heal me.

"Simple things like that had me wondering—why? Why would a man such as he—powerful, dangerous, and intelligent— be helping me? Should I even trust him? But despite my doubts, I *did* trust him and never detected anything in him that would make me think otherwise. Jon was, after all, the thread that grounded me within the Rhidge.

"On the eighth year of my service in the Rhidge, two things happened. First, Aedin became Lord of Lailan. It was a surprise to all members of the Rhidge to learn this, and a sign of hope. That someone could survive half a lifetime the Rhidge and live to become a *lord*? The thought, once impossible, had become a reality.

"Jon, however, was furious—he said that they meant to murder him, give him hope and then snuff it out. I thought I would never see him again. And I was afraid for him, afraid for his stability… When I looked at him, I still saw the small, quiet boy who had looked at Jon with such wonder. I hoped and wished he would survive."

Rebecca paused, noticing that Aedin had stopped sewing. He was now watching her quietly, his face impassive.

"The second thing that happened was I Dreamed of my future. I Dreamed of escaping from the Rhidge—and how to do it without being caught. Although it felt like an impossibility at the time, I knew I had to follow through and trust the Gift.

"Jon came to me the day after my Dream, to tell me his suspicions of being killed. He hadn't been passing his tests, he was growing old, and the Rhidge was too suspicious of his loyalty to take a second chance on him. He was what they called… disposable.

"He was in tears. He told me he had Dreamed of us together in the future—he had Dreamed of us living in the fortress, married and happy. But he didn't know how to get there… I then understood the reason for my Dream.

"So I told him of my Dream to escape. We quickly made plans, and that night we left." Rebecca paused, allowing a small laugh. "I'm sorry, I make it sound all too easy to escape the Rhidge. Let me clarify—it wasn't. That was one of the most difficult nights of my life. I was scared to death, and I assume Jon was as well. But" —she folded her hands and said simply—"we did. And then we sailed to the only place we knew we could hide.

"For all the years of my life, I will never forget the look on Aedin's face when we entered the villa on Lailan." She grinned at the memory. "I had never seen him so shocked. It was amusing—looking back—but terrifying at the time. He looked horrible—there were circles under his eyes, he hadn't bathed in a week, and he looked as if he ate hardly a meal a day.

"We stayed with him for two or three days, making arrangements to figure out a plan. Aedin found some ancient maps that helped us locate this fortress, and we decided that coming here was our best option. That was when we also found out about the eighth island… Something the Rhidge had never disclosed; something that only existed in folklore from my childhood.

"Those days we stayed with him… Aedin was unstable. Jon and I had to hide from everyone in the house except for him, but that wasn't so hard. What was hard was being around Aedin. During meals, he would carry a knife, visible on the table, next to his right hand as he ate with his left. I think some part of him thought we'd been sent by the Rhidge to kill him, but he never brought it up. I remember watching him at night—he hardly slept. He would stand by the door, gazing into the garden, occasionally glancing back to check on us. It unnerved me… but I loved him— as a brother or child—nonetheless."

Rebecca pushed back her hair with a smile. "So several days later, Jon and I left for the fortress. On the sailboat, he asked me to marry him, surprising me with a ring. I supposed I had always loved him, and I realized that I wouldn't want to spend the rest of my life with anyone else." She shrugged, leaning back in the chair, one hand on her stomach. "And that's that. When we arrived at the fortress, we found the place in complete disarray, so we worked on it for months. And soon enough, it was suitable to live in. And so we've made our lives here."

She stopped, and I realized that she had finished. I was unsure of what to say for a moment, until I finally settled for, "Thank you, Rebecca."

She nodded solemnly. "Of course."

Our heads turned to Aedin. He was staring at the floor, lost in thought. I hesitated, waiting for him to blink or for his eyes to focus. The fire crackled merrily.

Rebecca's chair scraped across the floor as she slowly exited the kitchen. "I'm going to get Jon for dinner." She patted me on the shoulder and left.

I counted to ten in the silence that followed and then whispered, "Aedin."

After a breath, he blinked and looked up at me, becoming the husband I had come to know. "Yes?"

Wordlessly, I stood and took the sail from his hands, then sat in his lap and wrapped my arms around his shoulders. I felt his body ease, his breaths becoming shudders into my breast. We were silent and still.

———

The trees rushed past me as I sped through the dense forest of the island.

Glimpses of the dark ocean were visible through the pines, but I trained my sight on the rocky ground. Ever-changing, it proved to be a difficult opponent. Jon had advised me to keep an active mind when running, but I nearly forgot his advice as I tripped on a root, my step breaking from the even rhythm I had fought to gain.

As usual, I listened for Jon and Aedin—but heard nothing.

Just when I was beginning to worry, I caught sight of a black shirt between a pair of trees, though it disappeared the next second. Comforted, I increased my pace—regaining the tempo I'd lost. I tried to control my breathing and ignore the growing stitch in my side, focusing on my next breath, the stretch in each step, until slowly the pain eased.

Occasionally, I would look up to gauge the trees ahead, decide which route between the obstacles would be best. Closer to the shore, there were more rocks and fewer trees. But the land nearer the fortress held thorny brush and tall pines that closely scattered the forest floor.

Since we'd started running every morning, I had grown accustomed to this difference, and chose to weave between both environments. Where there was a particularly tricky spot of trees, or an overgrown bush, I would neatly jump onto the rocks, continuing my course until the upper land became less dense.

I recollected the past two weeks—they had been the most enjoyable days I'd had since marrying Aedin. It was perpetual training, meals, and camaraderie.

And it was the feeling of belonging that was most satisfying. I had goals—and had achieved most. I spent almost every waking minute with Aedin—reveling in our mutual trust and understanding. And I had become close with Rebecca and Jon— despite the underlying threat of the Rhidge.

Each morning and evening, Aedin and I continued to walk the shore to scout the horizon. There was no sign of sails. I wasn't sure if this made me more or less anxious.

I felt constantly ready for the threat of the Rhidge, and yet they didn't appear. I wondered if we were safe—and if so, would we stay here? Make our lives at the fortress? The thought was terrifying on its own, so I didn't bring it up.

Jon's lessons had proved useful, and I had progressed rapidly. Not only could I now easily move objects, but I had also accomplished setting barriers, heightening my senses, and even healing wounds. The latter proved to be the trickiest and a delicate process. It required binding the skin with the Gift and then knitting it together.

The task was so precise, that, at first, it took me half an hour to mend a simple cut. But after numerous repetitions, I was able to do it quickly and cleanly. Jon and Aedin had no problem playing victim for my practice—but with each bit of progress I made, I didn't miss the surprised expressions that they shared.

Still, I struggled. Today was the longest we—or *I*—had run yet.

The route that Jon had coordinated totaled about three miles. Before, we had practiced sprints through the woods. But, as Jon had wisely pointed out, long distance was essential for escaping in a worst-case scenario. Which is most likely what I would be doing if we were to be attacked.

Ahead of me, to the right, I saw a long stretch of dirt, wide enough for five bodies to fit unobstructed by trees.

Excited at the prospect of not having to dodge through the pines, I made for the clearing, lengthening my stride as the ground remained even. I couldn't help but grin at my good luck—it was a relief to not worry about the earth any longer.

My ears twitched at the sound of a faint rustle to my right. I felt something—or someone—in the trees.

Slightly disturbed, I increased my pace, controlling my breathing and focusing my Gift. I felt the presence get closer and closer. Jon and Aedin were ahead of me—who else could it be? The Rhidge?

At that thought, I fled into a dead sprint, my hysterics rising, my legs protesting in pain. What if it was actually them? Should I call for help? I didn't dare turn my head, less I would lose speed. Maybe I should stand and fight—

Something large and solid hit my back.

Shrieking, I fell to the dirt, the air whooshing out of my lungs as my body hit the ground. Terrified, I turned over, reaching for the knife at my belt—but a dark shadow was now pinning me down.

Aedin smirked with satisfaction.

Panting, lying there in the dirt, my body aching from impact, I wanted to smack the smug expression off my husband's face and kiss him at the same time. I brushed away my hair, groaning at my previous anxiety.

Leaning forward, Aedin kissed me neatly and then grimaced. "You taste like dirt."

"I wonder why?"

He ignored my sarcasm, rolling off and lying down next to me. "You were running incredibly fast."

I wanted to laugh, but all that came out was a pant. "I thought you were the Rhidge!"

"If I had been, you would have been dead minutes ago."

"It could happen." I shrugged. "I thought you and Jon were ahead of me."

"It could." At this thought, Aedin grew serious, his dark brows lowering over his eyes. With the Gift covering my sight, I could see the flecks of color in my husband's gaze once again—dark azure, mahogany, coal... There were too many to count.

Sensing his concern, I brushed away a twig from his hair, kissing him softly. "But let's not dwell on that."

I saw the war in Aedin's eyes—he didn't want to give in to fear and apprehension. His lips tightened as he gazed at me, fingering our clasped hands, and I held my breath for a moment, releasing it slowly as my heart decelerated.

I sat up, pulling him up with me as well. "We should meet Jon."

"Yes," Aedin agreed shortly.

———

After drinking a jug of water, we returned to the weapons room. I rubbed my sore arms as we stood to attention for another lesson.

"Now, essentially, what you're going to be doing is *pushing* the Gift out of you, but hard enough to knock someone over." Jon motioned with his hands. "It's a common trick, but it takes your enemy by surprise and knocks them to their feet. The only downside is that it saps your energy fairly quickly because you're pushing out with so much force."

He turned to the dummy and pushed the air towards it, rocking the dummy back, but not enough to topple it.

"There—I only pushed slightly," Jon explained. "If I was to topple it, it would probably make me tired. Aedin"—he grinned at me—"was one of the few who could—or *can*—use it consistently, while only feeling slightly fatigued. I expect you, Gwen, to be even more efficient. This should be fun. Now—stand in front of the dummy."

I obeyed, my blood humming in anticipation.

"Now, unravel the thread as though you're about to push a weight—using your hands may work—and direct it towards the dummy."

Closing my eyes and concentrating, I caught the thread easily and pushed it outwards from my hands. I opened my eyes to watch the dummy lean back only an inch.

Jon nodded. "That's pretty good. But we want it to be instantaneous. Faster. Grab the thread as fast as possible and project it, no matter how small the power—that part takes time. Pull back and try again."

"Alright." I pulled the thread back and tried again, not even bothering to close my eyes. I knew where my Gift was. The dummy rocked from the feeble impact, but it was a push nonetheless.

"Again."

I nodded, inhaling, taking a minute to collect my thoughts and focus on the thread. Again, I shot my hands towards the dummy, pleased to see the Gift smoothly knocking it back harder.

"Now you need power," Jon said, evidently pleased, his blue eyes appraising me. "Try to get angry."

That wasn't hard. Thinking of Tours, I felt anger rush through my veins and pushed towards the dummy again. It was thrust backwards, nearly knocked over.

Jon cheered and Aedin smiled in appreciation. "Good one! Try again!"

The Gift ran freely through my veins, making it impossible to ignore. I wanted to hurt the thing and push it into the floor. I had never felt so powerful—as though I could take on an entire army of Rhidge. Grunting with effort, I pushed out my hands with a grin.

The dummy fell flat on its back, but I wasn't done with it. With my hands still out, I stalked towards it. It was pressed against the floor, sides straining from the effort of not collapsing in.

I smiled, lowering my hands above the dummy's chest, and forced the straw inside it to misshape. It looked crinkled, crippled. Amazed at my control, I pushed even harder.

There was a ripping noise as the fabric broke and straw spilled out of the dummy's head and body.

Shocked but pleased, I retracted my hands and stood. The dummy sprang up from its bottom weight, throwing straw everywhere.

I coughed, dusting off my shirt and turning to Aedin and Jon. They were watching me with wide eyes and open mouths—silent.

It was Jon who recovered himself first. "Well." He shook his head, regaining a smile. "You *are* quite powerful."

Aedin remained stunned, staring at me.

The Gift was leaving my hands, retreating slowly into my blood. My heart calmed. "Did I do something wrong?" I frowned, slightly winded.

They shared a look before Jon answered. "No, not at all." He paused. "I have an idea—why not try to do that to me?"

I raised an eyebrow. "You want me to… push you?"

"Yeah." Jon shrugged, pushing the dummy aside and taking its place. "Why not? Just don't rip out my insides please."

Glancing at the cleared space behind him, I decided it was safe. There wouldn't be much harm in it. "Very well," I began cautiously, and then focused.

Drawing the Gift back out, I pushed my power towards Jon. He flew into the air, nearly three feet, and collapsed clumsily on the mat. He groaned, shaking his head as my hand flew over my mouth.

"Jon?" I rushed towards him. "Are you alright?"

He laughed, grimacing as he rubbed his shoulder. "Of course! That was great! Let's try again!"

I frowned. "Are you sure?"

"Come on, Gwen." He rolled his eyes, standing up. "That didn't hurt one bit! I bet you weren't using your full power."

"I wasn't," I replied truthfully, stepping back and lifting my hands. "Are you *sure*?"

"Yeah." Jon braced his legs, leaning forward, "This time, I'm going to try to attack you, to startle you. Use all your power to get me away from you."

I nodded shakily and drew out the Gift.

He did take me by surprise, lunging towards me only seconds later and nearly catching me off guard. But just before he reached my outstretched hands, I threw all of my power at him.

There was a resounding BOOM, shaking the bones of my arm, and I saw the air almost solidify as it threw Jon away from me— nearly twice the length and height of last time. He landed hard, grunting as the air flew out of him.

Aedin was staring incredulously at the scene—I had never seen him so speechless.

From across the room, Jon coughed. I ran to him, holding out my hand to help him up. It took both of my hands to pull him up, but when I did, he caught me in a great big bear hug.

He shook with a laugh. "That was incredible!"

I frowned at him. "I didn't hurt you?"

"Don't worry about me." Jon grinned and looked over my shoulder. "Aedin, I think I've found someone who can finally beat *you*."

As Jon let go of me, I turned to my husband, startled. He was impassive as he gazed at me. "Do you really think so?" he asked, almost curiously.

I didn't want to fight Aedin. "No, Jon, I don't think I can…"

"Gwen, you just pushed me down like I was a twig, and we both know I weigh a lot more than that. Why not try? He won't hurt you… Aedin, are you up for it?"

There was no small comforting smile on his face. He turned to me seriously. "Yes."

I wanted to protest, but Jon pressed something into my hand. It was a dagger.

"It's about time someone put that to his throat," Jon joked, turning to the wall and leaning against it. "Gwen, are you tired?"

I assessed myself. "Only a little," I whispered, not wanting to look at Aedin.

Jon stared pointedly at Aedin; Aedin looked at the ground.

"Okay, Gwen." He gestured towards me. "Let one loose."

Shakily, I tucked the dagger in my belt, holding out my hands, terrified of what I was about to do.

"Go."

Aedin ran towards me, much faster than Jon had. We nearly collided, but I released my power an inch before he met my hands.

Like before, there was a deep sound that resonated within the stone walls. I watched Aedin fly back, as if in slow motion, and hit the mat. I wanted to stop it, but the Gift was pumping through my veins. It was intoxicating.

Holding out one hand towards him, I walked to where Aedin lay, pinned helplessly against the mat. He stared up at me wildly, in shock, almost terrified.

I pulled the dagger out of my belt.

Aedin's hands twitched as if to move to defend himself, but they were useless. I watched him struggle at my feet—powerless and unable to escape.

In a swift motion, I placed the blunt edge of the blade against Aedin's exposed throat.

For a second, neither of us moved. Trembling, I dropped the dagger to the floor and pulled back my power, suddenly tired. My knees shook and I collapsed on the mat, near Aedin's outstretched hands.

Even though the Gift was long gone, he didn't move.

Jon broke the silence again, saying softly, "Do you remember what I said, Aedin?"

"I haven't forgotten," Aedin responded tonelessly.

"She is your crossfire."

The sound of Aedin swallowing was loud. "I know."

I remembered Jon's words from my Dream as my lungs burned for air. *I'm teaching you this because someday you will meet someone who will beat you, Aedin… Someone who will take everything about you and tear it apart—make your life such a crossfire that you won't know if you'll come out broken or alive…*

Aedin was staring at me with a mingled expression of amazement, relief, and sorrow. I held my breath, unsure of what he would do.

Pushing the dagger away from where it lay between us, my husband turned till his body was pressed against mine, gathered my face in his shaking hands, and kissed me.

I felt something wet and opened my eyes to discover that his were brimming with tears. He was smiling.

And this time, Jon didn't interrupt us.

Chapter Thirty

WE FELL ASLEEP early that night. Whether from the emotional or physical toil, no one wanted to continue. Aedin and I retreated to our chambers and lay on the straw mattress in complete exhaustion.

"Are you afraid of me?" I asked quietly after some time, staring at the sliver of fading light through the arrow slit.

Aedin stirred, licking his lips. "I'm not sure…" He wrapped an arm underneath my shoulders and pulled me close. "Weren't you afraid of me?"

I couldn't help but smile. "Most definitely," I agreed.

"Then it's mutual." He chuckled darkly. The quiet chorus of crickets entered the silence between us.

Aedin's hand traced the length of my spine in a comforting gesture. I could feel the sleep begin to numb my mind and ease my aching limbs. After a while, I heard him cleared his throat. "Although I was trained, all of my understanding regarding the Gift came from the limited perspective of the Rhidge… There are some things we may not understand."

The sound of his words pulled me from the descending fog of sleep. "What do you mean?" I turned, hardly able to see his face in the darkness.

"I mean… your power could be… different."

"How so?"

"You've already demonstrated a deeper well than any of us have ever seen, and we have only *just* begun to tap into your capabilities..."

In the thick silence, I considered his words. "When I was using my Gift earlier—to push you down—I could *feel* an irresistible pull to use even more power... I felt so... alive," I ended in a whisper.

He was quiet as I struggled to pinpoint his reaction.

"What should we do?" I asked.

"What do *you* want to do?" Aedin countered softly. "We have to keep training, but we can't remain here forever."

"No," I agreed, snuggling my forehead against his and searching my mind. "I think we should leave... soon. Although I've enjoyed being here with Jon and Rebecca, the threat of the Rhidge grows more real each day that passes."

"I've been thinking the same."

"So then we take our chances," I concluded.

Aedin released a reluctant sigh. "Going to the eighth island?"

"Yes. The likelihood of us being killed *there* is slightly less than remaining within the Empire."

I felt his belly contract with a short laugh. "Our lives are now reduced to probabilities."

"Hasn't it always been that way?"

"I suppose," he muttered, leaning in to brush his lips against mine. We found each other in the black of the night as our mouths moved together—searching and soft. I gripped the coiled muscles of his arms as his lips pressed over my cheeks, my nose, and my forehead.

Smiling in the darkness, I inhaled his scent, a thick river of joy running through my blood.

No matter the stakes or where we fled, he would be there. We would be together.

He was the future. He was mine.

We fell asleep in each other's arms. But our rest was brief.

If I hadn't felt Aedin move from the bed, I wouldn't have awakened from my deep sleep. But his body shuddered with a start—as if breaking from a nightmare.

"Gwen," he whispered, pushing my shoulder.

I grunted in protest, blinking my eyes open until I saw his expression. With only two words, he sent my heart racing.

"They're coming."

He stood abruptly and began pulling out the knives and daggers from their hiding places and throwing them on the mattress.

I leaped up to grab my boots—sliding them on and putting the Gift under the soles. "Are you sure?"

"Positive." Aedin slid the daggers into his pockets and grabbed a knife. "I felt a presence on the shore."

"What about Jon and Rebecca?"

Aedin sent me a dark look. "We're leaving," he said with finality as I fought with trembling fingers to braid my hair.

He handed me a dagger. "Take this."

I grabbed the hilt—it still felt foreign in my grasp.

"Listen to me," he said forcefully. "We exit the fortress and head for the boat. We make for the eighth island—there's no other choice."

I nodded, and Aedin kissed me briefly on the lips. "I'm sorry it had to come to this," he muttered.

"Never apologize." I tightened my grip on the dagger. "I'm ready."

We exited the door with Aedin in the lead.

The hallway was still save for our soft breaths, the darkness thick given the early hour. But with our Gifted sight we were able to view the silent halls with clarity.

Aedin moved to the main entrance, his form crouched and quiet. My legs shook as I followed him across the stone floor.

A soft voice echoed from the gloom. "You can't leave."

We turned the corner to see Jon standing in front of the wooden doors. He held a dagger loosely in his grasp.

His blue eyes were cold.

"Jon, we have to," Aedin said slowly, straightening from his defensive posture and walking towards him.

"No... You can't... They will *kill* us if you leave." Jon's mouth was twisted in a humorless grimace.

Aedin didn't flinch, even as our worst suspicions were confirmed. "The Rhidge…"

"They found us months ago. They threatened Rebecca, they threatened my *child*—"

"I know." Aedin moved cautiously until he was standing only several feet away. "I know this must be hard…"

"You *can't* leave." Jon's voice rose in hysterics. His cheeks were flushed. "It's one life for another—I can't sacrifice—"

"We're leaving," Aedin said firmly. "Please let us go."

Jon swiped a broad stroke of the dagger across Aedin's midsection.

He jumped back quickly. "Jon," he said warningly, "I don't want to fight you—"

"There's no other option." Jon pointed his dagger at Aedin's chest. "Either you stay—and Rebecca and I live—or you go… and we—"

The door burst open behind Jon, exhaling a cloud of splintered wood and dust.

Instinctively, I stepped back and shielded my eyes. Dark shapes swarmed through the doorway and I heard the distinctive ring of metal on metal.

My heart pounded as my blood quickened in a rush of adrenaline and fear.

The Rhidge.

I saw feral shapes rush towards Aedin and Jon as they jumped into position and began the motions of battle.

A shadowed form sprinted towards me.

Steadying my feet, I pulled my Gift and pushed. It was a powerful hit—they flew nearly ten feet back, hitting the remains of the wooden door with a sickening thud.

My head whipped as I heard a cry and saw Aedin thrust his knife into a body—its dark form slumped against the wall.

He rushed towards me, positioning his body in front. "Go, *now*," he hissed as another moved towards us.

I eased backwards from the battle—sending a final push towards Aedin's newest opponent—and fled down the hall. The walls echoed with the sounds of the fray as I ran towards the back stairs. I sprinted as Jon had taught me—my breath coming light and easy.

A warning tugged in the corner of my mind. Suddenly, I detected a presence and slowed my steps—Rebecca emerged from a corner.

"Please—" I began quickly.

"Don't say a word." Rebecca motioned to her lips. "You have to go."

"Rebecca," I trembled in anger. "Jon *threatened*—"

"I know." There was sadness in her eyes. "And no matter what we choose, there is death."

I eyed her strong form and said hastily, "We can fight them—*together*—"

"I can't take that risk," she whispered fearfully, placing her hands protectively on her stomach. "You—*go*. Take the boat."

My heart pounded as I eased towards the doorway. "I will see you again."

Rebecca nodded gravely before disappearing back into the darkness of the fortress.

Running down the stairs, I pushed open the door to the smell of fresh pine and paused—the sound of my thudding heart was like a distant hammer.

I felt a presence ahead of me and tightened the grip on my dagger.

Something whistled through the dark and I intuitively ducked —a small knife embedded itself on the door where my head had been.

I crouched, terrified, easing my way through the brush and dirt.

It was following me.

My ears strained for any sign of attack, but there was little to betray its movements. I would die if it came to close combat—I needed to use the Gift. Though the advantage was slight, it might be enough to save my life.

I suddenly stood tall, exposing myself, and held my breath.

Another knife whistled through the air, but I thrust out my hands with a wave of power. The knife clattered uselessly to the ground as I located the direction of the attack.

Mustering my strength, I pushed out and saw a dark form fly through the air. I ran towards the thud as it fell, continuing to press out my Gift as I had done with Aedin and Jon. There was blood streaked on the stones beneath the struggling form on the forest floor.

It was a young girl—perhaps only five years my junior.

My heart skipped a beat as I studied her wild eyes. Her dark hair was cut short, and her chest rose and fell rapidly as her fingers squirmed at her sides.

She looked at me with… fear. I had to remind myself of the dagger in my fist.

It felt like a dream.

Something charged through the brush with incredible speed—I looked up, my attention suddenly broke from the fallen Rhidge.

The girl rushed to her feet, facing me with a knife that had somehow materialized.

In that second, I realized that my death was near. I had failed.

She took a step and then paused, her eyes growing wide in shock.

Blood filled her mouth as a long, silver blade jutted through her belly. It disappeared a moment later, as her limp form collapsed to the dirt floor.

A tall man towered over me, his green eyes glinting in the darkness.

A strangled cry caught in my throat as I stumbled backwards, throwing out my hands. He dispelled the pressure with a wave of his hand.

His long, silver sword was stained with the young girl's blood.

I shakily raised my dagger—pointing it towards him.

He slowly continued to advance with a stern look of warning. "Put down your weapon."

Summoning my Gift from the deep well of power, I threw the dagger to the ground and pushed out both hands. He stopped, then took a couple of steps back, raising his own hand in response.

Forcing harder, I gritted my teeth, setting my feet in the dirt. Crackles echoed through the night sky as my body stiffened— directing every ounce of power towards him. His expression shifted to a frown of concentration as he fought to remain standing.

"Gwen!" I heard Aedin yell and felt him running through the forest.

The sound of clashing blades emerged through the pines as Aedin was stopped by several others.

My jaw was clenched and tight, my entire focus fixed on my opponent as we struggled.

His tunic was dark in the thin moonlight, but it wasn't black. It was a color and material that seemed to shift and absorb the starless sky.

The realization hit me with a wall of fear and desperation—he wasn't from the Empire.

I dropped my hands and felt a blow hit my chest.

My body was thrown backwards—I tasted blood as my head hit something hard.

I stared up at the black sky and the shadowed branches of the pines; the man kneeled next to my body as I struggled to move.

"Don't move," he whispered, leaning down to cradle my head.

I felt a thin prick against my neck and blinked in surprise.

Someone shouted intelligibly.

Time seemed to speed up.

I saw my husband's dark eyes—wide and horrified.

And then I blacked out.

From the Author

Writing *Crossfire* has been an incredible journey spanning over a decade of my life. The story was first conceived circa 2008 and has since undergone numerous revisions—some small, others large. Although the essential story has remained the same, the larger context and side stories were given room to grow and have expanded into a second book, which will be released in the Fall/ Winter of 2022.

In early 2021, I finally mustered the courage and resolve to take my Apple Pages document and turn it into a published book. I would like to thank my editor, Laura Kincaid, whose patience and enthusiasm was invaluable. Diving headfirst into the self-publishing world was overwhelming (to say the least) and I am thankful for her guidance and advice.

To my husband—my partner and love of my life—now you finally know what occupied my time while you were traveling for work! Your kindness and humor continue to inspire me every day and I love our life together.

To my friends and family—you know who you are—thank you for your love and support. These past two years were a whirlwind of pandemic frenzy, long dinners with wine, DIY projects, days filled with laughter, and growing pains. We all survived somehow and have been made stronger through the process.

To my readers—thank you for spending your precious hours with this story. It is a wonderfully terrifying experience to publish a book, and I am very grateful that you chose to read mine. From the bottom of my heart—thank you.

A.G.K.
September 2021

Book II of The Rhidge coming Fall/Winter 2022

Sign up for my mailing list and check out my website for
writing updates.
www.agkarine.com

Thank you for finishing _Crossfire_
Liked what you read? Please leave a review on Amazon, share
on social media, or tell a friend. In this great world filled with
amazing literature, every bit counts and I am grateful for your
time.

This is the part where we stay in touch.

Follow me on Instagram for regular writing updates and all
things #bookstagram
@a.g.karine

www.ingramcontent.com/pod-product-compliance
Lightning Source LLC
Chambersburg PA
CBHW051754050726
47598CB00006B/2274